THE HOUSE OF SPIRITS

Mirrorscape

MIKE WILKS

EGMONT
USA
NEW YORK

EGMONT

We bring stories to life

First published in the United Kingdom by Egmont UK Limited, 2005
First published in the United States of America by Egmont USA, 2009
443 Park Avenue South, Suite 806
New York, NY 10016

10 9 8 7 6 5 4 3 2 1

www.egmontusa.com

Library of Congress Cataloging-in-Publication Data
Wilks, Mike.
Mirrorscape / Mike Wilks.
p. cm.
Summary: In a world where all pleasures are severely restricted, Melkin
Womper is apprenticed to a master painter where he discovers the
Mirrorscape, a world inside paintings, and becomes entangled in a war
between the restrictive Fifth Mystery and the rebels fighting to stop them.
ISBN 978-1-60684-008-5 (trade hardcover) —
ISBN 978-1-60684-040-5 (lib. bdg. edition)
[1. Apprentices—Fiction. 2. Adventure and adventurers—Fiction.
3. Artists—Fiction. 4. Art—Fiction. 5. Fantasy.] I. Title.
PZ7.W65438Mi 2009
[Fic]—dc22
2009016245

Book design by A. Castanheira

Printed in the United States of America

FOR LUCY JANE WILKS

(wherever you are)

Contents

Acknowledgments

This picture bears my signature but others have made indispensable contributions in getting it from a blank canvas to the finished work you see here. My literary agent, Ivan Mulcahy, saw some of the original rough sketches and gave me valuable early criticism and advice. Later, Cally Poplak and Rachel Boden of Egmont Press in London, as well as Elizabeth Law, Ruth Katcher, Doug Pocock, Mary Albi, and the team at Egmont USA, all made priceless comments concerning composition and technique. I would also like to thank Ben and Louise Jenkinson for their Latin scholarship and my friend Carol Smith for her unflagging support.

Lege nuntium turrium

prologue

IT SHOULD HAVE been darker than the darkest night, as black as Indian ink. But it was not. He held his hand in front of his face and could clearly distinguish its outline in the feeble light. It was both a blessing and a curse. If he could see, then he could also be seen.

The man quickened his pace. There was little risk of stumbling now but where the light was coming from he could not yet tell. The echo of his footfalls and the even floor told him that he was indoors and deep underground.

Then there was the smell. A smell of damp and decay laced with something sour and feral.

And sounds, too. Sounds that could only be footsteps somewhere behind him, getting closer. Periodically they stopped, and he was sure he heard sniffing.

There was a sudden movement to his left and the man froze, his heart pounding. He turned his head slowly and so did his watcher. With an audible sigh of relief, he saw his own reflection. He approached the mirror. Its ornate frame was cracked and draped with cobwebs, its glass scabby with age. But the shadowy reflection was his even if his own mother would not have recognized the gaunt features and the malachite-green skin. Escaping from the island of Kig had been the easy part. It had taken him only a matter of hours to travel the hundreds of miles from the horror of the mines to here—wherever here was. But when he finally emerged, fumbling, into the pitch darkness he found a new peril. It soon became clear he was being stalked.

As the man hurried on the light gradually increased until he discovered its source. A forgotten gallery stretched before him, one long wall hung with many paintings. But these were unlike any paintings he had ever seen before. Weird vines and plants spilled out of the images and on to the gallery floor. The branches of gnarled trees, originally crafted in oil paint, snaked and intertwined overhead. Streams formed by deft brushwork and pigment splashed their way out of the canvases and coursed along the gallery floor. Light was leaking from these pictures, casting rectangular pools on the bare, stone floor. It reminded the man of a deserted city street at night, lit by the windows of many shops.

The green man walked down the long gallery openmouthed, staring at the canvases. He stopped before one that depicted a clearing in the heart of a forest, overflowing with extravagant plants, where a band of traveling players dressed in gaudy costumes and masks slept. The scene was illuminated by thousands of candles that littered the floor of the forest and the branches of the trees as if the troupe were dreaming a collective dream that had materialized into the forest around them. Dark spaces between the trees suggested shadowy forms that lurked beyond the light of the candles. In the foreground of the picture were strange creatures the size of small monkeys and covered with piebald fur. One had left the picture and was scampering around in its pool of light on the gallery floor. The man knelt and picked it up.

Then the smell was suddenly stronger. Behind him he heard a sound and without looking he knew what it was. The nightmare form of a monstrous creature slowly emerged from the darkness beyond the gallery. It stood erect on immensely muscular hind limbs, its enormous jaws filled with needle-sharp teeth as long and transparent as icicles. It had huge, pale eyes as big as tea trays. From between them extended a long, curved barbel with a luminous tip like that of a deep sea fish. For a long moment they stood staring at each other. Then the monster folded its long wings and charged. As it hurtled towards the man, it uttered a bloodcurdling roar.

The green man thrust the small, piebald creature into his rags, turned, and sprinted down the gallery, his feet splashing in the watercourse. He knew from his pursuer's composition and fine detail that it was the work of Lucas Flink, and therefore was exceedingly dangerous. But this was not the moment for the finer points of art appreciation.

Ahead, an interruption in the light betrayed the presence of a painting with its surface still intact. There was no time to examine the dark canvas closely; he had to trust that the seal remained unbroken. He came to a halt and made a complicated gesture with his hand and, with a faint smile of satisfaction, he saw the surface ripple.

Then he vanished!

Flink's creature let out a howl of frustration and skidded to a halt in front of the canvas, its wicked jaws closing on thin air and its claws tearing great gashes in the floor. It sneezed loudly, spraying pellets of foul, black mucus on to the canvas, each droplet reflecting a tiny, distorted image of its maker as it slid slowly down. The ghostly light from the creature's barbel revealed a snowy landscape with a group of lamp-lit dwellings nestling in a hollow. Misty blue mountains graced the skyline silhouetted against the setting sun. If the creature had possessed the intelligence to comprehend the picture it would have seen a trail of footprints leading from the foreground down towards the village. And if it had followed that trail to its end it would have seen the beautifully painted form of a ragged man with a skin of malachite green cradling a tiny, piebald creature in his arms.

He was looking back over his shoulder and smiling.

1. the messenger

THE HARE LAY perfectly still. As a breeze stirred the long grass, her silky fur would ruffle and her whiskers twitch. Once, when a bee lifted off from a nearby gentian, she gave a quick flick of her long ear to send it on its way. Mel could see the nervous movement of her tiny nose as she sniffed the air for danger. Her bright eyes remained motionless but she was aware of everything around her. There was no sound except the faint buzz of insects and the whispering of the trees.

Mel had skived off to his favorite spot on the outskirts of the village. He had been dying to try out his new drawing materials. Lately he had been experimenting with a new, homemade ink. His first attempt had been soot mixed with water, but the ink it was thin and faded to a sickly yellow-brown when he drew with it. His brainstorm was to boil the sooty liquid the same way his mother thickened broth. The result was much more like the real ink that Fa Theum used to pen his sermons. For his pen Mel had a fine goose quill made from a long wing feather. With his father's sharp knife he had stripped away all of the feathery part and cut a fine point that he split to hold the ink. It was light—featherlight, in fact—and responded to the slightest movement of his hand.

Mel sat in the sweet-smelling grass with the warm midday sun on his back, resting his mother's chopping board on his knees.

On this was a precious sheet of paper that he had begged from Fa Theum.

He drew slowly but carefully, putting the quill to the paper only when he was certain that he understood what he was looking at. It was absorbing work, but he found the same old frustration gnawing at his concentration. If only he had colors to match the vivid splendor he saw all around him. The gray-brown of the hare, the green of the grass, the blue gentians, the yellow buttercups, the rich color of the soil. But color was out of the question. He might as well wish for a mansion to live in or velvet and silken clothes to wear.

"You haven't finished it, Mel."

The hare streaked away, a blur of movement. As startled as the wild creature, Mel spun around. Indistinct, with the sun directly behind his head, creating a kind of nimbus, stood the figure of Fa Theum. Relieved, Mel squinted up at the gray-haired priest. "Nearly, Fa. I was thinking that if I had some colors I could make it better. You know, more lifelike."

"It looks very lifelike to me. But that's not quite what I meant."

"Sorry, Fa. What did you mean?" asked Mel, puzzled.

"Why, you've forgotten the most important part, my son."

Mel stared back blankly.

"Your signature! All great works of art should be signed by their creator. Like I taught you."

Mel smiled at the compliment. He tilted his little pot, dipped his pen in the last of the ink, and slowly and carefully wrote in the bottom right-hand corner *Melkin Womper*.

"That's it." Then, after a pause as he continued to admire the drawing. "I guessed I'd find you here." With a grunt, the elderly priest eased himself down to sit alongside Mel and absentmindedly plucked a blade of grass to suck. "That's a fine sketch, Mel. You have a rare talent. But it's not your usual subject matter, is it?"

"No, Fa. I really like to draw, you know, *imaginary* things." It was his favorite word. "But sometimes I need to find an outside thing and use it as a starting point. Like, if I want to draw a creature with . . . with an owl's body and a hare's head, I'll need a drawing of an owl and another of a hare so that I can join the two up."

"We call such creatures 'hybrids.'"

Mel tried out his new word. "Hybrids."

"You know, Mel, in the House of Spirits—the Maven's palace in Vlam—there is a great library. And in that library there is a rare book called a bestiary, containing descriptions and pictures of all manner of beast from every corner of the world. There are also fabulous creatures—unicorns, mermaids, griffins, and manticores—and there are hybrids. There are cameleopards, hippardiums, allopecopithicums. And there are lots more besides. Do you know what these creatures are?"

Mel could only shake his head in bewilderment.

"Well, you know that when a donkey mates with a horse, their offspring is a—"

"Mule," finished Mel.

"That's right. Now, according to the bestiary, when a camel and a panther mate they create another kind of creature altogether—a cameleopard. But if that same panther were to bear the offspring of a horse, well that would be a hippardium. The offspring of a fox and a monkey would be an allopecopithicum."

"Do such creatures really exist, Fa?"

"Possibly, possibly. But there's something else about hybrids. You remember what a symbol is?"

"It's something that means more than itself. Like your diaglyph."

The old priest touched the tarnished pendant slung around his neck that rested on his shabby, brown cassock. A triangle within a square within a circle. He smiled at his quick pupil. "Just so. This is a symbol of my maker and my faith."

Mel nodded, eager for the old man to continue.

"So, a mermaid might symbolize temptation and a unicorn purity. As for the hybrids, well they might symbolize two things at once. A fox is cunning and a monkey full of mischief, so an allopecopithicum would have both those qualities. A kind of cunning rascal."

"Yes, but do they *really* exist?" insisted Mel.

"When I was a young priest in Frest, I met some sailors who swore that they once saw a mermaid and had traveled in a land where unicorns and other strange creatures lived."

"Mermaids and unicorns sound better than an owl with a hare's head," said Mel, disappointed that he had come up with such mundane components for his imaginary creature.

"Well, there you're wrong. According to ancient folklore, the owl possessed wisdom and the hare was the messenger of the moon. So your hybrid might symbolize a wise messenger."

Mel thought about this for a moment and smiled. "And do you think that my hare might have been bringing me a message, Fa?"

The priest smiled and looked down at the thirteen year old, ruffling his unkempt fair hair. "Come on, Mel, let's go home and see your parents. There's something very important we must discuss with them."

A wave of panic swept through the youngster. "It's all right.

I'm not skiving. I've done my chores; they know I'm out here drawing. They said I could come," he quickly lied.

"Don't fret. Come, help me up."

As Fa Theum and Mel made their way up the village street, the boy began to drag his feet, reluctant to reach home and the inevitable price he would have to pay for his truancy. Their footsteps raised puffs of pale dust in the rutted, unpaved street. An unpleasant smell rose from the central gutter where all manner of waste flowed. The low, single-story houses that lined the street had roofs of thatch and walls of wattle and daub. Some had once been whitewashed but most were now faded. The entire village seemed to be painted in shades of sepia, alleviated only by the green backdrop of the distant trees and the gray smudges of smoke from cooking fires drifting slowly upwards from the chimneys into the clear, azure sky. Doors and wooden shutters were thrown wide to allow the summer air to circulate.

The Womper cottage was on the far side of the village. It was little more than a shack with a lean-to at one side. The ceiling was low, the tiny windows unglazed, and the floor was of hard, packed earth scattered with dried rushes. Mel's father, Willem, worked incessantly at the wooden loom that filled most of the main room. What little space was left was occupied by the plain table and chairs and by Willem's fireside chair. Next to a small, mud-brick hearth there was a settle where Mel and his mother would sit of an evening, and in the far corner the straw pallet where Mel slept. The remaining accommodation was no more than his parents' tiny bedroom to one side and some storage in the lean-to.

As they approached, a gang of the village boys raced past them.

Fa Theum looked down at Mel. "Before we go in and see your parents there is something I must tell you."

Mel was not listening. Something was wrong. Everything was quiet where there should have been the steady clackety-clack of his father's loom. What had started as a sense of unease grew in Mel's heart to one of trepidation. He broke away from Fa Theum and ran the last few steps to his door.

The priest shouted after him, "Mel, wait!"

But Mel did not hear him. He burst inside and stopped dead. Seated in his father's chair by the hearth was a monster, its vast size dwarfing the room. The creature's leathery head slowly turned and its single eye fixed itself on the intruder.

2. dirk tot

THE MONSTER SLOWLY rose from the chair and would have stood erect if the ceiling had been higher. Mel uttered a terrified cry, turned on his heels, and fled, dropping his drawing. He collided heavily with Fa Theum, who blocked the doorway.

"Mel, whatever is the matter?"

The boy could only whimper as the priest held him fast, preventing his flight. He looked up at the old man and was astonished to see that he showed no fear. Instead, he was actually smiling. Mel half turned and was even more astounded to see his father and mother in the shadows, sitting calmly side by side on the settle. His mother, Mabin, was smiling nervously, but his father shifted uncomfortably. He glared at Fa Theum.

Then, the monster spoke. "Hello, Mel." The voice was deep and resonant but surprisingly gentle, his Vlamian accent refined.

Slowly, Mel turned to confront the dreadful sight and a strange thing happened. He began to look at the creature the same way he looked at a subject he was about to draw. Almost at once, his fear and preconceptions fluttered away like so many moths shaken out of an old blanket. What he now saw was not so much a monster as a tall and powerful man dressed in the finest clothes he had ever seen. And, what's more, they were *colored*. Mel had never met anyone before who was not dressed in tabby.

The monster wore a long, sleeveless tunic made from fine, richly embroidered purple brocade trimmed with tawny fur. Beneath this was a deep blue velvet doublet stitched with gold. The sleeves of his doublet were slit in many places revealing the white silk of his shirt. He wore a heavy chain around his neck. He carried a plumed, flat velvet hat and he had a jeweled reticule at his side, attached to his ornate belt. His black leather breeches were tucked into soft, high boots. He made a dazzling contrast to the drabness of the cottage.

But, the wonder of the colors aside, it was his ruined face that held Mel's attention. The whole of the right side seemed to be made of wrinkled leather, leather that had melted like candle wax. Set in this was his eye, now a milky dome. There was a deformed lump where Mel supposed his ear had been and on that side of his head there was no hair at all. The man-monster turned his head for a moment to look at Mel's mother and father, and Mel was surprised to see that when the ruined half of his face was turned away he looked perfectly normal. In fact, he was even handsome. By this time, Mel's initial dread had almost completely vanished.

"Mel, don't stare," admonished his mother.

Mel lowered his eyes momentarily, but raised them again as the stranger bent down to pick up his drawing. The man straightened up, forgetting the low ceiling, and bumped his head, sending a small shower of dust cascading around him. Mel stifled a laugh.

"*Mel!*" His father hissed.

"I-I'm sorry," stammered Mel sheepishly. He looked up at the stranger to see that he, too, was suppressing a laugh. He rubbed his head where he had bumped it and Mel saw that his left hand was made entirely of finely engraved silver. It was beautifully crafted, even down to the articulated joints.

The stranger looked down at the drawing of the hare he held in his good hand. "I can see that everything I've heard about you is true, Mel."

The stranger had heard about him!

The man looked at the drawing again, and then turned to place it on the table, where Mel was surprised to see lay many of his other drawings. "You are industrious, too, I can see."

"Mel, this is Dirk Tot. Say hello," said Fa Theum, as he stood behind Mel with his hands resting on the boy's shoulders.

"Hello," and after a sharp squeeze from the priest added, "sir."

"Come here, Mel," said Dirk Tot. Clearly discomforted by his stooped posture, he sat down again in Willem's chair, which complained with a loud creak as he settled his great bulk. Hesitantly, Mel approached. "How long have you been drawing?"

"I don't know in years," Mel answered. "Ever such a long time, as long as I can remember."

"What do you like to draw best of all?"

"I like to draw *imaginary* things best of all," Mel replied instantly.

A smile flitted across the undamaged side of Dirk Tot's face and then vanished. "Tell me, Mel, which do you think is the best of your works?" He gestured towards the drawings scattered on the table, some in charcoal and some in ink.

Mel quickly sorted through the drawings. "This one," he said, passing a picture of a set of bagpipes with dancing human arms and feet and the head of a nightingale with its beak open wide.

Dirk Tot studied it. "Why do you think this is good?"

There was a short silence before Fa Theum prompted, "Come on, Mel. Don't be shy."

"I like it because it's more than just an ordinary picture." He looked at his interrogator. "It's a picture that means two things at once." He shot a quick glance at Fa Theum, who nodded almost imperceptibly. "It's a symbol."

The old priest smiled the faintest of smiles.

"You see, it's a picture of a bagpipe, which makes a certain kind of noise, joined up to a picture of a nightingale, which makes another kind of noise—a noise much sweeter than the pipes. And the arms and legs are dancing—as if to the music. So, even though there's no sound, you can make believe there is. But you're not sure what kind of sound it is, bagpipes or bird, or both. And you wonder why he's dancing. Is it because of the music or because of something else?"

"Where did the idea come from?"

"I don't know, it was just there when I sat down to draw."

"Are your ideas always there?"

"Usually. Inside in my head. But if I ever can't think of one, I look at the shapes and get a new idea from them."

"Shapes? What shapes?" asked Dirk Tot.

"Just shapes. Sometimes I look in the hearth, at the ashes, and I see pictures there. Or in the flames in the fire. Sometimes I see them in the clouds or in the stains on the wall. I see people and animals and monsters with"—he nearly said horrible faces—"strange landscapes." Mel could feel everybody's eyes on him. He hated being the center of attention.

Dirk Tot seemed to sense his awkwardness and quickly asked, "Tell me, how often do you make mistakes?"

Mel thought about lying, but he realized this man knew too much about drawing. "Not very often. Well, sometimes . . . quite a bit actually."

"Every artist makes mistakes; it's nothing to be ashamed of. Only people who never try anything new never make mistakes."

The man sat forward, resting his elbows on his thighs. "Now tell me, which is your *worst* picture?" he asked.

Surprised at this question, Mel shuffled through the drawings a couple of times and then handed the man an ink portrait. "This one, I think."

The stranger studied it. "Tell me why."

Mel thought. Should he point out the mistakes or tell him how the pen kept clogging up or how lumpy the ink was or how dark it was when he made the drawing? As Mel rehearsed these themes in his head they began to sound like excuses. Eventually he said, "Well, you see, it's a picture of Fa Theum—but it's not like him."

"You're wrong, Mel, it is the very image of him," interrupted Dirk Tot.

"It *looks* like him—at least I hope it does—but it's not him. Fa Theum talks and laughs and does lots of things that my drawing can't show. He can read and write and say sermons and he tells funny stories and—"

"Well, I'm glad *someone* thinks they're funny," interjected the Fa.

Everyone laughed—everyone except Willem.

Dirk Tot continued. "You know, Mel, there is more to being an artist than being able to carry a likeness. A true artist knows the difference between what is good and what is bad and, more importantly, between what is merely good and what is great. Sometimes great masters make paintings that are bad—not as often as bad artists, but occasionally—and do you know what they do to these bad paintings?"

Mel shook his head.

"They destroy them."

Mel slowly nodded. "So that the bad apple doesn't spoil the others in the barrel."

Dirk Tot fixed his one good eye on Mel and stared so hard that the boy began to feel uncomfortable. Mel lowered his head and shifted his weight. After what seemed an age, Dirk Tot grunted, turned to Fa Theum, and nodded.

"Mel, gather up all these drawings now and come over to the fane with me," said Fa Theum. "We need to put them back up on display so that the rest of the village can continue to admire them." This drew an alarmed look from Dirk Tot that the priest pretended not to notice. "Besides, Dirk Tot has things he needs to discuss with your parents."

After a glance at his father, Mel did as he was told.

As soon as he was out of the door, the questions about the richly dressed stranger gushed from Mel's mouth. But he soon realized that he was not going to get any answers until Fa Theum was good and ready. He could not contain his excitement, however, as he virtually pulled the old priest past Dirk Tot's fine carriage and coachman in their matching liveries of deep blue.

They entered the cool, whitewashed interior of the fane and genuflected to the large diaglyph on the altar before sitting down on one of the scrubbed wooden pews. Sunlight slanted in through the small windows, creating patches of amber light and shade on the bare stone floor.

The old man held up a preemptive finger. "Sit still. Listen carefully to what I have to say."

What Fa Theum had to say began a chain of events that changed Mel's life, and, ultimately, the lives of everyone in the land of Nem, forever.

3. hopes and dreams

SOME TIME LATER Mel left the fane almost in a state of shock. He ran back through the village and burst into his tiny home. The stranger had left and his parents sat side by side on the settle, deep in conversation.

"Is it true?" Mel shouted, as he struggled for breath.

His father said nothing. He did not even look at his son as he rose, walked over to his loom, and began weaving again, his face set like stone. He wove at a frantic pace, violently stamping on the treadles and dashing the shuttle from side to side with a speed Mel had never witnessed before. He turned to his mother and noticed that her eyes were red.

"Mum, is it true? What Fa Theum told me?"

"Come outside with me, sweetheart, and help me pick the vegetables for supper," said his mother softly.

When they were alone in the vegetable patch, Mel asked, "What's the matter with Dad?"

"Leave him be. This whole business has come as a bit of a shock. He needs to adjust to the idea. We both do."

"It's true then."

"Yes, Mel, it's true."

"Fa Theum told me that I'm to go and—"

"Nothing's certain yet. Please don't get your hopes up." She gently caressed his cheek. "The gentleman had to continue his journey but he will return this way in a few weeks. There's a great deal to be discussed before then. It's best if you don't dwell on this too much."

An impossible request; from that moment on Mel thought of nothing else.

That night, as he lay in bed, Mel turned over the momentous events of the day. Fa Theum had explained to him that he had written to Fa Marten, an old friend in the Maven's household, to ask if he knew anyone in the capital who might be interested in commenting on Mel's artistic gift. He had received a reply that exceeded his wildest expectations. He had produced a thick sheet of paper from inside his cassock and unfolded it with a soft, crackling sound.

"The first part does not concern you, Mel, but this bit surely does." Fa Theum turned the page.

"'I found the story of your young protégé fascinating and the boy's precocious talent is amply demonstrated by the drawing you enclosed. I took it at once to show to Dirk Tot, steward to Ambrosius Blenk, the greatest artist in the Seven Kingdoms. Dirk Tot was as impressed as I was and took it to the great man.

"'Now, you may know that Ambrosius Blenk's studio employs many apprentices and is almost like a factory for producing paintings. These apprenticeships are usually purchased for large sums of money by wealthy families. Occasionally the master will offer a free apprenticeship to someone who is too poor to pay but who shows truly exceptional talent. I am pleased to report that your boy is so considered. However, artistic ability alone will never be enough to make an artist. Quite apart from a skill in draftsmanship, the boy would also need a discerning and inquiring mind, the right attitude, and, above all, a great passion for art if he is ever to succeed.'"

Mel did not hear the rest of the letter or Fa Theum's caveat that any apprenticeship depended on the agreement of his parents. He had been in an almost delirious state of excitement since Fa Theum read it to him, despite his father's odd behavior. Willem had not spoken another word to his family all day and went to bed without a glance at his wife and son.

Now, unable to sleep, Mel tossed and turned on his straw pallet. His entire universe had spun on a great, invisible pivot and now faced in a totally different direction. At breakfast he had been a happy enough boy who was good at drawing and who would grow up to become a tabby weaver like his father. By supper, another magnificent vista had opened up that held the promise of becoming an apprentice and, eventually, an artist who would spend all day, every day, doing what he loved most—making the most wonderful pictures. Mel's deepest wish, a wish he had scarcely dared to admit even to himself, had actually come true.

Obviously his parents could not sleep either and their muffled voices rose and fell in the bedroom. Mel lay there in the darkness until his curiosity got the better of him. He just had to know what they were saying. He rose from his bed and crept towards their room.

". . . not so loud, you'll wake Mel," he heard his mother say as he placed his ear to the door.

"But how can you bear to be parted from him? If he went away we might not see him for years on end."

"It's just as hard for me as it is for you, but think of his future. He would get away from here, make something of his life."

"And what do you mean by that?" shot back Mel's father. "Suddenly being a weaver isn't good enough for him. Let me remind you that weaving puts food on the table. Weaving keeps a roof over our heads. He might go off to Vlam, spend years playing about with paints, and never make it as an artist."

"Will, you know as well as I do how talented he is. And Fa Theum, he wouldn't have gone to all that trouble if there was no talent there."

"Don't talk to me about that interfering old priest, after he's gone behind our backs like that. Why didn't he discuss it with me first? I could have put an end to this nonsense then and there.

"Mel's shooting up," continued his father. "Soon his legs will be long enough to reach the treadles. I'll build him his own loom and can weave alongside me. Think what a difference that will make. Double the cloth, double the income. Why, we would be able to move out of this place into somewhere larger, with better light. I could buy the Pleasure to make finer cloth, and we could have the things we've dreamed of."

"You think I would want that rather than Mel's happiness?"

His father blew out loudly breath in exasperation. "And then there's Vlam. Do you know what goes on there? There's drinking dens and worse. Do you know that?"

"No, Will, and neither do you. Neither of us has ever been more than ten miles from Kop."

"But I've heard stories. I've got ears."

"All I'm asking is that you think about it."

"There's nothing to think about. My mind's made up."

Then the argument seemed to start again from the beginning. Mel stole back to bed. His mother would get her way. She always did. Well, nearly always.

Eventually he dropped off to sleep, where his dreams were full of fabulous hybrids romping about in the most glorious color. In the morning he awoke with a wonderful feeling of elation and anticipation. Mel also felt more than a little guilty at being the cause of his father's anger and the disharmony between his parents. Was he selfish to want to be an artist, to be so delighted about going away to distant Vlam?

His father's black mood lasted all the next day and into the one after but it did not dent Mel's joy.

By the fourth day following Dirk Tot's visit, Mel sensed things were beginning to return to normal and he and his father managed to exchange a few words. He took this as a sure sign that his mother had won the argument.

One week later, with normality more or less restored, as they sat around the table after supper, there came a knock at the door. Mel rushed up and opened it.

"Fa!" he exclaimed to the visitor.

"Good evening, Fa," said Mabin, as she gestured for the old man to enter. "Please join us. Will you have something to eat? To drink, maybe?"

"Thank you, but no." The old priest sat down. "It's been over a week now and Dirk Tot will be returning this way soon. I realize that there has been much for you to think about. We really must have an answer for him."

Willem looked at his wife and then back at their visitor. "Fa, this apprenticeship is wonderful, there's no denying it. I know opportunities like this rarely come along—and never to the likes of us. This has made our decision so very difficult. At first, I was confused and angry that you had done this thing. That you had approached someone else about Mel's future. A future that would mean us living apart. You should have discussed this with us first."

"I know, Willem, I apologize. But there was no certainty in this matter. I took it upon myself just to find out if Mel's work was as good as we all think it is. That Mel should be asked to join Ambrosius Blenk's studio was as much a surprise to me as it must have been to you both. And what a delightful surprise!" The old priest smiled.

Willem paused and lowered his eyes. Then, turning to Mel, he said, "I'm sorry, son. We're simple folk; artisans. This thing isn't for the likes of us. Surely you can see that? You can continue to draw in your spare time but this apprenticeship is out of the question."

Mabin sighed and leaned over to hug her son. There was a tear in her eye. "Your father's right, Mel. I know it seems hard now but it's for the best. This apprenticeship was a dream—for both of us—but now we must wake up. You'll stay here with us, just like it's always been."

"But Mum, Dad . . ." The words died on Mel's lips. He wanted to argue but the tone of his father's voice told him it would be futile. Willem's mind was made up. Mel fought an almost overwhelming desire to break into tears as the disappointment settled on him with an almost physical presence.

"Is there nothing I can say to make you change your mind, Willem?" said Fa Theum. His face betrayed a regret almost as bitter as Mel's.

"Nothing. This is how it must be." Willem turned again to his son. "Mel, I know how hard this must be for you but you'll get over it. Weaving is a fine trade. Why, it's almost an art in its own right. In a few months none of this will matter. It will all be forgotten. What do you say?"

Mel could say nothing.

That night, the tears did come. Rivers and silent sobs racked his small body as he cried himself to sleep. That night he did not dream in color. He did not dream at all.

4. the pleasure and the pain

THE WORLD DID not end. As one week stretched into two, Mel gradually became more resigned to his future. His desire to create slowly returned and he eventually found the time to draw the view of Kop that he had planned when the hare turned up. In fact, the landscape turned out so well that he took it at once to show to Fa Theum.

When the fane came in sight, he saw that there was a magnificent carriage waiting on the sward outside. Unlike Dirk Tot's, this one was a vivid scarlet, ornamented with fine carving and gold leaf. It positively throbbed with color. It occurred to Mel that he had seen more color in the last few weeks than in his entire life. Four huge black horses with hairy fetlocks, heads hanging towards the ground in exhaustion, looked up at the boy. Pale sweat streaked their flanks and froth hung around their mouths as if they had been driven hard. Hitched to the back of the carriage was a trailer with what looked like a large, domed birdcage resting on it, easily big enough to hold a man. Hanging from the thick bars were stout chains and manacles. Mel walked towards the fane wondering who Fa Theum's visitor might be.

As he reached the door, it struck him that the village boys were not around. No one was. He would have expected the villagers to be irresistibly attracted by such a spectacle. Even the birds had stopped singing. It was as if everything had fled.

Mel hesitated for a moment and then pushed open the door.

"Ah, and this must be the artist."

There were three of them, the one who had spoken and two other armed and powerful-looking men, who held Fa Theum between them in the small vestibule. The old priest stood in a pool of his own vomit. He was bleeding heavily from a deep scalp wound, his left eye so swollen that it was completely closed up. The lower half of his face was encrusted with blood and snot, and he held his right hand at an odd angle.

His captors were dressed in long scarlet robes that brushed the floor, with a large black eye emblazoned on the breast. They wore many jeweled rings in rows over their red gloves. All had faces painted with white makeup and straight jet-black hair that hung to their shoulders. This was shaved in a strange tonsure so that the front of their scalp and everything in front of their ears, including their eyebrows, was completely bald. Their leader was taller than the others and cadaverously thin. He had reptilian gray eyes with irises so pale they were only a shade or two darker than the surrounding whites. They were deep-set above a tiny, upturned nose. The man held a long multicolored staff with an ornate, gilded boss on top. He sneered at Mel, revealing uneven yellow teeth.

"So these are your masterpieces," he said, with an expansive, sweeping gesture towards the drawings decorating the vestibule.

Too frightened to speak, Mel nodded.

"I thought as much. Seize him!"

One of the other men grasped Mel roughly by his arms. His new drawing fell to the floor and was trampled underfoot.

"Leave the boy alone," Fa Theum managed to croak.

"Keep quiet until I tell you that you can speak! Unless you want another beating," said the leader, jabbing his staff in the priest's ribs. The old man gave a gasp of pain. "And *you*," he said, stooping so that he was eye to eye with Mel, "tell me who gave you permission for this exhibition."

His fetid breath made Mel wince.

"It's got nothing to do with the boy. It was my idea," rasped Fa Theum.

"I told you to keep quiet!" he bellowed, showering Mel with beads of foul-smelling spittle. Then, to Mel, "Well? What's the matter? Forgotten how to speak?"

"Can't you see he's terrified?" said the priest, fighting back his own pain.

The man grabbed Mel's hair so hard that a clump was torn out.

Mel screamed.

"Do you know how many laws you've broken with your pathetic little exhibition here? Do you realize how much trouble you're in?"

"Stop hurting me," screamed Mel. "Stop it!"

"So you can speak, after all. Well, now that you've found your voice, answer me. Or would you like another hairdo?"

"Mel, say nothing," came Fa Theum's voice.

"I'll not tell you again, skeg-breath." Turning to his henchman holding the priest, he said, "If he interrupts me again, hurt him. Hurt him badly."

"Leave him alone!" said Mel through gritted teeth.

Yanking his hair even harder, his interrogator said, "Don't try and tell me what to do, *Smell*. That is your name, isn't it?" He wrinkled his nose as if smelling something nasty. "You have no rights in this matter. None at all. You, Smell, and this disgusting old man, are mine. I will do with you exactly as I please."

"Don't hurt the b—" The priest's protest was cut short by a backhanded blow across the face.

"You have no idea who I am, have you, Smell? Not the faintest idea." He touched the emblem on his breast. "Have you ever heard of the Mysteries? Of course you have. Even out here in Feg, this stinking backwater. Well, I am the High-Bailiff of the Fifth Mystery. And as far as you and this old man are concerned, I *am* the Fifth Mystery. And it is *me*, and no one else, who says what goes and does not go, where pictures are concerned. Not that I'd grace such ugly scribbles with so noble a title as *pictures*." He prodded Mel's dropped landscape with the toe of his boot before grinding it underfoot as if it were a verminous insect.

Mel was scared that at any moment he would wet himself. His scalp hurt terribly where his hair had been yanked out, and his arms, held from behind, had gone numb. What had he done wrong?

At that moment there came a shrill whistle from within the fane.

"Ah, we're ready. Bring them both inside," announced the High-Bailiff. "Now we'll get some answers. Soon you'll both be eager to talk."

The men dragged their prisoners into the main body of the fane. The pews had been hastily pushed aside except for two, placed close together to form a kind of bed that occupied the center of the space. Fa Theum was roughly thrown down onto this and his hands and feet were tied to the legs.

"Are we ready, Mumchance?" asked the High-Bailiff.

In answer, a dwarf, dressed in the same scarlet robes, took a silver whistle attached to a chain around his neck and blew a note. He then selected a couple of evil-looking instruments from a small decorated chest and approached the helpless priest. Fa Theum's blood-stained cassock was ripped open, baring his pale and skinny torso.

There came a noise from the doorway. "Mel, Fa, what's going on?" said Willem, come to search for his truant son. He was followed closely by Mabin. They looked with horror at the scene.

"Ah, an audience. There's nothing I like more than an audience," said the High-Bailiff. "Are you the parents of Smell here? The resemblance is uncanny. There's something of the festering cesspit about both of you. A family trait, I'll warrant."

"Let go of them. You have no right." There was a tremor in Willem's voice.

"*No right*? On the contrary. I have *every* right. It's you who have no right. The only one who has less right than you is Smell here." He jerked Mel's head hard.

Mabin stifled a sob.

"W-what are you going to do?" Willem had difficulty saying the words.

"What am I going to do? I am going to watch my little man here create his own work of art. Then . . ." He placed a long, gloved finger to his pallid face and rolled his eyes in a showy gesture. "Mmm, let me think. What *shall* I do? Shall I have this pair of miscreants nailed to a tree and whipped and let it go at that? No, that would hardly fit a crime as serious as the theft of a Pleasure. Shall I hang them? No, not that either. Leniency was never my strong point. *I know!*" He held up his finger, pretending he had just had a brainstorm. "I'll send them to the mines! That's what I'll do. The old man won't last long, not in his present state, but Smell here"—he jerked Mel's head up by his chin—"might last for years before the Colored Death takes him. Who knows, he might even last long enough to pay for this stolen Pleasure. Not that it will matter to him. Not after a spell on Kig. Maybe I'll take you as well. And your woman. Make it a family affair. There's always room for more in the mines. The more the merrier, I say."

Willem hugged his wife even closer. "All the boy did was to pin up a few of his pictures."

"All the boy did was to steal a Pleasure. And whose Pleasure did he steal?"

"Ambrosius Blenk's Pleasure," came a deep voice. "Let the boy go."

5. escape

"DIRK TOT," SAID the High-Bailiff, recognizing the voice and turning to regard the newcomer. "I was wondering when you would turn up."

"Adolfus Spute, you have no jurisdiction over these two. Release them at once." Dirk Tot strode into the fane. He seemed even larger and more imposing than Mel remembered.

Adolfus Spute stood his ground. "I represent the Fifth Mystery here and these . . . these *vermin* have stolen one of our Pleasures. They must be made to pay. Even the great Ambrosius Blenk must pay for his Pleasures. That's the law."

"Oh, I quite agree. But, you see, Ambrosius Blenk has already paid for this Pleasure. This boy is one of Ambrosius Blenk's apprentices. And everything that Ambrosius Blenk's apprentices create belongs to Ambrosius Blenk. So, you see, this is actually my master's exhibition. Arranged, with great kindness I might say, by the good Fa. You are here on a fool's errand. Which seems fitting. Now let them go."

The High-Bailiff narrowed his pale eyes. His intense loathing of this man was obvious. Then he rounded on his men. "Why wasn't I told this Pleasure belonged to Ambrosius Blenk?" he bellowed. He kicked Mumchance in the ribs, sending him flying. "Which one of you scrot-brained, cretinous, half-wits organized this excursion?" he screamed. His men retreated backwards as he advanced on them.

Willem went over and cut Fa Theum free. Mabin rushed to her son's side and held him close.

Mel was distraught. "It's all my fault. It's my pictures that brought those men here. I nearly killed Fa Theum."

"Hush, Mel, hush." His mother hugged him closer.

"There's not a moment to lose," Dirk Tot said to Mabin quietly. "Take Mel out to my carriage at once."

Mabin stared at the giant man, uncertain.

"Now! Before it's too late. If we don't act at once all will be lost. Mel's life depends on it. Willem, do you know of a place where the Fa will be safe for an hour or two?"

Willem nodded.

"Good. Take him there and have someone tend to his wounds." He looked towards the back of the fane where the furious High-Bailiff had cornered his men and was laying into them with his heavy staff.

"Come, Mel, we must do as the gentleman says," said Mabin.

Mel turned to look at Fa Theum as his father helped the old man to his feet. *I shouldn't be leaving at a time like this. Leaving everyone to take the blame for what I've done.* Then he caught sight of the dwarf's case resting on a pew and shrugged free of his mother. "Wait, there's something I need." He gazed in at the tools of torture. He needed a weapon to make him feel less vulnerable. But they all looked somehow inappropriate, too specialized for self-defense. Then he spied a bodkin. *That's the one.*

"Mel, hurry." His mother tugged at his sleeve.

There came a pathetic whistle from the back of the fane and, as everyone turned towards it, Mel grasped the slim dagger, but it resisted. He tugged it hard and, as it came free, there was a soft metallic ping and a secret drawer inside the chest sprang open. Inside was a small decorated box. Without thinking, Mel grabbed that, too, and stuffed them both into his shirt.

"Mel, come *on*," said his mother as she pulled him towards the door and out to Dirk Tot's carriage, which stood alongside the scarlet carriage of the Fifth Mystery. A crowd of villagers had begun to gather.

Behind them, Dirk Tot followed them from the fane. "Put Mel inside and make your good-bye quick," he said to Mabin.

"*Good-bye*? But your outriders, surely they'll protect us."

"I don't have any outriders," confessed Dirk Tot. "There's just me and my coachman."

"But you can't snatch Mel away from us like this," said Mabin.

"There's no choice. Mel must come with me to Vlam. It's the only way he can survive now. Say good-bye. As quickly as you can." He turned away and said something quietly to his coachman, before disappearing back into the fane.

"Oh, Mel," said Mabin as she helped Mel into the carriage. She cradled her son's face between her hands and then pressed her handkerchief to his torn scalp. "It shouldn't have been like this."

"I'll be all right, Mum," Mel said, sounding braver than he felt. He gazed at his mother standing there and noticed a gray hair among her blonde tresses. *Why haven't I ever noticed that before?* He looked beyond her at the fane and the group of villagers, people he had known all his life. *Now that I'm leaving everything looks different.* "Mum, you know that—"

"No time. We must be gone," interrupted Dirk Tot as he joined Mel in the carriage, which dipped and groaned on its springs under his great weight. "You will probably want these," he said as he tossed the drawings from Mel's exhibition on to the opposite seat. He then sat alongside Mel, with the damaged side of his face towards him.

Mel's artistic eye no longer seemed to be working and he only saw the monster he had first encountered.

"Mabin, you and the villagers make yourselves scarce until those men leave. I'll send word as soon as we're safe in Vlam."

"But Mel has no food, no clothes, no money. How will he survive?"

"Fear not. What he needs will be provided. Yan, drive on!"

Mabin held on to Mel's hand, running alongside the carriage until it was moving so fast that she had to let go. Leaning out of the window, Mel watched his father join her. He attempted to see the expression on his face, but they were already too far away. He wished he could have spoken with him. He saw his parents clutch each other, and his mother waved until they were lost. Soon, even the village of Kop vanished behind the trees.

6. the mysteries

MEL HAD NEVER experienced such a complicated flood of emotions. There he was hastening off in the finest transport he had ever seen with a rich and important man to begin a new life. *But now that my dream's come true, why do I feel so wretched?*

"Here, Mel, let me look at you," said Dirk Tot. "Are you hurt? I can see bruises and a nasty wound on your scalp. Any broken bones? You belong to the master now. He won't want damaged goods."

Mel shook his head. He suddenly realized the danger he had been in and then, with a shock, the danger his parents and the whole village were still in. "Those men . . . what are they going to do? Mum and Dad, will they be all right?"

"I don't think that your parents—or anyone else—are in any immediate danger. If I know Adolfus Spute, as soon as he has vented his rage on his men he will be hot on our trail."

Mel looked alarmed.

"But he won't catch us. Not without these." He opened his good hand to reveal two greasy linchpins. "I had Yan remove them from the rear wheels of his carriage. I reckon he might get as far as ten miles before they finally fall off. The closest spares would be in Arpen and it would take a fast rider a day to make it there and back."

"I don't understand any of this. Those men, what did they want?"

Dirk Tot turned his good eye to look at Mel. "What do you know about the Mysteries?"

"Everyone knows about the Mystery. It controls weaving. Dad says that if he had more money he wouldn't have to make tabby. He could buy the Pleasure to weave fancy cloth."

"That's just the First Mystery. The Mysteries do rather more than that. Long, long ago, when Nem was just beginning to become rich and prosperous, all trade was unregulated. Unscrupulous traders began to take advantage of their customers. Wine was watered, flour was bulked up with sawdust, and all manner of shoddy goods were passed off as genuine. The honest merchants and artisans of Nem decided that this could not be allowed to continue. So they banded together and formed the Mysteries. If you wished to trade or produce any kind of goods, anywhere in the realm, then you had to be a member of your particular Mystery. Your work was carefully inspected before you were admitted and at regular intervals thereafter. The Mysteries only asked that their members pay a small tithe each year to cover the cost of seeking out the frauds and charlatans and policing the trade. Within a few years, the frauds had all but disappeared the customers grew content and bought more and more goods from the members of the Mysteries."

"If the Mysteries are so good, why does everyone in Kop always moan about them? And I still don't understand what this has to do with those men back there."

"Well, over the years, things went wrong. There will always be men who only think in terms of profit, never in terms of value. Men who have no interest in what they claim to represent.

Eventually, such men came to dominate, and under their control the Mysteries became increasingly corrupt. The tithes they demanded became bigger and bigger. When this form of income no longer satisfied, they came up with the idea of Pleasures. The bigger Mysteries began to gobble up the smaller ones until, eventually, only a few remained.

"Today they regulate all life in the realm beyond the bare necessities by their control of Pleasures."

"So if Heck the baker wants to bake a new kind of cake he has to buy a Pleasure?" asked Mel.

"That's right. Or if a seamstress wishes to decorate a garment with a new kind of stitch, then she must buy that Pleasure."

"So how many Mysteries are there?" Ever since he was small, Mel had always vaguely known that life in Kop was regulated by some shadowy authority far away.

"There are five, and each controls one of the senses. The First Mystery has dominion over touch and it controls, among other things, the production of cloth and tailoring. The Second Mystery rules over the sense of smell, and thereby the production of such items as perfumes and cosmetics. The Third Mystery concerns itself with the sense of hearing, and so with regulating all entertainment in the land. The Fourth Mystery is concerned with the sense of taste and its power lies over agriculture and the production and supply of food and drink."

"But everyone eats food. I've never heard of the Fourth Mystery."

"That's because the kind of food you would have been used to in Kop—bread, water, homegrown vegetables—doesn't come under their auspices. If things don't change, they probably will soon."

"But . . ." Mel paused, confused. Suddenly the world seemed huge and hostile. "I still don't see what those men wanted."

"That brings us to the Fifth Mystery, which you have just had the misfortune to encounter. Its domain is the sense of sight. It controls the use of color and anything to do with it with an iron fist." Dirk Tot's brow furrowed and his good eye narrowed. "You will be seeing a lot more of it in the years ahead. The Fifth Mystery is the largest, richest, and most powerful of all."

"More powerful than the Fourth Mystery? You can't eat color."

"Oh, color was just the beginning of its power. Its ascent began when it discovered deposits of pigment on the island of Kig. The Fifth Mystery has mines there."

"That's where that man threatened to send me."

"Yes. Anyone who crosses the Fifth Mystery can end up there. On Kig the Fifth Mystery became expert at mining—and not only pigments. It discovered gold, silver, precious stones, and other valuable minerals, which increased its wealth further."

"I've heard they're valuable but you can't eat them, surely."

"There are things even more valuable than gold, silver, and gems. It expanded its mining operations and discovered the coal and gas that powers Nem today. When we get to Vlam you'll see what I mean. The Fifth Mystery's wealth is fabulous—certainly greater than the King, the Maven, and the other four Mysteries combined."

"So you're telling me the Mysteries are all bad?"

"Bad? As things stand, yes. There are a few, a very few, within the Mysteries who still hold true to their original ideals, but their voice is weak."

"But none of that explains why the Fifth Mystery came all the way to Kop. How did they know about me?"

"You flatter yourself, Mel. Adolfus Spute didn't know you existed before today. He came to Kop looking for me."

"But why—?"

"That's enough questions. You must be hungry."

Mel had never imagined that there could be food like the delicacies the giant pulled from a wicker hamper. There were richly colored and delicately smoked slices of ham cut so thin they were almost transparent, and a great loaf of fluffy bread with tiny pieces of fruit. Even the water was alive with thousands of bubbles that danced on his tongue.

"Enjoying the picnic? We'll stop for something more substantial this evening."

Mel's eyes widened. "More substantial? That's the best food I've ever tasted."

"You can eat very well in Nem—if you can afford the Pleasures." Dirk Tot's tone had a bitter edge.

Afterwards, Mel began to doze, lulled by his full stomach, the warm day, and the steady rocking motion of the carriage as it made its way across the rolling countryside towards Vlam.

Suddenly, he was jolted awake. They were stopped in the middle of a thick wood and he realized he must have slept for some time. The door opened and Yan stood there. He looked at his master meaningfully and then twitched his head, indicating something over his shoulder.

"Wait here and keep quiet," said Dirk Tot sharply. "Don't try and follow me." He ignored Mel's questioning look and drew down blinds that blocked the view from the windows. "And don't look out. You belong to the master now and must do as you're told."

Mel was taken aback at the man's terse tone of voice. Was

this the same man who had spoken so encouragingly about his drawings?

As soon as Dirk Tot slammed the door after him, Mel felt very alone. Sitting in the darkened interior, he became fearful that the High-Bailiff and his men had caught up with them. He remembered the bodkin he had stolen and fished it out of his shirt. He grasped the sharp dagger firmly and sat very still, straining his ears for sounds of activity. After a few minutes he slowly turned the handle and opened the door a crack. Seeing nothing, he opened it fully and stepped down. There was no one in sight. Then he caught the faint sound of voices on the wind. Mustering all his courage, he patted the horses and then set off towards the sound.

After a few yards he heard the voices again, louder now, and turned down an overgrown track in their direction. He soon saw a ruined building ahead. It had clearly once been much grander than anything he had ever seen in Kop, with fluted columns supporting the door and windows, and the still recognizable remains of colored tiles set into the walls. He began to creep towards it. The walls were still upright and covered with ivy and brambles but the glass in the windows was missing, and only blackened, bare rafters showed where the roof had once been. He sensed movement inside and edged closer still. At the window he saw what he dreaded most. Three men, dressed in scarlet, were confronting Dirk Tot and Yan.

7. the road to vlam

MEL STOOD AS still as a heron, his whole body tense. He strained his ears but heard only the wind whispering through the trees and the song of birds. His senses were as alive as when he was drawing, aware of everything around him.

He edged towards the doorway. Sick with fear, he crept closer and saw that there was a sixth figure inside, dressed in the same deep blue livery as Yan. The odds seemed better now, but the men in scarlet were sure to be armed and Dirk Tot still might need his help. He watched as Dirk Tot unfastened his reticule, withdrew what Mel guessed was a bag of money, and a folded document and handed them over to the men in red. *They're robbing him.* Mel readied his bodkin in his sweaty hand. Then, in a gesture that shocked Mel, Dirk Tot embraced first one man and then the others as if they were old friends.

The meeting broke up abruptly. Mel ducked down. There was no way he could get back to the carriage before the others. He let them pass his hiding place and then set off back through the wood at an angle he calculated would bring him out near the carriage. When it came in sight through the trees he saw that Dirk Tot, Yan, and the new man were already there. Thinking quickly, Mel unbuckled his belt and emerged on to the road refastening it.

"Mel, where've you been?" asked Dirk Tot. "I told you not to leave the carriage." There was suspicion as well as anger in his voice.

"Just in there," Mel lied, indicating the trees. "That food was much richer than I'm used to. I had to go."

Yan and the new man exchanged a smile but Dirk Tot stared hard at Mel. He said, "Mel, this is Hennink," indicating the other man. "We just stopped by his house to pick him up so he could share the driving with Yan. We've a long way yet to go. We'd best be cracking on."

Mel did not feel quite so guilty about his deceit now that Dirk Tot was lying to him, too. As it turned out, his was only a half lie, as shortly after their journey recommenced he felt a stirring in his bowels. The food *had* been rich. The steady rocking motion of the carriage that had lulled him before had an altogether different and unwelcome effect now.

As evening approached, they halted at an inn and Mel was at last able to relieve himself. In his brief absence, Dirk Tot had arranged rooms for them all and ordered supper. The inn itself was bigger than Fa Theum's fane and much better furnished. The other customers stared at the new arrivals with thinly veiled distrust. Mel also looked around warily. Strangers rarely came to Kop and those that did were invariably dressed in plain, uncolored tabby. There was tabby to be seen here but augmented with brighter, better-made garments. To Mel tabby meant friend while colored clothes increasingly meant foe.

Mel felt even more ill at ease as he sat down at the dining table. Dirk Tot looked at him as if he could read his thoughts. *Why did he say such bad things about the Fifth Mystery when he was one of them?*

When the hot food came Mel wolfed it down. "Can I go to my room now?" he asked.

Dirk Tot nodded. "It's been an interesting day—for all of us. We won't be long from our beds. There's another four days of hard traveling ahead of us."

Mel had never had a room of his own before, nor a bed as large as the one he saw now. He could not believe how soft the feather mattress was. As he pulled off his shirt, the bodkin and the tiny box fell to the floor. He retrieved them, placed the dagger on the small table next to his bed, and examined the box by the light of the candle.

It was made of some veined material that he had never seen before, as dark as old pewter but with murky swirls of color forming the tiniest picture he had ever seen. It represented the inside of a cave, looking outwards. There were sharp rocks on the floor pointing upwards and others on the ceiling pointing down. Beyond the mouth of the cavern he could see a landscape, veiled in mist, stretching away to jagged, snow-capped mountains. There were stars in the evening sky but they described no constellation that he could recognize. On the cave floor a strange plant grew and in the folds of its leaves nestled an egg. Mel was astounded at the fine detail.

He turned it over in his hand but could see no way of opening it. He was about to give up when he pressed both ends at once and the lid popped open. There was powder inside it, every color of the rainbow all at once. It glowed with a beautiful iridescence as he turned the box in the candlelight. He raised the box to his nose experimentally but could detect only a faint, metallic odor. Mel licked his finger and dipped it into the powder. He put this to his tongue and tentatively tasted it. It was bitter. *Perhaps it's poison*. With horror, he remembered where he had stolen it from. He cried out and immediately spat it on to the floor. Mel then watched in amazement as the blob of multicolored spit swirled this way and that on the bare boards and then seemed to writhe more purposefully. It began to form a miniature picture all by itself: a view of Kop! Incredulous, he had just grabbed the candle so that he could examine this marvel closer when there came a knock at his door.

"Mel?"

Mel just had time to snap the box shut, hide it behind his back, and place his foot over the gently moving stain before Dirk Tot's face peered around the door.

"Are you all right? I thought I heard you call out."

"Oh, it was just a spider. It startled me, that's all." Mel was becoming a practiced liar.

The giant glanced around the low-ceilinged bedroom. "You're not in Kop anymore, Mel. You've got some growing up to do and you'd better do it fast. Good night."

Hurt and angry, Mel wanted to answer back, *Don't talk to me like that, traitor, or I'll tell* . . . Who? He was not in Kop anymore. He was all on his own.

As soon as the sound of Dirk Tot's footsteps had vanished down the hall, Mel removed his foot. There was now just a many-colored smear on the floor. *Did I imagine it?* He was puzzled but also weary. He blew out his candle and climbed into bed. Sleep overtook him almost instantly.

In the morning there was no trace left of the stain.

~

Mel would have liked to examine his box and its strange contents further but the inns they rested at each night were busier so he had to share rooms with Yan and Hennink.

After they had been traveling for five days, there came a rapping on the carriage roof and Yan's voice shouting "Vlam ahead, sir."

Mel looked out of the window. What he saw took his breath away. They had crested the brow of a hill, one of a long chain of hills that spread away in a great loop on each side all the way to the horizon. Nestled in the hollow within this vast natural amphitheater were many farms, fields, and orchards that became more numerous as they approached the center. Right in the middle lay their destination. Roads snaked towards Vlam from every direction, vanishing into the city walls through grand arches. These thoroughfares were crowded with people and vehicles. The buildings that flanked the roads became denser as they neared the city. A wide river and many smaller canals entered through other, broader openings. Mel made out barges and sailing ships. Yet more boats sailed high above them, entering on tall, stilted aqueducts over the city walls. Spaced at intervals around the walls were tall towers, on top of which were peculiar machines with articulated arms that moved up and down, left and right in odd, purposeful patterns.

When he finally found his voice Mel said, "I never imagined anything could be so *big*. Vlam must be very old."

"Some say it's half as old as the world."

"Are all cities like Vlam?"

"I've traveled throughout the Seven Kingdoms but I've never seen its like." Now that they were in sight of home Dirk Tot's mood had lifted. "You see those palaces?"

"Palaces," repeated Mel. He had never dreamed he would ever see a real palace.

"Those are the three Great Houses. To the west stands the House of Thrones, the palace of the King. You can see his purple banner. And there to the east, crowned with the golden diaglyph, is the House of Spirits. The other one to the north, the biggest of all, is the House of Mysteries."

"Who lives in them?"

"King Spen lives in the House of Thrones and the Maven in the House of Spirits."

"What, all on their *own*?"

Dirk Tot laughed. It was a deep, rich sound. "No, Mel, not on their own. The King and his entire court and council live within the House of Thrones. The realm doesn't govern itself. The Maven is the spiritual leader of Nem. He has the Hierarchs, the Fas Major, and lots of Fas Minor to keep him company. As for the Mysteries, well, there is a vast bureaucracy needed to keep *that* House and all its machinations functioning."

Mel could make out the five banners of the Mysteries fluttering from a tower so tall it seemed to scrape the underbelly of heaven itself. The topmost banner, bigger than the rest, was scarlet, emblazoned with the same black eye emblem that Adolfus Spute and his men had worn. The three soaring palaces each stood atop a steep hill. From the flanks of these hills the rest of Vlam seemed to tumble down, its headlong fall only checked by the city walls, which seemed to hold it in and prevent it from spilling out into the surrounding countryside.

Unable to take his eyes from the spectacle, Mel asked, "What're those hills called?"

"The hills are named after the palaces that stand on them. The Hill of Thrones, the Hill of Spirits, and the Hill of Mysteries."

As they descended the steep road, Mel's flood of questions slowed to a trickle and finally ceased, so enthralled was he by the splendor of Vlam.

By the time they reached the city gates it was evening and lamps were being lit everywhere. The guards at the gates recognized Dirk Tot's carriage instantly and respectfully ushered him through. The music of the wheels changed as they rumbled over the cobblestones of the city.

Mel had never seen so many people before in his entire life, and all rushing this way and that as if there was no time to lose. There was not a scrap of tabby to be seen on anyone. All of the streets were lit by lamps that burned within glass globes on top of tall, intricately fashioned posts. He saw buildings with brightly lit lower stories open to the street.

"Why haven't those houses got proper walls?" he asked, baffled.

"They're shops, Mel. You know what shops are? They sell things."

"Shops? I've never seen shops before. In Kop we make everything ourselves or barter with the other villagers for what we need. Once a year a tinker visits with pots and pans and stuff. We usually pay him in tabby. The people here must be very rich."

"Some are, but not everyone."

Mel rapidly became disoriented by their frequent twists and turns. At one point they crossed a wide river, although the bridge was so lined with shops and inns that at first Mel thought it was just another busy street. Mel saw that the three Great Houses were always visible above the rooftops from anywhere in the city.

"Mel, come away from the window," said Dirk Tot suddenly.

"Why?"

"Those men are from the Fifth Mystery. It's best you don't draw attention to yourself. And look, those others are members of the Fourth Mystery. And those are from the Second."

From the darkness within the carriage Mel saw people with the same arrogant air as the High-Bailiff but dressed in other colors and with different hairstyles. Mel saw that the citizens of Vlam would deliberately cross the street to avoid the men from the Mysteries and one man spat in the gutter at their passing.

At last, their carriage turned into an imposing square with tall houses on each side and a huge, elaborate fountain at its center. The architecture was intricate and made much use of herringbone brickwork, tracery, and colored tiles. The steep, gabled roofs were tiled in extravagant, geometric patterns with tall, barley-sugar brick chimneys. The roofline was punctuated here and there with pointed spires and turrets, and fierce-looking stone gargoyles projected from the carved eaves. The building they were headed for was larger than its neighbors, the upper part of it mostly devoted to an enormous clock surrounded by a multitude of small doors and windows. At that moment the clock struck the hour with a great, musical peal of bells. A procession of small, brightly painted mechanical figures appeared in the windows and filed out from the doors. As the clock chimed, minstrels played instruments, maidens danced, knights chased dragons from one side of the timepiece to the other. Above them, bright planets and constellations whirled and pirouetted until the chiming ceased and they all disappeared back into the clock face. Mel, whose sole concept of time was gauged by the height of the sun, was awestruck.

"What's *that?*" asked Mel.

"It's a clock. It's one of the wonders of Vlam."

"Who's it belong to?" Mel craned his neck to keep it in view.

"It's Ambrosius Blenk's clock. It's his house."

"What about the others?"

"All of the houses on this side of the square belong to the master. The other houses on the block behind belong to him, too. It's now one big mansion. The master has a large household, Mel, as you're about to see."

Beneath the wondrous clock was a set of gilded gates. As they approached, the gates swung open and the carriage passed through a tunnel into a large courtyard. Sure enough, what had seemed to be a row of individual houses from the outside was revealed as the façade of a single dwelling that occupied the entire side of the square. The courtyard was planted with low box hedges and flowering trees, interspersed with stone sculptures and surrounded by a cloister. Lamps burned everywhere, turning the twilight to noon. Servants in the same deep blue livery as Dirk Tot and his coachmen hurried to and fro. Grooms appeared and took charge of the horses. A footman opened the carriage door.

Dirk Tot stepped out of the carriage but Mel held back. Now that he had finally arrived, he felt nervous and painfully aware of how shabby and unsophisticated he was. Everything was so grand, so alien, so colored. *I look like a scarecrow. I'm never going to fit in here.*

"Come on, Mel. It's late."

Mel swallowed hard, grabbed his precious drawings, and stepped down from the carriage. Dirk Tot snapped his fingers impatiently. Mel held his drawings in front of him to hide his threadbare peasant clothes and followed. He was so captivated by everything around him that he did not notice when he stepped in a mound of horse dung before following Dirk Tot up a low flight of steps and into the mansion of his new master.

The long hall they entered rose above them seven stories to a brightly painted and intricately beamed ceiling. The floor was paved with pale tiles in a huge, circular design that was now tainted with Mel's filthy footprints. The entire mansion was illuminated by flickering gas lamps in brackets attached to the walls. Before them rose a wide staircase that branched and divided into galleries all the way to the top.

Then, in an instant, Mel's world changed. For the first time he came face to face with a great work of art. He had listened to Fa Theum's descriptions of paintings, but nothing could have prepared him for the raw thrill of actually seeing one. It seemed to him that it was not just lifelike but was even more real than the concrete objects all around him. It was as if he could step through the canvas and enter the immaculate world depicted there.

As he stared, he felt a great happiness enfold him, as he felt the borders of his life expand until they stretched for ever. He knew then that he had come home.

8. the apprentices

MEL STOOD TRANSFIXED at the foot of the stairs. There, just above him, at the head of the broad, first flight, on a great crystal throne, sat an enormous, robed figure with the head of a giant eagle. Around its feet were gathered a menagerie of hybrid creatures, and above it soared more strange and wonderful birds and insects than Mel could count. They all gazed down at the new arrival from out of the painting with a piercing, unblinking, and malevolent stare.

"One of Ambrosius Blenk's. Impressive, isn't it?" Dirk Tot's voice jolted Mel from his ecstasy.

"The master did that? *Really?*"

"Really. Look, Mel, it's late and I must report. Minch will look after you now."

As Dirk Tot strode away through a side door, Mel looked up at Minch. He did not need to be told that the fat servant did not like apprentices—it was evident in his sour expression.

"Shoes," said Minch curtly.

Mel followed the man's imperious gaze down to his own feet and, with a sinking feeling, saw the muck he had trailed inside. "Sorry." He blushed and quickly removed them.

"Follow," ordered Minch as he set off up the stairs.

Mel padded after the servant in his bare feet. At the first

landing he paused to examine the painting more closely. Up close there was even more detail visible than from below. There was no trace of brushwork. His own drawings seemed pitiful in comparison.

Movement attracted his eye. At the foot of the stairs he saw a young girl, probably no older than he was, on her hands and knees with a bucket and soapy scrubbing brush attacking the mess he had created. She saw him looking at her and glared back.

"*Boy!*" snapped Minch and gestured brusquely for Mel to follow. They climbed the stairs and turned down one corridor after another until Mel was hopelessly lost.

"Stop," ordered Minch. "Wait." He produced some keys and unlocked a storeroom. He looked Mel up and down. "Small." He entered the room and soon emerged with a pile of clothing. "Kit," he announced as he piled a shirt, doublet, hose, and boots in the household colors in Mel's arms.

Mel stood for a moment with his jaw hanging open. "Are these for me?"

Minch sighed. "Come." He set off again at once, Mel half-running to keep up. More corridors and stairways followed until they arrived at a door through which Mel could hear the murmur of many voices. Minch pushed open the door and announced, "Refectory. Apprentices," before turning and leaving.

Mel found himself looking into a long, brightly lit room with a colored mural running around the walls. Running down the center of the room was a long oak table, around which sat a dozen apprentices on wooden benches with their half-finished suppers before them. They all wore additions to their livery such as colored caps or patterned scarves or sashes, and all of their clothes bore paint stains. There was an evident hierarchy in the refectory, with the younger apprentices at the end of the table nearest the door and the older ones at the other. Seated at the head of the table, in an ornate, upholstered chair, was the eldest of all. He was skinny and much taller than everyone else, his spotty face in need of a shave.

At Mel's appearance the conversation ceased. All eyes were upon him. The head apprentice took a long drink from his goblet and wiped his mouth with the back of his hand. He had a ratlike, pointed nose and tiny gray eyes, above which ran a long, single eyebrow, and there was a large wine stain on his shirt beneath his open doublet. Slouching back in his thronelike chair, he asked in a slurred voice, "What've we here? Wash your name?"

Mel smiled and introduced himself, "Melkin Womper. But everyone calls me Mel. Pleased to meet you."

There was a moment's silence and then they all bellowed with laughter.

"A Fegie, we've got ourselves a real, live Fegie!"

"I do believe you're right," sneered the eldest apprentice. "Our very own country bumpkin. Look at what he's wearing—it's *tabby*. And he's barefoot. Have you ever seen anything like it? And where did a shoeless, tabby-wearing Fegie get the wherewithal to buy an apprenticeship with old Blenko?"

"I didn't buy it. It was a free one," answered Mel.

"*It was a free one*," mocked the other.

"And what makes you so special? What're those?" He had spotted Mel's drawings and pushed his right-hand companion roughly. "Bring it here, Bunt. Let me see."

"It's not bad, Groot, it's actually not bad," said Bunt admiringly as he retrieved a charcoal portrait of Mel's mother from under the new clothes Mel carried and handed it to the head apprentice.

"You don't know what you're talking about, Bunt. It's rubbish," proclaimed Groot. "A Fegie wouldn't be capable of producing anything but rubbish. I doubt if his hands have held anything finer than a plough or pitchfork. Still, it's nothing that a few strokes from a real artist couldn't improve." He dipped his finger into the gravy on his plate and wrote "Fegish rubbish" across the drawing.

"Hey! Don't do that."

Groot ignored Mel's plea. "There now. What do you think?" He held it up for the other apprentices to admire. When no one answered he grabbed the nearest apprentice viciously by the throat and asked again, "Well, Jurgis?"

"It's Fegish rubbish, Groot," answered the lad in a strangulated voice.

"Let's hear it from all of you," said Groot, releasing Jurgis.

There came an unenthusiastic murmur of "Fegish rubbish" from around the refectory.

"It's better than you can do," mumbled a boy about Mel's age, sitting at the foot of the table.

Mel looked down at the mumbler. He had very pale skin and dark hair. His hazel eyes had a dejected look that matched his hangdog expression.

"What did you say, Ludo?" asked Groot. "Let's all hear it."

"I said it's probably the best he can do."

"That's right . . . hey, what's that smell?" asked Groot.

Bunt approached Mel again and saw the shoes he was carrying. "It's the Fegie, Groot. His shoes are covered in scrot."

"Ugh, that's *disgusting!* But what more can you expect from a Fegie?" He turned to Mel, "Perhaps you're used to that smell where you come from but it's not allowed in *my* refectory. Ludo, take that smell out and get him cleaned up. I don't want to see either of you again until he's dressed properly and smelling like a human being. Here, take this with you," he said, flinging Mel's defiled drawing back at him before taking another great swig of wine and belching loudly.

"They call me a Fegie as if it's an insult," said Mel, balancing his new clothes and drawings as Ludo led him away. "None of us have the choice where we're born."

"Think yourself lucky. It could have been worse. They could have smelled your shoes before they heard your accent."

Mel laughed. "I guess Fegie doesn't seem so bad, after all. So those are the other apprentices. I can't say I think much of them."

Ludo laughed with him. He was taller than Mel and his demeanor was lighter now that they were out of the refectory. "They're okay, once you get to know them. But they're scared of Groot. And his sidekicks, Bunt and Jurgis. They can be vicious—especially when they're drunk."

"Isn't he, you know, a bit old to be an apprentice?"

Ludo gave a dismissive laugh. "He should have graduated years ago. But when the time comes each year to present the master with his apprentice piece he always comes up with some excuse or other."

"What's an apprentice piece?"

"It's a painting that we all must produce on our own at the end of our apprenticeship, before the master passes us as journeymen." He looked at Mel. "You don't know what a journeyman is, do you?"

"Afraid not."

"It's like a junior artist. The truth, is Groot's not that good.

He's lazy, too, prefers to spend his time boozing and gambling. The master would like to boot him out, but he's a Smert."

"What's a smert?"

"It's not a thing. It's his name. Groot Smert."

"What's so special about that?"

"Don't you know anything? The Smerts are only one of the most powerful families in Vlam, that's all. They're related to the Brools and the Sputes."

"Not the High-Bailiff?"

"The same. Groot's his nephew. What's the matter? You've gone as white as a sheet."

"It's . . . it's nothing. It's just that I've met Adolfus Spute."

Ludo and Mel mounted some stairs. "So the master gave you a free apprenticeship then. You must be good. May I see?"

"I don't know. Groot said it's rubbish."

"You don't get it, do you? If it *was* rubbish he would have ignored it." Ludo took some of Mel's new clothes so he could look at a drawing. "Wow! This is great, Mel! Groot couldn't draw like this until he'd been here years."

A broad grin cracked Mel's face.

Ludo pushed open a door. "This is the dormitory. You can sleep there, next to me." He indicated a vacant bed. "You can stash your stuff in there," he said, opening a cupboard and placing the clothes inside. "And look here." He knelt down and showed Mel where a board was loose at the back of the cupboard, revealing a shallow space. "Great for hiding things you don't want the others to see." He winked at Mel. "You can pin your drawings up next to your bed, we all do. I'll fetch some drawing pins while you get changed."

Mel quickly discarded his coarse tabby garments and changed into his new livery. They were the finest clothes he had ever worn. The shirt and the hose were made of white silk, the doublet of the softest deep blue velvet, and the ankle boots of supple doeskin.

Mel folded his old clothes and placed them inside his cupboard. As an afterthought, he secreted his bodkin and the little box behind the loose board, pushing the box especially far down so that only an arm as small as his could retrieve it. He laid his drawings on the bed, placing the defaced portrait of his mother to one side. With a few strokes of his hand the malicious Groot had turned a thing of beauty into no more than a piece of stained paper. It was as if he had assaulted Mel's mother. Mel felt a stomach-churning mixture of rage and sadness.

"Don't you look smart? Almost like one of us," said Ludo as he returned. "But you need to add something of your own that sets you apart from the other servants. Like this here." He touched the olive-green-and-gold sash around his waist. "It's the colors of the Cleefs—my family's house."

"Your family has its own colors? You must be awfully posh."

"No, not really. Certainly posher than Groot—not that it counts for anything round here. Not while he's in charge."

"I know!" said Mel. He reached inside his cupboard, pulled out his faded, tabby breeches, and tore off a wide strip. Tying it around his waist, he said with a sense of pride, "It's the Womper family colors."

"Great! That's one in the eye for Groot."

The two of them pinned his drawings up around his bed.

Ludo picked up the portrait of Mel's mother. "I'm really sorry, Mel. That was a squity thing to do. Even for Groot."

Mel could not respond because a great lump had formed in his throat. He placed the drawing in his cupboard. He felt tears forming but did not want to embarrass himself in front of his new friend. Changing the subject, he said, "I'm starving."

"I guess you don't want to go back to the refectory. Let's sneak down to the kitchens. It's strictly out of bounds but Wren will give you something to eat. But first, I think we'll get rid of these." He picked up Mel's smelly shoes, holding them at arm's length, and dropped them out the open window. "If only Groot was as easy to get rid of."

"There she is. Psst! Wren. *Wren*," called Ludo softly from their hiding place. Heat and bright light radiated out of the bustling kitchen into the cool, dimly lit storeroom.

"Who's there? Is that you, Ludo?" came a girl's voice from beyond the door.

"Wren, this is Mel. He's new here and he's missed his supper. He's starving—could you find him something to eat?"

"You know it's not allowed, Ludo. You shouldn't be down here. And if they catch me then I'll be out on my ear. We both will." She peered cautiously over her shoulder and stepped into the storeroom. "And who's this new . . . *you!*"

It was the girl Mel had seen earlier, cleaning up the mess he had created in the hallway. She was slim and wore a long cloth wrapped around her head like a turban. Beneath it she had long, auburn hair and green eyes and her cheeks were bright with exertion. Over her long dress in the Blenk household blue was a soiled, white pinafore. *When she's not scowling she might be quite pretty,* thought Mel. "Uh, hello," he said sheepishly. "Sorry about the . . . the you-know-what."

"Why should I risk my job to get anything for *you*—after all the work you made for me?"

"But Wren, he's really hungry. *Please*," pleaded Ludo.

Wren glared at Mel, but after a moment her expression softened and she said, "Oh, all right. You look half starved. Wait here. And keep quiet. If they catch you there'll be big trouble." She disappeared into the kitchen and returned shortly with an apple and a generous sandwich containing a thick slice of succulent beef. "I must go now. We're rushed off our feet at the moment. Just stay out of sight."

Mel had only ever eaten beef once before, at a village feast. It tasted even better than he remembered but he managed only one bite.

"Caught yer, thief!" A plump woman grabbed him by the scruff of his neck and held him fast. "Minch, Minch! Come and lend a hand. I've caught a thief."

Mel looked round quickly for Ludo. *Where was Ludo?*

Minch emerged from the kitchen, wiping his greasy mouth on his sleeve. He grabbed Mel's arm. "'Prentice," he said. He snatched Mel's sandwich away, proclaiming, "Proof."

"It's off to the steward with you, my lad," said the cook. "This could mean prison. I've seen people sent to the mines for less. Yer no better than a guttersnipe. The gutter's where yer belong and that's where yer'll be before tonight's out. Mark my words."

Mel's heart sank. *Ludo, please help.* A great feeling of dread overtook him. *Arrived and expelled on the same day.* How could he face returning home?

As he was marched away between Minch and the cook he looked around and caught sight of the toe of a boot as it withdrew behind some sacks. *Ludo.* The first sign of trouble and he'd left Mel alone to face the music.

Mel was marched up to the steward's office. Minch knocked and they entered.

Dirk Tot looked up from his papers. "Yes?"

"Thief," said Minch, pushing Mel forward. "Proof." He slapped the illicit sandwich on to the desk and indicated the cook with a jerk of his thumb. "Witness"

"Is this so?" asked Dirk Tot, addressing the cook.

"Yes, sir. Caught him red-handed, I did. Freshly baked bread and some of the best beef, straight from the spit. An' this!" she said triumphantly, producing the apple as if it were the clinching piece of evidence.

"Is this true, Mel?"

Mel hung his head and nodded.

"Very well, Cook, Minch. I'll deal with this. Please return to your duties."

"Just so long as he gets what's comin' to him," said the cook as she left.

"'Prentice," said Minch with a sneer, as if it were an insult. He cast a last, longing look at the sandwich and closed the door after them.

Dirk Tot fixed his withering one-eyed stare on Mel and said in a stern voice, "Is there anything you want to tell me, Mel?"

Still staring at the floor, Mel shook his head, "No, sir."

"Was there anyone else involved?"

Mel said nothing.

"Mel, there have been hundreds of apprentices through the studio in my time, and more than a few of them have stood where you're standing now for all manner of misdemeanors. But never after so short a stay. I cannot really believe that after only a few hours in this household, you made it all the way down to the kitchens, found where the bread was kept, helped yourself to a fat slice of the master's best beef, from the spit in the very heart of the kitchen, and then found yourself the means of preparing this sandwich. All on your own. Come on, Mel, who else was in this with you?"

Mel raised his head. *Scrot to you, Ludo.* "No one, sir. I just found my way there by . . . by accident and took the food. All on my own."

"Very well. You've disappointed me, Mel. Cook wanted you punished and punished you will be."

9. lord brool

BY THE TIME Mel found his way back to the dimly lit dormitory, everyone was busy retiring for the night and paid him no attention. From the far end, where Groot slept, there came the sound of heavy, drunken snoring. As Mel sat down on the edge of his bed, Ludo's face appeared over the partition that separated their compartments.

Great. Now *he turns up.*

"Sorry, Mel, I tried to warn you when I spotted Cook coming," Ludo whispered sheepishly. "I only just had time to hide myself. There was no point in the two of us getting caught, was there? It's not as if the punishment would have been halved if two people had to suffer. Besides, you're new here. They'd be bound to make allowances. You didn't say I was involved, did you?"

"Don't worry, Ludo, I didn't mention you." Ludo had let him down, but he was still the only friend Mel had in this strange new world.

"Thanks. If my family ever heard of this I'd really be in for it. By the way, what did you get as a punishment?"

"One month's loss of privileges and stipend, whatever they are."

"Privileges are permission to go out and about in the city every Sunday. The stipend's like pocket money. It doesn't amount to much, though—only one silver piece per year."

One silver piece sounded like a fortune to Mel, who had only ever seen copper coins—and never too many of those either.

He undressed and climbed into bed, feeling miserable and betrayed. He thought about his parents and Fa Theum and hoped that they had not suffered any more at the hands of Adolfus Spute. He wished he had had time to talk with his father before Dirk Tot had whisked him away. And then his thoughts turned to his new life. He would have the opportunity to study the many paintings that hung around the mansion. One day he would even create some of his own. In spite of his hunger, he drifted off to sleep with a smile on his lips.

At the same time, high in one of the lofty towers of the House of Mysteries, a heated meeting was taking place. Adolfus Spute and his dwarf Mumchance, weary and travel-stained, cowered before the huge bulk of Lord Brool. The Lord-High-Master of the Fifth Mystery sat, toadlike, at his desk. A single lamp illuminated Lord Brool's face, its flickering, yellowish glow emphasizing his warts and bloated features the master was angry; very angry.

"*Lost it!* What do you mean, *lost* it?" he bellowed. Flecks of spittle hung at the corners of his mouth. His complexion almost matched that of his scarlet robes. The silver goblet of wine he was holding buckled in his grasp.

"It was definitely with us when we arrived in Kop. Wasn't it, Mumchance?" Adolfus Spute glanced nervously at his diminutive companion for support.

Mumchance nodded.

"Yes it was. But after we packed away the Instruments of Interpellation the box no longer seemed to be there. It was, in a word, *gone*," the High-Bailiff confessed.

"It was such a simple task, Spute; I could have sent a child to do it. Perhaps I *should* have sent a child. An infant could not have made more of a mess than you incompetents have done. All you had to do was pay a visit to that meddling fool Floris and persuade him to return the Fifth Mystery's property."

"Just so, cousin." Adolfus Spute hoped that playing on their kinship might help to mitigate his superior's ire. "But Lord Floris was most reluctant to be parted from the substance. He needed to be persuaded to within *an inch of his life*. Could a child have achieved that, I ask myself?"

Lord Brool's tiny eyes bored into his subordinate. "Your persuasive powers, Spute, are not in question. What *is* in question is your trustworthiness. To *misplace* such a treasure seems to me almost disloyal. Disloyal to the point of treachery. The Fifth Mystery expects more from its servants. It expects much more. Do I make myself clear?"

Adolfus Spute's mouth was moving but no words were coming out.

"So, seeing as it was you who lost it, it seems only reasonable to expect that you should restore it before the next meeting of the High-Council. Otherwise, we might review your current position."

"But, my lord . . ." Finding his voice again, Adolfus Spute realized he was in no position to object. "As your lordship wishes."

"And you have yet to explain exactly what you were doing in such a godforsaken province as Feg in the first place. If I thought that you were pursuing your own, private ends—your personal vendetta against Dirk Tot, perhaps?"

Adolfus Spute's mouth dropped open.

"Oh, I know all about the history between you two, Spute. I know that you've been trying to entrap him for years, and he's thwarted you at every turn. Perhaps I should also bring this episode to the attention of the High-Council. We would take a very dim view of such dereliction of duty on the part of our High-Bailiff."

Adolfus Spute swallowed hard.

"Do I make myself clear, Spute? I'm sure I do. Now, get out! And don't let me see you again until you have it back."

As he reached the relative safety of the anteroom and his two waiting henchmen, Adolfus Spute rounded on Mumchance and kicked him viciously, bowling him over. "You were in charge of the box, you sniveling fraction of a man. How could you have let it out of your sight?"

Mumchance picked himself up and blew a series of notes on his whistle.

"What? Of course I was going to keep some for myself. It's me who should be Lord-High-Master, not that beslubbering, toad-featured scut in there."

Mumchance's tiny eyes twinkled and he blew a triumphant note.

"You're right, 'Lord Spute' does have a certain ring to it." The High-Bailiff bared his yellow teeth in a repulsive smile. Then his face darkened. "But now I'm right back at square one. I need to get my hands on it all over again." He looked down at Mumchance. "Now, where do you suppose it went?"

The dwarf blew a positive blast.

"Yes, that's what I thought, too."

Mumchance piped a tuneless warble.

"Succinctly put, my murderous midget. There's no chance of getting our hands on Smell while he's under Blenk's protection."

Mumchance's whistle blew again.

"Great minds think alike, my little man. The Fegish boy might be induced to leave the mansion if I chose the right bait." He turned to his henchmen. "You two are looking a bit peaky, a trifle run-down. I think you could do with a vacation. In the country, maybe. I hear Feg is rather lovely at this time of year. And while you're there, why don't you look up some old acquaintances of ours in Kop—the Womper couple and that disgusting old priest, Theum. I'm sure they would love to see their darling little boy again. We'll organize a family reunion."

10. ambrosius blenk

THE SOUND OF the great clock striking eight echoed through the mansion.

This is it! The start of my new life as an apprentice. Mel smoothed his hair, straightened his smart new livery, and peered around the studio door. Morning light flooded the large, whitewashed space from several skylights, highlighting the paint-stained floorboards. There were drawings pinned around the walls, along with several small canvases depicting details of the large unfinished paintings he could see propped on the massive easels at the far end of the room. Nine of the apprentices he had met the previous evening were busy, the elder ones painting at easels and the younger ones at workbenches, preparing materials. Even at that early hour the studio was a hive of activity. Hardly anyone spoke and the air of concentration was palpable.

"The master will be here soon," said Ludo. "I need to get on with my work. Take a look around until Groot gets here and tells you what to do."

Mel stood in the middle of the room, drinking in the intoxicating, alien smells. The other apprentices acknowledged him with nods of their heads. One even smiled at him.

Emboldened, Mel approached and peered over his shoulder at a drawing of a unicorn. "Did you do that?" he asked in a tone of awe.

The boy stopped working. "I wish. No, it's one of the master's. Don't touch it. It's not fixed yet. My name's Henk, by the way."

"My friends call me Mel."

Mel watched full of admiration as Henk confidently drew a grid of small squares all over the unicorn like a net, dividing it up into many regular boxes. Next to him, on his workbench, he had a much bigger sheet of paper with a grid of the same number of correspondingly bigger squares drawn on it. Into these he carefully copied the contents of each of the smaller boxes, and soon had a larger version of the master's original sketch.

"I wish I was that quick," said Mel.

"You will be soon. It's just practice. Using squares like this is called graticulation," explained Henk. "With this technique you can enlarge a drawing to any size you like."

"Or reduce it," said Mel, instantly seeing the possibilities.

"Turn the squares into oblongs and you can even distort things."

"That's *amazing*."

Mel wondered what task he might be given. *Probably something simple like mixing paints.* He could see another apprentice near the door shaking some coarse green powder into a mortar and begin to grind it with a pestle.

"What's this?" Mel examined a glass jar containing the bright pigment.

"It's malachite. It must be ground really fine before—"

Just then the door burst open, sending Mel flying and spilling the color in a great, long slash across the floor.

"*The smell!* I might have known it. You clumsy little scrot!" snapped Groot. "Do you realize how much that pigment's worth? You won't last long around here. Not if I have my way." He looked pale and sickly.

"Clean it up, Smell. I can see that you're going to be a *great* help in the studio," said Jurgis, as he and Bunt followed Groot into the studio. "Jump to it!" He aimed an unsteady kick at Mel, but missed and almost lost his balance. He looked no better than Groot.

"It wasn't his fault," said the apprentice with the pestle.

"Oh? If it wasn't his fault then it must have been yours, Teck. It certainly wasn't mine. Perhaps you should clean it up, eh?" said Groot, grabbing the boy's ear and twisting it cruelly. "So, whose fault was it?"

"It was Mel's fault," said Teck, grimacing with pain.

"*Whose* fault?" Groot twisted his ear harder.

"Smell's fault."

"That's better," said Groot, releasing him. "Now, clean it up, Smell."

"That's servant's work. Let the cleaners do it," said Teck as he nursed his sore ear.

"Thanks for reminding me, Teck. That kind of work's only for household scum. I expect you'd much rather be using a brush, wouldn't you, Smell?" asked Groot.

"Yes," answered Mel. "I thought that's why I'm here." He set the empty jar back on the workbench.

"I'm so sorry, Smell. Do forgive me." Groot half bowed to Mel. "Bunt." He snapped his fingers. "Fetch the new apprentice a brush, if you'd be so kind." He winked at his crony.

"Here you are, Smell," said Bunt, returning with a domestic brush and pan. "You fit the bill of household scum, all right. Now get on with it. Do as you're told, unless you want to feel my boot."

Mel sighed and knelt and began sweeping the spilled pigment into the little pan.

"Hungover. *Again*," explained Teck in a low voice as Groot and his cronies sauntered down the studio and took up their positions in front of the big easels.

"The master's coming," said Henk.

The master! At last, I'm going to meet him. Mel hurried to finish collecting the valuable pigment. He decanted it back into the jar, then noticed some he had missed. He disappeared under the workbench on his hands and knees and came face to face with a tiny pink face surrounded by a shock of pure white hair. The creature stared at him with wild eyes, bared its pointed teeth, and hissed loudly. Startled, Mel jumped up and banged his head hard against the underside of the workbench. The glass jar tottered and then fell, covering one side of the snowy white monkey, for that is what it was, in bright green pigment. Mel saw a pair of stubby hands with thick fingers and jeweled rings appear and gently lift the animal.

"Albinus, my lovely, what has he *done* to you?" said an agitated woman's voice.

Mel crawled out from under the table. The apprentices were staring at him, horror-struck. The agitated woman was stout and richly dressed. An enormous, stiff lace collar framed her face, atop of which sat the biggest hairdo he had ever seen with more jewels interwoven into her red curls. Her face was thickly made up and her cheeks heavily rouged. She cradled her pet in her arms. The monkey was divided almost exactly in half, one side white, the other green. *What have I done? She must be the master's wife!*

To her right stood Dirk Tot, and next to him, the man Mel knew must be the master.

Mel's first impression of Ambrosius Blenk was that he looked both very old and very young. He was tall and slim, with a long gray beard that hung over his elegant black robe like a hairy waterfall. The garment was covered with fine silver embroidery that sparkled as it caught the light. Around his waist was tied a sash in the deep household blue and he wore a tight-fitting black skullcap that extended over his ears. From beneath busy eyebrows two of the most piercing, blue eyes Mel had ever seen darted back and forth. Then, to Mel's astonishment, Ambrosius Blenk winked at him.

"So you are the Fegish boy," said the master's wife. "Well, Green-Knees, what have you to say for yourself? What do you mean by mutilating my beautiful Albinus, eh?"

Mel gazed down and saw that his new white hose was stained by the green pigment. "I'm . . . I'm very sorry, Mistress," he stammered. "I can bathe him, perhaps it'll wash off."

"Wash off? That is the finest Kig malachite. It costs its own weight in gold. It's not intended to merely *wash off*! If it did we'd want our money back, wouldn't we, Ambrosius? It's permanent. He's ruined, thanks to you."

Mel looked around anxiously at the many faces staring at him. He came to rest on the master's face and was sure he saw amusement in his eyes. He might even be smiling beneath his beard.

"Remarkable. *Quite* remarkable. Womper, isn't it?"

"Yes, Master." Ambrosius Blenk—*the* Ambrosius Blenk—was actually speaking to him.

"Tell me, Womper: are you familiar with the southern rainbow-ape? Related to the harlequin-mangabey? From the Pyrexian jungles, the home of the carnivorous butterfly and the tree-dwelling crocodile."

As Mel heard the names of these exotic creatures, ideas—dozens of them—began to ricochet around in his imagination; ideas for a whole new menagerie of fantastic creatures.

"No? Never mind. I have a likeness of one in my bestiary. You must take a look at it sometime. There's much else in there that will appeal to you. You'll find basilisks and catoblepas and chichevaches and cockatrices and the crocotta and—"

"Ambrosius, you're rambling again," interrupted the mistress.

"I'm truly sorry, Master. For the accident."

"Sorry? What on earth are you sorry for? This creature's coloration is a marvel. It's pure serendipity, Womper. We must talk more when I have time. I've seen your work; it's interesting stuff. Very promising. Once you get some technique at your fingertips you'll flourish. Here's a silver piece for you, you've made my day with this happy accident." The master patted Mel's arm. "Ah, Henk, how's my unicorn? Grown up, has he?"

Mel stared at the silver coin in his palm.

"What are you gawping at?" said the mistress. Then to Groot, "Put this . . . this, *mutilator* to work at once. Before he creates any more damage. And keep him away from the paintings until he has found at least a modicum of coordination."

"As you wish, Mistress. I'll see that he understands his duties and doesn't get into any more mischief. Come along now, young fellow, let me show you how you can help." The head apprentice placed a protective hand on Mel's shoulder and led him away.

When they were out of earshot, Groot leaned close to Mel and hissed, "Oh, you've really done it now, Smell. Albinus is the mistress's favorite pet. Just because old Blenko's taken a shine to you, you needn't think you'll be getting an easy ride.

And give me that. All gratuities belong to the head apprentice."
Groot snatched Mel's gift away and dug his nails viciously into
Mel's shoulder.

As soon as the master and his entourage had gone, Groot said
to everyone, "All right you scrot-stains, the show's over. Now,
Smell, if you're so good let's see how well you can draw. I want
you to draw water." Mel's face betrayed the briefest flash of hope.
"Oh no, Smell. You can forget all about *that* sort of drawing. I
want you to take that bucket over there down to the courtyard
behind the kitchen and draw enough water to fill it. Then, I want
you to carry it up here and begin to clean all of the stains off of
this floor. When it's clean to my satisfaction I'll see about the
next stage of your *education*."

Mel soon found out that artists' colors made stains that were
almost indelible. Throughout the long day he toiled down the
mountain of stairs between the studio and the pump and then
back again. On each visit to the courtyard Mel had to pass
Cook, who could not hide her delight at his treatment. Once he
caught sight of Wren but she was being kept busy and could only
exchange a sympathetic smile as their eyes met.

The great clock struck six as Mel reached the top of the stairs
at the end of yet another knee-trembling, arm-numbing climb
and was met by a thunderous wave of apprentices as they hurried
from the studio.

"Come on, Mel. Suppertime!" shouted Ludo. "I'll meet you in
the refectory."

Mel felt limp with fatigue. As he tidied away his cleaning tools,
he heard a noise coming from the storeroom that opened off the
studio. Curious, he crept over to the doorway. The room was

like an Aladdin's cave, packed with every imaginable type of art material. There were large chests with shallow drawers containing paper in a great variety of colors and weights, and shelves crowded with exotic oils and pigments. Large pots contained every kind and size of paintbrush, and long rolls of canvas and bundles of wooden stretchers leaned against the walls.

Among all of this was Groot. Mel crept into the room and hid himself behind a chest. From his hiding place he watched as Groot fiddled with a cabinet. He had a long, bent piece of wire, which he was poking into the tiny keyhole. After several attempts he managed to pick the lock and open the door. Arranged on shelves inside the cabinet were small glass jars of pigment. Mel guessed they were kept under lock and key on account of their value. On a table to one side there were several small sheets of paper. Groot took one of these and rolled it to form a cone. He shook a quantity of pigment from one of the jars into the cone and folded over the top and bottom. He repeated this with other pigments. When he had finished he closed and locked the cabinet. He concealed his parcels inside his doublet and, pausing to make sure no one was around, he left, closing the storeroom door behind him.

He's stealing pigment! Mel stood up from his cramped hiding place and flexed his aching legs. He approached the cabinet to examine it more closely, then heard the noise of footsteps outside. He turned to see the door begin to open with a soft creak.

11. the house of mysteries

MEL ONLY JUST had time to hide again before the huge form of Dirk Tot entered the storeroom. He went straight to the cabinet and unlocked it. He took down one of the glass jars and shook it gently, examining its level. He then took a vial containing a similar pigment from his reticule and tipped it into the jar. He repeated this several times with other pigments, replenishing the material Groot had taken. This task complete, he relocked the cabinet and left.

Mel did not understand the scene he had just witnessed. *Groot's a scrotty thief. No surprise there. But why is Dirk Tot covering up for him?*

Mel was the last to arrive in the refectory. He ignored the baiting from Groot's end of the table and sat down. A plate with a huge portion of rabbit stew was placed before him, much larger than everyone else's. He turned and saw Wren serving.

She leaned close and whispered, "Thanks, Mel. For not telling on me. I can't afford to lose this job. Now, eat up. You look like you could use it."

Mel noticed that Ludo did not seem pleased with the supper menu.

"What's up? Lost your appetite?"

Ludo looked sick and pushed his plate aside. "Rabbit for supper always spells bad news for the junior apprentices."

"I thought rabbits were lucky. Their feet, anyway."

"If you think scrubbing the floor's bad, just wait till tomorrow."

Puzzled, Mel glanced at Henk and Teck for an explanation. They said nothing and just smiled knowingly to each other.

Mel awoke the next morning to find that the weather had changed and a dense fog clung to Vlam. He looked forward without enthusiasm to the prospect of continuing his cleaning of the studio floor. Against all the evidence of his aching limbs, he had hardly made any difference. However, when he and Ludo arrived in the studio, Groot had something else in mind for him.

"Leave that, Smell," he ordered. "I have something that's more urgent for you and Ludo. Get on down to the kitchen courtyard. Ludo knows what's to be done."

Ludo groaned. "Told you supper was bad news."

Perplexed, Mel followed his friend down to the courtyard, where some servants had built a fire. Above it, suspended from a stout metal tripod, was a large, iron cauldron filled with water.

"Well, you wanted to be given something to do with making pictures and it looks like your wish has come true. We're to make size. I hope you're happy," said Ludo.

"What's sighing got to do with pictures?" asked Mel, puzzled.

Ludo rolled his eyes. "Not sighs, *size*! It's a kind of glue. Before a canvas is ready for painting it must be prepared with a coat of size, so that the paint won't soak into the fabric. Then more size is mixed with gypsum to make gesso."

Mel looked confused. "Gesso?"

"You know, the white ground on the canvas. It also helps to fill in the weave so that it's flatter and easier to paint on. They must have run out," he added gloomily.

Mel could not see why Ludo was so disheartened. "So, what do we need to make size?"

Ludo took out his handkerchief and tied it around his nose and mouth. He lifted the corner of some old sacking that covered a pile in the corner. "This," he said.

A cloud of flies rose up and the two boys reeled back at the sickening smell of a large heap of rabbit skins.

"That's disgusting!" Mel took out his own handkerchief and copied Ludo. From all around the courtyard came the sound of windows and doors closing.

"The water's boiling," said Ludo. "Grab a pitchfork and help me transfer the skins to the cauldron."

When the nasty task was complete, Ludo handed Mel a paddle. "Here, you stir the brew. Just keep it moving."

"What about you? Aren't you going to help?"

"I've got to clean this mess up." Ludo grabbed a broom and a bucket of water and began to scrub the gory stains from the cobbles.

Mel's arms were already beginning to ache. "How long must I keep stirring?"

"Till it's done. Use the ladle to skim off the scum as it forms on the surface. It needs to be the consistency of syrup before it's ready. And make sure you keep the fire fed. It must be kept boiling. I've got something to finish in the studio. I'll be back soon," said Ludo.

Within a very short time, Mel wished he was back scrubbing the studio floor. The rank steam from the cauldron got into his hair and into his clothes until he was dripping wet. Stirring the ripe brew as it thickened made his arms ache far more than yesterday.

Ludo only reappeared at midday.

"Where've you been? I thought you were supposed to help me."

"Sorry. Groot found something urgent for me to do in the studio. Here, I got you a sandwich."

Mel was not altogether sure he believed him. He raised the sandwich to his mouth and lowered it again.

"What's the matter? Aren't you going to eat it?"

"It stinks! It smells just like the size." Mel threw it, untouched, onto the fire.

"Ludo!"

The boys turned to see Dirk Tot standing in the doorway, a handkerchief covering his mouth. "Take over, will you? Mel, come here. I have an important errand for you."

Mel smiled to himself.

"First, go and see Minch. Tell him I sent you and that you're to have a new set of clothes. Then you must wash—try and rid yourself of that smell. You're to go to the House of Mysteries and present this warrant for cinnabar pigment at the commissary. Guard it well, it's very valuable. Now, is that clear?"

"The House of Mysteries?" The idea of another meeting with the Fifth Mystery filled Mel with dread. "How do I get there?"

"You must take a tramcar. Here's the number." He wrote the number sixty-one clearly on a sheet of paper. He told Mel where to find the tram stop and gave him the fare. "You can't mistake the House of Mysteries—it's the biggest building in Vlam. If you get lost anyone can point you in the right direction."

A little later, Mel, washed and dressed in his new clothes

but not smelling very much sweeter, found himself in the foggy square outside the mansion. He made his way to the busy tram stop and boarded a tram with a number that matched his piece of paper. After only a few stops he had the entire car to himself; the other passengers had dismounted, driven away by the strong smell that clung to him. Only the conductor remained, behind his glassed-in driving position. He occasionally looked back at his sole passenger with annoyance.

Mel listened attentively each time the conductor rang the bell and shouted out the names of the various stops but he did not hear the name of his destination. He soon lost all track of time and imagined himself exploring the city once he had regained his privileges.

"All change. End of the line." The conductor's voice shook Mel from his reverie. He looked up just in time to see the conductor step down from the cab and disappear into the fog. Mel was quite alone. He stepped off and looked around for someone to ask for directions but the place appeared to be completely deserted. In no time at all he was completely lost in the narrow streets. Mel sat down on a doorstep to think what to do next when he heard footsteps. He caught sight of two strangers wearing red robes emerging from the fog. *Fifth Mystery men!* He shrank back into the doorway and the two men walked past without seeing him. In a flash, he realized that they must be going to the House of Mysteries. Cautiously, he began to follow them.

Sure enough, they soon approached the veiled form of a huge building. The yellow lights from its windows were reflected palely on the damp cobbles of the street. It was easily the biggest building Mel had ever seen. A rectangle of light briefly appeared when a door was opened and closed as the two Mystery men entered the building. Mel dashed up after them but found the door locked. *At least I've found the House of Mysteries*, he thought.

It seemed oddly deserted for such an important place. Mel began to follow the wall, hoping to find the door to the commissary. Eventually, a thin sliver of light appeared, revealing a door. Mel pushed it open and stepped inside.

"Oi, what're you doing here?" Mel spun round at the sound of the voice. Confronting him was a tall man dressed in the uniform of the Fifth Mystery.

Mel backed away involuntarily. "I'm sorry but I'm lost. I'm new to the city. Please, is this the House of Mysteries? I'm looking for the commissary."

"This is the South-Eastern winding shed, you're miles from the House. You're a spy. What're you really doing here?" The man grabbed Mel roughly by the arm. "*Yargh!* You smell dreadful." He released him quickly.

"No, honestly. I'm looking for the commissary. See, I've got a warrant here for some pigment." He withdrew the document from his doublet and showed it to the man.

Whether the man was convinced of his explanation or simply wanted to be rid of the obnoxious smell, Mel was escorted brusquely to the door and pointed in the direction of the Great House. He began walking and soon heard a clanking sound, followed by a subdued groaning as a line of chained men in ragged clothes materialized from the fog. Mel stood aside to let them and their scarlet-clad guards pass in the narrow street. They were obviously headed for the winding shed.

"Hey, you there," said a quiet voice. "Apprentice. Blenk's boy."

"Silence. No talking back there!" yelled one of the prisoners' escorts.

Mel looked around for who had addressed him.

"Yes, you," said the voice even more softly. One of the prisoners was looking at Mel from the corner of his eyes, trying to speak without moving his lips. He was filthy, half-starved, with matted hair that might have been auburn. He had a scar across the bridge of his nose and stared at Mel with hollow, haunted eyes.

"How did you know I'm one of the master's apprentices?" asked Mel.

"You're wearing the most famous livery in Vlam. Do you know Wren? She's about your age, works in the kitchen."

"Yes," said Mel, surprised. He fell into step with the line of prisoners. "She's my friend."

"Tell me, is she well? How's she looking?"

"She's well. But how do you know her?"

"Can you take her a message—?"

"Who's talking back there?" One of the guards was walking briskly back down the line.

The man began to speak quickly. "Tell Wren I love her. I think of her all the time. Tell Wren her father said to . . . to look in the night."

Mel took to his heels and ran off at the guard's approach. Behind him, he heard the sound of a man being beaten. Shaken, he ran on blindly until he saw lights appearing through the fog. He was back at the tram. The conductor had returned from his tea break and was climbing into the cab. "Excuse me," said Mel, slightly out of breath. "I thought that this tram went to the House of Mysteries?"

The conductor paused. "Not this tram, son. From here at the South-East Winding Shed to the river. That's my route."

"But I was given this number. Look." He showed the man the paper Dirk Tot had given him. "It's the same as yours."

"So it is, number nineteen, right enough," the conductor said, examining it. "But wait a mo'; it could also be sixty-one." He turned the note upside down. "Now, a sixty-one goes right past the Mysteries. Hop back on. I'll tell you where to change." He caught a whiff of Mel. "But do me a favor, son. Ride on the running board outside, will you?"

Mel fretted about the delay during the two tram journeys that eventually set him down outside the House of Mysteries. The scale and splendor of the structure was obscured by the fog as he ran up the steps towards the entrance.

"And just where do you think *you're* going?" A doorman barred his way.

Mel showed him the warrant.

"Side door. The commissary's at the *side* door. How many times do they have to be told? I don't care if you are one of Blenk's apprentices, civilians are not allowed in the front. Whatever next?"

Mel reached the side door and entered. He found himself in a long corridor that curved upwards in a sweeping incline. Presently, he came to an open door and entered it to find himself in a long room lit from above by gas chandeliers. All along one wall was a long, continuous bench seat of mahogany beneath a wall-length mirror. On the bench sat customers awaiting their goods. Facing it was an equally long and high counter of the same dark wood, lit by more gas lamps. Behind it, on shelves that reached up to the ceiling, were arrayed thousands of huge, oddly shaped glass jars containing pigments of every imaginable color, including a few that Mel had never guessed existed.

As Mel advanced into the commissary, the customers waiting on the bench slid away from his unwelcome odor.

"Yes?" The man in charge eyed Mel over half-moon spectacles.

"I'm to give you this," said Mel nervously. "It's for some pigment."

"The young scut here says he wants some pigment. Have we got any pigment in at the moment?"

"All gone. Tell him to come back tomorrow," said his assistant, as he measured out a quantity of orange pigment into a complicated set of brass scales.

"What's all that then?" Mel pointed to the shelves where another man rolled back and forth on a wheeled ladder. "Please, it's really, *really* urgent. I've got to . . ."

The man in charge shook his head. "Give it here then." He leaned forward to take the proffered warrant. "*Poo!* You smell worse than you look." He snatched the document and quickly retreated. "Go and wait outside. You'll be called when it's ready."

Mel went out into the corridor to stand by a large archway, open to the air. The first puffs of a breeze that promised to blow the fog away ruffled his hair and made him feel less uneasy about being there in the headquarters of the Fifth Mystery.

That same breeze wafted along the corridor and into the ventilation shaft feeding fresh air down through the building and into the chambers below. In one such chamber the breeze oozed out of the ventilator, carrying with it the disagreeable odor of rabbit-skin size.

"What's that smell?" asked Adolfus Spute, wrinkling his stubby nose.

A negative note from his whistle indicated that Mumchance did not know.

"*Men!*" the High-Bailiff shouted for his assistants.

Mumchance's whistle.

"Yes, you're quite right, of course I did. How forgetful of me. I sent them to Kop to collect our guests, didn't I? We'd best go and find out for ourselves. What *is* that stink?"

"Red mercuric sulfide!" The completion of an order was announced in the commissary. When no one came forward the man bellowed at the top of his lungs, "Red mercuric sulfide! Cinnabar for Blenk!"

Mel rushed back in. "That's for me!" A parcel was pushed down the counter. He tucked the valuable pigment into his doublet and hurried back the way he had come.

"It's getting stronger. It's definitely coming from this direction." The High-Bailiff and his companion hurried along the corridor leading up to the commissary. "Whatever is that—*Smell!* How nice to see you again."

Mel froze. The High-Bailiff and Mumchance stood there, blocking his way. He suddenly felt very cold.

"So we meet again. Just when we thought that we faced a dreary afternoon, you've brought some color into our lives."

Mumchance smiled and piped a long note on his silver whistle. He and the High-Bailiff moved closer.

Mel wished he had his bodkin. *But I do have this!* He withdrew the parcel and flung the powdered cinnabar in their faces. Adolfus

Spute screamed and Mumchance doubled up, both coughing and clawing at their eyes. Mel turned and began to run back up the corridor, but the commissary servers emerged barring his escape.

Mel looked to his right, at the archway, but escape was impossible that way. It was high above the street; the fall would surely kill him. To his left was a door. In desperation, he lunged at it, and it opened on to a stairwell. There was a scuffle of feet behind him as his pursuers reached the doorway.

With no time to think, Mel took the down staircase as a hand grabbed his collar. He half-turned and saw the High-Bailiff's face, now stained red and contorted with an inhuman fury. "I know you took it, Smell. It's mine, you thief. It's mine, and I want it back."

Mel wrenched himself free and plunged down, the sound of feet close behind him. He reached the foot of the stairs and turned left, right, left again, as he tried to throw his pursuers off his trail. *They mustn't catch me. They simply mustn't.* Mel had a fleeting vision of the last time he saw Fa Theum but forced the dreadful image from his mind. He ran down a long, dimly lit gallery hung with large paintings. He stole a look over his shoulder. He could hear the drumbeat sound of running feet coming ever closer. The tattoo merged with the pounding of his own blood in his ears. Then he heard more running feet, this time from in front, doubling the rhythm. *I'm trapped.* He skidded to a halt in front of one of the paintings. Panting, he pressed his back to it. *There's no way out. It's all over.*

12. secrets

EVERYTHING WENT BLACK as a sack was thrust over Mel's head. Strong arms grabbed him and heaved him backwards. Abruptly, the sounds of pursuit ceased and were replaced by birds singing. He could hear wind blowing through trees and, somewhere nearby, the gentle tinkling of a stream. He felt the warmth of sunshine and, beneath his feet, grass. This sudden transformation was, in its own way, as frightening as the High-Bailiff and his pack.

"What're we going to do with him now?" said a man's voice.

"Shut up, I'm thinking," said another.

"*Yech!* Have you smelled him? We should have left him out there," said the first voice. "We don't need this. He's not our problem. Let's slit his throat and dump him back. One more body in the House of Mysteries won't matter. They wouldn't even notice."

There was silence for a while. All Mel could hear was the sound of his own rapid breathing.

"Listen to him, he's hyperventilating. He's going to croak soon anyway. Let's slit his gizzard and be off." It was the first voice again.

"I told you to shut up."

The sack was whisked off Mel's head and he received two sharp slaps to his face in rapid succession.

"Are you all right, lad?" said the other voice.

Mel blinked rapidly and gradually came to his senses. Then

he wished he was back inside the sack. He screwed his eyes tight shut. *I'm in the dormitory. I'm in bed; I'll wake up in a moment. I'm having a dream—a very, very weird dream.*

But he was not.

When he opened his eyes again he was still in a forest glade serenely lit with beams of clear, golden light. In the distance were snow-capped mountains, and birds with bright plumage wheeled overhead. Nearby, a unicorn grazed—a *real* unicorn. It looked up briefly and blinked its languid eyes at him. Mel shook his head. It was all too much. His legs turned to jelly and he collapsed heavily on the ground.

"What've you done now? He's seen where we are. We'll have to kill him."

"Are you all right, lad? Speak to me."

Mel looked up. *It's not a dream. I've gone mad.* The man bending over him was green: the color of grass. His hands and his fingernails were green. His skin and his hair were green, as were his teeth. Even his eyes were a paler shade of the same green, with dark green pupils. This was so bizarre in itself that Mel did not notice his strange clothes or the weird piebald creature clinging to his shoulder.

"He's in shock," said the other man.

Mel looked at him. He was blue. *This isn't possible. I'm hallucinating.*

"Of course he's in shock. So would you be. What's your name, lad?" the green man asked.

Mel just looked at him, uncomprehending.

"Your name. Who are you?" He shook Mel again gently.

"M-Mel. Melkin Womper."

"How long have you been Ambrosius Blenk's apprentice, Mel?"

"How do you . . . ?" He remembered his livery. "Just a couple of days. I got a free one."

"What's he talking about, 'a free one'? He hasn't been there long enough, he can't know anything. Now he's gone and seen us. Let's do him and dump the body back out there. We need to get out of here," said the blue man, drawing his knife.

"No one's going to do anyone. Not while I'm in charge," said the green man. "Put that knife away. If Adolfus Spute and the Fifth Mystery are after him, then he's on our side. Can you stand, Mel?"

Mel nodded. Unsteadily, he got to his feet.

"Well done. Now we're going to take you somewhere where it's safe to release you but I'm going to have to put the sack back on your head. It's for your own good."

Mel briefly fought back panic. The last thing he saw before the sack was placed back over his head was a softly shimmering and undulating wall of mist that rose up, sheer, from the grass to the sky just a few feet from him. Then they began walking, Mel guided by the firm hands of the two colored men.

They walked for what seemed like a long time. They climbed hills and clambered down steep inclines, picking their way over fallen branches. Once, the temperature dropped suddenly and they skidded across a broad expanse of ice. Then it became warmer and they were in some inhabited place where he heard music and the sound of many voices that faded as they marched on. Eventually, they halted.

The green man spoke. "Right, Mel. I'm going to let you go now. When I take the sack off you won't be in the House of Mysteries, you'll be somewhere else. You won't be in any danger but you mustn't linger. You must go straight back to Ambrosius Blenk's mansion. Do you understand?"

Mel nodded.

"And you can never talk about this. Not to anyone. Otherwise my mate really will slit your gizzard. Okay? Now, close your eyes."

Mel was gently thrust forward. He felt a tingling sensation all over and he sensed that the air around him changed again.

"Good-bye, Mel. And remember, not a word." The sack was lifted off his head.

Mel opened his eyes. He was in a strange room. In front of him was an open door with a short flight of steps leading down to a busy street. He turned around and saw a large painting. Before he had a chance to study it he was interrupted.

"I'm sorry, my son, but the House of Spirits is not open to visitors."

The House of Spirits? I'm back in Vlam! Mel turned to see a young priest walking towards him. He was smiling and his shining diaglyph sent reflections dancing around the walls.

"I'm sorry, Fa . . ."

"Ah, I see you're one of Ambrosius Blenk's apprentices. Well, we sometimes allow you to come here and study the Maven's paintings but you must make an appointment first."

"Excuse me, Fa. I'm new here. I only arrived in Vlam a couple of days ago. I'm lost. I must get back to my master."

The priest escorted him to the door and pointed at where the rooftops sloped down from the three hills to the center of the city. "Ambrosius Blenk's mansion lies at the very heart of Vlam. The fog's lifted now and you can see the Great Houses. When they're equidistant, you'll be near home. Now take care." The Fa waved him good-bye.

It was long after dark when Mel arrived back outside his master's mansion. Above him, the clock chimed midnight and the gates to the courtyard were locked. Weary to the point of exhaustion, Mel walked around the block, trying to find someone to let him in through one of the side doors. He felt hopeless as he began a second circuit. Then he heard his name.

"Mel. Up here."

He looked up and saw Wren at a second-floor window.

"I'll come down and let you in." A short while later a nearby door opened. Wren was not wearing her pinafore or turban, and her long auburn hair hung loose about her shoulders. She looked altogether different, less like a servant and more like she lived in the splendid house.

"Mel, where've you been? You look done in. The house has been in turmoil. They were on the point of calling the Watch to go and look for you. But I knew you'd come back."

"Wren, you won't believe what happened to me. First I got lost and then I was chased and *then*—"

"Slow down."

"But I have a message for you."

"For me?" She laughed nervously.

"From your father."

"My *father*. You can't have met him. He's—"

"A prisoner of the Fifth Mystery. Honestly, Wren. I'm not making this up. He has a scar, here, on the bridge of his nose," said Mel.

Tears welled up in Wren's eyes. "Oh, Mel, did you *really* see him? Where?"

"Near the South-Eastern Winding Shed. He was with some other prisoners and I think they must have been taking him to work there." Mel could not tell his friend that her father looked wretched.

Wren smiled sadly. "This means that he hasn't been sent to the mines. There's still hope."

"Why's your father a prisoner? What's he done?"

"Done? What do you have to do to fall foul of the Mysteries? *Nothing*, that's what! You know the great clock on the front of the mansion? Well, my father made it *and* the one at the House of Thrones. He's made clocks for all sorts of important people. He's the greatest clockmaker in Nem! The Mysteries—all of them—hated him because time didn't belong to any of them. You can't touch it and you can't smell it. You can't hear it, taste it or see it."

"There's no Pleasure attached to it."

"None. No one could make a profit from time. So they made up some kind of crime for his not having the Pleasure of time. No one ever knew what it was or which Mystery was responsible. They just came and took him away one night, about three months ago."

"I'm sorry, Wren, I had no idea. I didn't mean to upset you." He touched her arm in a gesture of comfort.

"We used to have a nice house, not far from here, and two servants, and now we have nothing. My mother has to work in a laundry and I have to work here, in the kitchens." She fought back the tears and raised her head proudly. "So what's this message my father gave you?"

"He said that he loved you and thought about you all the time. And then he said something else that I don't understand. He said that you should 'look in the night.'"

"Look for what? Which night? Tonight?"

"I don't know. That's all he had time to say."

The great clock chimed the half hour. "Come on, Mel. You need to get back to the dormitory. Stay here, I'll be back in a moment."

Wren disappeared down a hallway and returned holding a candle and a small key. "Here's something you 'prentices don't know about. Even I'm not supposed to know. I *borrowed* a key." Wren winked. She led Mel to some carved paneling on the wall and fitted the key to a tiny keyhole. The oak panel swung open and Wren stepped inside. "Come on."

Mel followed her. "A secret passage!"

"*Shhh!*" Wren closed the panel behind them and lit the candle. Her green eyes twinkled. "This is a service passage. The mansion is riddled with them. Most of the rooms can be accessed from the passages. It allows the senior servants to come and go without having to clog up the normal corridors. Come on, this way."

Mel followed Wren along the passage. They climbed uneven stairs, cobwebs sometimes brushing their faces. As they proceeded, Wren whispered to Mel what lay beyond the various doors they passed.

"That leads to the servants' hall and that one over there to the scullery. Here's the door to the linen store."

"You must have a good memory. To remember all the doors like that."

"No, not at all. The rooms are all written on the doors. Look." She held up the candle. "What's that say?"

Mel was silent.

Wren held the candle closer. "There, surely you can see it now." Then the truth dawned on her. "You can't read, can you?"

Mel hung his head. "Fa Theum, the village priest, wanted to teach me but he didn't have any books in Nemish."

"I've got some books. I can teach you."

"*Really?* You'll really teach me to read? I can write a bit."

"Then I'll teach you to write more. I'd like that, to have

something better to do after work than to gossip with Cook and the others. It would be fun."

Mel smiled for the first time that day. "Look, Wren, thanks for everything. If you hadn't waited up for me I'd still be wandering round outside. You're the only friend I've got in here."

"What about Ludo?"

"Ludo . . . He's . . ."

"Selfish?"

Mel nodded.

"He's not really; he's just a bit thoughtless sometimes. It's his upbringing. Ludolf Cleef comes from a very well-to-do family. His father's Lord Cleef. They used to be very rich—still are by anyone else's standards. But they love their Pleasures a tad too much. He's the youngest son and his parents dote on him. They bought his apprenticeship for him, probably with money they don't have. They're counting on him being a successful artist one day. He was bullied a lot when he first arrived. His life never prepared him for an apprenticeship under Groot."

"I don't think *anyone* could be prepared for that," said Mel.

They continued onwards and upwards. At length, at the top of a steep flight of especially rickety stairs, they reached the dormitory.

Wren opened the door a crack. "All's clear. Just get straight into bed." She held the panel open for him and Mel slipped through. Wren closed it after him and made her way back through the passages in the direction of the servants' quarters.

In the silence after she had passed, a flame flared, illuminating the green face of a man. He made his way down a different passage. When he came to the door he sought, he raised his candle to read the inscription: DIRK TOT'S STUDY. He knocked softly and entered.

13. more secrets

"SIX MONTHS' LOSS of privileges and stipend. You're ever so lucky, Mel," said Ludo.

"*Lucky?* What does *un*lucky earn you around here?"

"No, really you are. Apprentices have been thrown out for much less. It can only be because you're so talented. And the master likes you. I was here for six months before he even spoke to me. That's going to make Groot angry. He's bound to try and get back at you somehow."

Ludo was right. The following morning, Mel was given a final warning by Dirk Tot. He was then put straight back to work scrubbing the studio floor. Groot, Bunt, and Jurgis would periodically pass by, splashing fresh paint on parts he had already cleaned or kicking over his bucket. At lunch his food was sabotaged with a dead mouse and he left the refectory hungry. When he went to use the privy he found his precious drawings scattered around. This time they were smeared with something worse than gravy.

Mel ran straight to the dormitory, opened his secret cache, and withdrew his bodkin. He crossed to Groot's sleeping place. He stood there, looking at the head apprentice's drawings pinned up around his bed. His fingers tightened on the dagger.

The door opened and Ludo walked up the empty dormitory

towards him. "I thought I'd find you here. I saw what they'd done. Are you going to shred his drawings? I would."

Mel hesitated. He tucked the bodkin into his doublet. "No. It would just drag me down to his level."

Ludo was quiet for a moment and then said, "Look, Mel, things will be different from now on. You'll see. You covered up for me when you got caught in the kitchen and you're the only one here, apart from Wren, who treats me like a human being. You're my best friend. I'll make it up to you?" He offered Mel his hand.

"All right," agreed Mel, touched by his friend's concern as they shook hands.

"But there must be some way you could strike back at Groot. You could tell Dirk Tot what happened. He hates bullying."

"No, I can't do that."

"Why ever not?"

"There's something you don't know about Dirk Tot. He's—"

The door opened again and Wren entered. "Mel, I heard what happened in the refectory earlier. Here, I brought you some cheese. You must be starving."

"That's not the worst of it. They . . . they destroyed his drawings," said Ludo.

"Just wait till I'm serving again in the refectory. I'll give them a taste of their own medicine."

"No, Wren, they're not worth it. Thanks for the cheese." Mel gratefully took the food. "Look, there're things I've got to tell you both. Important things. I wish there was somewhere private we could talk."

"Maybe there is," said Wren. "Come with me." They made their way to the grand entrance hall. In one of the galleries that surrounded it, halfway up, she approached a panel.

Wren looked about to make sure they were not being observed and then ran her hand around some molding. There was a click and a small door, only half their height, sprung open. "Mind your heads and follow me."

"We're inside the great clock," said Mel as he gazed around in astonishment.

The space glowed with the light penetrating the translucent glass of the huge clock face. Its hands and back-to-front numerals were clearly silhouetted against the daylight. All around them moved gears and pulleys, and a large, brass pendulum swung back and forth. Coiled springs contracted and expanded. Escapements and well-oiled ratchets rocked to and fro, and large counterweights hung suspended. The whole machine ticked and tocked with a loud but friendly voice. Racks of bells, in strict order of size, waited to announce the hours.

"How did you know how to get in?" asked Ludo, touching the rows of brightly painted automated figures that paraded across the clock face each time the hour struck.

"My father made this clock. And I designed and painted all the figures." Wren ran her hand lovingly over the machinery.

"*You?*" said Ludo.

"I wasn't always a kitchen girl. I used to help my father in his workshop."

Up close, Mel recognized several of the faces on the figures. A scrawny dragon bore the unmistakable features of Adolfus Spute and a tiny, horned devil that of Mumchance. "Their faces. They look like . . ."

"Yes, they do. It was our way of poking fun at the Mysteries," said Wren. "Great, aren't they?"

"They're *amazing!*" said Mel. "So you can draw, too."

"Almost as well as you, I imagine. But girls aren't allowed to be apprentices so I just worked with my father until . . ." She looked away. "Look, now that you know how to get in, why don't we meet here every evening, after work. It can be our secret place."

"*Wonderful!*" said Ludo and Mel together.

"Now, we must all get back to our duties before someone misses us. Especially you, Mel. You can't afford another mistake. I'll see you both later."

Supper had finished and the three friends were back inside the clock.

Mel took a deep breath and started to tell them of all the things that had happened to him. He told them of his meeting with Dirk Tot in Kop and his encounter with Adolfus Spute in the fane, of their flight to Vlam and the meeting he had witnessed between Dirk Tot and the Fifth Mystery on the road. He recounted how he had seen Groot stealing the pigments from the storeroom and how his crime had been covered up— by Dirk Tot.

Suddenly, they were interrupted by a whirring noise.

"What's that?" said Ludo.

"The clock. It's about to strike the hour," said Wren. "Watch."

The machinery around them came alive. The bells, struck by an army of small hammers, pealed loudly in the enclosed space. The figures began to spin and jerk their limbs, and the belt they were attached to began to move. The figures filed out of the small door at the right of the space and their shadows danced across the glass clock face. Then they returned through the left-hand door. Above their heads the stars and planets did the same.

Laughing loudly, the friends collapsed on to the floor as the performance ended.

"You know, that's the first good laugh I've had since I arrived in Vlam," said Mel.

"Come on, finish your story." Wren was as eager to hear it as Ludo.

When the noise died away, Mel detailed his visit to the House of Mysteries, his escape from the High-Bailiff, his strange encounter with the colored men, and their journey through who-knows-where. His tale ended with Wren taking him through the secret passage back to the dormitory. The only thing he left out was the tiny box and its mysterious contents. If he told them about it he would have to admit he was a thief.

"That's quite some story," said Wren.

"We had no idea," said Ludo.

"But I just don't understand any of it," confessed Mel.

"Well," said Ludo, "Groot's a thief. That's no surprise. He must be stealing the pigment to pay for his drinking and gambling. You've got something on him now, Mel. Something you can use against him."

"And the colored men," said Wren. "They must be fugitives from the mines on Kig. The pigment gets into their skin and eventually it colors them completely. Not many ever escape. The pigments are toxic and it usually kills the miners after a while. It's called the Colored Death." Her voice trembled slightly. She could not help but think of her father.

"What I can't work out is why Dirk Tot should be working with the Fifth Mystery," said Mel. "Do either of you have any idea?"

"No," said Wren, shrugging her shoulders. "He always seems so dead set against them."

"Me neither," said Ludo.

"I bet we could find out if we explored the secret passages," said Mel.

"The *service* passages," corrected Wren.

"But what do you think about the strange journey that the colored men took me on?" asked Mel.

"Let's start with the things we can find an answer for," said Wren. "Then, perhaps, we'll find out a bit more about the other things."

She produced the little key and three candles from the pocket of her pinafore. "I think we should start with Dirk Tot's study."

"Secret passages? What are we waiting for?" said Ludo.

Opposite the clock, just across the gallery, was an entrance into the passages. After the door was closed, normally busy sounds of the mansion were shut out, and they felt enclosed in their own parallel world. The air was very close and the yellow light from their candles cast shadows tall and grotesque on the wall.

"Now, keep it quiet. Remember, there are rooms with people just the other side of the paneling," warned Wren. "I just hope we don't meet anyone while we're in here."

"What, you mean like monsters or ghosts?" joked Ludo. "*Whooooo!*"

"*Shhhh!*" said Wren. "No, silly. I hope we don't bump into any of the other servants. Now, come on."

Mel and Ludo followed Wren but could not help casting the occasional uneasy look behind them as they threaded their way along in single file.

"Dirk Tot's study is just up here," whispered Wren. She carefully began to mount the uneven stairs, and then, halfway up, Ludo stumbled into Mel. The trio froze and held their breath.

After a while, they continued until they stood outside the study. Wren put her ear to the door. She turned to her friends and shook her head.

"There's someone in there. We'll have to come back some other time," she whispered as she led them back.

"Where to now?" asked Mel.

Before she could answer, they heard the sound of footsteps. Wren pushed the two boys down a side passage. They blew out their candles and waited in blackness darker than any of them had ever known.

Please don't let us get caught, thought Mel. *Not now. Please, please, please.*

Slowly, the footsteps faded. A few moments passed before Wren said, "Okay, I think it's safe to light our candles again."

"Let's get out of here," whispered Ludo.

"I thought you wanted to help us find out what's going on," said Wren.

"It's too risky."

"We're in here now," said Mel. "We might not get another chance for ages."

"Please. Let's go on for a bit longer," said Wren, "or we're never going to find anything out."

They both looked at Ludo.

"I suppose so. What's down there?" he asked, indicating a new direction.

"That the way to the master's private studio," said Wren.

"No one's ever allowed in there," said Ludo, "not even Groot."

"Let's just take a look," said Mel, his excitement winning over caution.

"Okay," said Wren. "But let me lead. *And keep quiet.*"

They set off towards the studio. Eventually, Wren signaled for them to halt. She put a finger to her lips and then pointed into the darkness ahead of them. A tiny sliver of light indicated where a door stood slightly ajar.

If I never get to see anything else in my life, I've got to see this, thought Mel.

They crept up to the door. Then, Mel crouching, Wren standing, and Ludo on tiptoe, each put one eye to the crack.

The master stood before a painting on a large easel that dominated a spacious, whitewashed room lit by gas brackets around the walls. From their hiding place, the watchers could not see what the canvas depicted. Mel took in the bright tapestries and a number of large, unframed paintings that leaned against the far wall. Several tables were stacked with tottering piles of books and artist's materials, and a huge, richly colored rug covered most of the floor. In the far corner he saw a bulky cage in which several strange creatures chattered and swung to and fro. With surprise he realized that they were white monkeys like Albinus but colored in different ways—one striped, one in harlequin quarters, one spotted, and another patterned in rainbow hoops.

As they watched, the master raised his hand in front of the canvas and moved it in an elaborate gesture as if he were tracing a complicated design in the air. He moved closer to the canvas and—

The trio gasped. "He's vanished!"

14. the fugitive garden

THE FRIENDS WERE so astounded by what they had witnessed that they fell headlong through the door into the studio and landed in a heap. Their candles were extinguished in the fall. The patterned monkeys began screeching loudly and jumping around inside their cage, rattling the bars.

Wren picked herself up, rushed to the main door, and looked out into the corridor. "All clear."

"Quiet, *please* be quiet," pleaded Ludo with the monkeys.

"You've a knack with animals," said Wren as the shrieking died down. "I'm impressed."

"It's nothing, really, when you know how." Ludo smiled to himself. "Hey, Mel, the master must have liked what you did to Albinus so much that he's tried something similar on these guys." A sketch of the newly green and white pet was pinned up next to the cage.

But Mel was studying the canvas. "Come here, you two. There's something you have to see."

The canvas depicted a landscape in the unmistakable, hyper-real style of Ambrosius Blenk. It was so finely painted it seemed to glow. An ethereal blue sky was studded with white clouds. In the foreground grew odd, alien trees with spiral trunks and ripe, speckled fruit hanging from their branches. A variety of brightly colored hybrid creatures grazed contentedly on the lush pasture that led down to a placid lake. On a small island, right in the center of the lake, stood a head-shaped building that seemed to have crystallized out of the rock on which it stood. It had an expansive, thatched roof that resembled shaggy hair, peppered with random plants and the occasional stork's nest. Thick ivy grew around it like a beard. There were two great windows for eyes, above which projected shallow, sloping roofs like brows, and the entrance was in the form of a gaping mouth. A portcullis appeared like teeth, reinforcing the carefully crafted illusion. From the shore of the lake, a tonguelike bridge, built from red brick, spanned the waters and disappeared into the entrance. On the bridge, dressed exactly as they had seen him moments before, was the perfectly painted form of the master.

"It's beautiful," said Wren.

"It's completely different from anything that he sends across for us to work on," observed Ludo.

"You don't understand," said Mel. "A moment ago, the master was depicted here, in the foreground. Now look."

The master had moved farther along the bridge.

"How did he do that?" said Ludo.

"I don't know. Look again."

The master had gone.

"Now he's inside the building," said Mel.

"What're you saying? That it's painted with some kind of vanishing paint?" suggested Ludo.

"No. I'm saying that I think the master's somehow managed to get inside his picture."

"How can you get inside a painting? It's ridiculous." Ludo prodded the surface of the picture. It was still wet but as solid as any other stretched canvas.

"You saw the master vanish," said Wren.

"Yes! And remember I told you about the colored men, the ones that grabbed me? Well, before they put the sack back over my head, I had a moment to look around. The landscape was different from this one but it feels the same. The way everything's perfect. It isn't like nature at all. Just before I was whisked out of the House of Mysteries I had my back to a painting. And when I was released, there was a painting there as well. I know it sounds crazy, but I think I was inside a picture with them."

"Which picture?" asked Wren. "The one in the House of Mysteries or the one in the House of Spirits?"

"I don't know. Both of them perhaps. Or . . . I just don't know," said Mel, shaking his head.

"That's impossible," scoffed Ludo. "Even if you could get inside a picture—which you can't—how could you be inside two pictures at once? There must be a trapdoor here somewhere and the master used it when we weren't looking."

"But we *were* looking, Ludo," said Wren. "We never took our eyes off him."

"You're both talking rubbish. There's a trapdoor. I bet it's under the rug." Ludo relit his candle from one of the gas lamps and began inspecting the floor. He crawled behind the easel.

"Look!" Wren and Mel gasped.

"Leave the candle there and come and look at this, Ludo," said Wren.

With the picture illuminated from behind by the candlelight, the underpainting became discernable. All of the complicated brushwork that underlay the master's technique, that made his pictures seem so real, was revealed. But more than meticulous brushwork was visible. In the center of the picture, and painted in some denser medium that rendered it opaque, was a circle within which other lines twisted and whirled, creating a knotlike design.

"What is it?" asked Ludo.

"I think it's a symbol. Like a Fa's diaglyph," said Mel.

"What do you mean?" said Wren.

"It's something that means more than itself. Maybe it's got something to do with the master vanishing."

"But he *didn't* . . . Look, it's just a shape," said Ludo. "It can't actually *do* anything. It's just a paint stain."

"The painting wouldn't look like it does without the underpainting. So maybe this is a part of the illusion as well. You saw the master trace something in the air just before he vanished. It could be this symbol."

"Come on, Mel. Are you telling me that it's magic?"

"No, it's *art*. Fa Theum says that's the only type of magic that exists in the real world."

"But art's about things we can see," insisted Ludo.

"You can no longer see the underpainting," said Wren. "Or the skill or time it took to paint—but they're all locked up in there, too."

"That's different."

"Is it? My guess is that this thing's an important part of the picture," said Mel, as he took a sheet of paper and a pencil. "I'm going to make a copy. See what else you can find."

Ludo shrugged and began sorting through the piles of books with Wren. "There's a book full of drawings of animals here. I've seen some of these before in the master's pictures."

"It's his bestiary," said Mel. "I'll have a look, as soon as I've finished this."

Ludo wandered over to inspect the large paintings stacked against the wall. "These must be in the master's private collection," he said as he sorted through them. "Wow! There're a couple here by Lucas Flink."

"Really? They must be worth a fortune," said Wren.

"Who's Lucas Fink?" asked Mel absently as he concentrated on his copy.

"*Flink*. Only the greatest master of fantastic paintings—along with our master, of course."

"Does he have apprentices, too?" asked Mel.

"He might have had once, but he's been dead two hundred years. That's odd. This canvas is still wet. How could the paint on something this old not be dry yet?"

"*Quiet!*" Wren crossed to the door and placed her ear against it. "Quick, someone's coming."

Ludo snatched his candle from the floor and followed her to the service passage. "*Mel*, come on!"

Mel hastily finished his sketch and stole one last look at the canvas, which appeared normal again now with no trace of the hidden design. He joined the others and they closed the door to a crack just as Dirk Tot entered the studio. He looked suspiciously about the room. Then he approached the painting before withdrawing some phials of pigment from his reticule and arranging them with the master's other painting equipment. He took another look around the room before leaving. They heard him turn the key in the lock after him.

"Wherever there's a mystery, he turns up," said Wren.

"Well, we've learned something this evening. If you know how, you can get inside a picture," said Mel.

"No, you *can't*."

"Ludo, what's it going to take before you accept what your eyes told you?" said Wren.

"If you're so certain that you can get inside a picture, there's one way to find out for sure," said Ludo. "We can make one of our own."

The next morning the master visited the apprentices in their studio as usual. Mel looked up from his scrubbing as he and his entourage strode by. They exchanged smiles and Mel detected a wave of jealous hostility from Groot and his sidekicks. Mel contrived to clean a patch near Ludo so that they could talk.

"He looks okay," said Mel in a low voice. "Wherever he went hasn't done him any harm."

"That's because he hasn't been anywhere. Meet me in the clock after supper and I'll prove it to you. Watch out." Ludo made himself look busy as Groot scanned the studio, looking for Mel.

During one of his many visits to the courtyard to replenish his cleaning water, Mel noticed a door standing ajar. He looked about him, then approached it and entered. The door led, by way of a short covered passage, to the strangest garden he had ever seen. Along one side of the high-walled space were several beds of brightly colored flowers. One contained only the primary colors, red, yellow, and blue, and another the secondary colors, green, orange and purple. Yet another held an entire rainbow spectrum. Not only were there red, orange, yellow, green, blue, indigo, and violet plants, but between them many intermediate shades, so that the whole effect was of a rainbow laid out on the ground. Still another bed contained earthy, tertiary colors, and one more was planted with unusual, achromatic plants: black white and every shade of gray in between. As if all this was not strange enough, the opposite side of the garden contained the mirror image, except that the plants there were made of painted wood. Some of the colors were as vivid as their natural counterparts, others less so. Kneeling there, tending these artificial plants, was Dirk Tot. Without looking up from what he was doing, he said, "Skiving off from your cleaning, Mel?"

"No, I . . ." He could not think of an excuse.

"It's all right. Can't say I blame you. If I had my way you'd be doing something more useful than scrubbing floors. I know the master feels the same—but Groot's in charge of the apprentices and we won't interfere. Don't be downhearted, though. All apprentices start out with a few days of menial labor. It never lasts long."

Mel knew Dirk Tot was mistaken in this. He would never be given anything useful to do while Groot was in charge.

Dirk Tot looked up. "This is my Fugitive Garden. Fascinating, isn't it."

"What's it all for?"

The giant rose to his feet and dusted some dirt from his knees with his good hand. "It's a kind of ongoing experiment. You see, all artists' colors are fugitive to some extent. That means that they fade when they're exposed to daylight. Some are highly fugitive and fade rapidly while others are less so and hardly fade at all. Look here." He pointed to some brown artificial flowers with his silver hand. "Generally speaking, those that are painted with earthlike colors are the most permanent, and others—like those faded pinks over there—the least. I take a sample from every batch of pigment that we use in the studio and paint one of these wooden plants. The real plants, over there, are our control group, the ones I compare them to, so that I can gauge the extent of the fading. It's important to know how a painting will age. They'll be around a lot longer than you or I. Some pigments are more expensive than others, as you have already learned to your cost, but the most precious is this one here." He indicated a deep blue.

"That's the household color," said Mel, fingering his own doublet.

"It's called ultramarine. It's made from ground-up lapis lazuli, a semiprecious stone. The master likes that color as it impresses his patrons, makes them aware of how rich and successful he's become. How much his pictures will cost them. It's good salesmanship."

"He must be very rich to have us all dressed like this."

At that moment, a gust of wind blew open a gate at the far end of the enclosure. Mel caught a fleeting glimpse of another garden beyond. It was also planted with artificial flowers but they seemed to be much less faded than the majority of those in this. Dirk Tot was not aware of the open gate at first, as the undamaged side of his face was towards Mel, but the boy's expression must have betrayed his curiosity and the giant turned to look at what he found so interesting. Immediately, Dirk Tot dashed over and closed the gate.

He spoke gruffly. "Shouldn't you be working? Run along. That floor isn't going to clean itself."

Reluctantly, Mel left wondering why Dirk Tot did not want him to see the other garden.

After supper, Mel, Ludo, and Wren gathered inside the clock. Ludo had smuggled some sheets of paper from the studio storeroom and had glued several together until they formed a sheet about as big as the master's painting. He had also brought a small pot of gesso and a paintbrush. They pinned the paper up on to the wall and Mel carefully copied the knotlike design on to it from his sketch. The gesso rapidly dried and the white-on-white symbol was invisible.

"That's the first part done," said Mel. "What have you got for us to make the picture with?"

"These are all I could nab." Ludo held up a bunch of pencils apologetically.

"They're no good," said Mel. "The master's landscape, and the one where I was kidnapped, were both colored. And as real as here and now—realer."

"Mel's right," said Wren.

"But paintings are usually made for other people to look at. They *have* to be detailed. If the picture was just for us, then we'd know what color everything was supposed to be. Like, if we drew some grass, then we'd know it was green, or that the sky was blue. Wouldn't we? That way it wouldn't matter that it wasn't as perfect as the master's. It's only us that are ever going to see it."

"Then why did the master make his picture in color?" asked Wren. "I bet he's the only one that's ever going to see it."

"There's no way we could get enough paint and canvas and stuff to make a picture like that. Everyone would know it's missing," said Ludo. "And we'd need an easel and everything. Anyway, it's only a test. It's just to find out if it works—which it won't."

"All right, but let's keep it simple. Just a basic landscape. Ludo, you start that side and Wren the other. I'll begin in the middle. We'll make it up as we go along."

They had been drawing for only a minute before Mel and Ludo stopped.

"That's really good, Wren," said Ludo. "You weren't lying when you said you could draw."

"I think it's unfair there're no girl apprentices," said Mel. "You're far better than Groot."

"And prettier, too." She fluttered her eyelashes. "Now, get a move on or we'll never finish."

By the time the light began to fade, they had not made much progress.

"Look, tomorrow's Sunday and we don't have to work," said Ludo.

"*You* don't have to work," corrected Wren. "The kitchen will still be busy."

"Yeah, but Mel and I can carry on with the drawing first thing and you can join us when you get the chance. We should have it finished by the afternoon."

By the time Wren was able to free herself from her duties the next day, the picture, such as it was, was complete. "I don't think much of that," she said critically.

What she saw was a crude landscape in shades of gray. In the foreground was a stunted tree standing amid hastily scribbled grass. The middle and background were smudged and vague, with just the merest suggestion of hills and valleys. A roughly drawn building occupied one of the hilltops. The sky was an all-over uniform gray and there were odd blotches where they had inexpertly rubbed out mistakes.

"It's not very good, is it?" said Mel. "Perhaps we should begin again?"

"It'll do. It's not as if it's going to work, after all," said Ludo.

"I don't know, Ludo." Mel looked concerned.

"You're being a perfectionist. Just think of it as a working drawing. Are you staying to watch, Wren?"

"I can't. I've got a mountain of pots and dishes to wash up. Good luck. And, if it works—"

"No chance of that."

"—be careful. Promise?"

"What do we do now?" asked Ludo after she had gone.

"We copy the master." Mel sounded unsure. He held his sketch of the symbol up in front of him. "Here goes."

"Wait! If you do that you might go into the picture but I'll be left standing here on my own," complained Ludo.

"I thought you said it wasn't going to work."

"It won't. But just in case it does."

"Why don't we link arms? That way we'll both go."

"I've got an idea." Ludo unpinned the drawing from the wall and, with a couple of dabs of glue, stuck it to the translucent clock face. They could see the symbol underneath the drawing clearly silhouetted against the daylight. "That's more like it."

"*Brilliant!* Right, here goes. Take my arm." They looked at each other, and each took a deep breath. Then, hesitantly, Mel traced the design in the air in front of him.

15. the ill-conceived world

NOTHING HAPPENED.

"What did I tell you?" said Ludo.

"Maybe I wasn't trying hard enough. Let's do it again." Mel screwed his eyes tight shut, willing it to happen. He traced the design in the air. *Come on, come on, come on, come on.* He opened his eyes.

They were still inside the clock.

"It's never going to work. We're wasting our time."

"It's got to. I *saw* it work. There's something I'm not doing right. Think back, which hand did the master use?"

"His right!" said Ludo confidently. "No, his left. At least I *think* it was his left."

"No. It was his right hand. The one nearest to us. Then what?"

"Then he . . . I can't remember. Why don't you try starting at the top? Make a kind of spiral, like a whirlpool. Whirlpools suck things into them, don't they? And look, some of the lines are drawn on top of the others. That means that the bits underneath were made first, before the other bits were laid on top."

It took a bit of working out but soon Mel had it. He glanced up at the clock face. Its back-to-front hands indicated that it was midday. Behind them, the works began whirring as they prepared to chime. "All right. Clockwise or counterclockwise?"

"How should I know? Oh, clockwise!"

The boys took another deep breath as Mel traced the motif once more. This time the drawing shimmered and seemed to rotate, just like a whirlpool. The world around them—the real world of the clock and the mansion—grew indistinct and distant. They felt a sensation like pins and needles all over as they were drawn forward. Everything seemed to blur for a moment. When they regained focus, they stood, side by side, inside their own, newly created world.

The friends looked at each other.

"*Scrot!*" exclaimed Ludo. "It *does* work!"

"That tingling feeling," said Mel. "It was the same as I felt before."

They looked behind them. There, close by, rose the undulating wall of mist that Mel remembered seeing.

"That must be the surface of the drawing," said Mel.

"The master calls it the 'picture plane,'" replied Ludo.

"It's the way back to the real world." Mel touched it but it felt strangely resistant.

They turned again to gaze at their world. Everything looked particularly sketchy and unfinished and very, very gray.

"It doesn't look very, you know, *real*," said Mel.

"Maybe if we imagine the colors that'll help. I'll try with the grass." Ludo narrowed his eyes and dramatically pointed at the grass like a stage magician. "Alacaboozle."

"*Alacaboozle?*" Mel stifled a giggle.

The grass remained gray.

"I felt I had to say *something*. Maybe it needs the two of us. Come on, Mel, both together now. Imagine it's green."

The boys concentrated and slowly the grass took on a definite greenish tinge, like a gray sponge sucking up colored water.

"Did we do that?" Mel was astonished.

"You're not the only one with ideas," said Ludo.

"Just imagine if we could do that in the real world. We could put the Fifth Mystery out of business. Now let's try the sky."

The sky became bluer but the grass lost some of its previous greenness. "And the tree," urged Ludo.

Soon they had colored their world.

"Doesn't it look a bit washed-out to you?" asked Mel.

"It's difficult to keep the colors there," complained Ludo as they started to fade. Beneath everything, the rough texture of the pencil drawing showed through.

"It works while we're concentrating, but as soon as we think of something else the colors start to fade again. It's as if we can only imagine a certain amount between us. It's not enough to spread over the whole world."

"You've proved your point. It works. Now, how do we get back?"

"But we've only just arrived. No one's ever been here before. We're the very first people in this world." Mel folded his sketch of the symbol and tucked it inside his doublet.

"I don't know . . ."

"Come on, Ludo. Just imagine what Wren will say when we tell her."

They approached their tree. Mel reached up to grab a leaf but it turned to dust in his hand, leaving a dirty green smear that rapidly turned gray like powdered graphite. Disappointed, he wiped it clean on his sleeve. "Come on, Ludo, let's go and visit the house."

But walking was hard work. Their scribbled grass was more like a low-lying vine that snagged their feet and tugged at their ankles. The house did not appear to be getting any nearer. But they did reach it and they found that, rather than being full-sized, it was tiny and barely reached up to their knees. It was no bigger than when they first saw it.

"That's *really* odd," said Mel.

"It's the same size as it was in the drawing. Perhaps if we knew more about the laws of perspective, things would behave like they do in the real world. It's not much of a house either, you can't get inside." The doorway and windows were simply hollows in the surface. He kicked it and the tiny house crumbled like a sandcastle into gray dust.

"Where to now, Explorer?" asked Ludo.

"I think you're right. There's nothing much to see here. Let's go back."

"But which way?"

The wall of mist had vanished. Everything looked the same in all directions except for the tree, which had not diminished in size at all even though they had walked away from it. Their eyes told them that it had grown enormously.

"That way," said Mel, pointing to it. "The way out's right next to the tree."

But it was not. Their eyes told them the tree shrank as they approached it, but, in fact, it remained the same size.

"What's going on, Mel?"

"I don't know. I think it's because we drew it big, in the foreground, to make it seem closer."

"Or maybe this world's got laws all of its own."

When they reached the tree the landscape still looked exactly the same in all directions. There was no sign of the mist wall anywhere.

"I just don't understand any of this," said Mel. He leaned

against the tree and fell on to his back as it crumbled to dust, just like the house. There was no landmark left in their world.

"What now?" asked Ludo.

Mel picked himself up and dusted his clothes. "I don't know. The way out has got to be around here somewhere. Maybe the wall of mist is only visible from a certain angle."

"What's that? Something's moving out there." Ludo was pointing into the distance, or what passed for the distance in their topsy-turvy world. An amorphous shape was thickening and solidifying. "It looks like one of your mistakes that you rubbed out."

"It could be one of yours. You made as many as I did."

As the shape came towards them it began to assume a form. A smudge near the bottom began to grow legs—three of them. The center flowed and solidified into what looked like a skeletal rib cage. Scrawny, fingerlike wings unfurled from behind and spread wide. For the moment the top could not decide what it wanted to be and hovered as an indistinct blur before it resolved into a cloud of buzzing flies. Then two eyes formed within the cloud as sinister dark slits.

"Run!" shouted Mel.

The scribble-grass caught Ludo's ankle and he fell headlong. Mel helped him to his feet. The creature was getting nearer or, if not, it was certainly getting bigger. The buzzing of the flies grew louder and the creature loped towards them with its awkward gait, like a one-legged man on a pair of crutches.

Mel looked desperately around the nondescript landscape. It looked somehow thicker in one direction and the pair set off that way, hoping it was the wall.

But it was another mistake.

This hastily erased error was transforming itself into a second nightmare creature with long legs supporting a hard carapace. Antennae, as slender as whips, sprouted from the top in place of eyes, and two mantislike arms hung down in front.

"Come on, Ludo. This way." The boys changed direction yet again.

The scribble-grass grew bigger and thicker, as thick as rope, slowing the boys further. Ludo stumbled again. Mel made a grab for his friend and the two overbalanced and tumbled down through the oversized undergrowth, which parted and then closed over their heads to form a kind of imperfect, interwoven roof. They lay there breathlessly on their backs and watched as the two Mistakes stalked backwards and forwards above their heads.

"Now where are we?"

"Who cares," said Ludo. "We're safe from your Mistakes for a bit."

"More like yours. Come on. We can't stay here. Those things will find us in a minute."

They got to their feet and found themselves in a maze of low tunnels beneath the undergrowth. Under their feet was flat, dirty-white ground that Mel associated with the surface of the paper. He looked up and saw that a third Mistake had joined the other two. It was like a huge spider with a long, barbed trunk, which it stabbed down through the undergrowth at them. The boys ran down one of the tunnels as the Mistakes followed the sound of their footsteps.

"This way," said Mel as he branched off to the left.

"Mel, *help!*" Ludo had caught his ankle in a loop of undergrowth projecting from the tunnel wall.

As Mel turned back to help him, the barbed trunk shot through the canopy, tearing Ludo's sleeve and grazing his arm. Before Mel could reach his friend, it flashed down again, wounding Ludo in the leg. Mel drew his bodkin and slashed at the trunk as he freed Ludo with his other hand and dragged him away. The trunk, spraying arcs of gray blood, continued to stab at the space where they had been and was soon joined by the multi-jointed arms and the thrashing antennae of the second Mistake probing cruelly down into the tunnel.

"Can you walk?"

Ludo tried to stand but fell as his leg collapsed under him. "I guess not."

"Here, grab hold of me." Mel helped his friend to his feet. "Use this." He hacked off a length of undergrowth to use as a stick.

"Why's this so solid when the house and tree turned to dust?"

"Good question. Perhaps we were pressing harder when we drew it."

Ludo looked around. "What now?"

"Let's keep moving." They set off slowly down another tunnel. Mel glanced behind and saw the thin trail of Ludo's blood quickly turn gray as it soaked into the ground. As they moved through the tunnels Ludo became weaker.

"This is no good," said Mel. "We could be going round and round in circles down here. We need to get back to the surface." He eased his friend to the ground and began snapping off pieces of the undergrowth until he had created a hole big enough for them to escape through. Cautiously, he raised his head and peered out. Some distance off, he had no way of telling how far, he saw two of the Mistakes stabbing and probing the undergrowth where they imagined their prey might still be. The third Mistake, the one with the long legs, was prowling in a circle around them.

Mel looked around. "The going seems easier away from the Mistakes." He ducked back down and helped Ludo through the hole. The two made their way as fast as they could, Ludo leaning heavily on Mel. The size of the undergrowth grew less until it was like the previous low-lying vine. The going was easier but not easy, and a soupy gray-white mist began to rise from the ground.

Ludo cried out in pain. "Mel, I think that barbed trunk thing must have been poisoned. I feel cold."

The Mistakes had heard Ludo's cry. They were coming towards them. Ludo's color was beginning to leave him. He and his clothing were slowly turning gray.

"I can't go on any further, Mel. I'm sorry."

Mel shot a worried glance towards the Mistakes.

"Don't leave me here."

"Don't worry; I'm not going to leave you. The way back's got to be around here somewhere. Come on, Ludo. Ludo?"

Ludo did not answer.

Mel heaved his semiconscious friend on to his shoulder and stumbled on, away from their pursuers. He began to fight hard for breath. The mist started to thicken and clot in front of him. The clots began to resolve themselves into trees. *How could that be? The world we drew had only the single tree.* A sparse wood opened up around him as he hastened along. Their drawing had taken on a life of its own.

Mel stopped for a moment and lowered his friend to the ground. He eased Ludo's wounded arm from his doublet and tore his shirt, revealing the gash. With revulsion he saw that it was crawling with tiny gray worms. The maggots were eating Ludo's flesh and as they ate, more color drained from him. Mel tore his hose and saw the same thing on his leg. With a rising sense of disgust, he picked as many as he could off the wounds but for every one that he picked off another took its place.

He looked about him desperately. *Which way, which way? If only I could see a landmark.* All he saw were the Mistakes. He heaved his friend back up on to his shoulder and staggered on, but after only a short way had to rest again.

Thin, icy tendrils snaked towards them along the sketchy ground, like shabby skeins of gossamer. Beyond them Mel saw nothing but gray indistinct shapes dissolving into the fog. Only the few trees nearby had any substance and even those were changing themselves as he watched. They were now more like giant, many-fingered hands. Here and there the gray bark fell away like rotting flesh to reveal not bare wood but sinew and bone.

Mel regretted drawing the grass so casually. He had thought it would be so much quicker than drawing in every single blade. *How could I have been so stupid?* He should have realized they might need a landmark or two, to give a sense of direction in this world.

Then, very faintly and at the limit of his hearing, he heard a familiar tune. It was the sound of the carillon in the clock. It was coming from behind him, from where they had been. He must have been walking away from it all this time. Where the grass had become thicker, where it had seemed as thick as rope, must be near the front of the drawing. That's why it did not break like the house and tree. They *had* pressed harder with their pencils to make it seem darker and nearer the foreground of the drawing.

"We're near to the picture plane and the wall of mist, Ludo," said Mel.

With great effort he heaved Ludo up on to his shoulder again and half-ran, half-staggered in the direction of the music.

The bells became louder, the undergrowth thicker. Just as he thought he could carry Ludo no farther before his lungs would burst and his legs collapse under him, he saw it. The wall of mist shimmered and undulated gently, silver against the dead gray of the landscape.

"Nearly there, Ludo. Just a little farther."

Then, out of the fog they stepped, barring the way. The three Mistakes stood in a line in front of the wall, awaiting their prey.

16. the uninvited guest

MEL LOWERED LUDO to the ground. The chiming of the bells continued from beyond the wall and the creatures cocked their heads as they listened to the first music ever heard in their world. Mel reached into his doublet and withdrew his bodkin, though he doubted that it would be of any real use against the three towering monsters. He knew instinctively that this was not a problem that could be solved with cold steel. It was a problem for an artist's hand and mind.

No sooner had Mel formed these thoughts than the Mistakes seemed to grow less formidable. *They're only mistakes. I just need to correct them. But how?*

"Hey! Errors! Botched Jobs! Blunders! Here I am! Come and get me!" He darted to the side and led them away from Ludo.

The Mistakes began to move slowly towards him. Then the spider-creature, its hairy body glistening, lunged at him with its venomous trunk. Mel tried to sidestep it, but snagged his foot in the undergrowth and fell. He felt the whoosh in his hair as the barbed weapon shot over his head. He quickly rolled over and stabbed at the creature's long legs with his dagger, but missed. Then, from where the first creature's head should have been, a swarm of flies flew towards him, temporarily blinding him and inflicting cruel bites. Mel swiped wildly at the attacking flies but his bodkin was useless. It was like trying to cut smoke. He reached back with his free hand and touched something powdery. The remains of the tree. He grabbed a handful of the graphite dust and flung it at his attackers. It made a great arc in the air that hung there suspended, as if it had stuck to a sheet of invisible glass. The long-legged Mistake rushed at him, but as it touched the dust its legs became entangled and then fused together. It toppled down and landed with a great crash, shattering into powder and sending up a great, gray cloud of dust.

Mel rolled towards the cloud and, as he did so, the flies moved with him. As they reached the cloud, its mass added to theirs and they began to coagulate and form a single, large accretionlike pools of quicksilver flowing together, too heavy to take wing. Mel rose and jumped on it with both feet and it exploded in another cloud of dust that slowly drifted to the ground. The bulk of the Mistake, now deprived of its head, also crumbled away.

The final Mistake advanced towards him on its eight hairy legs, swinging its barbed trunk before it like a swordsman entering a melee. Mel kicked a pile of dust into the path of the approaching creature. Its trunk scythed through the cloud, shredding it into streaks. As it swung back, the streaks attached themselves to the trunk and transformed into hissing snakes. They opened their many mouths wide, revealing sharp fangs. *I've just made it ten times worse!* He backed away but the undergrowth snagged his feet yet again and he toppled backwards. If only the scribble-grass was as friable as the other artifacts of this world.

That's it! He grabbed and tore up handfuls of the undergrowth as he scrambled away from the Mistake. When he had an armful he flung it at the creature like a *retiarius* gladiator tossing his net. As it flew, the grass spread and flattened in the air into a shaggy pancake, enveloping the creature and pulling it to the ground. The creature screamed and then, like the other Mistakes, exploded into a cloud of dark gray dust.

Mel dashed back to Ludo. His friend felt cold and lifeless. "Ludo, speak to me." The familiar musical carillon continued through the barrier. "Come on, we're going home." He lifted his friend in his arms and walked towards the wall of mist, but as he neared it he felt resistance. For an instant the dreadful prospect of being trapped there forever flitted through Mel's mind. He laid Ludo back down, withdrew his sketch from his doublet, and unfolded it. Making sure he was touching his friend, he traced the design in the air. He expected to feel the tingling feeling and to be drawn back into the real world but nothing happened. *Think*, he told himself. He recalled how they had got there and imagined the drawing stuck up on the clock face, illuminated from behind by the great face with its back-to-front numerals. *That's it!* The symbol would be reversed. He traced the design counterclockwise in the air. Then came the spinning, the tingling, and they were back, collapsing on the floor of the clock.

The carillon reached its crescendo and ceased. The animated figures completed their motions and returned to their resting places. The door to the clock opened and Wren ducked in, clutching two apples.

"*Mel! Ludo!* Whatever's happened?"

"Help me." Mel eased Ludo's doublet from him, exposing his wounded arm, which writhed with the tiny worms. He began plucking them out of the gash.

Wren knelt beside him. "What're *those*? How did this happen? I only left you a moment ago."

"We've been in the picture."

"But you can't have been . . ."

"We *were*, the symbol worked. Ludo was attacked. He's dying. *Help* me."

They quickly picked the worms off Ludo's arm and leg, squashing them with their hands into mush. They were brightly colored inside.

"*Yuck!* They must have been drinking Ludo's color," said Mel.

"His color's beginning to come back," said Wren.

As each worm was removed, a little more color seeped back into the boy. Soon Ludo's wounds were free of them.

"What happened to you in there, Mel?" asked Wren.

Mel caught sight of himself reflected in a shiny brass counterweight. Graphite dust covered him from head to foot. His blue eyes stared back at him—the only color on his black body. "It's a long story."

Ludo moaned.

"He's coming around!"

"He's so cold," said Wren, rubbing his hand. She rolled his doublet and placed it beneath his head for a pillow.

Mel took off his own and placed it over his stricken friend.

Ludo opened his eyes. Suddenly coming to himself, he tried to sit up. His eyes shot about him in panic. "Mel, Wren, what—?"

"It's okay, Ludo. You're safe now. We're back home," said Mel.

Ludo forced himself up on his elbows. "I've just had the strangest dream." He looked up and saw the drawing hanging on the clock face. "Except, it wasn't a dream, was it? Look, Mel, the drawing's changed."

In place of their ill-conceived world there was a misty landscape dotted with the vague forms of stunted trees and, in the foreground, several large piles of gray dust.

"And what's all this mess? It's like the studio floor."

"Nothing, Ludo," said Mel. "Just take it easy."

"This is all crazy," said Wren. "There's not enough time for anything to have happened. As soon as I got halfway down the stairs I remembered I'd forgotten to give you these apples. I came back at once and found you like this."

Mel looked up at the clock. Sure enough, it was barely past midday. "But we've been gone ages. Time must be different inside the picture."

"You'll have to tell me later. I've got to get back to the kitchen before I'm missed." With a last, concerned look at Ludo, she left.

Mel inspected Ludo's wounds again. Now that they were free of the maggots they were healing visibly. "It's like magic."

"I'm all right, Mel," said Ludo, standing up, although Mel could see that he was badly shaken.

Mel pulled down the drawing and tore it into many pieces. "That's somewhere we won't *ever* be going back to."

As the two boys left the clock, neither noticed a tiny worm hidden under the machinery. After the door had closed behind them, it crawled out of its hiding place and began to eat the colored remains of its kin. Then, its hunger unsatisfied, it slithered through a crack in the floorboards and on through the mansion.

The night was stifling. Even though the dormitory windows were open wide, no air seemed to circulate. Mel lay on his back staring at the ceiling, feeling small rivulets of perspiration tickle his body like crawling centipedes. Shadows painted sinister shapes on the ceiling. One shadow seemed to change into the silhouette of a tall man accompanied by a dwarf. Mel found that he could not move. He thought he heard sinister laughter. From the corner of his eye he saw a hand appear over the sill of the open window and then a man hauled himself into the dormitory. Another followed him and then another until a dozen or more stood there in the dim light. They were all dressed in gray robes and were obviously members of a Mystery he had yet to encounter. Two were carrying a long, rolled bundle. They formed a semicircle around his bed. The bundle was unrolled, revealing a huge, color-eating maggot. The shadows above him solidified and the dreadful, gray face of the High-Bailiff leaned close. Mel could smell his vile breath.

"Smell, you thief. It's mine. Your color's mine. All the color in the world's mine. You stole it and now I shall have it back," he hissed.

Mumchance's shadow beckoned to the others and the maggot was brought forward towards Mel's face. Nearer and nearer it came. Mel struggled to rise but only managed a few feeble movements as it was brought closer, its drooling, color-sucking mouthparts pursed as if for a kiss. Mel struggled harder against his paralysis.

"Mel, wake up! Wake up."

Someone was shaking him. Mel slowly surfaced from his nightmare and blinked. "Ludo? What time is it?"

"It's dawn. Mel, come and look at this. I think we're in deep trouble."

17. the vermiraptor

MEL CLIMBED OUT of bed, pulling on some clean clothes, and followed Ludo to the window. They looked down into the courtyard. Even in the thin light of early dawn, they could see that the far corner beneath the clock tower had lost its color.

"It looks just like—"

"Our drawing," said Mel. "There's something moving down there. Come on."

Downstairs, the full extent of the damage was evident. Many of the flowering trees and low box hedges were completely gray. Some of the marble statues near to them had lost their delicate pale pinks and blues and a small gilded fountain looked as though it were fashioned from dull and lifeless metal. The ground writhed with a carpet of slimy, gray creatures.

"It's the *worms*. But it can't be. Wren and I pulled them all off you and squashed them."

"*What!* You mean those things were on *me*?"

"The ones that attacked you were tiny. These are huge. Some are as big as sausages."

"You must have big sausages in Feg. Some of them are nearly as big as the whole pig."

Now that the maggots were bigger their features were more defined. They were covered in fine hairs and trailed sticky mucus behind them. Beneath bulging, pale eyes their mouthparts had slug lips like gaping wounds, and they made an ominous sucking sound as they fed.

"They're drinking the color from everything."

"I think they're multiplying."

"What're we going to do? The servants will be up and about soon. It won't be long before this is discovered."

Mel began stamping on the mucus-covered worms that were squirming about ankle deep. They made a squelching noise underfoot and a satisfying *splop* when they burst and their colored innards shot out.

"This is revolting. I feel sick."

"You must help me, Ludo. No one must know about this. If they ever find we brought them here we'll both be kicked out."

After a short while, both of the boys were skidding about on the slick, multicolored surface of the courtyard. Their boots were thick with the colored residue of the squashed worms and their white hose were splashed with bright stains. But the maggots kept multiplying.

The task seemed hopeless to Mel. "We need help. Go find Wren."

By the time Ludo returned with Wren, the oversized maggots had increased visibly.

"I thought a broom might help," said Wren.

Ludo took it from her and began frantically brushing yet more worms from the trunks of the trees and from the statues. Wren hitched up her skirts and joined in the stamping but it was a lost cause.

"We need more help," said Wren. "I'll go and get the other

servants and one of you go and wake up the 'prentices. *Get off!*"
She kicked one of the larger worms that had sucked her shoe,
leaving a gray patch.

"No, we can't do that," said Ludo. "This is all our fault."

"We must do *something*," said Wren. "The mansion's full of
the master's paintings. Just imagine what would happen if they
get inside. And what if they escape into the city?"

"Wren's right. We'll never wipe them out on our own," said
Mel. "But no servants. I've got another idea. Wren, can you get
the key to the passages?"

"I've got it here."

"Will the master be in his studio this early?" Mel asked her.

"No, he never starts work until after his morning rounds."

"Good. Come on, you two."

The friends raced through the service passages to the master's
studio.

Mel asked, "Where's the bestiary you found the other day,
Ludo?"

Ludo rummaged around and soon found it. "Here it is. What're
you thinking?"

"Perhaps we can find a creature in the bestiary that we could
use to fight the maggots and we might find that same creature in
one of the master's paintings." Mel nodded towards the master's
canvas. "One of us could go and get it."

"Sounds like a pretty feeble plan to me," said Ludo.

"I still think we should get help," said Wren.

"But we *can't*," said Ludo.

"Do you have a better idea?" said Mel.

Ludo sighed. "Okay, let's try your idea."

The bestiary was a richly illuminated tome bound in worn, tan leather. It had reinforced metal corners and hinges and a heavy iron clasp holding it shut.

"Where do we start?" asked Wren. "There must be hundreds of pages."

There *were* hundreds of pages and each one featured several creatures painted in bright colors. The illustrations were obviously by many different hands and the older ones, near the beginning, were faded.

As they turned the pages, the beasts depicted on the crinkled vellum became stranger and stranger. In the later half of the book the illustrations were fresher. Next to each was a handwritten inscription in sepia ink.

"What's that one?" Mel pointed to a likely looking brute. "It looks like it might eat worms for breakfast."

"I don't know. It's in some strange script," said Wren. "Can you read, it Ludo?"

The fierce grothling defends itself with its sharp tusks and antlers. It spends its days half submerged in swampy where the tufted carbuncles of its shell resemble floating islands of bog debris. Any flying megaphine that is unwary or foolish enough to approach is seized and dragged into the depths of the mire where it is left to decompose for several days before it is devoured by the grothling. The eggs of the grothling resemble green, spiked balls. In the absence of flying megaphines the grothling has been seen to consume its own eggs or, on occasion, small parts of itself.

"No, I can't. It looks like you should be able to read it but when you try it doesn't make any sense. I'll tell you what, though; it's the master's handwriting."

"Perhaps it's in code," said Wren.

"I'm sure it's in Nemish, but I still can't read it," said Ludo. "There's something odd about it."

"Why does everything have to be so difficult?" said Mel, frustrated that he could not read. "Even getting back from the picture was hard. Everything was back to front and I had to—"

"Wait! Hang on . . ." Ludo looked about the studio. "Yes!" He unhooked a small mirror from the wall and held it at an angle against the book. "Can you read it now?"

"Ludo, you're brilliant," said Wren. "It's mirror writing."

The fierce grothling defends itself with its sharp tusks and antlers. It spends its days half submerged in swamp where the tufted carbuncles of its shell resemble floating islands of bog debris. Any flying megaphine that is unwary or foolish enough to approach is seized and dragged into the depths of the mire where it is left to decompose for several days before it is devoured by the grothling. The eggs of the grothling resemble green, spiked balls. In the absence of flying megaphines the grothling has been seen to consume its own eggs or, on occasion, small parts of itself.

"What do you suppose a megaphine is?" asked Ludo.

"It doesn't matter. It says they fly, which the worms don't," said Mel. "What about that one?"

Wren tilted the mirror. "It's a 'thringle.' It seems they feed on things called 'fustinbules.'"

"What're *they*?" asked Ludo.

"Wait." Wren turned to the back of the book. "There's a glossary here. Let's see—here it is—'thringle.'"

Neither "thringle" nor "fustinbule" looked promising. They tried several more creatures but with the same result.

"We're wasting time," said Wren.

"Wait a minute. What's that? I've seen it before," said Mel, pointing to a white-scaled, lizardlike beast.

"Where?" asked Ludo. "In a bad dream?"

"No," said Wren. "He's seen it there." She pointed to the master's painting. Sure enough, in the foreground, beneath a tree, lazed the selfsame creature.

The friends looked back at the bestiary. The beast had a triangular, crested head with large eyes rimmed with lemon yellow, a stout body, and a long, thin tail that curled up over its back in a tight spiral. Wren read out the annotation in the mirror.

The vermiraptor is normally docile but has been seen to enter into a frenzy after feeding upon chromophages. On no account should the vermiraptor be approached during such a frenzy. Vermiraptors are normally solitary and inhabit rocky wasteland only venturing to richer climes when they have the need to drink or seek a mate. The beast depicted here is an immature female but the adult can become aggressive and grow to enormous size should sufficient food be available.

She looked up "chromophage" in the glossary. There was no illustration, just a brief note that said,

Chromophages are pernicious worms (probably mythical) thought by some to inhabit the half-worlds. If such entities exist

they are probably formed within the saliva of such creatures as the hogfire and arachnophant.

Wren drew her finger down the glossary. "Harpy . . . Hippogriff . . . Humbata . . . Hydra . . . There's no hogfire here."

"How about 'arachnophant'?"

She flipped back. "Ajatar . . . Allopecopithicum . . . *Arachnophant!*" Wren turned to the indicated page.

Ludo gasped. "It's the spider creature that wounded me."

"Well, we've found our creature," said Mel. He approached Ambrosius Blenk's canvas and studied the vermiraptor more closely. "You two wait here, I'll go into the painting and fetch it."

"Are you sure?" said Wren.

"It doesn't look as though it'll be too much to handle."

Mel stood up straight and composed himself. He traced the unlocking symbol in the air and Wren and Ludo saw the surface of the canvas gently ripple. They watched Mel vanish, only to see him reappear almost instantly, panting heavily. His hair was disheveled and his doublet was muddy.

"Too much to handle?" asked Wren with a smug grin.

"It's bigger than it looks," he gasped. "It doesn't seem to want to leave. I'll need a rope or something."

"Here," said Ludo, taking a length of velvet cord that held back the curtains.

"That should do the trick," said Mel.

Almost as soon as he disappeared, there was a loud thump and the vermiraptor appeared on the studio floor immediately in front of the canvas. It looked just as it had in the painting except it was about as big as a small crocodile and much fatter.

"Get this great lump off of me," came Mel's muffled voice. One of his arms appeared from under the creature.

Ludo grabbed the velvet rope attached around the beast's neck and tugged, while Wren helped Mel out from under it.

"She's a stubborn brute," he said, rubbing his bruised ribs. "I had to chase her for miles."

"We'd best get her down to the courtyard right away," said Ludo, tugging gently on the rope.

"Careful, she's vicious. She tried to bite me."

"I think I'll call her Munchie. You're not going to give me a hard time are you, Munchie?"

Munchie looked up at Ludo with her big, long-lashed eyes and blinked mildly. If a lizard could be said to smile that is certainly what she was doing to Ludo.

"I don't believe it," said Mel.

"Just like the monkeys," said Wren. "Ludo has a way with animals."

Ludo led the unresisting vermiraptor towards the door to the service passage. She moved with a comic, exaggerated waddle, her potbelly dragging on the floor. They entered the passage and Wren lit the way. When they came to some stairs, Munchie was reluctant to descend.

"You two are going to have to carry her," said Wren. "Give him a hand, Mel."

"*Me?* She hates me." Mel took Munchie's tail, keeping well clear of her head as she twisted and hissed and spat at him.

"Munchie. Stop that," cooed Ludo.

Munchie complied.

They heard the great clock striking the hour. "Hurry! Everyone will be up and about soon," urged Wren.

In their absence, even more of the courtyard had lost its color. Munchie saw the chromophages and strained at her leash.

"Okay, Munchie. Let's see what you can do. Grub's up," said Ludo, releasing her.

Munchie's funny waddle became more purposeful. When she had covered half the distance towards the maggots she rose up on her front legs and uncurled her tail to balance herself, and her long, sticky tongue flashed out and returned to her open jaws with the speed of a piece of elastic snapping back on itself, cleaning a wide swathe of the courtyard of the maggots.

"I'm glad I'm not on the receiving end of *that*," said Mel.

"That really was an inspired idea of yours, Mel," said Wren as Munchie collected and swallowed whole scores of the fat worms.

"What about me?" said Ludo. "Munchie wouldn't be here if it wasn't for me."

"Well done, *both* of you." Wren shook her head. "*Boys*."

"Er, Wren, Ludo. Look at Munchie. She's changing."

Munchie's scales had begun to swell. Before, they had laid sleek and flat against her body but now they were globular like pearls. They then elongated into sharp spines until she was covered in them like a sea urchin. The crest on her head transformed into a sharp horn and the loose skin around her neck became a broad frill that also bristled with spines. Long spikes grew from the end of her tail. Her white complexion vanished, replaced by vivid streaks of color that flashed over her hide, rapidly changing shape. Her eyes lost their appealing, doelike quality, and sharp teeth appeared in rows in her jaws.

Munchie grew visibly as she ate more and more of the fat maggots, and her demeanor changed into something decidedly unpleasant. Within a short space of time, there were no more worms left but Munchie was obviously still hungry. She stared at Mel, Ludo, and Wren balefully.

"I have a funny feeling that getting rid of the worms will turn out to be the least of our worries," said Ludo.

"She's coming this way," said Wren.

"Back away slowly," said Mel. "Make for the door. Try not to make any sudden moves."

"Scrot to that. *Run!*" shouted Ludo.

Munchie broke into a lumbering gallop.

They just made it to the mansion before a fat, sticky tongue splashed against the jamb. They slammed the door behind them and braced their backs against it, holding it shut as Munchie rammed it.

"What do we do now?" asked Wren.

"We have to get her back inside the picture somehow," said Mel. "She still has the leash attached. Ludo, you're going to have to grab it and lead her back to the passageway."

Thump! Munchie rammed the door again.

"*Me?*"

"You're the only one with any control over her," said Wren.

"It was Mel who fetched her; he should take her back. It was all his idea."

Thump! The door shivered.

"Ludo, we're all in this together," said Wren. "If we don't do something very soon, we'll be caught. I'll lose my job and you and Mel will be thrown out."

"Getting thrown out may be better than being ripped to pieces by—"

Ludo was cut short as the door finally gave way. Silhouetted against the shattered doorway, and eyeing them malevolently, was Munchie. She advanced towards Wren as she got back to her feet.

"Wren, your pinafore!" shouted Mel.

Wren looked down and saw several pale chromophages still attached to her. She flapped her apron and the maggots flew off, to be instantly captured by Munchie's long, sticky tongue in a whiplash motion. "You two. There're more on your hose," cried Wren.

Mel and Ludo quickly brushed them off. The chromophages instantly disappeared on the tip of the vermiraptor's long tongue.

"Looks like she's still hungry," said Ludo.

Hissing, the vermiraptor stalked towards Mel.

"Mel. *Run!*" shouted Wren. "Here, catch!" She tossed him the little key. "Ludo, grab the rope!"

Wren and Ludo seized Munchie by her leash and attempted to slow her down, but the beast was too strong and pulled them off their feet.

"It's no good. It's only Mel she's interested in," said Wren as Munchie dragged them along behind her on their stomachs until they were forced to let go.

Mel made it to the door to the passageway and opened it. He grabbed the still lit candle from the small table where they had left it. Once inside, he retraced his steps, shielding the candle flame from the draught with his hand as he ran. He could hear Munchie rapidly padding after him, banging into the sides of the passageway, which was only just wide enough for her new form. The new Munchie no longer had any trouble mounting the stairs. Every now and then, her long tongue would flash out and, once, caught Mel a wet blow on his back. He could feel his doublet being tugged back by the sticky projectile, but he only slowed for a second as his momentum carried him forward.

Mel climbed higher until he reached the master's studio and burst in. He went straight to the painting and prepared to unlock it using the secret gesture. The service door into the studio was alive with flashing colors as Munchie arrived. She saw Mel and let out a great croaking howl. It rattled the windows and toppled some articles from a nearby table. Her breath was rank and filled the cool room with a sulfurous reek. Her tongue lashed out and connected with Mel's doublet just as he formed the symbol and was drawn into the canvas.

Munchie penetrated the canvas with a powerful bound that carried her past Mel and into the land beyond. He was counting on this and, as she flashed past him, he grabbed her trailing leash and wound it several times around the nearest tree, wedging its end into a cleft. He knew this would not hold her for long and quickly returned to the misty wall, performed the reverse gesture and jumped through.

Mel stood back in the master's studio, panting and gagging. He looked at the canvas. Everything appeared the same, except that the image of the gentle, white vermiraptor that had lain so contentedly beneath the tree was now that of a multicolored monster with a terrifying mien. There was no way it would go unnoticed. He touched it with a fingertip and found that the paint was wet, while everything else on the canvas was dry. He opened the window wide and took a deep breath. He snatched a spare candle from a table, entered the passageway, and made his way back to his friends.

18. another piece of the puzzle

LATER THAT DAY there was much conjecture in the household as to the cause of the baffling events in the mansion. Some thought that the gray courtyard was the result of a prank by the apprentices. Servants were set to cleaning off the supposed gray paint but without success. It was as if all the color had been bleached away by magic. Dirk Tot dismissed the idea of a prank. He knew that such a feat was beyond the capabilities of any apprentice and probably beyond those of Ambrosius Blenk as well. Another theory ran that the plants had been infected by some obscure, botanical disease, but that failed to explain why the statues and fountain had also been affected. Most were agreed that the colored sludge that covered the ground had fallen from the sky. But no one could explain why the sludge had only fallen in that part of the courtyard where the color had vanished. It was as if the color had somehow coagulated and dripped off its hosts on to the ground. And no one could deny that it stank dreadfully.

Everyone was in complete agreement as to the cause of the shattered door: burglars! The only thing that could not be accounted for in the entire household was a cord used to hold back the curtains in the master's studio. This seemed to be an improbable item of loot but the Watch was summoned and alerted. Assurances were received that the nightly patrols about the district would be stepped up.

Whatever the cause, the effect was unwelcome and involved lots of additional work for everyone. Gardeners uprooted the "diseased" plants and replaced them, the fountain was regilded, and carpenters were brought in to repair the shattered door and replace the ruined floorboards. Nothing, alas, could be done to rectify the color that had disappeared from the statues.

However improbable the theories about the courtyard were, the master and Dirk Tot were much more concerned about the change to his painting.

"This is most perplexing. Is it possible that someone else knows the secret?" asked Ambrosius Blenk.

"No, Master. The only people in the household who know are you, me, and the mistress. Are you certain that the painting hasn't deteriorated in some way?"

"Now you're sounding like the servants. It's just not possible. Look, the alterations to my vermiraptor are deliberate." The master offered Dirk Tot the magnifying glass he had been using to inspect the painting.

"So it *has* been altered?"

"Undoubtedly. But not by me." Ambrosius Blenk moistened the corner of a rag with turpentine and wiped away the creature's tail. "There's no original image underneath. It's just changed of its own accord."

Both men knew this was impossible.

"Could it have anything to do with the arrival of Womper, the Fegish boy?" asked the master.

"I can't believe that. He's talented but not *that* talented.

Besides, he's only been here a few days. He can't possibly have found out anything."

"All the same, I think we should keep an eye on him. He reminds me very much of myself when I was his age. He's very sharp."

"Very well, Master."

The riddle of the courtyard aside, work for the apprentices continued as normal. For Mel that meant more scrubbing and torment at the hands of Groot. The end of the working day came as a welcome relief.

After supper the friends reassembled inside the clock.

"Do you think we've got away with it?" asked Ludo anxiously.

"I don't know, Ludo. There're all kinds of ideas floating around the servants' hall but none of them are anywhere near the truth," said Wren.

"That's just as well," said Mel. "I think Dirk Tot suspects something, though. He's been giving me funny looks. And the master must have seen the new addition to his painting. My guess is it won't be as easy for any of us to go there again."

"I don't want to go there again," said Ludo. "I don't want any more to do with this." He unconsciously rubbed his leg where he had been wounded.

"But there's so much we need to find out. Why is Dirk Tot in league with the Fifth Mystery? Why are the colored men living inside the paintings? We need you, Ludo; you've been here longer than either of us," coaxed Wren.

"No one's going to force you to do anything you don't want to," said Mel. "But we still have to get a good look inside Dirk Tot's study. You can help us with that, surely."

"I don't know. What if we meet somebody while we're in the passages?"

"I'll go on ahead and make sure that the coast is clear. I know the way by now," said Mel. "You and Wren can follow on behind if it's safe."

"I don't know . . ."

"Come on, Ludo," said Wren.

Ludo looked at his friends. "I suppose so. We're all in this together, aren't we?"

Five minutes after Mel had gone Wren said, "If he'd met anyone in there he would have been back to warn us by now. Let's go."

"Wren, I . . ."

"Don't worry. I'll be right beside you all the way."

Once inside the passageway Ludo began to tremble. "You're not up to this are you?" said Wren.

"I want to, Wren. I really do . . ." Ludo looked sick.

"Come on, I'll let you out. You've been through a lot lately."

Normally cautious, Wren would have opened the door a crack to make sure they could emerge unobserved, but in her concern for Ludo's well-being she forgot this simple precaution.

"What're you two up to?" It was Groot and he was drunk. He grabbed them firmly by their arms as they emerged. "What's in there?" He nodded at the open passageway. "Where's Smell? You three are as thick as thieves."

"Look who's talking," said Wren under her breath.

"What?" Groot narrowed his eyes. "He's in there, isn't he?" Groot nodded towards the passageway.

"No. Mel was exhausted after all of that stupid scrubbing you've put him to. He went straight to bed," said Wren. "He's in the dormitory right now. Go and see for yourself if you don't believe me."

Groot looked at Ludo, who refused to meet his gaze. "That's just what I *will* do. You, get back to the kitchen, where you belong. I'll be telling Cook about this. Ludo, I'll deal with you later. Leave the door," he said as Wren tried to close it. He confiscated their candles and key and watched them until they were out of sight.

"Gone to bed? Like skeg he has," he said to himself. He stepped unsteadily inside the open passage.

Mel could not read the nameplate on the door but he recognized the shape the letters made as belonging to Dirk Tot's study. He could not hear anything inside so he opened it a crack. The room was deserted. He entered, leaving the door ajar. He had no idea where to start or even what he was looking for.

The desk was littered with papers, covered in dense writing. He tried the desk drawers. One contained quills, a penknife, a ruler, sealing wax, and sundry odds and ends. The others were locked. He sat back in Dirk Tot's chair, exasperated. *Where have Wren and Ludo got to?* Then his attention was caught by the top shelf of books on the wall opposite, spotlighted by the rays of the setting sun streaming in through the window. To Mel it seemed too neat, too orderly, compared with the other shelves, which were crowded and overflowing. A giant like Dirk Tot could reach it but it was too high for anyone else.

There was a chest under the window and Mel dragged it to the bookshelves. He manhandled the heavy chair towards it and struggled to lift it on top. He climbed his improvised ladder but it was still too short, so he removed some thick books from the lower shelves and piled them on the seat. He found that he could now reach the top shelf from his wobbly perch. *The books were dummies!* The spines from real books had been removed and glued on to a panel. One book looked slightly different to the rest, as if it had been used more than its neighbors. Mel pulled it towards him. The bottom was hinged and it tipped forwards. There was a low rumbling accompanied by a creaking noise and a section of the bookcase to his right swung open. *That's more like it*, he thought and climbed down.

He gazed into a long room much larger than the adjoining study. Down its length were two trestle tables crowded with scientific equipment. There were a great many different-sized glass vessels, some full of transparent, brightly colored liquids that glowed like gemstones. Gas flames burned under several of the flasks, causing their contents to bubble. They were connected by a complicated maze of glass tubing in loops and spirals, inside which tiny beads of moisture were condensing. Alongside them lay open books filled with long lists and calculations. In the far corner stood a large copper boiler with many pipes. Vapor escaped from a valve with a quiet hiss. Next to it was a small, unlit furnace.

Mel walked slowly down the room. He watched as a blue-black liquid slowly dripped from the mouth of a retort through a muslin filter into a beaker. Next to it were a pestle and mortar and several large jars full of pigment in the familiar household ultramarine. If it was as valuable as Dirk Tot had said, then the contents were worth a fortune. Nearby were other jars full of different colored pigments. More were arranged on shelves around the room. He also found a sheaf of the wooden flowers similar to the ones he had seen in the Fugitive Garden.

Still wondering where Wren and Ludo were, Mel left the laboratory and shut the door. He dismantled and replaced the components of his ladder, relit his candle, and left through the service door.

He walked swiftly back towards the others and soon saw the light from their candle coming from around a bend farther down the dark passageway.

"Wren, Ludo, you'll never guess what I've found," he called.

"And what's that, Smell?" said Groot as he rounded the corner. Mel stopped dead in his tracks.

"There's no one else around now. It's just you and me. And very soon there'll just be me. Fegish scum like you should never have been allowed in here in the first place. Your scrotty drawing isn't going to help you now and neither is your friend Blenko." Groot advanced towards Mel, grinning wickedly. He drew a knife from his belt.

There was no way Mel was going to get into a knife fight with someone as big and vicious as Groot. He turned and ran. He knew the passageway better than the head apprentice and the distance between them soon increased, but he could never hope to lose him completely. He ran on and up but habit unconsciously led him back to the door to the master's studio. It was right at the top of the mansion and the passage went no farther. His only escape was through the door. The room was unoccupied and Mel rushed to the window. There was a sheer drop to the courtyard far below. He was left with only one way of escape. As the service door flew open and Groot lurched into the studio, Mel made the secret gesture and found himself inside the painting.

19. the irascible house

MUNCHIE WAS WAITING for him. Most of her tail was missing and she was ferociously angry. Her tongue shot out and lassoed his legs and she began to reel him in like a fish on a line.

"Oh, no you don't," said Mel. He snatched out his bodkin and stabbed her tongue.

Munchie uttered a howl of pain and let go, her tongue recoiling as if spring-loaded. Mel scrambled to his feet and backed away, bumping into something solid. He looked behind him and saw that he was trapped against a rock face. The vermiraptor leaped at him. Mel raised his hands and cowered but Munchie's leap was checked in midair and she dropped, choking, to the ground a few paces from him. Against all odds she was still attached to the leash, which remained fastened to the tree. She screamed in frustration and lashed her bloody tongue once again at Mel. He had his bodkin ready and parried her attack and was able to retreat to one side, beyond her reach. A moving scene of pure malice erupted across her hide. Mel saw a stylized representation of himself being torn apart by the vermiraptor. It would have been fascinating had it not been so horrible.

He looked beyond her, but the wall of mist had vanished. He moved around in a wide arc, careful to stay outside the range of Munchie's tongue, and the mist came back into view. It was as he had thought—the way home was only visible from a head-on angle. With dismay, he realized that Munchie, at the limit of the leash and with her long tongue, commanded the way out of the painting. He imagined getting her to chase him round and round the tree until her leash shortened as it wound around the trunk, but then remembered the way the flow of time was altered inside the pictures. He could stay here a week and Groot would still be waiting for him when he came out. *What I need is another exit.*

Mel made his way down to the shore of the lake and stared across at the strange house. He could not escape the feeling that the house was staring back at him. He stepped on to the bridge, which unexpectedly felt as soft and pliant as a thick carpet, and crossed. The building not only looked human from the outside, the interior also mimicked the inside of a mouth. He found himself in a cavernous hallway with a vaulted, redbrick ceiling. Underfoot was a rich, red carpet, and the walls were loosely draped with scarlet tapestries. At the rear was a huge spiral staircase leading down. Suspended immediately above the stairwell was a great chandelier made from a multitude of sparkling rubies. *It must be so perfectly imagined that even the bits the master didn't paint are as detailed as the bits he did.* Mel approached the staircase and shouted down into the void.

"Hello, anyone down there?"

". . . down there . . . down there . . . down there," his voice echoed back.

He did not like the thought of descending wherever that led, so he withdrew. Then a vibration began under his feet that grew until the entire space trembled. The rubies on the chandelier tinkled loudly. An almighty wind filled the chamber, accompanied by a roaring belch and a nauseating smell. Mel was blown off his feet, catapulted out of the entrance, and hurled down the bridge. The soft surface left him shaken but otherwise unscathed. He picked himself up and, as he approached the entrance once more, the ivory white portcullis dropped shut with a heavy thud.

"Bog off!" came a deep, gruff voice. "Yer needn't think yer coming back in 'ere."

"What?" said Mel, startled.

"I said bog off. How would you like it? Something crawling around inside yer gob like a spider. 'Sorrible. Sling yer 'ook. Scarper. Vamoose."

"Who's there?"

"What're you, blind as well as stupid?"

"Who said that?"

"Ruddy deaf, too. *Struth!*"

"I—I—"

"*And* the little scut stutters. What 'ave I done to deserve this?"

With a shock, Mel realized that the *house* was talking to him. He looked up at the two great windows and saw the overhanging thatch rumple as if the facade was frowning. "I'm sorry if I've offended you but—"

"*Huh!*"

"—but I'm lost. I need to find my way back home."

"Right behind you, Sonny-Jim, past yer pet crocodile. Couldn't be plainer. Just do a sweet little one-eighty and Bob's yer uncle. And while yer at it, tell yer pet to put a sock in it. That racket's doing me 'ead in."

"I can't go back that way, there's . . . I can't go that way."

"Not my problem, squire."

"I need to find another way. Can you help me?" pleaded Mel. The house did not answer.

148   MIKE WILKS

"If you won't help me then I might as well stay here."

No response.

"In fact, I think I might pitch camp on this bridge."

"*Tongue!* It's not a bridge, it's me tongue."

"Whatever. I think I might make it my home."

"No, you skegging won't." There was a long silence. "All right, Pip-squeak, if I tells yer where to find another way back, will yer bog off and leave me in peace?"

"That's all I want. I'll be out of your face as quick as you like."

"See that hill over there to the right? My right, blockhead, not yours. Well, just beyond that there's another way out. Climb to the top and yer'll see it. But yer not going to like it."

"Oh? Why not?"

"Look, d'yer want a way out or not?"

Mel was about to press the building further but thought better of it. "Yes, I do. Thank you. I'll be on my way. Good-bye."

He returned to the shore and set off for the hill. After he had gone a little way the house called after him. "Out of yer face. I like that." It gave a little chuckle. "Out of yer face. That's a good 'un."

When Mel climbed the hill and reached the summit, he understood the house's warning.

There was a town at the foot of the hill. It looked to be completely in ruin and the shells of the buildings were burning fiercely. Thick black smoke rose and made an already overcast sky as dark as night. There were a great many partially naked people running around, pursued by misshapen demons that were scourging them with whips or prodding them with long, many-pointed spears. They were herding them towards an enormous, yawning chasm that had opened up in the earth, belching flames. A broad river with the remnants of a bridge bisected the town. Some of the hunted had swum out to seek refuge in the cool waters or on an island but, as Mel watched, dark creatures rose from the depths to snatch them and drag them below.

On the far side of the river, beyond the town and some open ground, just as the house had said, he saw the wall of mist and his way home. *How am I going to get all the way over there?* he thought in despair.

Several figures ran up the hill towards him. As they drew nearer Mel was surprised to see that they were imperfectly formed. They had only the most rudimentary faces, almost like a child's drawing, with just two dark holes for eyes and a gash for a mouth. Their limbs—such as they were—were in proportion but without any detail. They silently mouthed something at Mel.

"What? I can't hear you."

Mel jumped out of the way as an equally ill-formed demon rushed past in pursuit. *I hope the others show as little interest in me,* he thought as he started down the hill. Other people fled past him as he descended and he saw that their features were more defined the farther he advanced. Then it struck him that these figures were in the background of the scene, farthest from the wall of mist and the picture plane. He had entered this canvas from the rear.

By the time he had reached the outskirts of the town everyone whom he saw was perfectly formed and detailed. The place was hideous but of one thing he was sure: this place wasn't made by Ambrosius Blenk. The technique and the subject matter were unfamiliar. Mel had stumbled into someone else's depiction of the underworld.

Whether from anxiety or from the noxious fumes oozing out

of the ground all around him, Mel began to feel unwell. *I need to get out. But how to get across the river?*

There were demons everywhere and they took a huge variety of forms, among them snail-like fiends with warty skins and huge shells on their backs. Tubes led from these, out of which the demons squirted gouts of flame at the damned. Mel saw that some of their shells had become floppy and realized that they weren't actually part of the creatures. They were soft and more like bladders attached to their backs. Near the river's edge a couple of them knelt and refilled these with the gas that bubbled to the surface. When they were inflated once more, Mel noticed that they leaped much higher now because the gas in the bladders made them lighter.

I wonder . . . He saw two snail-fiends who had been overcome by those they were tormenting, their bladders now as slack and as lifeless as their bearers. He crept towards them and removed the sacs, which were attached to their backs by shaggy ropes, and dragged them to the edge of the river. Tying them securely to a large rock, he began to inflate them with the gas bubbles as he had seen the others do. The gas made him feel increasingly nauseated and he tried to hold his breath as the sacs filled. When they were full, Mel grasped the ropes firmly with one hand and cut himself free. He rose into the air. Now he could get across to the wall of mist.

"Yaaahhh!" *I'm flying. I'm actually flying.* It was a mixture of terror and pure exhilaration.

The wind took him in the direction of an island. Then, to his horror, a flock of airborne demons swooped down at him. They had lizardlike bodies and weasel heads, with snapping jaws full of sharp teeth. They were borne along on bat wings that were incongruously patterned with butterfly markings. Mel kicked wildly at them as they attacked him, but one soared over his head and tore a long gash in the side of one of his balloons. Foul-smelling gas gushed from the puncture, and he began to plummet downwards. He only just made it to the central island before it deflated completely and landed with a bump as another wave of the flying creatures dived on him, forcing him to release the other bladder.

As he searched the bleak vegetation for a hiding place he began to feel movement underfoot. The island wobbled and lurched as it began to rise, dripping glutinous river water as it did so.

"What the—?" Mel soon saw that what he had taken to be an island was the carapace of a grothling like the one he had seen in the bestiary. He lost his footing on the slimy surface and began to slide down towards the river, trailing the tattered remains of his balloon, which snagged on the encrustations and slowed his descent. The creature's long, antlered head broke the surface and snapped at the flying demons. *Those must be megaphines!* thought Mel as he desperately tried to stop his headlong slide. The grothling blew a mighty jet of dirty water from a blowhole on top of its head. Mel slid towards this and, when he reached it, jammed the limp balloon into the beast's air passage. For a moment nothing happened, and then the creature gave out a series of choking, gurgling noises and uttered an enormous sneeze that blew the obstruction—and Mel—high into the air. As Mel began to fall back to earth and certain death, the ripped balloon opened above him with a sharp snap and became a parachute that glided him slowly down on to the far bank of the river. His panic vanished as relief flooded his body. He felt an absurd urge to laugh out loud.

Mel abandoned his parachute and ran through the far side of the town towards the wall of mist that lay beyond the open ground that Mel soon found was a mire. A band of demons gave chase as a strange contraption rolled on to the bog after him. It moved on four broad paddlewheels studded with suckers. Inside each of these wheels sat a muscular demon peddling furiously. Mounted on top were several more fiends with spears and ropes and a larger version of the flame-squirter. The machine was bedecked all over with human scalps and skulls and a carved prow with a hideous figurehead projected from the front. It advanced over the boggy surface as easily as a boat over water.

The wall of mist was now only a short distance away, but it might as well have been a mile as the bog sucked at Mel's feet. With a roar, the demons' flame-squirter fired and Mel felt a searing heat at his back. Nearby bubbles of swamp gas ignited, which in turn lit others, and then still more, until the whole surface of the bog was alive with leaping columns of flame.

Eventually, Mel reached the wall of mist. He made the unlocking gesture and leaped at the wall just as a lasso fell over him. But the strength of the portal pulled him through.

Unfortunately, it also pulled the demons and their entire swamp-machine through with him together with the flock of megaphines.

The far side of the portal was in pitch darkness, broken by only the feeble glow of the fire drizzling from the end of the demons' flame-squirter. This then spewed a long tongue of fire that swept in a wide, roaring arc, brilliantly illuminating the surroundings. The demons spotted Mel and began cackling wildly. He could now see that they had arrived in a huge hall. The flame-squirter fired again. Several of the flying megaphines were caught in the jet and burst into flame. They flew about the space screaming and colliding with the remainder of their flock, which also caught fire. As the flickering light of the conflagration increased, Mel glimpsed the painting they had all emerged from, seen this time from the viewpoint the artist had intended. It was terrifying. If he had seen it from this perspective he would never have attempted to travel through it.

He felt a sharp tug on the lasso as he was yanked helplessly towards his tormentors. The flame spat again, this time aimed directly at him. The heat was intense but did not reach him. The rope caught fire and, as Mel struggled against it with his remaining strength, snapped. He threw off the smoldering remnant and took to his heels, in a kind of racing stagger for the safety of the darkness. It felt like he was running in slow motion. The demons were right behind him, shooting more gouts of flame and throwing their spears as they stampeded after him, jabbering with excitement. He ran as fast as his trembling limbs would allow, but after a short distance he was overcome by nausea. His legs turned to jelly and he collapsed forward on to his stomach. He raised his head and something in front of him caught his attention.

Tiny pinpricks of light like a swarm of fireflies hovered in the darkness. These sparks grew bigger and brighter and with a great, whistling swoosh shot over his head, followed by a rapid series of wet thuds and screams. He turned and saw that each of the demons had collapsed with a flaming bolt embedded in them. They shrieked as they were engulfed in fire. Mel looked back in the direction the bolts had come from and out of the darkness emerged twenty or more figures carrying discharged crossbows. They were illuminated by the flickering light of the burning fiends.

"We meet again, Mel."

20. the rainbow rebellion

THE GREEN MAN walked into the light. This time he was accompanied by a whole palette of colored comrades, who finished off the screaming demons with their swords.

Mel vomited violently.

"You're pleased to see us, then." It was the blue man Mel had met before.

"You'd better tell us how you got here," ordered the green man.

Mel raised himself to his knees and wiped his mouth on his sleeve. He pointed a shaky finger back at the painting.

Blue let out a long whistle. "I'll say this for him: he's got guts if he's been in there. That's a Flink."

"How long were you in there?" asked Green.

"I don't know. Awhile. Before that I was in the master's picture. That's how I got here. Wherever here is."

"That's why you're feeling sick," said Green. "You can't stay too long inside the pictures before it gets to you. Believe me, I know. It starts with the body but before long it gets to work on the mind. It's a good job you got out when you did." He helped Mel to his feet. "You'll be feeling better soon. Come with us now. You've got a lot of explaining to do."

Mel was not blindfolded this time; there was no need. Several of the men lit torches from the bodies of the blazing demons and the wreckage of their chariot and set off after their leader in single file. From time to time, the flickering torchlight lit the walls of crumbling galleries hung with old paintings, but it was too dark for Mel to see what they depicted. He saw abandoned treasures—statues, furniture, huge ceramics, and tapestries. Everything was rotting and festooned with cobwebs.

After about half an hour they stopped.

"This is our camp," said Green. "You'll be safe here. We'll rest for a while."

"I'll get the fire going," said Blue. "Killing demons always gives me an appetite. How about you, Mel? A nice greasy hunk of rat?"

Mel thought he might be sick again. "No, thanks."

Several of the men joined in Blue's laughter.

The large fire cheered Mel but failed to illuminate the vast space. The blaze was fed with pieces of broken furniture, and a number of skinned rats and a haunch of some unidentifiable meat were put to roast on a spit. Mel gazed around at his saviors, the firelight illuminating green, blue, yellow, red, mauve, and orange faces and an extraordinary collection of clothes. Their garments had been fashioned from carpets, tapestries, and curtains held together with crude stitching and lengths of rope. They had armor improvised from silver and gilt plates or salvers, and bowls for helmets with candles stuck to them. Some wore oversize jewelery recycled from crystal chandeliers and interspersed with the skulls of small rodents. All eyed Mel with suspicion.

"Now," said Green, "I want to know everything about how you came to be here—and I mean *everything*." He sat stroking an odd, piebald creature of a type Mel had never seen before. "I'll know if you're lying to me."

As if to reinforce the point, Blue began to sharpen his knife.

Should I tell him everything? thought Mel. He met Blue's icy stare. *Yes.*

So Mel recounted his discovery of the secret symbol and his journey through the master's picture and then through Flink's underworld. He also told them what Wren had said about the colored men.

After he finished, Green studied the multi-hued faces of his comrades before looking back at him. "That's quite a tale. How many of your friends know about us?"

The sound of Blue's knife being sharpened seemed very loud in the silence. "Just two. I'm sorry."

Mel's answer did not anger the man as much as he had expected. "You've found out a lot and guessed much of the rest. You're right, all of us here once worked in the mines on Kig. One by one, we managed to escape before the worst symptoms of the Colored Death became evident, but not before our skin became stained. We'll be like this for good. Now we hide here, beneath the Great Houses."

"*What?* You mean . . . ?" Mel gazed up.

"Yes, that's exactly where we are. Most people imagine that Vlam is built on three hills but those hills are only the ancient and abandoned cores of the palaces. They've just gone on building and building on top of them over more than a thousand years. The foundations are so extensive that down here they actually all join up. Right now we're beneath the House of Thrones. A few hundred feet above our heads King Spen is probably at his table. Tonight we'll also be dining in the palace."

Everyone laughed.

"It suits us just fine, down here. There's always something to eat—if you're hungry enough."

"Some rat?" said Blue, offering Mel his tiny drumstick.

Mel put his hand to his mouth.

More laughter.

"Nobody alive remembers these halls and no one ever comes down this deep. We scavenge the forgotten galleries for most of what we need: clothing, armor, and even weapons. Very fine weapons they are too, originally crafted as collectors' pieces and made to hang on walls. But they work just fine." Green proudly stroked his jeweled sword.

Mel now saw that their crossbows were ornate and made from rare materials.

"We can travel under the city unseen and if we need to go anywhere in a hurry then there's the Mirrorscape."

"The Mirrorscape? What's that?"

"It's the world within the paintings."

"So you *can* get inside the pictures. All of them. Not just the master's. I *knew* it. They're all joined up, aren't they?" Mel's mind went into overdrive. If every painting was its own world then they could all join up to make another universe. A universe where anything artists had ever imagined became real.

"Only some," said the green man. "Those bearing the secret symbol. The mirrormark it's called." He guessed Mel's next question. "Not every artist can make the mirrormark, only the greatest. Ambrosius Blenk and Lucas Flink before him, and a few others. Lesser artists can mark the canvas but it won't open a door into the Mirrorscape, and not every painting bears the mirrormark. The Mirrorscape recognizes its own."

Mel asked, "How big is the Mirrorscape?"

"I don't know; no one does. And it's getting bigger all the time. Whenever your master makes one of his paintings it grows."

"And other masters will add their own bits to it in the future," observed Mel. His eyes grew wide with wonder at the notion. "But what happens if a painting is destroyed?" he asked, thinking of the ill-conceived world he, Ludo, and Wren created. "Does that piece of the Mirrorscape disappear?"

Green thought for a while. "I don't know. My guess would be that it remains, but that the portal into it is closed. The only way you could get there again is from another painting."

"That makes sense. Once something's imagined, it can't be un-imagined. And is it all like . . . like inside the Flink?"

"Some of it is. Some of it's beautiful and some of it's dangerous—often it's both—and everything in between. It depends on the artists and what they painted. We have a rough map of some of the less hostile regions and we try to stick to those. But it's not always possible. And there's something else about the Mirrorscape. The mirrormark, the seal that keeps people out, also keeps the inhabitants locked in. There's plenty in there that we most certainly don't want out here."

"Like the demons."

"Like the demons—and worse."

"*Worse?*"

"You don't want to know. They're not like us, the creatures of the Mirrorscape; figments they're called. If some of those creatures ever got free . . ." He let the thought hang there.

You don't have to tell me, thought Mel. "Time's different, too. It's frozen—compared to here."

"The Mirrorscape's a very big place. In some parts time stands still and in others it's different, more different than you can imagine."

"And the insides of things, bits that you can't see in paintings, that the artist never painted. They're real as well."

"You've noticed that, have you? I believe that some artists imagine things so clearly, so perfectly, that every tiny detail of their world is realized in the Mirrorscape. One more thing: the seal's not permanent, it's fugitive."

"Fugitive? Like colors that fade in daylight?"

"Yes. After a few hundred years it breaks down. In the very oldest and deepest parts of the Great Houses there are paintings that are so old the seal will be weak. It's a place you don't want to go."

"How do you know all this?" asked Mel.

Green almost smiled. "I just do." Then, after a short silence, "As for us, we're just a small band at present; more are joining the Rainbow Rebellion all the time. There are a few people in Nem—very rich and powerful people—who sympathize with our cause."

"Like my master?"

Green did not answer, but by the way he looked at him, Mel knew he had guessed right.

Green continued. "And others. Despite what you may think, there are those in the Mysteries—yes, even in the Fifth Mystery— who are sympathetic to our cause: to put an end to their worst excesses. Lord Floris, the former governor of the Colored Isles, for one. He helped us—while he could."

"How?"

"Lord Floris is an art lover. He had a very fine Blenk in his quarters on Kig."

"That's how you escaped," said Mel.

Green nodded. "And now, Mel, whether you like it or not, you're also one of us. In fact, it would suit us very well to have someone else who can travel about up top without attracting attention. Our topside ally is not exactly inconspicuous. I want you to keep your eyes and ears open in the mansion and to let me know if anything unusual happens."

Who's this "someone else"? Something told Mel not to ask. Instead, he said, "I've been in Vlam for less than a week. I don't know anything."

"You know a great deal, Mel. You're a very observant and resourceful boy. There're apprentices who've been in Ambrosius Blenk's studio for many years and haven't worked out the hundredth part of what you have in a few days. So?"

Green had saved his life—twice now. Mel felt he could trust him. "I'll help you if I can. I owe you that."

"Good lad."

"I'm feeling much better now and I really ought to get back to the mansion. Am I free to go?"

"Of course you are. We can escort you back by a different route. My mate here will show you the way."

Mel stood up and Blue laid his hand on his shoulder. He winked at Mel and cocked his head, indicating that he should follow.

Mel looked at Green. "How can I get in touch with you?"

"Can you get inside the big clock that overlooks the square?"

"Yes."

"Good. If you need to talk to one of us tie a shred from your sash around the dragon."

"The one that looks like the High-Bailiff?"

"He's quick, this one," said Blue.

"Do that and we'll come and find you. We're closer than you think. Now, off you go."

"Erm . . . what do I call you? I don't know your names."

"Just call us by our colors. That'll do fine," said Green. "Now, skedaddle."

Blue grabbed a torch and led Mel away from the fire until they came to a wall hung with paintings. "You know how this works. Grab hold of my arm." He performed the gesture that unlocked the mirrormark.

Mel felt the familiar tingling and found himself side by side with his guide in the midst of a city made entirely of ice. From there they traveled through a bleak landscape littered with the bones of enormous, long-dead animals and, after that, through some kind of botanical hothouse where all the plants had human faces. Then they stood before another wall of mist.

"This is where we say good-bye for now, Mel. We'll meet again, soon enough."

21. missing persons

"HOW MANY OF them were there?" asked Wren.

"I counted twenty-six, including Green and Blue. Green said there were a few others. And they've got a spy up here in Vlam."

"Oh, if they've got twenty-six *and* a spy, then that makes *all* the difference," said Ludo.

"So who is this spy?" asked Wren. "The master?"

"No," said Mel. "I think the master's on their side but he's not the spy. Green said the spy's conspicuous."

"How about Dirk Tot," said Ludo. "You can't get more conspicuous than him."

"It *can't* be him," said Mel. "I know what I saw on the road to Vlam. It's got to be someone who hates the Mysteries."

"That narrows the field a bit," said Wren. "*Everyone* hates the Mysteries."

"Everyone hates the Mysteries for good reason. You've seen at firsthand what they're capable of, Mel—and that was just because of a single Pleasure." Ludo took another mouthful of porridge. "Imagine what they would do if they caught someone who was helping the rebels. Better still, don't. Did they *really* eat cat?"

"Keep your voice down." Mel gazed around the empty refectory. "I promised I would. It wasn't cat, it was *rat*." He looked at the remains of his breakfast and pushed it aside. "What about you?

What do you suppose Groot's going to do? And what are you going to do about losing the key to the service passages?"

"Nobody knew I had it," said Wren. "I'll have to try and get another. And Groot was probably too drunk to remember he caught us." Wren cleared away the last of the breakfast plates.

"Don't count on it," said Ludo. "When it comes to being spiteful, he's got a memory like an elephant. Aren't you going to eat that?"

Mel pushed his bowl across the table to Ludo.

"We'll cross that bridge when we come to it," said Wren. "Now, eat up and get a move on, you two. You're already late. All the other 'prentices went up to the studio ages ago."

"Yeah, I can hardly wait," said Mel.

Later in the day, Ludo went into the storeroom for some varnish. As he was searching the shelves for what he needed, he heard the door close quietly and Groot's voice say, "Here, you dropped this, Ludo."

"I didn't drop anything." He turned and saw the head apprentice holding a small paper parcel. He knew at once what it contained.

"You know what happens to sniveling little apprentices who steal pigment from the master, don't you? It'll be a shame to see you go. I've so enjoyed tormenting you."

"Everyone knows who's been doing the stealing around here, Groot. I'm surprised you've not been rumbled before now."

"Rumbled? Me? Oh, I'm much too careful for that, Ludo. I learned from the best. You're forgetting who my family is."

"A bunch of thieves?" said Ludo bravely.

"Why, you little scut . . . You know, I think we'll go to old Half-Face now. We'll see who he believes."

"He's not the fool you take him for."

"You think so? Can you be absolutely certain that you won't be packing your bags and heading home before the day's out? And, you know what; I think I'll ask my uncle Adolfus to open an investigation into the Cleefs. See if they can account for every single Pleasure they consume. And they do consume an awful lot of Pleasures; don't they? Shall I do that?"

"Leave my family out of this."

"It's you who brought up families, Ludo, not me. What do you imagine a thorough audit might turn up?"

Ludo felt sick. His family, like many others, often bought additional Pleasures on the black market. "You wouldn't."

"Oh yes, I would. Just think how much your family would enjoy a stay in the dungeon at the House of Mysteries. I think I'll go and mention it to my uncle this evening." Groot paused for effect. "Unless, that is, you were to tell me how he did it."

"What?"

"Come on, Ludo. You know what I'm talking about. How did Smell manage to vanish like that?"

That evening the office of the High-Bailiff of the Fifth Mystery was a happy place.

"Well done, Groot my boy, well done! You are to be congratulated. This is a triumph!" The High-Bailiff held up Mel's sketch of the mirrormark. "Look, he's even signed it for us. How did you manage it?"

"It was nothing, Uncle. After all, I learned from the best."

Adolfus Spute treated his nephew to one of his repulsive smiles. Mumchance was happy, too. With his master in such a good mood there was little chance of his receiving a kicking.

"Now, are you sure you've got this right? There's another world inside Blenk's paintings? And he uses this . . . this thingamajig to go there? And we can use it, too? And those infernal rebels you say, under the House of Thrones?"

"Yes, Uncle."

"You know, dear boy, this is the opportunity I've been waiting a long, long time for. Blenk has always been a thorn in the side of the Mysteries. With his wealth and influential friends, he's always been able to buy Half-Face out of trouble before now. I think we'll arrange a little surprise for him inside this Mirrorscape, something to lure him in and keep him there. As soon as Blenk is removed from the scene, that repulsive giant will be mine for the taking. Once he's in my hands I'll make him pay for all the humiliation he's heaped on me over the years." Adolfus Spute's eyes glowed. "This is everything I could have wished for. Well, almost everything. You searched the Fegish runt's possessions thoroughly, I take it?"

"Yes, Uncle. Including his hidey-hole."

"And there was nothing else there? Nothing of mine?"

"Only his scribble."

Adolfus Spute's brow darkened for a moment. "You won't go unrewarded. We'll soon see if Half-Face has indeed been fabricating counterfeit pigments, as I've long suspected. There's always been too much blue in that household for my liking. Even Blenk would have been stretched to afford that much. Then the monster and his silver hand will be packed away to end his days on Kig, and I will sit at the head of the Council table. Lord Spute! Everyone will be so grateful. There are great times ahead for you and me, dear boy, great times."

"And Smell, Uncle?"

"After I retrieve my property, you can have him. You can do whatever you please with him. My gift. The first of many once I'm Lord-High-Master. The time is ripe for us to pay a little visit to Ambrosius high-and-mighty Blenk's mansion, don't you think? This is wonderful, simply *wonderful!*"

The following day, Mel returned to scrubbing a floor that had acquired a great many more stains overnight. Groot caught his eye and smiled a triumphant smile.

Mel edged towards Ludo. "He's up to something."

"Not now. Can't you see I'm busy?"

What's got into him? wondered Mel.

Ludo said nothing else to Mel all day.

Normally, the master would have visited the studio in the morning to inspect and comment on the work in progress, but he failed to show up. By the afternoon, the household rumor mill was again in full swing.

"The master's unwell."

"*Rubbish!* He's never had a day's illness in his life."

"A friend of a friend saw him going into the House of Thrones. They said one of his pictures is falling to pieces."

"*Piffle!* There are no paintings better made than the master's."

"He's locked in his studio, working on a secret commission."

"*Nonsense!* In that case, why are the mistress and Dirk Tot also looking for him?"

He still had not shown up by bedtime.

Something's wrong, thought Mel. *Very wrong.*

Late that night, there came a fearful noise of pounding. "Open up! Open up in the name of the Fifth Mystery!"

The commotion filled the courtyard and penetrated the dormitory, waking Mel. He got up and opened the window near his bed. The other apprentices crowded the windows that ran the length of the dormitory. He saw that Groot, Bunt, and Jurgis were not among them. Ludo remained in his bed.

"Ludo, wake up! There's something going on down there."

Ludo appeared to sleep on.

Mel watched from his window as two score of men-at-arms carrying lanterns burst into the courtyard and surged towards the main door. Then, Adolfus Spute, with Mumchance in tow, strode out of the tunnel.

Minch, still in his nightshirt, emerged from the mansion and confronted the High-Bailiff. He attempted to block his way.

Mel watched as Mumchance crept behind Minch and got down on all fours.

"How *dare* you! You bucket of lard," screamed Adolfus Spute. "No one stands in the way of the Fifth Mystery. Especially not a flabby, offal-brained, privy-licker." He pushed Minch, who fell over the crouching dwarf. Adolfus Spute strode into the mansion laughing.

"Mel. *Mel.*"

Mel looked round for the whispered voice.

"Over here."

Wren's hand was beckoning him from the crack of the door to the service passage. Mel looked at the other apprentices but they were too engrossed in the scene below to pay any attention. He crossed to the passage and briskly stepped inside, closing the door after him.

"What's going on?"

"I don't know. They're ransacking the place," said Wren.

"They've got a nerve. Is the master back yet? He'll give them what for."

"No. No one's seen him since yesterday. Dirk Tot will throw them out."

"You really think so?" Mel chewed his fingernail. "What's up with Ludo? He won't talk to me."

"Perhaps he's unwell."

"Perhaps."

"I think you'd better stay out of sight, Mel, till the High-Bailiff's gone."

"You don't need to tell me. I'll hide in the clock."

"The sooner, the better. Come on, follow me." When they reached the door opposite the clock, Wren opened it a crack and quickly closed it again.

"What?" said Mel.

"They've got Dirk Tot. He's in chains. They're taking him away."

"*What!*" Mel stole a look. "Trying to, more like." Six burly men-at-arms had to restrain the giant as they bundled him down the stairs. Several more followed, carting away laboratory equipment and boxes full of illicit pigment. "Looks like they knew exactly where to go."

"Still think he's one of them?" asked Wren.

"Yeah."

"You don't sound so certain."

That night, Mel slept in the clock, waking on the hour, every hour.

In the morning the men of the Fifth Mystery had gone. Mel ventured from the clock, dressed, and made his way up to the studio. Without anyone to tell them what to do, the apprentices stood around idle. All of them that is, except for Mel, who was ordered to continue scrubbing, and Ludo, who said he was ill. He had taken to his bed and refused to talk to anyone.

Soon the skylarking began as balls of paper were flung about the studio. This quickly escalated into dollops of paint. When this paint fight was in full sway, and Mel's hopes of ever getting the floor clean were rapidly disappearing into infinity, Minch entered the studio, receiving a large glob of cadmium yellow full in the face. He wiped this from his eyes and pointed a fat finger at Mel. "You. To the mistress. *Now!*" he ordered.

Mel followed the angry, paint-stained servant up to the top of the mansion. *It's the monkey. I know it's the monkey. I'm going to be punished for what happened to Albinus.*

Minch knocked on the door to the master's private studio.

"Yes?"

Minch opened the door and ushered Mel in before departing. The mistress was sitting in a large upholstered chair with Albinus in her lap and her lady-in-waiting standing at her side. She was dressed in much more sober clothes than the last time he had seen her and she looked less frivolous and more noble, almost a different woman. Mel noticed that the master's canvas had its face turned to the wall.

"Mistress, if it's about Albinus, I'm really sorry," gushed Mel.

"What? No, it's not about that. In fact, now that I've got used to him, I really rather like it. My husband made me a gift of some more. They've become quite the rage among my friends." Turning to her companion, she said, "Thank you, Gerta. That will be all. You may leave us now."

When they were alone, the mistress sat studying the apprentice before she spoke. "My husband and Dirk Tot have been watching you for some time, Womper. They tell me that there's more to you than meets the eye. Is that true?"

Mel did not know what to answer.

"They even think that you might know a secret. A secret that you shouldn't know."

"I'm sure I don't know what you're talking about, Mistress."

"Closemouthed, I like that. Your circumspection does you credit."

Mel waited.

"My husband has vanished and I think that both you and I know where he might be."

No reaction.

"Let's stop beating around the bush, shall we? Do you or don't you know about the Mirrorscape?"

The mention of the word caught Mel off guard.

"Ah, that's better. I can see from your face that you do. Who else in this household knows?"

There was no point in pretending anymore. Mel told her.

"Well, my husband has gone into the Mirrorscape and has not returned. I believe he is being held there against his will. It can be no coincidence that as soon as he's out of Vlam Spute and his men ransack our mansion and arrest our steward. They would never have dared act that way if he was still here. My husband is one of the few people who is powerful enough to stand up to them. Ambrosius has been in the Mirrorscape for some time now. If he's remained within the part he created, then he won't get sick. But my fear is that he could be enticed outside and become as vulnerable as anyone else. I must remain here and attempt to hold this household together and try to fend off that odious High-Bailiff, should he return. But you know about the Mirrorscape and you know how to follow your master. I want you to go in there and to bring him back."

"Yes, Mistress. If that's what's necessary, then I'll try and find him. But I'll need some help. Can I take Ludo and Wren?"

"You may. But before you and your friends get into this, there's something you should know. Something that may change your mind." The mistress rose from her chair with a soft rustle of silk and went to the easel. She swung it around on its castors.

Albinus uttered a terrified shriek and ran up the curtains.

"What the—?" Mel nearly choked. "It's just not possible!"

The canvas had changed, *utterly*.

22. the temporal labyrinth

MEL WAS OUT of breath by the time he finally found Wren in the kitchen. On his way he had gone to the clock and tied his signal around the neck of the dragon for the Rainbow Rebels. He told Wren about his interview with the mistress.

"So? Will you come?"

"Of course."

"I was hoping you'd say that. Without the master there'll be no household, and without a household there'll be no job. I know how much you need it."

"There's a more important reason than that."

"There is? What?"

"Friendship, you dummy." Wren shook her head. "Let's go and get Ludo."

"You think he'll come?"

As they approached Ludo's bed, he saw them coming. He turned away and pulled his blanket over his head. "Go away. I'm not well."

"What's wrong, Ludo?" asked Wren as she sat on the edge of his bed. "This isn't like you. Shall we ask to send for a doctor?"

"Don't need a doctor. Just go away."

"While you've been in bed, the whole place has gone to pot," said Mel. "Dirk Tot's been arrested. They found his secret laboratory and masses of pigment that he's been making. All the stuff I told you about."

"You know, I think it's why he didn't want you to see his secret garden," said Wren. "He was probably testing his own colors there."

"Yeah, and come to think of it, he must have been using it to top up the pigment Groot was stealing." Mel looked down at Ludo. "And the master's vanished as well. He's gone inside the Mirrorscape and he hasn't come out."

Ludo groaned and pulled the blanket farther over his head.

"The mistress has asked Mel to find him and bring him back. I'm going, too. If you were feeling better then we'd ask you to come with us," said Wren.

"Leave me alone. Can't you see I'm not well? I don't want anything to do with the Mirrorscape anymore. Or with you."

"But, Ludo . . . ," pleaded Mel.

Wren put her hand on Mel's arm and shook her head. "We're sorry to see you like this, Ludo, but we understand. We'll see you when we get back."

"*If* we get back." Mel bit his lip. *Stupid! Why did I say that?*

Wren shot him a withering look. "Good-bye, Ludo."

"Yeah, hope you're feeling better soon." Mel rose and followed Wren towards the door. "You go and get any stuff you might need and I'll meet you in the master's studio."

After she had left, Mel opened his cupboard and removed the loose board to his cache. He thrust his arm into the space, searching for his sketch of the mirrormark, but it was not there. *Has someone taken it?* He thought about this for a moment. *No one knew it was there.* The chimes of the great clock echoed through the dormitory. He mentally shrugged. *If it's gone, it's gone. I can't worry about that now.* He worked his arm deeper inside the narrow space and his hand closed on the tiny box. He drew it out and looked at it. *Maybe I'm not coming back. I should take this with me.* He tucked it inside his doublet next to his bodkin and hurried off to meet Wren.

As soon as Mel had left, the door to the service passage opened with a creak and Groot stepped into the silent dormitory. He carried two bottles of the finest Vlamian wine. Having discovered the passages, it had not taken him long to find his way into the master's wine cellar and he had since become a regular visitor. He had returned to the dormitory to hide his loot and had overheard the conversation. "What a touching little scene, Ludo. You know, it almost brought a tear to my eye."

"Go away, Groot. They were my best friends and now I can't even look them in the eye. Leave me alone."

"Oh, I will. Very soon now. I've an appointment with my new friends here." He clinked the bottles together. "But there's one more thing you're going to do for me." He sat on the edge of Ludo's bed, leaned down, and whispered into his ear.

Mel was not the first to arrive in the master's studio.

"Green! How did you get here so quickly?"

"The Mirrorscape might be dangerous but it's quick. What's up?"

"Dirk Tot's just been arrested. And no one's seen the master since the day before yesterday. The mistress thinks he's being held against his will inside the Mirrorscape."

"That's really serious news. I'd best get back at once and warn my men. Bad luck always comes in threes."

"I'm going to look for him and bring him back."

"What, in *there*?" Green looked at the master's canvas. "All on your own?"

"Not quite on his own." Wren entered the room.

"The Mirrorscape's no place for either of you," said Green. "But Mel will need all the help he can get."

"I can look after myself," said Wren. "I've scrounged us some food. I didn't know how long we'll be gone." She held up a small sack bulging with provisions.

"Wren, this is Green."

"Nice to meet you, Wren. But it's hello and good-bye, I'm afraid. I must hurry. We'll meet again." He left by the door.

"Mel!" Wren gazed aghast at the canvas. "What's happened?"

Before, where the picture had been full of sunlight and bright, luminous colors, it now looked totally different. The blue sky had vanished, to be replaced by a leaden, overcast sky. Swirling shapes within them suggested screaming heads. The delicate trees had been either felled or blackened where they had been burned. The corpses of many of the fabulous creatures lay about, dismembered, and more rotting bodies floated in the now filthy lake. Vultures with blood-matted feathers picked at the bloated carcasses. The island in the lake was empty. There was no sign of the half-human house that had formerly stood there, just an enormous crater. It was an awful transformation. The scene looked like the last place they would ever want to go, but it was their doorway into the Mirrorscape. They must follow the master.

"How could that have happened?" asked Wren. "Who'd do such a thing?"

"I don't know. Perhaps the person who stole my sketch of the mirrormark."

"It's gone?" Wren looked alarmed. "But how are we going to follow the master?"

"Don't worry, I've got it memorized. Now, I wonder if there's anything here that might help us find him?" Mel began searching the studio. He found a large leather satchel and placed some pencils into it. He added a small telescope with curious dials and knobs along its length, which he thought might come in useful. He picked up a leather-bound book.

"What's that?"

"It's the master's sketchbook," said Mel, opening it.

"Really? Let me see."

"It's beautiful. I've never seen drawings as fine as these." Mel traced the exquisite lines with his finger, imagining he was drawing them himself.

"They're drawings from his paintings—preparatory sketches."

"Are you sure? That means they're drawings of the Mirrorscape. We should take this, too."

"Well, there's no putting it off any longer," said Wren. "We should get going."

"I'm coming, too," said a voice from the doorway.

"Ludo!" they both exclaimed.

"What made you change your mind?" asked Mel.

"Oh, it was the thought of you two recounting your adventures after you get back and forever saying 'You should have been there, Ludo.' Besides, with you two gone, there's nothing left for me here. I'm sorry if I offended you." Ludo sounded cheerful enough, but he was avoiding eye contact.

"Are you *sure* you're feeling better?" asked Wren.

"Look, are we going or not?"

"What's got into you?" said Mel. "First we couldn't drag you into the Mirrorscape, then you can't wait to go."

"We're all going now. That's all that matters," said Wren.

"All right, let's do it. You okay, Wren?"

"Not really. I'm scared."

"Me too," said Mel.

"When you two are *quite* ready," complained Ludo.

The three friends looked at the painting for a moment and linked arms. Mel took a deep breath and traced the mirrormark in the air. The surface of the painting shimmered and they vanished.

"Come on, it's gaining on us," shouted Adolfus Spute. "Surprising turn of speed for a building, don't you think?"

Mumchance blew an extended trill on his whistle.

"I'll thank you not to rub it in, you rancid manikin. My plan was perfect—*perfect*. We had Blenk nicely trapped inside that peculiar house of his while we arrested Half-Face. The last thing anyone could have expected was for that jumped-up bungalow to get up off his foundations and come after us like that."

Another blast.

"Now what?"

And another.

"You mean that crag over yonder? For once in your miserable little life that's not a bad idea. I doubt if that hooligan of a hovel can climb. Or maybe there'll be some cozy cave where we can hole up until it gets tired of chasing us through the Mirrorscape. Come on, Mumchance; whistle up the rest of the men. Let's go mountaineering."

The first thing the friends found inside the Mirrorscape was Munchie's leash attached to the stump of a tree. It was bloody and had been cut or gnawed through. There was no trace of the vermiraptor—not that Mel was anxious to meet her again. He scanned the ground and saw a trail of footprints. *She got away.*

"This is *amazing*," said Ludo, gazing around. He knelt and touched the grass. "Feel this. It's all so real, not at all like the world we made."

"Amazing? It's *appalling*," said Wren. "Being real's what makes it even more horrible. Even down to the cries of those vultures. How can the master paint sound?"

"This isn't the master's work," said Mel, "not anymore. It started out as his. It was just as real but smelled a whole lot better."

"Death stinks wherever it is," observed Ludo.

"When we first saw the painting it was so beautiful," said Wren. "How can it have changed so much?"

"I don't know. But I've a feeling that we're going to find out soon enough. Come on, you two," said Mel. "The master's not going to find himself."

The friends hurried away, circling the lake where the house had been. On the far side they came upon a huge, almost human footprint in the mud. It had left a deep impression.

Mel jumped down inside and examined it. "I bet the house left this. It must be able to walk."

"There's another one over there," said Wren. "And there're more leading off into the distance."

Mel climbed out of the footprint. "Look, we saw the master going into the house when we first saw the painting. Remember? Maybe he's in there again."

"And maybe he's not," said Wren. "Maybe we chase it and just find the house."

"At least that'll get us somewhere. When I was here before, the house helped me. Maybe it will again. Let's go."

"You two go on, I need to pee. I'll catch you up," said Ludo.

"I'm not sure you should be peeing on the master's painting," said Mel.

"Sorry, I've got to." Ludo emphasized the point by crossing his legs. "Besides, it's already been ruined." Ludo went behind the remains of a tree. When he was sure that his friends were walking away, he crouched down and took a small paper parcel from his doublet. He opened a corner and, on the blackened grass, drizzled a trail of orpiment. When he had finished, the yellow pigment traced a vivid arrow pointing in the direction they were headed. He refolded the parcel and tucked it away before running to catch up with his friends.

When they reached the fourth footprint from the lake, they found out who had been responsible for the desecration.

"Yuck, that's gross. What was it?" Wren shuddered.

"Not what, *who*," said Mel. "Judging by the red robes, I'd say it was a Mystery man. It looks like the house has deliberately squashed him."

"Best make sure we don't annoy it if we catch up with it," said Ludo.

"How do you suppose the Fifth Mystery managed to get into the Mirrorscape?" asked Wren. "Could they have taken your drawing when they raided the mansion?"

Mel shook his head. "I shouldn't think so. Even if they did they wouldn't know what it was."

Ludo looked away.

As they trekked towards the background of the master's picture the grass underfoot became progressively smoother until it was like walking on an undulating billiard table. The vegetation also became cruder and more stylized, and the trees like spheres perched on poles. They reached the top of a hill and stopped to survey the way ahead.

"It's different," said Mel.

"Of course it's different," said Ludo, "unless we've been walking around in circles."

"No, I mean it's been created by another artist."

"It's a very subtle difference," said Wren. "What makes you so sure?"

"Texture. Brushwork. Technique. Whatever you like to call it, it's different."

"You've missed the most important thing," said Ludo.

"What's that?"

"Subject matter. The master's never painted anything like that."

Before them towered an enormous green pyramid. It was so high that wispy clouds clung to the side here and there and the top seemed to be dusted with snow. All around it the Mirrorscape was as flat and plush as a well-tended lawn and dotted with weirdly shaped trees or large bushes. Mel fished out the telescope and studied the pyramid before he handed it to Wren. "What do you make of that?"

"Those steps are like terraces. They go all the way up," observed Wren. "Here, what can you make out, Ludo?"

"All that vegetation around it is formed from clipped bushes and trees. Topiary. They've been shaped like monsters or huge, deformed heads."

The telescope was returned to Mel and he raised it to his eye again and idly twiddled one of the knobs. The image in the device grew dramatically. "That's a good trick. This thing's got a knob that makes things appear closer. Hey, that's no ordinary pyramid."

"So what's an *ordinary* pyramid?" said Ludo.

"You know what I mean. This one's a skegging great maze! A three-dimensional maze. The sides are made from some kind of clipped, evergreen plant. And the giant footprints lead right up to it."

They set off across the Mirrorscape but stopped after only a short way.

"Where's Ludo got to now?" asked Mel.

"Perhaps it was something he ate?" said Wren. "Ludo!"

"I'm coming. I just had to look at those topiary heads again."

"Gardening a new hobby of yours, is it?" she asked.

"Just interested."

They arrived at the great arch that formed the entrance to the pyramid-maze. It was guarded by two giant topiary monsters that towered above them.

"It looks like the house stopped here," observed Mel.

"Do you think it went inside?" asked Wren.

"There's no sign," said Ludo. "Something as big as a house couldn't get under that arch. And it couldn't have leapt over. Maybe it went around the outside."

"You two wait here. I'll go and see if I can find any tracks." Mel placed his satchel on the ground and followed the wall of the maze.

"See any, Mel?" called Ludo.

"That's odd!" said Mel.

They turned around at the sound of his voice and saw him coming towards them from the other direction.

"*Mel*?" Wren quickly turned and saw him walking away from them. He slowly became indistinct until he vanished. She turned back and looked at him again. "Did you see *that*?"

"I saw it but I still don't believe it," said Ludo. "How'd you do that, Mel?"

"I didn't do anything. I was going that way and then you two appeared in front of me and I found myself back here." He scratched his head.

"I don't like this place," said Ludo.

"Let me have a go in the other direction." Wren walked off and slowly disappeared, reappearing from the other side. "It's just like you said, Mel."

Ludo had to try it before they became convinced. "Well, if we're not able to go around, then neither was the house. It must have gone inside."

They stepped through the arch into the labyrinth and looked to the right and the left. Both directions looked identical and the dead-straight path seemed to stretch away to infinity. It must have been miles long either way. They turned left and began walking. At regular intervals they passed tall lampposts, but otherwise there was nothing to indicate how far they had gone.

"Listen. Did you hear that?" asked Wren.

"Hear what?" said Mel.

"Are you sure you didn't? Like a faint, low boom."

"You're cracking up," said Ludo.

After they had walked for about a mile he stopped. "Look, this is hopeless. It just goes on for ever. All we seem to be doing is walking around the base of the pyramid. We can't even see the end."

Mel got the telescope out and looked down the path. "Hang on, there's something up ahead. Let's take a look."

It turned out to be a broad ladder. They climbed it and found themselves on another path identical to the first.

"See if you can find another ladder," said Wren. "At least that would take us farther through the maze."

"Let's see." Mel raised the telescope to his eye. "*What the—?*"

"What is it, Mel? Is it another ladder?" asked Wren.

"Yes. But not only that. It's *us*! I See for yourselves."

"Us? What do you mean *us*?" Wren took the telescope and saw the three of them in the distance. "You're right. Here, Ludo, you take a look."

"This gives me the creeps," said Ludo, handing back the telescope.

"Me, too. But at least we know there's another ladder down there. Come on." Mel led them towards the distant ladder. It took a while, but when they got there he had an idea. "I wonder . . ." He raised the telescope to his eye and looked back the way they'd come. "It's us all right. Just as we were a little while ago when we saw . . . us."

When they reached the next level, Mel surveyed the maze in both directions. He saw himself, still a great way off, waving.

When they finally reached that spot they found another ladder. Before they climbed it, he said, "Just a minute, there's something I need to do." He waved back down the pathway.

"Now *he's* going off his rocker, too," said Ludo.

At the top of that ladder, Mel said, "If my theory's right, then we should see ourselves at the next ladder." He looked in both directions with the telescope but the path was deserted.

"So much for your great theory," said Ludo.

"I've been thinking about this," said Wren. "Time seems to be trapped in here somehow. It's as if . . . *there*! Did you hear that deep boom? I'm sure it's coming from inside the pyramid."

"There's no sound," said Mel. "At least, none that I heard."

"If you didn't hear that, then your ears need washing. Both of you. Now, time—"

"—is something we don't have much of," said Mel. "We've been in here awhile now. Before too long we're going to start to feel sick, remember. We'll need to find a way out soon. And we still haven't found any trace of the master. Come on."

After they had walked down the path for a while, they came to the mouth of a tunnel, lit by more lampposts, that seemed to lead into the heart of the pyramid.

"Do you suppose they—we—went down here?" asked Wren.

"Must have done. But there's only one way we're going to find out for sure," said Mel.

"I'll catch you up," said Ludo. "I just want to see ourselves when we come into view. I'll give us a wave so we can find this place."

They entered the tunnel and presently Ludo ran up to join them.

"Did you signal us?" asked Wren.

"What? Oh, yeah. All done."

"That's funny, I didn't see you waving at us," said Mel. He stopped and looked back down the tunnel. "What's that?" He took the telescope from his satchel. Behind them, running in and out of the pools of light cast by the lampposts, was a band of scarlet-clad men-at-arms, each with a drawn sword in his right hand. "It's Mystery men! Let's get out of here."

The friends took to their heels and sprinted down the long tunnel.

Suddenly it ended. The heart of the pyramid was one humungous, hollow space. It was lit by hundreds of spherical lamps that hung from the inward sloping ceiling high above. The walls looked and, certainly smelled, like earth, and the huge, hairy roots of the maze protruded through into the interior, creating a sinuous jumble of twisted tendrils on an immense scale. Many more formed springs, wheels, and ratchets that interlocked and moved with one another like a great machine. At the very heart of the pyramid swung an immense pendulum. It was so huge it moved slowly and took a long time to complete each swing. As it reached the limit of its arc, they heard the deep boom that had so puzzled Wren.

Mel's eyes soon adjusted to the gloom. Above and below him he took in many more doorways similar to theirs that opened on to the interior. They were all joined together by a confusing tangle of slender walkways like rope bridges, formed from the same root material. They overlay, underlay, and joined to others like another vast labyrinth. Yet more, like rope ladders, joined them vertically. On this impossibly complicated cat's cradle they could make out dozens more of the men from the Fifth Mystery running to and fro. Each carried a sword in his right hand.

"They're all coming towards us," said Mel.

There was an anguished shout.

"Where's Ludo?" said Wren.

Their tunnel was joined to its own swaying walkway. Mel and Wren ran out on to the flimsy structure and looked over. Below them, screaming and falling into the fathomless void, was Ludo.

23. mirrortime

"LUDO!" **WREN'S CRY** echoed inside the cavernous space.

"No," said Mel, almost under his breath. Then he shouted, *"No!* Maybe he . . ."* Mel looked over the edge but any hope he might have had about Ludo landing on a walkway evaporated. There was no sign of him anywhere. "It's all my fault. I persuaded Ludo to come with us."

But before the loss had a chance to properly register, his attention was torn back to their immediate peril. Surging towards them from every direction along the walkways and in the tunnel behind them were the sword-wielding men-at-arms of the Fifth Mystery. Scores of them. Their scarlet robes billowed out behind them as they raced in the friends' direction.

"Wren. Grab hold!"

Wren's attention snapped back as the walkway lurched to one side. "Mel! What're you doing?"

Mel was frantically cutting through the roots that attached their walkway to the inside of the pyramid. "It's the only way. Grab a root. Just one more. Hang on!" He severed the final root and grabbed on to a free-hanging fiber. The pair swung down in a vertiginous arc into the heart of the pyramid, clinging to the stout tendrils. Above them red-robed bodies, unable to stop in time, spewed out from the mouth of the tunnel into thin air. One after the other, they tumbled through the void, disappearing far below.

Mel and Wren crash-landed on another walkway fifty feet below their starting point. It shuddered violently and groaned at their impact.

Winded, Mel picked himself up. "We're not safe here!" he shouted, as more Mystery men surged towards them. He sawed through the roots of their new perch. They swung down again and landed heavily on yet another walkway even farther down. The Mystery men skidded to a halt above them, but two of them lost their balance and plunged headfirst into the void.

"There's something very odd about them," said Mel. He fished his telescope out and scanned their pursuers. He handed it to Wren. "Take a look. Tell me what you see."

"*Mel!* There's no time for this." But she took it anyway. "Lots of armed men chasing us. What did you expect?"

"Look harder. Use the knob to make things bigger."

"They're . . . they're all the same. They're identical!"

"Yes! You remember how we kept seeing ourselves, as if there were lots of us? Well, I'm pretty sure it's only one man. Perhaps the invaders were here and he got left behind. The weird time in here has somehow multiplied him."

"Maybe. But even if there is only one, he's really big. And he's carrying a skegging great sword."

Just then their walkway started swaying as more Mystery men reached it and ran towards them.

"It certainly feels like there's more than one."

"Here we go again." Mel hacked through the roots of the flimsy walkway. This time their pursuers—or pursuer—were nearly upon them before the roots parted and they swung away and crashed on to the temporary safety of another, deeper walkway.

The new Mystery men fell screaming from the slack gantry as it collapsed. Far above them, yet more men were scampering about, trying to find a new route to them through the rearranged tangle of walkways.

"This is hopeless, Mel. We could spend the rest of our lives swinging from one walkway to another," said Wren in despair.

"If we don't, there won't be a rest of our lives. You know about time. What do we do?"

Wren collected herself. "I don't know. This isn't like normal time. It's *mirror*time." She looked around at the strange root mechanism. Then it came to her. "Mel, it's a *clock*! We're inside a clock. It's pretty strange but it's got a pendulum, gears, springs, escapement. Everything. If only there was a—"

"Wren, *look*! Down there." Mel fixed his telescope on a spot deep below. He handed it to Wren with a broad smile.

"How can you smile at a time like this?"

"Just look, will you?"

Wren took the proffered telescope and followed Mel's pointing finger. A broad smile also spread across her face. She laughed out loud. "It's us. It's you and me . . . and *Ludo*!"

"Think, Wren, *think*! How do we join up now, to the future, down there? What's the missing piece?"

"Okay, we're in a clock, right? What we need is a regulator."

"What's it look like?"

"It'll be a dial of some kind, probably with a knob or lever."

Wren scanned the inside of the pyramid with the telescope but could see nothing. She tried again. She almost missed it, but then jerked the telescope back. "There's something over there. Let's go. But this time, please, no swinging."

The pair clambered along, through and down the swaying cat's cradle of gantries until they reached the spot Wren had identified.

"It could be a regulator but it's unlike any I've ever seen." It was about the size of a dinner plate and covered with clinging earth. She brushed some away to reveal a broad circle of root with others arranged eccentrically inside. "Lend me your bodkin for a moment." With the blade she scraped away damp earth from the face and then used the point to dig out more, revealing a scale incised into the surface. There was a plus sign at one end and a minus at the other, with graduated markings in between. About halfway between the two was a kind of lever formed from a filament of hairy root. She grabbed it but it was stuck fast. "Mel, I need your help. We have to move this."

Mel also grabbed the lever. "Which way?"

"Towards the minus sign, this way." They heaved it together but it was stuck fast. Then the long walkway beneath their feet started swaying as twenty or more Mystery men reached it and began running towards them.

"It won't budge, Mel. If it was a real clock I'd give it a shot of oil."

Mel knelt down, opened their sack of provisions, and took out a flask of water. "Here, use this." He shot a worried glance at the scarlet men who were approaching rapidly.

Wren poured the water on to the regulator turning the earth to thin mud that drizzled off. They both tried again, working it to and fro. Ever so slowly, the lever began to move. Time slowed down.

As if in slow motion, the first of their pursuers reached Mel. He raised his sword high over his head and struck down.

With a jolt, the lever came completely free and went all the way to the minus end of the scale. The razor-sharp blade halted a bare hand's breadth from Mel's skull. It then rose away. Slowly at first, but gathering pace, the man began to move backwards. He reached his doubles and they too began to reverse their course down the walkway as the mirrortime unwound.

"That was close," said Mel, rubbing his head.

"Come on," said Wren, "I don't know how long this'll last." With a mighty wrench, she pulled the regulator off its support and stashed it in Mel's satchel. They grabbed their belongings and ran after the retreating men.

Then their whole pursuit went into rapid reverse. When they reached the dangling ends of the severed walkways that they had descended on, they grabbed them and were whipped up into the air. It happened so fast that they nearly lost their grip. This was repeated several times as they retraced their descent, until they found themselves speeding upwards towards the mouth of the tunnel where they had entered the interior. Just before the walkway reattached itself to the inner wall of the pyramid, eleven men-at-arms shot from the darkness below and into the mouth of the tunnel. Mel looked down the passage and saw them running backwards and then he and Wren following them—or preceding them; it was all very confusing.

He looked over the edge of the walkway and saw Ludo rising towards them at great speed. As he neared the walkway, he slowed down. Mel reached out, grabbed his friend, and hugged him tight. The three of them watched for a moment as they saw themselves disappearing backwards into the tunnel.

"Ludo! It's so great to have you back."

"Have me back? I haven't been anywhere—and let go of me."

"Come on!" shouted Wren.

They hurried out on to the restored walkway. After they had gone a short way, it began to sway.

"We'd better hurry. You can't treat a clock like that and expect it to work normally," said Wren.

"What are you talking about?" asked Ludo, puzzled.

"We'll tell you later," said Mel and Wren together.

They rushed on, descending through the walkways as the entire interior of the pyramid began to vibrate. The noise of the pendulum—more of a "moob" than a boom now—became increasingly frequent.

"Just a moment, Ludo," said Mel as they arrived at the spot where they had seen themselves earlier. It stood at the entrance to another tunnel that seemed to lead out of the pyramid. "Come here and stand by us. Look up there and wave." He pointed back up into the heart of the swaying tangle of walkways.

"You've both gone mad," said Ludo.

"Just humor us," said Wren. "It's for your own good."

The three friends waved energetically, repeating the scene Mel and Wren had witnessed earlier.

"You're cracked," said Ludo. "Both of you."

"You fell into the pyramid," said Mel.

"We thought you were dead but then we saw us all standing here. We reversed time and got you back," added Wren.

"Dead? *Me?*"

"We'll all be dead if we don't get out of here before the entire place shakes itself to pieces," said Mel. "Let's go."

They were bouncing off the walls by the time they reached

the outside. They emerged through a doorway at ground level and ran out on to the grassy plain beyond for some way before they stopped in front of an enormous topiary head and looked back. The pyramid went through an instant autumn as the leaves of the towering maze all fell at once, revealing a bleak terraced structure through the suddenly bare branches. This tottered and, for a moment, seemed as if it was about to implode. The terraces leaned against each other at drunken angles and came to rest. Then, like a shockwave spreading out from an explosion, all the topiary figures on the plain also shed their leaves, leaving huge, skeletal branches behind.

The friends looked around, and beneath the bare vestiges of one of the giant heads that now resembled a skull was the entrance to a wide underground passage. Leading out from the tunnel entrance and disappearing towards the horizon was a trail of giant footprints.

"Well, that answers one question," said Ludo. "The house didn't go around, it didn't go over and it didn't go through. It went *under*." They all peered down into the hole.

"Do you suppose the house knew about the tunnel?" asked Wren.

"Maybe the Fifth Mystery chased him here," said Ludo.

"From what I know of the house, it would have been the one doing the chasing," said Mel. "Are you two all right? You don't look well."

"To tell the truth, I don't feel too good," admitted Ludo.

"Me neither, Ludo," said Mel. "It's the Mirrorscape sickness Green warned me about. We need to get out for a break. Can either of you see a wall of mist anywhere?"

"You mean like that, over there?" asked Wren.

"That's just what I mean. Come on, you two."

"I'll catch you up. I've got a pebble in my boot," said Ludo.

The wall of mist shimmered and parted. On to the black and ruined shores of Ambrosius Blenk's lake stepped Groot, Bunt, and Jurgis. They were wearing scarlet robes and each had the freshly shaved tonsure and pallid face of the Fifth Mystery. Groot looked about with satisfaction at the work of his new colleagues. He folded Mel's sketch of the mirrormark and handed it to Jurgis, who tucked it inside his robes. They searched around until they found the yellow arrow.

Groot laughed. "No strength of character, that boy. None at all."

The friends soon found themselves back in Nem and feeling better. It only took a short while before the symptoms of the Mirrorscape sickness disappeared. They were in a small, octagonal room hung with paintings. Wren opened the sack and shared out some of their provisions.

As they ate Ludo was incredulous at their story of how they reversed the mirrortime. "If I'd fallen down into the pyramid I'd know all about it. Look." He rolled up his sleeves. "Not a scratch."

"But you *did*," insisted Mel. "And then Wren worked out how to rewind time—and you didn't."

"You're just trying to confuse me. Either I did or I didn't."

"What's this then?" Wren showed Ludo the shaggy regulator.

"How should I know? What is it anyway?"

"We used it to rewind time. It's something my father would be interested in. I'm going to show it to him. One day." She put it away. "Where do you think we are?"

"We must be in the House of Mysteries," said Mel, pointing at the view through the windows.

"Figures," said Ludo. "The Mysteries have most of the best paintings. What's that one? Next to the pyramid."

"It's called *The World Turned Upside Down*," said Wren, reading the nameplate. It portrayed a scene where birds swam in rivers, fish flew in the sky and horses rode their riders. "But this is my favorite."

Mel and Ludo joined her at a canvas of an artist's studio.

"Look, the perspective's impossible," said Mel. "You look at it one way and the wall's the floor, and then you look at it again and it's the other way round. And there're figures going up the staircase and under their feet there're others coming down. It doesn't make sense."

Ludo did a handstand. "If you do this, it still looks wrong."

Mel and Wren twisted their heads.

"I think I know how it's done," said Mel. "It's got three vanishing points, one for each way you can look at the picture. Let me show you." He searched in his satchel for a pencil and the master's sketchbook.

"Not now, Mel. Show us after we've found the master," said Wren.

Restored, and back in the Mirrorscape, the friends picked up the trail of footprints and followed it until they came to a huge, smooth rock face at the base of a towering crag, where the trail stopped abruptly.

"Now what?" said Ludo. "This time there's no tunnel and it obviously didn't go around."

"Maybe it flew over," said Wren.

"A flying house? I don't think so," said Mel, craning his neck to see the top of the crag. "Perhaps there's some explanation in here." He took the master's sketchbook out from his satchel. The friends flipped through the pages but could find nothing.

"Oh, this is hopeless," said Ludo. "We might as well give up now. I don't know why I ever agreed to come along with you. The house—if it actually exists—just vanished into thin air."

"Perhaps it went inside the mountain," said Wren, studying the smooth rock face. There, at head-height was a sculpted, hemispherical boss of rock about the size of a thumbnail. Incised over it in small, neat letters was the word DELIVERIES. "Why don't we ring and ask?"

Mel shrugged. "It's no crazier than anything else we've come across in the Mirrorscape." He pressed the boss. There was the sound of a large bell striking somewhere far away. After a minute or so he pushed the boss again. Then there came a cracking sound, like someone snapping a bunch of twigs, and beneath the boss a pair of carved, human-shaped lips appeared out of the solid rock.

"All right, all right, keep your hair on. *Yes?*" said the lips in an irritated voice.

The friends looked at each other amazed. Mel said, "Can you please tell us, has a house passed this way?"

"Speak up! What? Speak up, I said . . . Oh, scrot. Just a minute." There was another snapping noise and a pair of carved ears appeared either side of the boss. "I can't hear you. Speak into the ears."

Ludo leaned closer and said in a raised voice, "A house! We're looking for a house!"

"*Ouch!* No need to shout, I'm not deaf. Now, what was it you wanted?"

"A house," said Mel in a more moderate tone.

"Do I look like an estate agent?"

"Err, no. But—"

"Then what're you bothering me for?" There was another snapping sound and the ears and lips disappeared back into the stone.

Undaunted, Wren pushed the bell again.

The snapping sound, much louder and angrier this time, was followed by the appearance of the lips and ears. ". . . don't put it there, it's bound to . . ." There came the muffled sound of something crashing to the ground. ". . . fall over. Why doesn't anyone ever listen to me? *Yes?*"

"Look, we're sorry to disturb you," said Wren. "You sound very busy but we're looking for a house. Did a large, funny-looking house come this way?"

"Who the skeg's that? Hang on a minute. Which switch was it?" There was a double crack and two carved eyes popped open just above the boss. There was now a complete, flattened-out face in high-relief with the boss as a nose and DELIVERIES forming a long eyebrow. "Ah, that's better." The eyes blinked and surveyed the trio. Then in a curt tone, "What now?"

Mel said, "We've been following a house and he seems to have come here. We were wondering if you've seen him . . . it."

"What's that say?" said the face, raising its eyes to look at its brow.

"It says 'deliveries,'" said Ludo. "But—"

"And have you got a delivery?"

"Not exactly—"

"Then what are you bothering me for? Haven't I got enough to do without time-wasters?"

"Well, we might have one, if we knew what this place was," said Wren. "What exactly are you?"

The face huffed and rolled its eyes. "We're a *mine*, ducky. What do you expect to find inside a mountain?"

"What sort of mine, exactly?" asked Mel.

"A mine of *inspiration*," said the face in a tone that clearly suggested it was talking to an idiot.

"Don't you mean a mine of *information*?" asked Ludo.

"Where do they get 'em these days?" said the face in an exasperated tone. "Whoever heard of a mine of information? Information's already out there. It's everywhere. You only have to open a book or a newspaper or talk to people. *Inspiration*, on the other hand, is much more difficult to come by. You have to delve for inspiration, ideas that no one's had yet. It's not just lying around anywhere now, is it? Inspiration's new stuff. Once it's been dug out and used it becomes information. Even an imbecile can work that one out, can't they?"

"Yes, I suppose so," said Mel.

"Well? Have you got any or not?"

"What, inspiration? Between the three of us, I guess we must have," said Wren. "In fact, we've got lots."

"Why didn't you say so in the first place? Come on in."

There was a much louder cracking sound and a huge carved door appeared in the rock face. It opened with a hollow, scraping sound, permitting the friends to enter.

Groot watched Bunt and Jurgis being sick with morbid fascination. He did not feel too well himself, but he was not going to let it spoil his enjoyment at seeing his companions suffer. They had picked up Ludo's trail on the far side of the pyramid. Since the root-clock had ceased working they were able to simply walk around the outside. Groot knelt and picked up a hastily scribbled note anchored by a stone next to a yellow arrow. Having read it, he screwed it up and threw it away.

"Come on, you pukes. Apparently it's being in here that's making us feel unwell. We need to get out for a spell." He led them away towards the wall of mist, which had been clearly marked by Ludo.

When they emerged into the small chamber in the House of Mysteries, Groot had an idea and sent Bunt to procure some paints, brushes, and canvas. Jurgis was sent to the High-Bailiff to fetch the models. All he now needed was a studio to work in to bring his plan to fruition. He did not need to search far.

24. the mine of inspiration

"ARE YOU SEEING what I'm seeing?" gasped Ludo.

"It's hollow," said Mel. "The whole mountain's *hollow*."

"It's like an enormous sculpture," said Wren.

Bright shafts of daylight streamed down from openings high above in a ceiling supported by hundreds of columns hewn from the living rock. Between these columns, and covering most of the vast floor space, were dozens of carved islands with square-rigged, stone ships plying back and forth across a stony sea. Stone beaches gently rose to support a confusion of sculpted mangrove roots. Nestling within the honeycomb formed from the leafless, twisted limbs of the mangrove trees were a mind-numbing assortment of items in every imaginable shape, size, and color. There were jellyfish and sycamore trees, clouds and unicycles, Ferris wheels and dinosaurs, cathedrals and euphoniums. High above the islands, suspended from a network of cables, hung bullet-shaped silver craft that cruised the upper reaches of the mine.

At least, that's what it would all have looked like if the house had not already been there. What the friends saw as they stood on a ruined pier that projected into the mine was altogether different. To either side, the mine still retained its original design, but right through the center was a broad swathe of destruction.

Many of the islands forming the archipelago had been flattened, and their inspirational contents were now so much flotsam and jetsam bobbing on the carved waves of the stone floor. Shipwrecked mariners clung to this wreckage or to the floating remains of their foundered vessels. Some of the sounder crafts plucked their unfortunate colleagues from the mineral waves or fended off circling stone sharks. Several of the overhead cable cars had lowered rope ladders to the distressed seamen and were ferrying them to intact islands. It was a scene of great activity and utter confusion.

"*Ow!*" A rope ladder had fallen from above and hit Wren a glancing blow on her shoulder. Above them, swaying gently, was one of the cable cars. "Perhaps we're meant to climb up into that contraption," she said. "It's the only way off this pier."

Just then, the lips briefly appeared on the lowest rung of the ladder. "Come along now, don't dillydally. There's work to be done."

"Hang on. Where's Ludo?"

"He was here a moment ago," said Wren. "Perhaps he's gone back outside."

"I'm right here," said Ludo, hurrying back to his friends. "You needn't think I'm going down there," he said, pointing out into the sea of flagstones and disorder.

"It looks like we have to take the cable car if we plan on finding out more," said Mel as he began to climb the ladder.

The cable car was covered in sheets of polished metal riveted together. It had sweeping fins, large air scoops, and exhaust pipes along its sides, which anyone could see were just for show. Inside, the car was constructed like a rowing boat with several benchlike seats running from side to side. Where the oarlocks would have been there were stout pulleys that were attached to the cables from which the car dangled. At the front was a small, semicircular glass windshield and beneath it, at an angle, was a polished and riveted dashboard. In the center of this was a button, above which were embossed the words PUSH FOR ATTENTION.

Mel pushed the button. There came the sound like a door opening on rusty hinges and the same face appeared, but this time formed from the polished metal around the button, with PUSH FOR ATTENTION for a brow. The rivets looked like pimples.

"Oh, there you are. You took your time." It sounded harassed. "So, what've you got?"

"Got?" said Mel, puzzled.

"Oh, *really*! You're making a delivery," said the face tetchily. *"Remember?"*

The cable car took them out to one of the undamaged islands. One by one, they were lowered down to vacant cells in the sculpted mangrove tree. Inside each was an odd metal helmet that looked like an upturned pudding bowl encrusted with coils, dials, and colored lights. As instructed, they placed these on their heads, closed their eyes, and imagined something. The helmets hummed, causing their scalps to tingle and the lights to flash and then, with a sound like a nightingale trapped inside an accordion, the object they imagined materialized in front of them. It was like making art without any of the hard work of drawing or painting.

When they were all back inside the cable car once more Mel pushed the button again.

"*Very* nice, very nice indeed," said the face as it reemerged. "You may have only a single brain cell between the three of you, but that's some quality inspiration, I must say. We could do with a lot more of that—to replace the damaged stock."

"We wish we could stick around and help some more but we must be after the house," said Mel.

"Perhaps you didn't hear me right. I said, '*We could do with a lot more of that.*'"

"I'm sorry, but we haven't the time right now. We have to go."

"Go? You're not going anywhere. Not until all the stock's been replenished. That house you seem to be so friendly with was the cause of all this damage. And now you're going to put it all to rights."

"I thought you said you hadn't seen the house," said Ludo.

"I didn't say I had and I didn't say I hadn't."

"But we *have* to go," pleaded Wren. "We've already spent far too long here as it is. If you could just show us the way out, we'd be ever so grateful. *Please.*"

"Oh well, if you have to go, you have to go," said the face, relenting. "It's a pity. We sure could have used your inspiration. You don't see quality like that every day. Hold tight." The face vanished and the cable car sped off with a lurching motion, into the heart of the mine.

They headed for an island towards the periphery of the flagstone sea. This one had a large, cone-shaped volcano on it rather than the ubiquitous mangrove trees. When the car was immediately over the volcano it came to a swaying halt and the face reemerged from the dashboard.

"Here we are."

"Where?" asked Wren. "This doesn't look like a way out to me."

"Way out, ducky? Whatever could have given you that idea?" asked the face. "Like I told you, you won't be going anywhere until the mine's been restocked. I'll find out what's needed and come back for you. Until then, you can keep the other one company. He looks like one of your lot. *Alley-oop!*"

"What other—?"

Mel's question was cut short by a whirring noise as the pulleys all along one side of the car engaged and the whole conveyance abruptly tipped upside down. The friends spilled out of the car and through the air into the volcano. Down and down they tumbled, landing on a great pile of junk that filled most of the interior. The debris broke their fall and they clattered helter-skelter down the slope, landing in a heap on the floor.

Mel looked up and saw the mouth of the crater, a disc of light no bigger than the full moon, high above them.

"That lying scrot," said Ludo as he staggered to his feet, dusting himself down.

"We shouldn't have been so inspirational." Mel angrily kicked a piece of junk.

"What're we going to do now?" said Ludo.

"We need to find a way out—in a hurry. Before too long we're going to become sick again, remember?" said Mel. "Perhaps we can find something to help us in all this rubbish."

"I suppose a ladder would be too much to hope for," said Ludo, sorting through the junk.

"It'd need to be a really long ladder," said Wren. "Even from the top of the heap it'd never reach the opening."

"This is all junk," said Ludo. "Everything's broken or useless."

"It must be the mine's dump," said Wren

"I've found a kettle. *Yuck*, it's made from butter." Mel wiped his greasy hands on his doublet.

"Here's a chocolate frying pan," said Ludo. "And a teapot made from feathers. What have you found, Wren?"

"I've got a velvet cartwheel, an elastic wrench, and a sewing machine that seems to be made out of smoke. Nothing here's the least bit useful." Wren sat down on the scrap heap.

"There's got to be a way out," said Mel as he knelt and unfastened his satchel. He withdrew the telescope and began to pan around the interior of the dimly lit volcano but there was very little to see in the feeble light filtering down from above. The far side of the volcano was obscured by the scrap heap. Even using the magnifier, he could find nothing. The only way out was the mouth of the crater high over their heads.

"*Ahem!*" A polite cough sounded behind the friends. "Young sirs, miss, if I might be so bold as to venture a small suggestion?"

"This is more like it, eh, Mumchance? Who's doing the running away now? Look at that cowardly cottage run!"

The High-Bailiff looked down from the cabin of his flying command vehicle at his men-at-arms far below, thundering across the Mirrorscape in their newly plundered conveyances. Fleeing before them in a cloud of dust was the house.

"Amazing what one can find inside a mountain these days. These machines are just the job." Adolfus Spute gazed admiringly at his fleet of bizarre vehicles, plundered from the Mine of Inspiration. "Mumchance, we're losing altitude. Adjust the buoyancy, my little man. Give us a trifle more elevation, if you please."

The dwarf mounted a ladder and opened a trapdoor in the roof of their weird flying machine. From the outside it resembled the rotting carcass of a rhinoceros. He blew a violent blast on his silver whistle. Above his head flew a huge flock of birds attached to the passenger compartment with myriad fine wires. When his whistle blast had no effect he reached inside his scarlet robe and withdrew a small catapult. Fitting a pebble into the sling, he took aim and fired into the midst of the flock. There was an enraged cawing and a cloud of shed feathers as his missile hit its mark. The birds flapped harder and the vehicle rose.

"Ah, that's better. Not long now, my manky miniature. Soon we'll have Ambrosius Blenk in our hands once more."

25. down and out

STARTLED, THE FRIENDS turned at the sound of the voice. He was about their height and dressed exactly like them in the Blenk household livery. But there the similarity ended. He was more or less human in shape but his bald head was completely spherical and his face recessed into it.

"Perhaps I should introduce myself. My name is Swivel and I am Master Blenk's butler." He inclined his round head in a bow.

"No, you're not," said Ludo. "I've never seen you around the mansion."

"Forgive me, young sir, but I serve the master here, in his residence in the Mirrorscape. Like all inhabitants of the Mirrorscape I am a figment. In my case, of Master Blenk's imagination."

Mel quickly made the connection. "You mean you work in that funny-looking house?"

"Precisely, young sir. And it's rather important that I get back as soon as possible. The master needs looking after."

"Then you'll know what's happened here?" said Wren.

"Indeed. Master Blenk was visiting his house by the lake when a large band of red-robed ruffians from the Fifth Mystery arrived and began vandalizing the grounds and mistreating the wildlife. Then they attempted to enter the residence, quite without invitation.

Such *appalling* manners." At this point the strangest thing happened. Swivel's face, which up until then had been composed, swiveled around within his head with a metallic, scraping sound, to be replaced by another with a look of disdain on it. It then swiveled back and he continued. "Billet, who you rather questionably refer to as 'that funny-looking house,' took umbrage at this and, after excusing himself to Master Blenk, set about teaching that rabble how to behave towards their betters. But they wouldn't be told. It was all most regrettable." He sighed and his face rotated in the other direction to display one of resigned sadness before flipping back. "They fled and he—we—gave chase. To cut a long story short, we ended up here, at the Mine of Inspiration, where things took a turn for the worse. Up until that time, Billet had the upper hand and the hooligans were in full flight. But once inside the mine they managed to appropriate several important articles of inspiration and caused quite a *furor*. I'm sure you've seen the result. Not to put too fine a point on it, the tables were turned. Master Blenk and Billet fled from the mine, this time with the hooligans in pursuit. Unfortunately, during the unpleasantness, I was accidentally ejected and left behind. I believe I may have been held to blame by the management for the unfortunate events and found myself sequestered here."

"It looks like the master needs our help now more than ever," said Mel. "The question is, how do we get out of here?"

"I was just about to suggest something, young sir. But first, if you'll permit me?" Swivel's hand retracted into his sleeve and when it came back out had a clothes brush attached. He began to brush the dust from Mel's velvet doublet.

"Never mind that now. What's your suggestion?" asked Mel.

"As you wish. It's just that I see you have the omniscope."

"The what?"

"The omniscope, young sir." The clothes brush hand withdrew into Swivel's sleeve and his open hand popped back out. "May I?"

Mel realized that he was referring to his telescope. "This thing? I've used it but I can't see a way out anywhere." He passed it to the butler.

"But perhaps the young sir is not aware of its rather special attributes."

"You mean making things appear closer?"

"Forgive me, but the omniscope does rather more than that. You have perhaps been wondering about the various attachments along its length, only one of which is the special enlargement facility. This control here, for instance, allows for better illumination of the subject and this one here—"

"Let me see," said Ludo, snatching the object from Swivel's hand. "*Wow!* You should see this, Mel. Everything's as bright as day."

He handed Mel the omniscope and Mel began to reinspect the interior.

"Excuse me, young sirs, but you won't find a way out there. I've already looked." At this, Swivel's face rotated again, this time from his chin upwards, revealing a face with huge, nocturnal eyes.

Its ghastly appearance made Ludo jump.

"I'm sorry if I startled you." The butler's face swiveled back to his normal one.

"So there's no way out?" said Wren, disappointed.

"Perhaps if I may continue? This control *here* will permit you to see a distance *through* things." Swivel indicated another knob on the omniscope.

Mel returned the apparatus to his eye and twiddled the knob.

At first nothing seemed to change, but as he turned the knob further, the walls of the volcano paled and vanished and he could clearly see the surrounding islands and ships. "That's *amazing*, but I still can't see a way out of here."

"*Ahem!*" The polite cough once more. "Perhaps the young sir is looking in the wrong direction?" The butler nodded towards the pile of junk.

Mel turned the omniscope on it and looked down deep into the heart of the scrap heap. "There's a great big hole in the floor, right in the center, like a massive drain or something. But it's blocked. There's a big whatnot wedged in it. Perhaps all this junk's supposed to vanish down there."

"Exactly," said Swivel.

"But that still doesn't help us much," said Mel. "There must be hundreds of tons of junk in this pile. We'll never shift it."

"Maybe this'll help." Wren held out a battered and dented helmet similar to the one they had used to produce their inspiration. "I've just found this on the scrap heap. It's been through the wars but perhaps we can get it to work."

"How very enterprising of you, miss. If you'll permit me?"

Wren passed the helmet to Swivel. He held it in his left hand and his right withdrew into the sleeve of his doublet and reemerged as a stubby screwdriver. He tightened a few screws, changed his hand for a pair of pliers, remade a connection or two, changed his hand back to normal, blew some dust off the helmet, and handed it back. "That might serve tolerably well, although I sincerely doubt it will function perfectly. After all, it had been thrown away."

"Go on, Wren, you found it, you use it," said Mel.

Wren put the helmet on and closed her eyes. Her brow furrowed in concentration and the lights flickered and then glowed dimly. There was a sound like fingernails scraping on a blackboard, and something amorphous began to materialize on the floor in front of Wren. At first it was vague and transparent and then it started to fade away altogether.

"*Do* excuse me, miss." Swivel whacked the side of the helmet with his hand. "Most frightfully sorry, and all that."

Wren recovered from the blow as the lights glowed brighter and, with a pop like a champagne cork, a python with the head of a flamingo sprang into existence at her feet.

"Well done. That's fantastic. It works!" said Mel, slapping Wren on the back.

"No, it doesn't," said Wren, disappointed. "I tried for a rope with a hook on the end. Something we could use to drag this junk aside."

"At least we're getting something," said Ludo.

Wren tried some more and then Ludo and Mel took turns, but after an hour of attempts at imagining something useful all they had produced was another pile of worthless junk. More by luck than design, they had created several more or less round wheels, lots of nondescript tubes, and more than a fair share of useless and malformed animal parts before the helmet gave up the ghost with a flash, a bang, and a puff of multicolored smoke.

Mel removed the smoking helmet. "Well, I guess that's it."

"What now?" said a downhearted Ludo.

"We're not necessarily finished yet, young sirs, miss. Between the items you have imagined and the scrap heap here, we now have at our disposal a rather large quantity of raw material. A kit of parts, as it were. If you were to describe exactly what you were aiming for, with my skills I might just be able to fabricate such a device."

Mel retrieved a pencil and the master's sketchbook from his satchel and turned to a blank page. "What about some kind of excavating machine?" He sketched out what he had in mind. Wren and Ludo made some helpful suggestions that he incorporated before handing the finished design to the butler. Swivel set to work.

Swivel was amazingly industrious and, after going through an impressive repertoire of different faces and hands, had Mel's machine fully assembled. It would have been finished a lot sooner if he had not stopped periodically to tidy up after himself. The friends inspected the finished machine.

The main part of it was built from the ribcage of an enormous fish. Inside was a four-seater tandem bicycle frame. This was bolted on to a flat bed from beneath which protruded a multitude of feet. Some were human-looking (with and without shoes), while others were distinctly animal in origin. Still others were mechanical, built from small pistons, bolts, and springs. For the excavating end there was a huge dinosaur's head with a formidable array of sharp teeth. Its eyes had been replaced with lanterns. It was anchored in front of a rather dangerous-looking steam engine, topped with organ pipes of varying length. The excavated waste was to be channeled along the machine by a complicated tangle of intestine-like flexible pipes and finally expelled from the rear via something that resembled an oversized sousaphone. This emerged from a great big bottom. All in all it looked as if it would be rather more dangerous to the operators than to the scrap heap.

"Look, I'm not so sure this is a good idea after all," said Ludo, studying the machine. "I think I'd rather stay here having inspiration than getting in that jerry-rigged thing."

"Excuse me, but I rather think you are laboring under a misapprehension," said Swivel. "When the Mine of Inspiration wishes to uncover a large amount of inspirational ore, it uses what any other mine would given the same situation."

"Oh, and what's that?" asked Ludo.

"Why, *explosives*, young sir."

Ludo was the first to climb on board the strange machine. He took the rear saddle with Wren in front of him, then Mel, who fastened his satchel to the crossbar. Swivel, who knew how to operate the contraption, sat in the driving seat immediately behind the steam engine. As they built up a head of steam the organ pipes began to whistle musically. The butler started the excavator and it rose on its feet and edged forward like a huge, weird centipede.

"And just what do you think you're doing?" The face emerged with a metallic *boing* from a malformed gondola at the edge of the scrap heap. It was evidently angry.

"With your permission, young sirs, miss?"

"Be our guest," said Ludo.

Swivel pulled one of the many levers arrayed along the handlebars and the head of the machine turned and crushed the boat with its massive jaws.

The face immediately reappeared on the other side, this time on a church steeple that appeared to be constructed from dried moths. "Oh no, you don't. I know what your little game is. I'll fix you."

The face vanished and moments later the gloomy light inside the volcano dimmed even more.

"What's that?" said Wren.

Mel looked up. "Whatever it is, it's bad news."

They all gazed up through the ribs of the excavator and saw a black cloud obscuring the mouth of the crater.

"I didn't expect them to have weather in here."

"That's not weather, Wren," said Mel as he trained the omniscope on the cloud. "That cloud's made from *beetles!*"

"Let's get out of here!" shouted Ludo.

Swivel pulled a lever and the jaws of the machine bit into the scrap heap. The friends could hear a clanging noise in the pipes as the masticated morsels of junk were channeled along, to be expelled behind. Suddenly, Wren screamed. The interior of the excavator was invaded by the beetles. Their bodies were as big as goose eggs and their scratchy legs began crawling over the occupants, nipping them painfully with their pincerlike jaws.

"Keep going, Swivel. I'll deal with this," shouted Mel over the din. Flailing his arms to bat away the beetles, he jumped off his saddle and grabbed one of the flexible pipes running alongside the excavator. "Everyone cover your faces!" He wrenched the pipe away, then used it like a machine gun to hose down the insects with the shredded junk that shot from the end with great velocity.

By this time, the excavator was wholly inside the scrap heap. No more insects could get in and those behind were being pelted with the debris thrown out from the rear of the machine. Within a short time Mel had shot them all, and managed to reattach the pipe.

The friends tended to their painful bites between coughing back the choking smoke as the excavator chomped on into the heart of the scrap heap. It was very dark.

After a while, the butler turned. "Not far now, young sirs, miss. There appears to be a large cavity all around the drain."

The cavity itself was formed by the upturned hull of a truly enormous galleon. Most of the decks were missing, exposing its ribs and keel, and the gigantic masts and yards had crumpled and were wedged crossways in the drain, causing the blockage.

The friends could all breathe more easily now that the smoke was escaping into the cavity, but even above the rhythmic noise of the steam engine and the musical pipes, they could hear the ominous creaking of the countless tons of rubbish above them bearing down on the hull.

"The scrap heap's about to collapse!" cried Ludo.

Swivel navigated the excavator through the jungle of fallen rigging and spars that littered the floor. As he maneuvered up to the drain, he worked a handlebar lever that engaged a circular saw. It bit into the debris that was causing the blockage, sending a fountain of bright sparks high into the air. Then, suddenly, the obstruction tumbled down into the drain. Without hesitation, the butler drove the excavator forward and into the hole. After a brief, vertical plunge, the passage of the drain evened out into a steep downward slope. Swivel wrestled with the controls as they dived deeper and deeper.

"You won't be getting away that easily."

"Look!" cried Wren in alarm.

The face had appeared out of the wall of the drain. It was much bigger and angrier than before and was moving along at great speed, keeping pace with their descent.

"That brain cell of yours is getting a real workout," it sneered. "But you won't be getting out of the mine just yet."

Muscular arms emerged from the wall and their powerful hands grabbed two of the excavator's ribs, snapping them apart as if they were matchsticks. One hand thrust into the excavator and made a grab for Mel. He leaped from his saddle as the hand crushed the bicycle frame, and his satchel fell to the floor. It burst open and the contents spilled out. Wren grabbed the regulator, and Ludo the sketchbook with one hand and the omniscope with the other. Mel lunged for the pencils but they rolled out of the machine. The hand reached in again and seized Ludo and Wren.

"Help! Help!" cried Ludo.

Ludo and Wren wailed in pain and struggled vainly to free themselves from the face's grasp.

Mel reached down, grabbed one of the snapped-off ribs, and thrust it out of the excavator and into the face's left eye. "Let go of my friends!"

The face howled and dropped the youngsters. "You vicious little tyke!" spat the face, rubbing its wounded eye. It formed its other hand into a fist and punched hard into the machine, catching Mel a hefty whack that bowled him across the floor of the excavator. He made a fruitless grab for one of the ribs on the far side but was hurled out of the machine as it reached a fork in the drain. Mel fell into one side-branch, while the excavator with Swivel, Ludo, and Wren careered on into the other.

Mel forced himself on to his back so that he was sliding feet-first. Fortunately, the lining of the drain was smooth, but this also prevented him from slowing himself down. He veered wildly from side to side, striking his elbows, his ribs, and, occasionally, his head. One half of his mind fought against mounting panic while the other half tried to concentrate on avoiding any more collisions. He came to a halt with a jarring thud, stopped by a heavy grille blocking the end of the drain. Though its crisscross bars he could see a long slope of ejected scrap and, beyond, a green, flat landscape.

The face appeared from the opposite wall of the drain and stared balefully at Mel with its uninjured eye. The other one was swollen and closed. "I'm going to wring your ruddy neck, you whelp. *Come here!*" The muscular arms emerged from the drain wall and made a grab for him.

Mel jumped back and the face's powerful hands closed on thin air just in front of him.

"Come here, you little blighter." The face vanished and reappeared on the opposite wall but Mel jumped back the other way. It then flowed sinuously around the inside of the drain and on to the floor like quicksilver. Mel leapt on to the circular grille and climbed to the center just as the face smashed its great fist into the wall where he had been standing only an instant before. The face made another vain attempt to grab him, this time from above. But Mel was just beyond its reach. As long as he stayed put right in the center of the grille, the hands could not reach him.

Then he heard a clanking rumble echoing down the drain. There was no mistaking what it was. It was getting louder and the drain began to shake. A sizable proportion of the monstrous scrap heap was hurtling towards him where he was perched like the bull's-eye on a target.

"Now we've got him. There's nowhere left for him to run to." Adolfus Spute rubbed his hands together. "We've got him and his atrocious abode surrounded. Mumchance, my leprous leprechaun, signal the men to attack. This is finally the end of Ambrosius Blenk."

26. the excavator excavated

"SLOW DOWN!" YELLED Ludo as the strange excavator hurtled on through the dark and winding network of drains.

"No, go faster! Or we'll all be crushed," shouted Wren as the rushing scrap heap grew increasingly louder behind them.

Then Swivel spied a heavy iron grille over the end of the drain ahead of them. "The young sir is correct, miss. We really need to brake." He frantically engaged another lever on the handlebars, and the feet beneath the machine dug in their many heels. But this served only to create sparks and make the excavator unstable.

"There's the end of the tunnel. We're going to crash!" Ludo raised his arms to shield his face.

"No, look!" said Wren. "It's opening."

The grille covering the tunnel exit began to rotate upwards and outwards with a nerve-jangling, mechanical squeal.

"I do believe the way ahead's clear," said Swivel, just as the colossal bolus of debris reached the rear of the excavator. The machine shot out of the end of the drain into thin air, along with the geyser of junk.

They had emerged on the far side of the crag high above a wide, deep pit. The butler operated another of his levers and a pair of scruffy wings unfolded from the top of the machine, flapping wildly. With the aid of the wings the contraption landed with a jarring bump in the bottom of the pit, just a few yards beyond the end of the outflow.

"Phew, that was close," said Wren. "I thought we were done for when the face grabbed us. You saved us, Mel. Mel? Where's Mel?"

"He was just behind us." Ludo looked around for his friend.

"I'm sorry, young sir, miss, but your companion parted company with us some way back," Swivel informed them.

"*What?* You mean he's still in there? We have to go back and get him," said Wren.

"That's impossible," said Ludo flatly. "That drain was miles long. There's no way we could climb back up there. Besides, the grille's closed again. You saw how many other drains branched off to the side. He could have gone down any one of them."

"The young sir's right, miss. I'm afraid we've lost him for good."

"We can't just abandon him. Perhaps he's come out of another exit. We have to try and find him," pleaded Wren.

"But where, Wren? We don't know if there *is* another exit. We don't even know where *we* are," said Ludo.

Wren looked desperately from one to the other. She sat down on the edge of the excavator and felt tears begin to well up behind her eyes. After a moment she choked them back. "No. That's not going to help us find Mel. He's still alive; I know he is. We came into the Mirrorscape to do a job and we owe it to Mel to complete it. We must go on and find the master." She wiped her eyes with her sleeve.

"I agree, miss. The young sir struck me as an eminently resourceful chap. Why, he's probably got out of the mine and is searching for us right now. He'll surely make his own way to the master." The butler seemed to have a face for every occasion. This time it swiveled to display one with a sad but hopeful smile.

Wren was grateful for the reassuring gesture but felt no better. She knew as well as the others that the odds were against Mel.

"At least we've still got the satchel and most of the stuff. We stand as much chance as we did before of finding the master," said Ludo.

They studied their surroundings. The pit had steep rocky sides from which the occasional gnarled tree grew out horizontally. Perched on them were strange birds whose forlorn cries echoed off the walls. There was a long, sloping pathway that spiraled around the inside of the pit to the top.

"It's an awfully long way up to the rim," said Ludo.

"Why don't we take the excavator?" suggested Wren.

"A splendid idea, miss. However, our supply of fuel has diminished considerably. Perhaps if you and the young sir would be so kind as to search the scrap and procure anything that is in any way combustible to fuel the boiler, we might proceed."

Impatient at the delay, Wren and Ludo rushed around collecting anything from the ejected junk that might burn.

As they set off, neither Wren nor Swivel noticed the yellow arrow pointing up the path behind them.

When they finally reached the top of the pit, Swivel brought them to a halt.

"Any idea of where we are? Which way do we go?" asked Wren. She glanced back towards the grille in the pit far below them, and the scavenger birds picking over the junk. "Where are you, Mel?" she said under her breath.

"I believe it would be constructive to consult the omniscope," answered Swivel. Ludo took it from the satchel. "If you were to try this knob here, for instance, we might learn something to our advantage."

Ludo put the omniscope to his eye and twiddled the control the butler indicated. "I can't see a thing. Everything's gone black." He removed the contraption and looked at the lens, but it was unobstructed. "Maybe it got broken in the mine."

"Perhaps if the young sir were to pan around in the other direction."

As Ludo swung around the light in the device increased and he could see clearly. He continued panning and the image darkened again before he swung back to where it appeared brightest. He fumbled with the other knobs until he found the magnifier.

"There it is! There's not just a single track of footprints but a great churned-up mass of them leading away. We've found the trail."

"That particular function of the omniscope is somewhat like that of a compass, young sir; a rather intelligent compass. It is always brightest in the direction of what one is searching for. In this case, the master."

"Then why can't we use it to search for Mel?" asked Wren.

"We can, miss, but not yet. It can only point in one direction at a time. You may have noticed that our master is rather . . ."

"Absentminded?" suggested Ludo.

"Liable to go off at a tangent, shall we say. Therefore, I took it upon myself some time ago to set the omniscope to always point the way to the master. Once that's been achieved it can be reset to look in another direction," explained Swivel.

"So let's hurry up and find him," said Wren.

They set off across the Mirrorscape, leaving the comparatively delicate footprints of the excavator alongside the broad furrow ploughed up by Billet and his pursuers. They made good time on the flat terrain and soon Swivel called back to Wren and Ludo. "I can see a cloud of dust up ahead. Why don't you two see what you can make out?"

The friends clambered up and on top of the rapidly moving excavator. When they were seated side by side on the dinosaur head, Ludo used the omniscope to study the cloud.

He raised his voice so that Swivel could hear him above the musical tune of the pipes. "I can see the house—I mean Billet. He's surrounded by a whole herd."

"A whole herd of what?" asked Wren.

"Here, see for yourself."

Wren took the omniscope and trained it on the distant cloud. She recognized Billet from the master's canvas, and milling around him were huge shapes made indistinct by the dust. Occasionally, a burst of light erupted within the cloud, followed seconds later by the low rumble of distant thunder. As they got closer, she could make out progressively more detail. "There must be a dozen strange contraptions circling Billet."

"Yeah, and each one is crammed with men-at-arms," said Ludo.

Each contraption seemed to have been cobbled together from items plundered from the Mine of Inspiration. Some spat bolts of lightning, and had succeeded in setting fire to the thatch that crowned Billet's head. Other machines sported huge iron fists or a variety of wickedly sharp blades of various shapes and sizes. Still more war engines were like long-legged steamships that fired nets and miles of sticky string that tangled Billet's feet and prevented his escape. One rhinoceros-shaped machine, which seemed to be in command, hovered in the air above the battleground. It was suspended from many wires attached to a great flock of birds of all shapes and sizes. The omniscope now clearly showed the High-Bailiff and his dwarf peering out from between the exposed ribs, organizing the assault and telegraphing instructions to the ragtag squadron with a small semaphore machine hanging beneath them.

"It looks like we got here too late," said Ludo.

"There must be something we can do." Wren anxiously scanned the scene with the omniscope. "Wait a minute. I can see . . ."

"What? *What?*"

"Ludo . . . it's the master! He's alive! He's on the roof trying to beat out the flames. We're not too late."

"We've found him. Swivel, we've found the master and he's alive," said Ludo.

"*Ahem!*"

"What now, Swivel?" said Ludo. "Don't tell me you've thought of some urgent tidying up to do."

"In a way, young sir, I have. It occurs to me there's an awful mess down there surrounding the master that simply must be attended to. I can't abide mess."

"What did you have in mind?" asked Wren.

"Might I suggest that it is not beyond your decidedly superior creative abilities and my more humble, workaday skills to engineer, as it were, a way out of this predicament."

Swivel set the excavator on automatic pilot. The smoke from the steam engine now worked to their advantage. The butler rearranged some pipes that blew thick clouds from the mouth of the excavator to mask their approach. The moth-eaten wings fanned this towards the enemy.

Through the smoke and din of battle they could make out Billet's booming voice. "Call that a slap, yer limp-wristed twerp? I've been hit harder by snowflakes."

Before the attackers knew it, the excavator was in among them and using its powerful jaws to hamper and maim the assailants. Blinded by the smoke, the monsters were unable to receive instructions from the High-Bailiff hovering above. In the confusion they began to set about each other.

"Our smokescreen seems most effective," said Swivel. "Now, if we remove the enemy's head we might be able to make inroads into his body." Swivel launched a carefully aimed circular saw blade at the flying contraption from an improvised catapult strung between the handlebars. The spinning projectile found its mark and severed many of the lines that attached it to the flock of birds.

"Good shot!" Wren and Ludo cheered as the machine crashed into the midst of its brothers, sowing yet more panic.

While the enemy contraptions were busy laying into each other, Swivel maneuvered the excavator right up to Billet and dismounted. "A spot of gardening is called for, I believe." With a sickle attachment on his hand he began to cut away the entanglements that bound the house.

Meanwhile, Ludo and Wren had noticed that the smoke was beginning to clear. Adolfus Spute had climbed from the wreckage of his aerial vehicle and mounted a tortoise contraption. It had a tall steel pylon on its domed back from which swung a spiked, iron ball on a chain like a rotor. The High-Bailiff used this to blow the smoke back towards the excavator.

"There goes our smokescreen," said Wren. "Time for another of Mel's machine guns, I think."

"Two are better than one," said Ludo as the pair grabbed pipes from the excavator to use like Mel's improvised weapon.

"But what are we going to use for ammunition?" asked Wren. "There's no scrap heap here."

"There's one thing," said Ludo. "The excavator!" He tried several of the handlebar controls until he found a combination that set the excavator to begin devouring itself. It started to gyrate like a puppy chasing its own tail. Beginning with the sousaphone and moving steadily along the length of its sinuous body, it chomped while the friends stood to one side and aimed the remains at Billet's attackers like firemen dousing flames.

"It's working," said Ludo, "but not fast enough."

"We're running out of ammunition," said Wren. They could see that the excavator would have totally consumed itself before the assailants could be put to flight.

"We might not need much more. Look!" Wren nodded towards Billet. Swivel had finally cut the house free from its entanglements.

"Right, yer bogey-chewing sticks of rhubarb. Let's be having yer!" bellowed Billet as he weighed into the melee. "How d'yer like *that*!" Those monsters he could not flatten with his enormous feet, he butted with his head. From one of his great windows, the master rained down pieces of furniture and other household items.

"We're winning!" said Ludo, seeing the High-Bailiff in the tortoise-machine wheel around and flee the battlefield, followed by his men in the remains of their battered contraptions.

With a final and seemingly impossible contortion, the excavator munched its own head and the last of the debris was fired from Wren and Ludo's truncated hoses as parting shots before they became limp and useless in their hands.

As the dust settled, the friends were able to get a clear view of Billet. He was much as they had first seen him in the picture, except that now he stood on two giant bare feet that seemed to be attached to his great head without the aid of very much in the way of legs in between. Strangely, he had no arms, and much of his exterior was battered and in need of redecoration.

"That showed 'em! That showed 'em good," roared Billet. Then, noticing his smoldering thatch for the first time, "Cripes! Me hair!"

While the house was complaining loudly to anyone who would listen, Swivel led the two friends in through a postern door in Billet's heel and guided them up innumerable stairs.

"It's much bigger in here than it looks from outside," observed Wren.

"That's because Billet is a figment. Each part can be any size his creator imagines," explained Swivel.

As they ascended, they passed many doors that opened on to all kinds of rooms. One or two were secured with formidable locks. Near the bottom they passed a dark, smelly chamber that seemed to be full of fat pipes and drains.

"Poo! What's in there?" asked Ludo.

Swivel explained. "Just as Billet has a more or less human countenance—"

"Rather less than more, if you ask me," interrupted Ludo.

"—so his interior has many functions that also equate to the human body. Here, near the bottom—"

"Thank you, Swivel. We get the picture," said Wren.

As they mounted higher they passed a kitchen and several well-stocked storerooms.

"Stomach?"

"Just so, miss."

"And this must be the studio," said Ludo as they climbed higher. They looked in on a lofty room lit by the two tall windows of Billet's eyes, with a splendid view of the Mirrorscape beyond. The contents were in total disarray.

At the very top, and out of breath, they came to a paneled, book-lined library. Many of the books lay scattered on the polished floor and a tall library ladder had toppled over. Amid this mess, sitting in a comfortable leather armchair, was the master. His skullcap was askew and he was consulting a large book open on a low lectern before him.

The butler gave his habitual polite cough and the master looked up. His pale face was smudged and his beard was singed. "Ah, Swivel, there you are. Where've you been? I could have used your help a while ago. I was just consulting my atlas of the Mirrorscape, trying to find exactly where we've got to. We've come far off the beaten track. There's a long way to go before we can get back out into the mansion." He removed his reading spectacles and looked up. "And we have guests. Young Cleef, isn't it?"

"Yes, Master."

"And?

"Wren, Master. I work in your kitchen."

"Upon my word. Now, what are you two doing here? And where's your friend Womper? But forgive me, I'm forgetting myself. You must be exhausted after the fracas. Swivel, tea for my guests."

As they sat in the library sipping tea, Ludo and Wren recounted the arrest of Dirk Tot, the ransacking of the mansion, and their journey through the Mirrorscape searching for the master. As they spoke, they watched Ambrosius Blenk's face darken. He twirled his long beard round and round in his fingers and fixed them with his piercing blue eyes.

"The impudence of Brool! This explains why Spute and his men have been preventing me from returning. With me out of the way there's no one to stop the Fifth Mystery from doing as it pleases." Then his expression lightened. "That sounds like quite an adventure you've had. Dirk Tot and I suspected that young Womper might know a little. Now I see that he knows rather a lot."

"Excuse me, Master, but Mel's sure that Dirk Tot is working for the Fifth Mystery."

The master began to laugh but stopped himself. "Young lady, nothing could be further from the truth. Believe me."

"But he saw him meeting with some Mystery men—when he was coming to Vlam."

Ambrosius Blenk smiled. "Did he now? Or did he just see my steward with some men in red? The kind of red you get mining cinnabar?"

Wren and Ludo looked at each other, the light of realization in their eyes.

"Now, does anyone else know about the Mirrorscape—besides the High-Bailiff and his men?"

"There are the colored men, the fugitives," answered Wren. "They do."

"The colored men, you say?" The master grunted. "So you've met them, have you? They've more reason than most to hate the Mysteries. Anyone else?"

"I don't think so, Master."

Ludo looked down at his feet and shook his head.

"Very well. That still doesn't tell us how the Fifth Mystery managed to get into the Mirrorscape in the first place." He twiddled his beard and thought some more. The only sound was the rhythmic sighing of the ventilation that sent fresh air around the room from an ornate brass grille set low in the wall. Somewhere below, the sound of Swivel tidying up drifted towards them. Then the master clapped his hands and rubbed them together. "All right, there's much to be done. We must get back home as quickly as possible and see about freeing Dirk Tot. The confounded nerve of the Mystery to ransack my mansion like that!"

"But what about Mel? We can't leave him here," said Wren.

"Quite right, young lady. We really ought to find young Womper and take him with us. I can't have my apprentices going astray now, can I? You say you lost him in the Mine of Inspiration?"

Wren nodded. "We don't even know if he's . . ." She couldn't complete the sentence.

"If only I'd thought to bring my omniscope with me."

"It's here. We have it," said Wren.

Ludo produced it from the satchel and handed it to the master.

"My word. Thank you. How very prescient of you." The master stroked the contraption fondly. "Let me explain a little about the omniscope. Do you know that each of these knobs and sliders along its length operates one of its many functions? This one, for instance, enlarges the subject and—"

"Please, sir, we know all about the omniscope. It helped us get here. But I—"

"I'll thank you not to interrupt me, young lady!"

Wren blushed.

"Now." The master paused and stared hard at the youngsters. "Now, I'm sure you don't know *all* about the omniscope. You may have fathomed that this wondrous instrument can enlarge things, can illuminate things, can see through things, and can even indicate a desired direction, but there's one function that I'm sure you have *not* discovered. As well as perform all of these undoubtedly useful services, it can also peer some distance into the future. Make it appear a little closer, as it were."

"You mean we can use it to see if Mel's all right—or going to be all right?" Wren's face shone with renewed hope.

"In a manner of speaking, yes. But first we need to know where to look. Come over here." Wren and Ludo followed Ambrosius Blenk to a dormer window in the corner of the library. "Before anything else, this needs to be reset. There, that should do it." Attaching the omniscope to a heavy brass tripod, the master bent and put his eye to it and turned what the friends now knew to be the direction-finding knob. "Are you sure you wish to see this? It may tell us something we don't want to know. Once something's been seen it can't be unseen."

Wren and Ludo looked at each other. They looked back at the master and nodded.

"Very well." He put his eye to the omniscope again. Suddenly the color drained from his face. "Oh dear. This is much worse than I feared; much, much worse."

27. the world turned upside down

A WARM BREEZE blew softly across Mel's face, lifting the hair off his forehead and waking him ever so gently. It carried a familiar scent, comforting and evocative; the smell of home. He stirred. He did not want to open his eyes, not while he was enjoying the delicious floating feeling. The sunshine felt so good, but he knew he had slept too long. He lay there listening to the birds singing and the insects buzzing in the grass. But he must be getting home. His parents would be wondering where he had got to. He slowly opened his eyes. Such a blue, blue sky. The clouds could almost be angels smiling down on him.

Mel sat up and his head reeled—he had certainly slept too long. The world swayed as he got to his feet, and he needed to brace against a tree to steady himself. After a moment he felt better, but there was something nagging at the back of his mind. But that could wait until later. *This must be what heaven's like*. The thought brought a smile to his lips. He looked around, oriented himself with the spire of the fane, and set off for home. He passed through a glade dappled with sunlight and stopped to pick some bluebells for his mother. Such big and succulent flowers and every one of them perfect. She would be delighted and he could draw them later.

When he reached the fane he turned left and took the familiar path for home. But after he had gone a short way he found himself out in the fields again. And such fields! Acre upon acre of blue-flowered flax, lush and heavy, stretched away to the flat horizon. It would be a bumper crop this year and no mistake. He turned and retraced his steps and continued past the fane. *How odd!* The way home lay to the right. He had certainly befuddled his brain with too much sleep to have made a silly mistake like that. *Why did I take the left-hand path?*

He skirted Kop, passing the back of the houses. Someone was drawing water from a well and he waved, but his greeting was not returned. He passed another house and saw someone at an upstairs window. He looked harder but could not recognize them. He had not heard of strangers in the village. Could it be someone visiting from Bols? He would have to ask his mother when he got in.

He saw his cottage bathed in an ethereal light, with no harsh shadows anywhere. Two stories tall, with carving around the gables, and a weaving shed at the bottom of the garden. *When had Dad added that?* He tried to remember but his head ached so. He approached down the well-tended road and swung open the gate. Mel entered through the front door and went down the corridor to the kitchen.

His mother looked up from preparing food in her well-cut tabby dress. "Hello, Mel. Are those bluebells for me? You are a thoughtful lad. Just leave them there. How was your day?"

"Oh, fine, except that I . . ."

"Yes?"

"I . . ." He shook his head to clear it but without success. "Oh, nothing. Where's Dad?"

"He's still weaving in the shed but he'll be up in a minute. It's nearly suppertime. You've time to go up to your room and change." She smiled at her son and pushed a lock of hair behind her ear with a ringed hand.

Mel smiled back uncertainly, noting that his mother had taken to wearing makeup a little too heavily applied. He climbed the stairs, but when he came to the landing he could not remember which his room was. *How could I forget something like that?* He pushed open the first door he came to and saw all his drawings pinned up around his bed. *Of course—this is my room.* He went in and looked round. It was all strangely unfamiliar. Then he caught sight of himself in the mirror. The mirror? Nothing looked out of the ordinary as he studied himself. His white hose and blue doublet looked dusty but apart from that . . . what? He went closer and, on a whim, breathed on the glass and idly drew a knotlike design with his finger in the misty condensation. *Why does the mist remind me of something?*

He looked at his reflection. What was that on his forehead? He touched a scab of dried blood and traced it up into the matted hair on his scalp. No wonder he was feeling groggy. He felt a wound there, still bleeding, and suddenly pain exploded through his skull. For an instant a great rush of thoughts dashed unbidden through his brain. He saw a studio full of boys dressed just like him and the floor covered with spots of paint. There was a boy smiling at him and a girl with auburn hair. Then it was gone.

"Mel! Supper's ready." His mother called up the stairs.

When he entered the dining room, his parents were already seated, and he said hello to his father. Willem smiled back at his son and then stood and began to carve the roast chicken while his mother served the vegetables. He could not remember his mother cooking chicken before and he wondered what it tasted like. He was disappointed; it was completely tasteless. He could have been eating warm cardboard. After the meal was finished and his parents had drunk the last of their wine, his father leaned back in his chair. Strange that they had not mentioned the wound on his scalp. Mel felt confused.

"Mel, there's something I need you to do urgently." His father's voice was oddly distant.

"Yes, Dad, of course."

"You must take this message to Dan Feen. He lives in the old house beyond the fane. Go straight there, as fast as you can. Will you do that for me, Mel?" He handed his son a folded piece of parchment sealed with red wax and the Womper crest.

"Old house? Dan Feen?" His head hurt.

"He's new to the village, sweetheart, but he buys lots of your father's cloth," said his mother. "He's become our best customer. Hurry along now. That letter won't deliver itself."

Mel walked out of the house in the direction of the fane. As he approached, he heard another familiar voice.

"Mel, my boy. Where are you off to in such a hurry?" Fa Theum emerged from the doorway. It was almost as if he had been waiting for him.

"Hello, Fa. I have to deliver this message for my dad. It's very urgent."

"If you'll slow down a bit, I'll come with you."

The pair walked on in silence for a way before Fa Theum spoke again. "So, Mel, what have you been doing lately?"

"I've been . . . I've been . . . I can't remember, Fa."

"Never mind. You've probably been up to no good. It's best I don't know."

"It's just that I . . ." Mel touched the bump on his head again. More pain, accompanied by a confusing flood of images. Men in red robes and jars full of bright colors. And something else. There was . . .

"What, Mel?"

"I don't know. Nothing really. It's just that I don't recognize where we are."

"Don't worry your head about that, my son. Dan Feen lives this way."

"How did you know I'm going to Dan Feen's?"

Fa Theum did not answer.

Mel looked around and saw that the landscape had changed completely, as if in a dream. The expansive flatness of Feg had been replaced by steep-sided hills covered with bare trees. Had they really come so far, so soon? Down the valley echoed the haunting song of a whale, answered by others from farther away.

Ahead of them lay a bridge across a broad stream. As they were crossing, Mel looked to his right and saw a silvery pike perched on the branch of a riverbank tree. It was such a peculiar tree. As if it had been uprooted and stuck back into the ground upside down. It looked like the roots had become its branches. Roots? What is it about roots? Was it a dream he had? He watched as the fish dived from the branch into the swift-flowing stream, only to emerge a moment later clutching a struggling blackbird in its jaws and regain its perch. Why did it seem so odd?

"Penny for them, Mel?"

"What, Fa?"

"Wool-gathering again?"

"Doesn't it seem strange to you that . . ."

"What, Mel?"

"That fish back there . . ." He looked up at the wise old face of the priest. "Fa, is this heaven?"

The priest smiled down at Mel but said nothing.

The lane led on until it joined a broad road. Mel and Fa Theum turned left and continued on their way. There was a noise to their left and a small flock of lobsters scuttled out from beneath a hedgerow.

At the sound of running feet behind, Mel turned. Coming down the highway towards them was a brightly colored cart drawn by six dapple-gray men. The horse driving the vehicle raised its beribboned hat and shouted a friendly "Good day" as he passed. Fa Theum waved and Mel, feeling as if he was doing something wrong, did the same.

"Well, would you believe it? Here's a fog bank. What is the world coming to? Such strange weather here lately. You know, Mel, I have a secret charm, taught to me by the Maven himself. It's a charm for dispelling fog. Would you like to try it for me? Here, take this piece of paper. On it is a charm that you must draw in the air. That way the fog will vanish."

Mel stared at the symbol. It looked like his doodle on the mirror. It made him think of so many strange things. Of houses that looked like people, of underground clocks, of volcanoes and faces that appeared out of walls. Things he would rather not think about. He handed the paper back. "Please, Fa, I don't like this. I feel unwell."

"Go on, Mel. Do it for me."

Mel put his hand to his bump again. It was coming; the thing he was supposed to remember.

"Come on, Mel. Do as Fa Theum asks." It was his father's voice.

Mel turned, and his parents were standing right behind him. "Dad, Mum, how did you get here?"

"Mel, be a good boy," said his mother. "We followed you to make sure you delivered the letter. It's very important. Draw the symbol and make the fog go away. Go on."

Mel felt confused. His head hurt. He raised his hand again and touched the painful bump. Pain, bright lights and it all came flooding back like the sudden unblocking of a drain. The drain full of inspiration!

Mel had been clinging to the grille just out of reach of the face in the mine when the debris from the scrap heap had exploded into the drain in front of him. He barely had time to leap into the depression the face had smashed in the wall. He had curled up tight inside as the thundering wall of rubbish hurtled past, hurting his ears and making them pop. It seemed to go on for ages until the flow eased and then came to a stop. When he peered out of the hollow, a tardy item of inspirational junk—an enormous amoeba whose sticky mass had slowed its descent—had struck him from behind with a wet *thwack*. He was propelled out of the drain, over the outflow of debris, and into the Mirrorscape beyond, smacking his head hard against the trunk of a tree.

"Mel! Do as you're told," his father barked.

"*No!*"

"Don't speak to your father in that tone," said his mother sharply. Then in a pleading tone, "Please, sweetheart. Do it for me. There's a good boy."

"No, I won't. This is all wrong." He looked closer at his parents, so familiar and yet so strange. His senses came alive and he saw that his father's face was the same but his clothes fitted too well. And his mother's complexion was too florid. He studied her hair, searching for the strands of gray he had noticed as he fled Kop with Dirk Tot. There were none. And the jewelery. She never wore jewelery, for the simple reason she had none.

"Come on, Mel," said Fa Theum. "Behave yourself and do as your parents command." There was subdued anger and threat in his voice.

"You're not real. None of you are real. This is all wrong. What's going on?" Mel looked around, increasingly desperate. He had been here before—or, at least, seen it somewhere. Then it came to him. It was the painting he had seen with Ludo and Wren in the House of Mysteries! "This is *The World Turned Upside Down!*"

"Mel, my son, you're talking nonsense," said Fa Theum. "You're not well. Just make the sign and deliver the letter."

Mel looked at the letter in his hand. The Wompers did not have a seal. None of his family could read or write. He broke the seal and tore open the letter. It was blank. He looked at his parents but their faces were expressionless.

"Mel, that's enough of your tomfoolery. You're to go through the fog this instant," ordered Fa Theum. When Mel did not move he grabbed him by the wrists. "You're going through there even if I have to drag you."

Mel struggled in the old priest's grasp, which was surprisingly strong. He got one hand free and grabbed the dangling diaglyph, yanking it downwards. The corner of it caught the priest's habit and tore a broad, diagonal rip across his chest—his bare canvas chest. "*None* of this is real!" Mel kicked the apparition in the shin and struggled free.

The phantom that was supposed to be his father made a grab for him, but Mel pushed him away. He felt sticky. He looked at his hands. They were smeared with wet, tabby-colored paint and he could see raw canvas on his father's chest. Mel began running back the way he had come.

"Where do you think you're going, Smell?"

Groot, Bunt, and Jurgis were standing across the road, barring his escape. They were dressed in the scarlet robes of the Fifth Mystery and their freshly shaved heads bore the distinctive tonsure.

Mel stopped. *I see it all now. I need to pass through the wall of mist to escape after all. That would take me back to the octagonal chamber in the House of Mysteries. Then, all I have to do is unlock the picture with the pyramid and the temporal maze—and I will be able to follow Wren, Ludo, and Swivel. They could be waiting for me there now.*

"What did you think of my depiction of a Fegish village, Smell? I just painted the most sordid hole I could imagine. And how about your skegging parents? Pretty good, eh?" asked Groot.

"It was pathetic. Poor observation and sloppy technique. A classic Groot."

"It fooled you easily enough, Smell. Or else you wouldn't be here. And where do you suppose I got my models from?"

Mel felt a sickening feeling in his stomach. Groot's sloppy depiction of Kop would not have fooled him if he had not been so groggy. His dazed mind had done as much of the work as Groot. But the portraits of his parents and Fa Theum were too good. They could only have been painted from life. Suddenly he felt icy cold. The thought of his mother and father and Fa Theum at the mercy of Adolfus Spute and Mumchance seemed almost too horrible to contemplate. The blood drained from his face and he swallowed hard.

"Look at his face, Bunt. He's only just worked it out."

"Where are they?" Mel's voice trembled as he asked the question.

"Wouldn't you like to know. Let's just say that my uncle Adolfus is looking after them. Isn't that kind of him? So what do you think of my technique now, Smell? It was easily good enough to fool you."

It was true. There must be something else going on here, otherwise he would have seen through Groot's shoddy work sooner. Then he remembered what Green had told him: *You can't stay in the Mirrorscape too long before it gets to you. It starts with your body but it soon gets to work on your mind.* The image of Kop must have been formed as much in his own mind as by Groot's brushwork.

"So when did you join the Fifth Mystery?"

"Oh, I've always been a member, Smell. It's a family tradition. They like to keep an eye on everything, especially where color's concerned."

"What tradition? Treachery?"

"I've had as much as I can take of you, you little scrot. And now I have more important things to do."

"Like what? More second-rate paintings?" Mel glanced to one side as a flock of startled octopuses took to the air.

"Like take over old Blenko's studio. That and everything that goes with it."

Out of the corner of his eye, Mel tracked the octopuses as they flew towards him, their soft bodies expanding and contracting as they pulsed through the air. He stooped and picked up a rock.

"Throwing stones, Smell? That's a child's weapon. It's no match for a knife. Especially not for six knives."

"I only count three of you, Groot."

"Count again. Look behind you."

Mel shot a glance over his shoulder. The images of his father, his mother, and Fa Theum were also wielding knives and advancing towards him. Mel flung his rock at the lead octopus. It landed with a rubbery thud on its soft body. The octopus's blue-green spots flashed a fiery red in warning as it dived, infuriated, towards its attacker. Mel turned and ran towards the wall of mist.

Several of the mollusks descended on Groot, Bunt, and Jurgis like fleshy umbrellas. Jurgis screamed and hacked with his knife at a tentacle clinging to his face. It fell away, revealing a livid pattern of circles. Mel dived flat on the ground just as the lead octopus attacked. The flying creature swooped over his head and collided heavily with the image of Mel's father. A dense cloud of ink filled the air like smoke, masking Mel as he ran headlong. He made the mirrormark in the air as he leaped at the shimmering mist. But something was different. The air seemed as thick as porridge and he seemed to move through it in slow motion. It felt as if invisible hands were tugging him back. He hung there for several moments. Then the resistance faded and he was through.

But the painting was no longer hanging on the wall in the octagonal room in the House of Mysteries. It had been moved. It was now propped on the window ledge high above Vlam, and it was facing outwards. Almost as soon as Mel emerged he realized he had made a terrible mistake. His back foot was on the window sill, but his front foot and all of his weight was resting on . . . nothing! *Oh, no! I walked right into a trap!* He pitched forward and began to fall down towards the city far below. He was back in the real world; back in Nem. There was no topsy-turvy mirror-logic to save him now. There was just thin air and gravity pulling him down to certain death.

28. the garden at the end of days

WREN APPROACHED THE omniscope, afraid of what she would see. Her hand trembled as she put her eye to the instrument. It only took a moment for her to take in the vertiginous scene. She drew in her breath sharply and took a step backwards. She looked at the master and Ludo. A great, desperate sob escaped her throat.

"That's quite enough of that, young lady. Tears never solved anything."

The master's words checked her and she fell silent.

Ludo came forward and looked through the omniscope. He put his fist to his mouth and uttered a stifled cry. "This wasn't meant to happen." He sat down hard on the floor, his head in his hands. "What've I done?"

Wren looked confused. "What're you talking about?"

"No one's done anything," said the master. "What you saw *hasn't* happened. But it will if we don't do something to prevent it. The important thing is, I recognize where Womper is."

"You mean that we can still save Mel?" Wren sniffed loudly.

"We can certainly try. You must have noticed something about the way time flows in the Mirrorscape."

"It's frozen," said Wren.

"That's not entirely true but time does flow at a different rate relative to Nem—in most places, that is. We can make use of that."

The master crossed to a bunch of flexible speaking tubes in a labeled rack on the wall. He selected one, unplugged the stopper, and spoke into it. "Billet, we must be off. Take us in the direction of *The World Turned Upside Down*." He put it to his ear to hear the reply. "What? I don't care how sore your feet are. You can rest them later." He listen again as Billet responded. The master sighed. "Billet, I'm not about to argue with you. Will you do as you're told?" The speaking tube went back to his ear. "And the same to you!" He slammed it back on its rack. "What nerve! Why does he have to argue about everything? The next time I'll create a more compliant residence."

Wren smiled. "Still, he is rather good when it comes to the rough stuff."

"I don't know where he gets it from. It certainly doesn't come from me. Now, you two are going to need all your wits for what I have in mind," the master said as Billet set off.

"What do you want us to do?" said Ludo.

The master ran his hand along the shelves and pulled out a large catalog of paintings bound in deep red leather. "Now come here and look at this."

The master explained his plan and then insisted they rehearse it. But however many times they repeated it Ambrosius Blenk was never satisfied.

"Oh dear," he said, shaking his head, "it's not going to work. You're just never going to be able to move fast enough. There's simply not enough time." He chewed his fingernail in frustration.

"But there must be some way we can get it to work," said Ludo.

"The regulator!" exclaimed Wren. She retrieved the hairy object from the satchel.

"Where did you get that?"

"I kind of found it."

"Did you now? You weren't thinking of taking this back as a souvenir." The master shook his gray head. "What belongs in the Mirrorscape must remain in the Mirrorscape. You can't imagine the trouble you could cause if anything ever got out."

Ludo and Wren exchanged a glance. They knew only too well.

The master looked at the regulator again. "Swivel! Ah, there you are. I'll need you to help us with this."

The rehearsal recommenced, now with three participants, and it soon became apparent that it might work.

"Now, have you got this straight?" asked the master.

"We're to wait by the wall of mist until you give the signal," said Wren.

"Once we cross back into Nem coordination will be lost," said Ludo, "so we must wait for you to tell us the plan's working before we go into the picture."

"Good," said the master. "If we get the timing right—precisely right—we might just get Womper out of this fix."

"We are approaching *The World Turned Upside Down*," said Swivel. "If you'll excuse me, I'll go downstairs and prepare."

Presently, the house stopped moving and one of the speaking tubes whistled for the master's attention.

"Very well, Swivel. You know what's to be done. Good luck." The master replaced the tube and selected another. He unplugged it and spoke into it. "Billet, you're to take us to *The Garden at the End of Days*—as quickly as you can. Lucas Flink will not mind in the least if we briefly trespass in his garden for a worthy cause."

Wren and Ludo could hear the curses issuing from the tube. They learned several new words in the space of just a few seconds.

"Just do it!" Red in the face, Ambrosius Blenk hung up the speaking tube and took several deep breaths to calm himself.

The butler slipped through the small door in Billet's heel and closed it behind himself. He climbed high into the roots of one of the strange, upside-down trees next to a bridge over a stream. A shoal of fish chirped above him and a fane stood balanced on its steeple in the distance. Swivel settled himself and watched as Billet disappeared in a new direction before he turned his attention back to the Mirrorscape below him and waited.

And waited.

And waited.

Little by little, his watchful face began to slip down back into his head. Then, with a soft click it disappeared altogether, to be replaced by one with closed eyes and an open, gently snoring mouth.

Wren and Ludo stood in the library window watching the Mirrorscape fly by through the leaded panes as Billet strode towards their destination.

"Ludo, what did you mean back there when you said, 'What've I done?'"

Ludo turned away from the window and stared at his feet. "Oh, it's just that I feel responsible . . . for . . . for Mel falling out of the excavator like that. If I'd been quicker, I could have grabbed him."

"Are you sure that's all?" Wren touched his arm. "Why won't you look at me?"

"Wren, please don't . . ."

"Come on, you two," said the master. "This is not the time for idle gossip. We're almost there."

~

Swivel's watchful face sprang back into place with a sharp jolt. Approaching over the bridge was Mel with an elderly priest. When they had passed Swivel's tree, he climbed down and followed them. At one point he disturbed a small group of lobsters that had been feeding, and he froze as they scuttled away under the hedgerow and across the dusty road in front of Mel and the old man. To his relief he saw that their attention had been distracted by a cart driven by a horse in charge of a team of dapple-gray men. When Swivel felt it was safe, he continued to follow them. Presently, they came to the wall of mist that the master had explained to him led to a chamber high in the House of Mysteries. A couple of tabby-clad peasants came up unseen behind Mel and the Fa. Then some kind of argument broke out between them and Mel. Mel turned and ran back in the direction they had come from. This was not part of the plan! He was supposed to go through the wall of mist. This would ruin everything!

Swivel set off in pursuit, shielded by a hedgerow, through which he caught a fleeting glimpse of three members of the Fifth Mystery. What was he to do? He had to get Mel running back towards the wall of mist. Distracted, he disturbed a nest of grass-green octopuses. The frightened mollusks instantly shed their camouflage, ejected a cloud of ink, and rose angrily into the air. He waited for a moment and then parted the hedge, just in time to see Mel throw a rock at the lead octopus. *Good thinking, young sir.* In the ensuing confusion, Mel turned on his heels and began to sprint towards the wall of mist.

Now was the time. Swivel withdrew the regulator from his doublet and planted it in the ground, willing it to take root. Then, with relief, he saw slender tendrils emerge from the side and burrow down into the soil. When he felt the rapidly growing roots were established, he took hold of the regulating lever and tugged it towards the minus end of the scale.

For a moment, the fishes ceased singing in the trees and the scudding clouds halted in their tracks. The next time Swivel looked, Mel had vanished.

Ambrosius Blenk stared hard at the ornate clock on the library wall. "Come on, come on. Can't you say anything except tick and tock?" He listened for a moment. "Obviously not. Come on, Swivel. Do your stuff. Plant the regulator and slow down time." He peered out of the window at Wren and Ludo far below, waiting impatiently in front of the wall of mist in *The Garden at the End of Days*. He looked at the clock again. "It's not going to work. I've miscalculated. By now, Womper will be decorating the rooftops of Vlam. Shut up, you old pessimist. Of course it's going to work!" He looked again at the clock. The pendulum was definitely slowing down. Slower and slower . . . and then it stopped! He leaned out of the window, his megaphone already at his lips. *"Now!"*

"Come on, Ludo! Just like we rehearsed," said Wren.

Ludo made the mirrormark but in his haste fumbled it. "Scrot, it's not working!"

"Here, let me try." Wren concentrated, then traced the mirrormark in the air—and they were through.

"There's *The Garden at the End of Days*. Help me unhook it from the wall," said Wren.

"Ooofff! No one said how heavy it'd be."

They staggered backwards, almost overbalancing, as the canvas came free.

"Careful! Don't drop it. Have you got it?"

Wren nodded. "Let's get it up on to the window sill. *Heave!"*

They struggled to lift the upright painting on to the sill.

"It's stuck! The window's too small!"

"What now?" Wren shoved the canvas harder.

"Stop. You'll wedge it. Lean it at an angle. So it's diagonal to the window frame."

It *just* went through, scraping some of the gilding from the frame in the process. Once through, there was enough room on the sill for it to be laid flat, picture-side up. The friends clambered on to it and their weight held it in place jutting out over the void.

"We've done it! We've done it!" crowed Ludo.

"I've just thought . . . ," said Wren, turning serious. "What if Mel doesn't realize what's going on and hits the surface without making the mirrormark? His weight will catapult us out into the air and—"

"—we'll *all* die."

The rushing air tore at Mel and roared in his ears as he fell. As the rooftops of Vlam raced up to meet him, he thought of his parents and, briefly, of his friends. Then he started to hallucinate. He saw a wonderful garden appear below him. Tiny at first, it grew rapidly as he rushed to meet it. Perhaps it really was heaven this time. But this vision of heaven had a great house in it shaped like a human head. *Billet!* In an instant, he understood what it was. He just had time to form the Mirrormark in the air before he tumbled head over heels into the garden inside the Mirrorscape. He picked himself up from between the giant feet of Billet, laughing hysterically.

Wren and Ludo were not launched into the air. The blur that was Mel fell into the picture as smoothly as if he were diving into water.

"He did it. Mel did it!" shouted Ludo. "Come on, let's go."

"Not yet, Ludo. We must stay put. The plan—remember?"

A few moments later, another blur—Swivel—fell into the canvas without a splash.

"Now!"

Wren and Ludo hauled the huge canvas back into place. Wren made the mirrormark once more and the gallery was empty. Only an eddy of dust motes swirling in the still air and a glint of gold on the window frame betrayed that anyone had been there.

"Come on. Get inside, the four of you," called the master from the library window. "And *do* stop giggling. You can congratulate yourselves later. We must be getting back home without delay."

"Mel, we're so glad to see you again. We thought we'd lost you for good."

"Me, too, Wren. When I saw the funny-looking house in the picture I couldn't believe my eyes."

The friends reached the top of the stairs and burst into the library.

"Well, Womper, I'm glad to see you back safe and sound and all in one piece. Your friends have been to a great deal of trouble to get you back. And now—"

The master was interrupted by a shrill whistle from outside. Everyone crowded round the window. Far below them stood Mumchance.

"What's *he* doing here?" said Mel.

"What's that he's waving?" asked Ludo.

"It looks like a white flag," said Wren.

The master's face bore a puzzled expression. "I do believe he wants a truce."

29. the crystal bridge

SWIVEL CLEARED HIS throat and read aloud from the scroll the dwarf had presented. "To Ambrosius Blenk, artist and master, greetings. Let it be known that I, Lucas Flink, artist and master, late of the city of Vlam in the land of Nem, Lord of the Mirrorscape and proprietor of *The Garden at the End of Days*, do hereby challenge you to a duel."

The master almost choked. "*A duel!* What's the man talking about. He's my oldest and dearest friend. Go on, Swivel."

"The reason for this said duel being that Ambrosius Blenk has given shelter and succor to the enemies of our gracious friends the Fifth Mystery, whose faithful service and magnanimity we greatly respect. These felons include, but are not limited to, one Dirk Tot, steward and counterfeiter, and one Melkin Womper, apprentice and thief."

All eyes in the room fixed on Mel. He shifted uncomfortably from foot to foot.

"Moreover, Ambrosius Blenk has also permitted his residence, known as the Mansion, located in the city of Vlam, to be used for the preparation of and dissemination of substances injurious to the benefices of the aforementioned Mystery. Namely, counterfeit pigments of a most inferior quality. This duel to take place forthwith, with weapons to be mutually agreed."

Mel laughed nervously. "It's a joke, right? Lucas Flink's been dead for two hundred years." He glanced at Ludo, who nodded.

"Dead? Now there's an interesting concept, Womper. In fact, he's as alive and well as you and me here in the Mirrorscape. You see, great artists never really die. They live on forever in their work. *The Garden at the End of Days* is Lucas's retirement home, in a manner of speaking."

"So it's not a joke."

"No, Womper, it's no joke. Lucas would never make light of a thing like this. One thing's for certain, though: he didn't write that overblown piffle of a challenge. Come on, Swivel, let's go and get to the bottom of this."

"Sir? If I may be so bold? A duel requires two seconds."

"Don't you mean a second and a third?"

"Two *seconds*, sir," repeated the pedantic butler. "Protocol demands it."

"All right. One of you must come with us. Not you, Womper, there's a price on your head. Nor you, young lady, I think. Cleef, you'd better accompany us."

"*Me?* A duel sounds dangerous. Please don't make me go."

"There's not going to be any duel; not if I've got anything to say about it. Come on, Cleef! The sooner we get this over with, the sooner we can get back to my mansion."

"Go on, Ludo," said Wren. "You helped save Mel. You can do this."

Dragging his heels, Ludo followed the master and Swivel out of Billet, certain the High-Bailiff would give him away.

"Do try and keep up, Cleef," called the master as they marched down a shaded tree-lined avenue.

For a moment Ludo almost forgot his fear as he gazed down on to a beautiful valley tightly enclosed by tall, colored mountains and cliffs etched with terraces. Dozens of sparkling waterfalls cascaded into a circular lake below. The effect was of entire mountainsides embroidered with liquid, silver filigree. Everything in the composition led the eye to Lucas Flink's magnificent house. It stood alone on its own promontory, which jutted out into the lake. The building was made of the purest crystal and took the form of a giant sea anemone. Its many spines flexed gracefully against each other in the breeze, softly chiming like bells. The sunlight that fell on this structure was multiplied by the prismatic walls, and rainbows sprang from them like flying buttresses down to the surface of the lake. Silver-scaled flying fish glided back and forth in their glow.

"Ever the showman, old Lucas," observed the master.

"Indeed, sir, most artfully contrived," agreed the butler.

"Are those what I think they are?" asked Ludo, pointing upwards.

"Certainly. They're angels," said the master as a pair flew overhead. "An artistic conceit, of course, but a nice touch."

As they reached the crystal house, Lucas Flink emerged. With his long, gray beard, Ludo thought he looked like Ambrosius Blenk, although from his deeply lined face he was evidently somewhat older. He was dressed in a gray robe in the high fashion of two centuries ago. Ludo was sure he looked embarrassed. Accompanying him in his scarlet robes was a smirking Adolfus Spute and Mumchance. Ludo tried to make himself as inconspicuous as possible behind his companions.

"Lucas, my old friend," said the master, "what's all this nonsense about a duel?"

Mel and Wren sat cross-legged on the library floor.

"What did that challenge mean when it called you a thief?" asked Wren.

"Does the Fifth Mystery ever need a reason for anything it says or does? They took your father without a reason."

Wren's shoulders slumped. "Yes, they did."

"And now they've got mine as well. And my mother."

"*What?* How do you know?"

Mel told her. "That's why we've got to get back to Nem as soon as possible. I've got to rescue them. But right now something else is worrying me."

"What's that?"

"I've been thinking. First the master's lands in his painting are wrecked to lure him into the Mirrorscape and then he's trapped here. With him out of the way, Dirk Tot is arrested, the mansion ransacked, and the artificial pigments that pose such a threat to the Mystery are seized. Everything the Fifth Mystery's been doing since is to prevent the master from returning to Nem."

"You think they're still trying?"

"Yeah, I do. And another thing. The master's been in the Mirrorscape ages and he hasn't got sick. The mistress said that while he's in a part that's created by his own hand, he's protected."

"And now, he's been lured outside. Into Lucas Flink's bit of the Mirrorscape—where he can get sick if he stays too long."

They both said it at once: "It's a trap!"

Mel and Wren crouched behind the trees at the end of the avenue and peered down into the valley. Below them Ambrosius Blenk spoke with Lucas Flink, while the High-Bailiff and Mumchance stood to one side. If there was a trap Mel could not see where it was coming from. Then they saw Adolfus Spute bend his tall frame and whisper something to Mumchance. The dwarf raised his silver whistle to his lips and blew a long, shrill blast.

For a moment everything was still. Then Mel and Wren saw the mirrorlike surface of the lake begin to shimmer. The faint ripples grew bigger until waves began to lap the shore. Bubbles erupted from the surface and a shape, hung with dripping lake-weed, rose out of the roiling water, an enormous tortoiselike contraption on long spider legs billowing filthy black smoke from its funnels and polluting the unspoiled air. It stalked towards the shore.

"It *is* a trap!" said Mel.

"It's a machine like the ones that attacked Billet," said Wren. "They must have cobbled it together from the leftovers of those we destroyed."

From the space where the tortoise-monster's head had been, a watertight door squealed open and a gangplank emerged that thudded down on the shore. From the body of the machine ran a score of scarlet-clad men-at-arms of the Fifth Mystery. They surrounded the two old masters, Ludo, and Swivel, crossbows aimed at their throats.

Wren got to her feet. "Come on. We've got to help them."

Mel grabbed Wren's arm and pulled her back. "No, there're too many of them. Let's stay hidden until we can work out what to do."

"What's going on?" said a strange voice from behind them.

Alarmed, they turned and there, radiating light in the shaded avenue, stood a white-robed angel. From above them came the soft flutter of wings and a second blond-haired angel landed beside its companion, casting its own pool of light.

"Here, let me see," said the second angel.

Wren's mouth was hanging open. "I should be used to the Mirrorscape by now, but *angels*. Are you *really* angels?"

"Of course we are. What did you think we were, shuttlecocks?" said the first.

"There's our master," said the second.

"Lucas Flink?" said Wren.

"Certainly. But who are all those other people?"

"That's *our* master, Ambrosius Blenk—and the funny-looking one's Swivel, his butler," said Mel.

"And the boy's our friend, Ludo. The ones in red are from the Fifth Mystery," added Wren. "And they've taken them all prisoner."

"Why?" asked the angels together.

"Because . . . ," began Mel. "Look, it'd take too long to explain. The important thing is that we need to rescue them. Will you help?"

"Will it involve any . . . you know . . . *devilry*?"

"I'm afraid it will," said Mel.

"In that case, I'm your angel. How about you, Farris?" asked the first angel.

"Count me in, Bathor," answered the second. "I'm always up for a spot of devilry. It's so boring flying around all day looking angelic."

"But what good can just four of us do?" said Wren.

"I've got a plan," said Mel. Turning to Farris and Bathor, he asked, "Tell me, how well can you two fly?"

Adolfus Spute and Mumchance had locked Ludo, Swivel, and the two old masters in a room high in Lucas Flink's crystal house. The crystal was so pure it did not seem to have any walls. Or a ceiling. Or a floor. Ludo could feel the solidity of the building beneath his feet but his eyes told him he was standing in midair. It made him feel very queasy. The room had a panoramic view of the lake, and if he looked down he could see the men-at-arms milling about on the shore.

Ludo saw the High-Bailiff and Mumchance as they clumsily ascended what must be a staircase. They kept missing their footing and bumping into things.

Adolfus Spute's going to give me away. Ludo looked around. *Where is there to hide in a crystal house?*

"*Now* do you see that you've been misled?" said the master, attempting to convince his old friend that he had been the victim of a cruel deception.

Lucas Flink shook his head. "But surely there's some mistake, Ambrosius. The Mysteries are a force for good."

"Your view of them is over two hundred years old. Since your day they have become corrupt."

"But they say it's *you* who's become corrupt. The High-Bailiff assured me he had evidence that you'd been fabricating synthetic pigment in your household. Is this true?"

"Yes, Lucas, it is. We've been making pigment that ordinary people can afford. Color belongs to everyone, not just a few. In your time everyone could afford color in their lives but now the price of the Mystery's Pleasures has become exorbitant."

"Pleasures?"

"So Adolfus Spute forgot to tell you about those, did he? Well, Pleasures are—"

"Pleasures are what make the world go round; my world, that is." The High-Bailiff and Mumchance entered the room. "And this old fool and his half-faced servant have stolen more Pleasures than your feeble brain could possibly imagine."

"How dare you talk to me like that!" said Lucas Flink. "And in my own house."

"Now I have your skeg-bellied friend here, you and your house have served their purpose."

"*Now* do you believe me?" asked the master.

Ludo edged towards the farthest corner of the room.

"Stay where you are, my little stool pigeon," ordered the High-Bailiff. "Trying to fly the coup, were you? Wouldn't you like to stay and sing us another song, Birdie?"

Ludo suddenly felt hot. Beads of perspiration broke out on his brow. He looked about for somewhere to hide. Anywhere. And then he saw it. "*Look!*" he shouted.

Everyone turned. Out over the lake, two angels had begun an aerobatic display. Ludo looked down and saw that all of the Mystery men had seen this, too, and stood transfixed by the spectacle.

"Yours?" asked the master, nodding towards the angels.

"Mine," confirmed Lucas Flink. "Misbehaving again."

"It's *fantastic!*" said Ludo, thankful for the distraction.

Mumchance blew his whistle and pointed to the lakeshore below, where the men-at-arms were jostling each other to get a view of the performance.

"Fools," said Adolfus Spute. "Gawking when they should be plundering. Come with me, Mumchance. We'll soon put an end to these shenanigans. *Ooph!*" He had walked into an unseen wall. It took two more collisions before he succeeded in finding an exit.

Just then, the angels began an especially spectacular series of loops, whirls, and arabesques that elicited gasps of wonder from their audience below.

"Do they often do this?" asked Ludo.

"If ever they get the chance," said Lucas Flink. "Sometimes I wonder why I created them."

"I have the selfsame problem with Billet," said the master.

Ludo's eye was caught by something else. Below them, snaking their way upwards on an invisible staircase towards the rear of the house crept two figures—blue figures! He nudged Swivel.

A smiling face swiveled into place. *Ahem!* Swivel coughed his polite butler's cough.

The masters glanced up and the butler nodded in the direction of the back staircase.

With his finger to his lips, Mel beckoned them silently.

"Womper, how good of you," whispered the master. "You too, young lady."

"Did you put those angels of mine up to this?" asked Lucas Flink.

"I hope you don't mind," said Mel.

"Mind? If I'd been as quick as you, I wouldn't find myself in this pickle. I see now that I've been deceived by the Fifth Mystery. I think we should leave." He led the small party through an invisible door onto the landing. For an instant, Ludo's eyes strayed to the angels' exhibition outside and he slammed hard into a transparent wall and cried out in pain.

"Birdie! *Smell!* Stay where you are, all of you, you lizard-drool!" bellowed Adolfus Spute from below. "*Guards!*"

A loud blast from Mumchance's whistle reinforced the alarm.

"Come along. Walk exactly where I do," ordered Lucas Flink. He led them, single file, through imperceptible doors and along invisible corridors. They saw the building below them fill up with men-at-arms running in from the shore, turning the diamond crystal of the house into the blood-red of a ruby.

"We're trapped," cried Ludo.

"*Now* how do we get out?" said Mel.

"Lucas?" said the master.

"Oh, dear. I was hoping things would never come to this." Lucas Flink removed a gold chain from around his neck. Hanging from it were three small tuning forks. He unthreaded them and knelt on the floor, where he struck the largest fork and stood it upright. Its clear note hung in the air and then the whole structure began to sing in sympathy.

"It sounds like that trick you can do with a wineglass," said Wren.

Mel looked around. "It's coming from everywhere at once."

Lucas Flink then opened an invisible door and stepped through and took a few paces into thin air.

"We must take the crystal bridge to the far side of the lake." So saying, he strode off. "Quickly now. You'll be in no danger just as long as you follow me precisely."

The others edged out cautiously, feeling their way as they went.

"Come along, don't dawdle," called Lucas Flink.

"You heard the man—keep up," said the master as the two artists strode ahead.

Mel, Wren, and Ludo were barely halfway across the lake when they saw Lucas Flink kneel down ahead of them, tap the second of his tuning forks, and set it upright on the bridge. All around, the noise swelled and became discordant as the structure began to vibrate unpleasantly.

Out over the lake where the angels were continuing their aerobatic display, the friends saw a lightning bolt shoot from the tortoise-monster and detonate in the air. As they blinked away the after-image all they saw was a shower of white feathers drifting down to the lake.

"Farris! Bathor!" cried Wren.

Suddenly, there was a sharp tattoo like hailstones hitting a glass roof as crossbow bolts struck the underside of the bridge, leaving star-shaped crazing where they had ricocheted off. Below them the men-at-arms were busy reloading.

"Don't stop," said Ludo. "Keep moving. We're protected by the bridge."

Again there came the blast of a whistle behind them, and Mel turned to see the High-Bailiff and Mumchance edging out on to the crystal bridge. Adolfus Spute smiled broadly and began to stride towards them.

"It's as if they can see the bridge," said Mel.

"They're going to catch us up before we can reach the other side," said Ludo.

"What's that?" said Wren. "It looks like a trail of yellow powder on the bridge. That's how they can see where to step."

"Ludo, it's coming from you," said Mel.

A trickle of powder fell from Ludo's doublet like superfine yellow snow. "It's . . . it's pigment. I, er, thought we might need some. The parcel must have burst when I ran into the wall back there."

Wren looked puzzled. "What's going on, Ludo?"

"Nothing." Ludo's eyes darted from side to side. "Nothing's going on."

"How much have you got?" asked Mel.

"Not much," answered Ludo, producing the crumpled paper parcel. "Please, let's get out of here."

Mel grabbed it. "Come on, follow me." He opened the corner of the parcel and gently threw some before him. "There. We can see where the bridge is now."

They hurried on after Lucas Flink, the master, and Swivel, who had already reached the far side of the lake and were disappearing into one of the caverns in the cliff face. Mumchance's whistle sounded very close behind.

"Come on!" shouted Mel, flinging the parcel aside. "Run for it!" They dashed straight for the opening and ran inside.

"Ah, there you are," said the master.

"If you'll just step up off the bridge," said Lucas Flink. He tapped the last of his tuning forks on a rock and stood it upright on the end of the crystal bridge. The dissonance was now unbearable and the bridge began to shake violently. Great cracks appeared in it. The sound echoing around the cavern was very loud and everyone covered their ears.

Mel looked back and saw that the High-Bailiff and Mumchance were nearly upon them. Then, as the sound reached an ear-splitting climax, the entire bridge shattered into crystal dust. On the far shore, the crystal house imploded. The music stopped abruptly and the two scarlet-clad figures plummeted feet-first into the lake.

Everyone cheered.

They saw Adolfus Spute and Mumchance bob to the surface, spewing water.

"Now I wish I'd stocked my lake with sharks. Come along, follow me." Lucas Flink led them up an irregular flight of steps. The tunnel led deeper under the mountainside. Eventually, they emerged into the light at the far end of the tree-lined avenue. Waiting for them in front of Billet were two very disheveled angels.

"That *was* fun," said Farris.

"Beats being angelic any day," said Bathor, smiling. Their gowns were in shreds. Both had singed hair and eyebrows and their faces were covered in black smuts. There were featherless gaps in their wings and their inner radiance now flickered on and off as if it was short-circuited.

Lucas Flink shook his head. "You needn't think I'm going to paint you all over again."

The angels hung their heads shamefacedly.

"What happened to you two?" asked Wren.

"Direct hit with that lightning gun by the look of it," said Ludo.

"Come along now," said the master. "Let's get back inside Billet and repair his damage."

"The sooner, the better," said Mel. "*Look!*"

30. iconium

A VIVID FLASH of lightning erupted followed by an instantaneous explosion as the tortoise-machine hauled itself up onto the avenue and opened fire on Billet.

"Oh, no!" said the master. "If the studio's been hit, we're really in trouble." Everyone ran to Billet and raced upstairs. The lightning bolt had blown in one of the windows and wrecked the place. He swore under his breath. "This is simply terrible. Every pot of color's been smashed. I was counting on having sufficient materials with which to create something to confront that abomination out there."

"You mean paint something?" said Wren.

"Something that would come alive in the Mirrorscape, like your other creations," added Mel. "But surely that would take time?"

"Too long, perhaps. But it was our only hope," said Ambrosius Blenk. "Now, without any materials . . ." He shrugged.

"So now what do we do?" said Ludo.

"Might I suggest we ponder that while we are on the move?" said Lucas Flink.

"Of course. Quite right. Swivel, a chair for my friend—if you can find one intact." The master navigated the debris and took up a speaking tube. "Billet, I think you should put some distance between us and that infernal contraption out there."

The lightning gun spat again and everyone staggered to maintain their footing as Billet lurched under the impact.

"Surely there must be something we can use amongst all this," suggested Lucas Flink.

"Ludo, did you bring any more pigment?" said Mel.

The master turned to Ludo. "You have some pigment, Cleef?"

Ludo shifted uncomfortably. "It's all gone."

"Pity. There must be *something* we can use. Everyone turn out your pockets onto the table. Let's see what we've got between us." From his own capacious pockets the master produced a small notebook, a pencil stub, a two-headed silver piece, two biscuits, and a jay's feather.

Swivel, Farris, and Bathor had nothing (figments rarely do) but Lucas Flink found a pair of spectacles with one lens missing, a piece of colored glass, a dried seahorse, and a diary two hundred and seven years out of date.

From Wren's pocket came a seashell, a pine cone, a pressed poppy, a small selection of tiny cogs and gears, and a pendant watch with cracked glass on a silver chain. On its tiny face was a double portrait of her parents.

Ludo's haul amounted to a few scraps of crumpled paper, a half-eaten sugared almond covered in fluff, a split pebble with a fossil inside, and a small purse embroidered with his family's coat of arms. From the clunk it made on the tabletop it evidently contained a sum of money.

All the while, Mel became increasingly anxious. *Everyone will know I'm a thief now.*

"What do you have, Womper?" said the master.

Dreading what Wren and Ludo would think of him, Mel laid his bodkin and the little box on the table.

The master picked the box up. "What's this?"

"It's . . . a box. Just a box."

"A rather beautiful one it seems. What's in it?" The master held it to his ear and rattled it gently.

Mel shook his head. "Nothing really."

The master tried to open it. "It's locked. Let's see if I can prize it open with the bodkin."

They have to know sooner or later. "No need. It opens like this." Mel pressed both ends at once and the lid sprang open. Inside, glowing with its own color-shifting iridescence was the strange powder.

The master gasped. "It's not possible! Lucas, is this what I think it is?"

Lucas Flink gazed at the shifting colors. "Where did you get this, young man?"

I found it. It was given to me. I won it. I'm looking after it for a friend. All of these thoughts raced through Mel's mind. What he said was, "I kind of stole it." And, anticipating the next question, "From the High-Bailiff."

The two old masters looked at each other. Then they burst out laughing.

What's so funny? thought Mel.

Wren and Ludo stared at each other, equally confused.

The old men's laughter was the kind that would have carried on for ages if it had not been interrupted by a flash and another lightning strike nearby.

"So that's what 'Melkin Womper, apprentice and thief' meant in that challenge," said Wren.

"I'm sorry," said Mel. "I didn't mean to be a thief."

"I know that," said Wren. "Anyway, I bet Adolfus Spute stole it himself."

"Is someone going to tell us what it is?" said Ludo.

"It's our salvation. That's what it is! Eh, Lucas?"

"Young man, what we have here is iconium." There was a boyish sparkle in Lucas Flink's old eyes. "I have only ever seen it once before—more than two hundred years ago—and never such a large quantity as this."

"It's unbelievably valuable," said the master. "Why, with what's in this box you could buy as many Pleasures as you wished and still have money left over."

"Just think of the devilry we could cause with that." Farris nudged Bathor and their eyes twinkled.

"Many, many years ago," continued Lucas Flink, "when I was no older than you youngsters are now, a meteor fell from the sky near the western shore of Kig. A fragment was retrieved by the Fifth Mystery and it was found to contain this extraordinary pigment. A little more was extracted, but unfortunately the impact of the meteorite made the substrata of the island unstable. It was already fragile, due to the extent of the mining. It triggered a number of earthquakes, which caused great fissures to open up. The meteor was swallowed by one of these and was lost."

"Then the iconium that had been extracted from the meteor also vanished; no one knows where. It's never been seen since." The master tapped the box and watched the play of the shifting iridescence.

"But how did the High-Bailiff get his hands on it?" asked Wren.

"That's a good question, young lady," said the master.

"There doesn't seem to be very much of it," said Ludo.

"'Much' is a relative term, Cleef. 'Much' is probably all there is in the world."

"Yeah, but how's it going to help us?" asked Ludo. "There's nowhere round here where we can sell it."

"Sell it?" said Lucas Flink. "We must *use* it. Iconium has almost miraculous properties. It can—"

"Make pictures all by itself?" said Mel.

"Just so, young man. This apprentice of yours, Ambrosius, has a rare head on his shoulders. Is he as nimble with his hands as he is with his mind?"

"Indeed he is, Lucas. I expect great things from Womper. That is, if we ever manage to get back to Nem." The master smiled at Mel. "I myself have never seen iconium. It is reputed to be highly fugitive. Is that so, Lucas?"

"Yes. It is the most powerful *and* the most fugitive of pigments. Whatever is created with the iconium lasts but a short time— minutes, no more."

"So, Womper, what are we to do with this serendipitous substance?" asked the master.

"Well, we could make our own creations to destroy the tortoise-machine. Using iconium they'd be done in no time at all."

Ambrosius Blenk looked at Lucas Flink and they both smiled. "That's exactly what we would do. Come on, to work—all of you."

"We've stopped moving," said Wren.

Ludo pointed. "No wonder. Look out the window."

Beneath them, and curving away to either side, was an enormous chasm. It had sheer cliffs and was perhaps a mile wide and just as deep. Even though it was full daylight, the sky above the far rim was darkest night seeded with brilliant stars. Deep below, at the bottom of this natural barrier, flowed a glowing river of molten lava.

"Ah, we've reached my moat," said Lucas Flink. "I created it to surround my valley and keep unwelcome guests out. Now it rather looks as if it's keeping us in."

"How do we cross it?" asked the master.

"There's a causeway. Unfortunately, it's behind us, on the far side of the valley. This is regrettable, to say the least, for just over there is my latest addition to the Mirrorscape, *The Empire of Sleep*, the painting I gave to you recently, Ambrosius."

"The one in your studio," said Mel.

"The very same," said the master.

Lucas Flink pointed to the far side of the chasm. "On the other side of the moat is the way back to your mansion."

"Well, maybe Billet can hold the monster off for long enough." The master clapped his hands. "Come on, time's against us. To work!" He carefully removed several blank sheets of paper from his sketchbook and handed them around. "We must take turns with this pencil stub. And be quick. Just lightning sketches."

"Lightning sketches. Very good, Ambrosius. But you can't expect us to work in all this mess."

"Of course not, Lucas. We'll repair to the library. Swivel, why don't you tidy up?"

"Farris, Bathor, lend him a hand," said Lucas Flink.

"Do we *have* to?" said Farris.

"Why can't we do a bit more *devilry*?" said Bathor.

Lucas Flink sighed and rolled his eyes.

Once in the library, everyone in turn made a quick sketch. By the time it was Mel's turn the pencil stub was almost too small to handle.

"Now, let's see what you've come up with," said the master. "Lucas, that's classic." The monster he had conceived was indeed horrible, with massive, hairy arms and razor-sharp horns that extended in front to form a deadly crescent.

"Yours, too, Ambrosius." Lucas Flink stood there, admiring the master's sketch. "It's a giant Pyrexian vampire-orchid, a natural predator of tortoises, if I'm not mistaken. Let's create both. I'd love to see them in action."

"Is that wise with so little iconium? What have the others created? Fine work, Cleef. What exactly is it?"

"I call it a forceposaur, Master. See, it uses its long, pointed jaws to force open the tortoise-monster's shell and expose its soft body inside."

"Very imaginative, Cleef." Turning to Wren, the master said, "I had no idea you could also draw, young lady. This sketch is not unlike the dragon that adorns my clock."

"Yes, Master. I designed it."

"You did? Remarkable. Are you related to Thomas Delf, the clockmaker?"

"He's my father."

"Indeed." The master looked hard at Wren. "Now, what does this dragon of yours do?"

"The usual dragon trick. It breathes fire. But this one bores into the shell with its corkscrew snout and injects the fire. The monster cooks from the inside out."

The master was delighted. "Any one of these inventions would be the equal of that old humpback." Ambrosius Blenk placed them on the table with the others. "Now, what have you come up with, Womper?"

Mel's sketch depicted a bridge. He explained how it was going to work.

"That's great, Mel," said Wren.

"I wish I'd thought of it."

"It doesn't matter who thought of it, Cleef. We now have a way out of our dilemma."

"Two birds with one stone, eh, Ambrosius?" said Lucas Flink.

"I think we're all agreed that this solution is the best. Lucas, as you're the only one here who has experience of the iconium, perhaps you would like to realize young Womper's sketch while we all watch and learn?"

Swivel had salvaged a battered canvas, an easel, some brushes, a palette, and a selection of oils from the wreck of the studio. Farris and Bathor helped him to set them up near the window.

Lucas Flink explained. "To use the iconium one simply mixes it with two media: oil and imagination." He selected a large brush, prepared some iconium, and began to apply it to the canvas in broad strokes. As he worked, he could not suppress a broad grin. The first marks he applied initially looked like nothing more than multicolored smears but as they watched, the blurry stains organized themselves, swirling about the surface of the canvas until they came to rest as a perfect representation of the view through the window.

Wren and Ludo gasped out loud. Even Mel, who had seen the power of the iconium before, felt a great surge of excitement as the image swam into place. Ambrosius Blenk seemed outwardly detached but his hand was trembling.

Farris nudged Bathor. "If we had some of that—"

"Enough of that, you two!" warned Lucas Flink.

As the first marks of Mel's design began to appear, Wren called out, "Look at *this*!"

Through the window they saw the painting becoming real as the first faint outlines of Mel's bridge appeared in the air, soaring out towards the middle of the chasm. As Lucas Flink continued, they saw the outlines fill in and the great bridge begin to take shape. Impossibly tall piers rose from the depths of the moat to support the wide spans. Along its length, colorful towers and graceful arches sprang into existence, interspersed with tall statues. Banners fluttered from pinnacles and the surface of the roadway was patterned with bright mosaics featuring giant serpents that intertwined with each other. The entire bridge looked, and indeed was, magical.

Billet shook with the impact of another lightning bolt. The smell of burning invaded the library.

"Time we were off," said Wren.

"Lucas, you'll have to complete it as we advance." Taking up a speaking tube, the master said, "Over the bridge, Billet. No dillydallying. Next stop home." Then to the youngsters, "Come with me. I know where there's a better view to witness the fun. You angels had better stay and help your master."

He crossed to the far corner of the library and swung open a section of bookcase that concealed a narrow staircase just wide enough for them to squeeze up. Beyond a small door at the top was a large attic. As their eyes adjusted to the dim light, they made out the rafters of Billet's sloping roof, with narrow shafts of daylight piercing the slats and damaged thatch. The attic itself was covered in a thin film of dust, and cobwebs hung everywhere.

"Here, help me with this," said the master as he dragged a large trunk across the floor. He climbed on it and opened a trapdoor in the roof. Bright light flooded in. "Come up here and watch the second part of Womper's plan. You won't want to miss this."

Mel, Ludo, and Wren mounted the trunk and, side by side with the master, they all looked back along the bridge as Billet strode onwards.

"*Duck!*" Mel's warning was just in time as a searing lightning bolt detonated just above their heads. "That was close."

Ears ringing, they raised their heads again to admire the rapidly forming bridge.

"It's . . . it's *incredible!*" said Mel. He had merely suggested the towers that flanked it in his sketch, but Lucas Flink had elaborated these into fantastic pieces of architecture complete with tracery, statues, and gargoyles.

"You must feel very proud, Womper," said the master.

"I'd feel better if it wasn't for that."

Close behind came the tortoise-monster, stalking after them on its spider legs. They could hear the whine of the lightning gun recharging.

"Master, it's gaining on us!" exclaimed Ludo.

"Calm down, Cleef. I'm sure Lucas has made provision for such a likelihood."

As the pursuing monster reached the first arch, the row of stone gargoyles that sat atop it came alive and sprang onto the monstrous contraption. Several squeezed into the lightning-gun port and began attacking the occupants. Others clambered up the tall tower, breaking off anything that protruded from the monster with their powerful arms.

"Look at the statues," said Wren. The stone figures that lined the bridge, agile as monkeys, had begun to scale the long legs of the machine.

"Now it's the mosaic," said Ludo, jumping up and down. "Look!" The pattern of snakes reared up from the surface of the roadway and began to entangle the machine's many legs. Soon they had stopped it dead in its tracks. "Looks like chucking-out time."

As they watched, they saw red-robed figures being flung from the machine by the gargoyles and statues.

"Oh, dear," said the master. "The iconium is much more fugitive than I expected."

"The bridge is fading away behind us," observed Mel. "I hope Billet gets a move on."

As the bridge paled and vanished beneath the tortoise-monster, it toppled into the chasm. As it fell, the top of the tower opened and a flock of birds flew out. Hanging from them by thin ropes were two figures—one very tall, the other very short—being carried away.

"Who's the birdie now?" said Ludo.

"Birdie?" said Mel. "Oh, I see what you mean."

"Rats deserting a sinking tortoise, eh, Mel?" said Wren.

"Yeah, scum always floats."

"*Ahem!*"

"Yes, Swivel?" The master turned from the action.

"Master, when you have a moment. Master Flink has

encountered a slight technical problem. He would be grateful for a word with you."

The master led his butler and the friends back down to the library.

"Swivel tells me that you've hit a snag, Lucas. Anything I can do to help?"

"A snag? Yes. I'm afraid that I've run out of iconium. I know I should have eked it out but I rather got carried away and used too much and now"—Lucas Flink showed them his almost empty palette—"there's not enough left to get us to the far side of the chasm."

31. child's play

"A SIMPLE CAUSEWAY might have been the prudent option, Lucas," chided the master.

"Yes. I'm sorry. But I felt inspired by the lad's sketch, truly inspired, and this iconium is fantastic to work with. If I had more I could—"

"But you don't have more, old friend. The question is, what do we do now?"

"How about stilts for Billet?" said Wren. "There might be enough iconium left."

"Mile-high stilts?" said the master. "To walk in molten lava? A trifle impractical, I think."

"What about a tightrope? That wouldn't need much either," suggested Ludo.

"Billet is many admirable things, but a funambulist he is not. In any event, I don't think the tightrope's yet been made that could bear Billet's weight."

"A safety net then," persisted Ludo. "At least we'd still be alive."

"That might save us for a while," observed Wren, "but it wouldn't last for long. Is there enough left for a flock of birds? They worked for the High-Bailiff and the dwarf."

"We would need a flock each, and a simply enormous flock for Billet. I don't think that's an option," said the master sadly.

"Excuse me, Master Flink," said Mel hesitantly, "but I was in one of your paintings, the one with the bladder-demons . . ."

Lucas Flink's old eyes lit up. "You know, young man, I think you might have it." His brush searched the entire surface of the palette and collected what little iconium there was left. With it, he painted as large a disc as he could in the air over the rapidly fading bridge. He trailed the brush and with the last vestiges of the wondrous paint flicked in a fine line with the point. "That's it. It's all gone now."

Before their eyes, the mark transformed itself into a spherical balloon and the fine line into a dangling rope.

"*Ahem!* If you'll permit me?" Swivel nodded towards the open window where a stout, hooked line had appeared. He extended a concertina-like arm and attached the line firmly to the window frame. The shadow cast above them by the large balloon dimmed the room.

"I hope for all our sakes your idea works, Womper," said the master.

From the window, they saw the last of the bridge become dimmer and dimmer and dimmer until it faded away altogether.

Then Billet started falling.

"*Scrot!*" wailed Ludo. "It's not working."

"Language, Cleef!" scolded the master.

"The balloon's giving us *some* buoyancy," said Mel, "but the trouble is, we're too heavy. Why don't we throw anything we don't need out the window?"

"Yes, Womper. Everyone jettison all the useless stuff. Start with the studio."

The friends cast debris from the attack out of the damaged studio window while the angels threw a similar amount of weighty items from the kitchen. Swivel emptied the house of all his cleaning materials, which lightened it considerably. Everyone rushed back to the library.

"Our rate of descent has slowed but we're still falling," said the master. "Now for the furniture. We don't have much time. Soon the balloon will begin to fade."

By the time the last of the furniture had been thrown into the chasm, they hung stationary in the air but altogether too near the lava for comfort—especially Billet's; he yelped in pain from his toasting feet.

"It's no good. There're just too many of us in here," said Lucas Flink. "Some of us will have to leave."

"*Leave!*" said Ludo. "You can't throw us out." The friends looked at their master, the alarm evident on their young faces.

"He means us," said a delighted Farris. "Come on, Bathor."

"*Yahoo!*" they shouted as they leapt from the window.

With their tattered wings spread wide the angels soared in wide spirals on the powerful thermal currents rising off the lava. Immediately, Billet began to rise.

"Great," said Ludo. "All we've done is increase the distance we'll have to fall. We're still no nearer the far side."

"Womper, you seem to be the one with all the bright ideas," said the master. "If you've got another one tucked away, now's the time to produce it."

"Only this." Mel picked up a jar of turpentine from beside the easel and dashed it against the canvas. The image of the balloon smeared and began to run down the canvas in streaks like tears.

"What're you doing?" cried Lucas Flink. "That's all that's holding us up." Then, after a moment, "We're falling!"

"No time to explain." Mel rushed at the canvas and, with

both hands, began to stir the loosened iconium into a great spiral. Round and round flew his hands, and as they did so a roaring noise swelled and entered the library. The room grew dramatically darker.

"What's happening?" shouted Ludo. He put his hands to his ears as the air pressure dropped dramatically.

Wren rushed to the window. "Look, everyone!"

As they all peered out, they saw the air continue to darken and a towering tornado materialize around them. It seized Billet in its powerful vortex. Slowly at first, then faster and faster, they revolved in the irresistible current. It drove Billet towards the far wall of the chasm and then back the way they had come and then forward again. But, as its speed increased, it began to exert a lifting force. Billet spun helplessly in the overpowering spiral and everyone in the library was hurled around like blobs of paint flicked from the end of a brush. Books flew about like missiles.

As Mel dragged himself to his feet and fought his way back to the easel, a hefty volume caught him a glancing blow on his forehead. Clinging on to the easel with one hand, he kept working the spiral with his other. He could feel the iconium drying. The whirlwind would last only as long as he could keep the pigment in motion.

Wren struggled to the window and saw the rapidly approaching wall of the chasm. "*Mel!*"

Mel saw it, too, and redoubled his efforts. Then, just as it seemed they would all be smashed against the wall, the tornado lifted them the last few feet and they were over the solid ground of the far side. The iconium finally dried beneath Mel's fingers and faded. The wind outside dropped suddenly. So did Billet.

"Me feet. Me skegging feet!" he shouted as he landed with a bump.

"Womper, you've saved us," said the master. "Who would have thought that we'd be rescued by a spot of finger painting? Call Farris and Bathor back in. The way home is clear, if I'm not mistaken."

But the master *was* mistaken.

A hot breeze caused the candles to flicker as the brocade drape that formed the tent flap to Lord-High-Master's pavilion was drawn aside. Through the flap could be briefly glimpsed the red desert of Lucas Flink's *The Empire of Sleep*. Lord Brool's secretary, Skim, entered and bowed his emaciated frame low before his grotesquely fat master.

"We have found Groot Smert, my Lord. He was in the House of Mysteries, drunk as a boiled owl, celebrating the demise of Blenk's Fegish apprentice. We have sobered him up and he is being put to work straight away as you ordered. He has the Mystery's finest bestiary to work from. All he now needs is the pigment. I'll stay with him to ensure he uses it wisely." The secretary glanced at a casket standing open on a table beside his master's chair. It was so full of iconium the lid would not shut. "And the High-Bailiff and his assistant have just arrived. They crave an audience."

Lord Brool spat some half-chewed sweetmeat on to the carpeted floor at the foot of one of the easels that supported two large paintings. He reached out and selected a candied snail from a dish on the table. He crunched it noisily and gave a flick of his scarlet-gloved hand as a signal to bring Adolfus Spute in.

Skim bowed again and left, taking the casket with him. Normally a rigidly controlled man, the thought of the inconceivable wealth represented by the shimmering pigment he cradled in his skinny arms induced a fit of hiccups. "The Lord-*hic*-Master will see you now."

Adolfus Spute's stained and creased robe hung shapelessly from his tall frame. His white makeup was streaked and Mumchance looked no better.

"*Spute!*" bellowed Lord Brool. "Don't just stand there; you're letting that confounded desert air into my pavilion."

The High-Bailiff and his dwarf entered, but the former's eyes were transfixed by the casket. "That's . . . that's . . ."

"Yes it is, isn't it? Amazing what one can find if one knows where to look." In spite of the heat, Lord Brool was beginning to enjoy himself for the first time since entering the Mirrorscape. "You see, that piddling quantity of iconium you collected for me is no longer the only iconium that the Mystery possesses. Ever since I became Lord-High-Master I have had a team of my own miners searching Kig for the fallen meteorite. And, while you were away extracting that tidbit from Floris, they found it. Not that I really expected you to return it to me. At least, not all of it."

"I don't understand . . ."

"Of course you don't, Spute, of course you don't. That is why you are merely the High-Bailiff and I am the Lord-High-Master. A little bird told me. Just as you have had your little songbird listening to the goings-on in the Blenk mansion, I have had my own little bird singing to me about the goings-on between you and your nephew. Some might go so far as to call it a conspiracy. He has been keeping me up to date with all your scheming. Isn't that so, little bird?"

Groot's sidekick Bunt emerged from behind the drapes. With his layers of puppy fat, scarlet robes, white makeup, and freshly shaved tonsure, he seemed a younger, reduced version of the older man. He stood grinning next to Lord Brool.

"And my little bird made a copy of that symbol that your little bird took from the Fegish boy. Which is how I came to be here. I knew all along that you would bungle things—you always do. I thought that I should be here to make certain that events turn out for the good of the Fifth Mystery—that is to say, for *me*. I've known all along what you've been up to, Spute. Everyone conspires against me. Why should you be any different?"

"Tweet, tweet," said Bunt with a mocking smile.

Suddenly there were far too many birds in Adolfus Spute's world, as he realized he had been outmaneuvered.

"You know, I do believe you have outlived your usefulness, Spute. However, as a treat—a *final* treat—I think I will allow you to witness the little reception I have arranged for Ambrosius Blenk. You've failed miserably to thwart his power and influence in the past. Now I'll show you how it should be done. It'll be child's play. Here, Bunt, help me up. The fun is just about to start."

Billet hobbled on scorched feet over the brick-red sand of *The Empire of Sleep*, complaining volubly. The night sky above was overpopulated with stars that bathed the arid wilderness in a crepuscular light. All around, towering sandstone heads emerged from the desert floor as if they were the tops of giant statues buried up to their necks. Burning wicks protruded from the crowns of these heads, adding a flickering counterpoint to the starlight and casting puddles of dancing yellow light at their base. Other heads seemed to have burned down like candles, their stony features distorted like melted wax.

The three youngsters lay curled up on the library floor, sleeping soundly. Exhaustion had overtaken them now that they were so close to home. Swivel dozed in the corner, leaning against a bookcase, while Farris and Bathor were preening each other's wings, which were nearly whole once again. The old masters stood side by side at the window, gazing out admiringly over Lucas Flink's creation.

"I wonder what the world would be like if there was more iconium available. If you could just think a picture into existence would there be any need of us artists, do you suppose?"

"I'm sure there would, Ambrosius. Technique is always hard won but surely it's our imaginations that make us different." They both ruminated on this for a while in silence. "That's odd."

"What is, old friend?"

"*That*. That's not part of *The Empire of Sleep*."

The master followed Lucas's pointing finger. Silhouetted against the distant wall of gray mist that marked their exit from the Mirrorscape and the portal back into the mansion, was a large, squat shape. He picked the omniscope from the floor and steadied it against the window frame.

"It's a *baby*. An enormous baby."

At least that is what it looked like. But as they drew closer he was not so sure. It certainly appeared to be a baby, and a rather ugly one at that, but its vast size suggested otherwise. It sat cross-legged on the sand, occasionally making jerky movements with its chubby limbs and looking from side to side. A thin trail of drool hung from its chin. Closer still, and they could see a large scarlet tent, with many smaller ones off to one side. The black-eyed red banner of the Fifth Mystery flew from the center of this camp, and a group of men-at-arms moved through it bearing flaming torches. The baby spotted Billet as they came nearer. Its face first registered a look of curiosity, which soon changed to one of consternation and then petulance. It screwed up its podgy features and opened its mouth wide in a howl. But instead of noise something else came from its throat.

A monster!

Behind the emerging creature's swordfish snout was a warty, lizard body tipped with a venomous scorpion sting. It was borne aloft on butterfly-patterned bat wings.

"That looks like—"

"I do believe it is, Ambrosius. It's one of my monsters."

The baby screamed its silent scream again.

"And one of yours, too."

The second monster that flew at them definitely had some stag beetle and dragonfly present, but the overall theme was undoubtedly spider, with more than a hint of wasp in its pointed abdomen. "They're setting our own creations against us!"

"Monster time, again is it?" boomed Billet. "All right. Let's be 'aving yer, yer flying fatheads."

The creatures flew around Billet twice and then attacked. The first monster hurled itself towards them where they watched from the library window. Billet shook with the impact as a long snout penetrated the wall, barely missing the masters and stopping just inches from the sleeping friends. Mel woke with a start, but had the presence of mind not to leap up. He lay on his back, staring at the lethal spike just above him. Then the library window shattered as the creature's scorpion tail thrust into the room, its deadly tip thrashing and searching for something to sting. Drops of amber venom dripped from its end, searing the floorboards like acid. There was another impact away from the window, followed by the ominous sound of gnawing. The second creature was using its powerful mandibles to chew through the wall.

"*Ahem!* If everyone would care to move to the far side of the library." Swivel's face rotated to one wearing welding goggles, and a cutting torch appeared from his sleeve. Its flame roared into life and a cone of fierce blue light stabbed the twilight. Carefully avoiding the probing sting, the butler crossed to where the swordlike snout pierced the wall and, amid a shower of bright sparks, deftly cut it off. There was a great howl of pain and the monster dropped to the desert floor.

The butler's masked face swiveled away and he extinguished the torch and drew it into his sleeve, replacing it with a long auger. He put his ear to the wall, gauging where the gnawing sound was loudest. Satisfied he had found the spot, he set the augur spinning and began drilling. He lurched forward as the drill reached the far side of the wall. There was another wail as the giant insect felt the auger's bite and fell off the house.

Wren hesitantly peered down from the broken window at the two bodies lying on the sand. "They're dead. They've lost their color and . . . they're *vanishing!*"

Mel joined her. "It looks like someone else has got their hands on some iconium."

"Yeah. And rather more than we had," said Ludo. "*Look!*"

From out of the gaping mouth of the babe came another monster; bigger, uglier, and infinitely more dangerous.

"We're so close to home," said Wren. "And this time we've got nothing left to fight back with."

"If only we had some ordinary materials," said the master. "It'd take longer to create our riposte, but at least we could go down fighting."

Mel looked at the wall of mist. *It's not far. I can do it.* "Let me try to get through, Master. I know how to use the mirrormark. I could bring back the materials from the mansion."

"Me, too," said Wren. "I can help. Between us we could bring back easels and brushes and oils and colors—as much as you like. Ludo will help us as well. Won't you?"

Ludo nodded unenthusiastically.

"Ambrosius?" said Lucas Flink. "It's probably our only hope."

"Very well. You've all been in the Mirrorscape awhile now. If you're not feeling unwell already, you will be soon. You need to get out for a spell anyway. Take Swivel with you."

"I believe Swivel will be of more use here. Take my angels." Lucas Flink turned to his creations. "You two, keep an eye on them."

"*Great!*" said Farris and Bathor as one. "A chance for more mischief."

"Right, off you go. But take care. I don't wish to lose you now; not after all we've been through." The master smiled at the three friends.

Mel, Wren, Ludo, Farris, and Bathor raced down the stairs. At the bottom, Mel signaled them to halt. "It's dark outside. Two shining angels are going to give us away. Here, put these on." He unhooked two hooded traveling cloaks hanging next to the door.

An enormous two-headed dragon was busy attacking the house from the front as the small party dashed from the postern door in Billet's scorched heel. They ran to the wall of mist, using the deep shadows cast by the giant heads as cover.

"Look at the baby," gasped Wren.

Its giant profile towered over them. As they watched, they saw the whole of its side vanish. It, too, had been created with iconium.

There were two people inside, lit by a dozen tall candelabra. A tall, skinny man loomed over Groot. The head apprentice stood before an easel copying monsters on to a large canvas from a book open on a lectern to one side. To his right was a smaller easel with the image of the baby on it.

The thin man looked up and pointed to the transparent patch. "If you concentrated as much on keeping us hidden as you do on your monsters, I'd feel a lot happier."

Groot glanced up. For a terrible moment Mel thought he had seen them, but soon realized that he was only regarding the flaw in his masking illusion. Groot spooned some iconium from the nearly full chest at his side. He mixed it and applied some to the portrait of the baby with one desultory swipe of his brush. "Happy now?" The giant baby became opaque again, but not before Mel saw Groot pocketing a handful of the priceless pigment while the other man's back was turned.

"It's *Groot* creating the monsters," said Wren.

"He's just copying them from a book," said Ludo. "No originality."

"Yeah, but more importantly, did you see how much iconium he's got to work with? Come on, we must hurry." Mel led them, crouching, to the wall of mist, made the reverse mirrormark, and they were through.

Their sense of relief was palpable as they reemerged into the daylight in the master's studio directly opposite the canvas through which they had left. The knot of anxiety that had been in Mel's stomach ever since he entered the Mirrorscape unraveled. They began to laugh and they felt the strength returning to them as the Mirrorscape sickness flushed from their bodies. They began collecting together materials.

"We should warn the Rainbow Rebels," said Mel. "I'll go and tie the signal onto the dragon."

"We'll all go," said Wren. "We ought to get some bandages and things from the infirmary to take back." Wren quickly led them to the service passage and ushered them inside before the angels could think up some new mischief.

"Wait—we'll need some candles," she suddenly remembered

"Allow us," said Bathor. The angels removed their hooded cloaks and lit up the narrow space, enabling Wren to lead them to the entrance hall. From there they entered the clock without being seen. Mel tore a strip from his sash and tied it around the neck of the miniature dragon. As he was doing so, his elbow dislodged the figure next to it. The knight tottered and fell to the floor, snapping its head off.

Wren knelt by the broken figure. "I'll need to fix it before the clock chimes again. Its absence is bound to get noticed and someone will come to investigate."

"While you do that, I'll go and get the stuff from the infirmary," said Ludo.

"Use the service passages," said Wren. "Meet us in the master's studio."

"We'll go with you," said Farris.

"To light the way," added Bathor.

When they were alone, Mel retrieved the head, which had rolled under the machinery. "They're beautiful figures. Did you really design them yourself?"

"Certainly I did. I designed them and my father cast them."

"They're lighter than they look." Mel picked up and hefted the body of the figure in his other hand.

"They're hollow. Look in the knight."

Mel suddenly remembered what Wren's father had said. "'Look in the knight'? *Wren*, that's the message your father gave me for you. Remember?"

"I thought he meant night, like in nighttime," said Wren, looking inside the head. "There's something in here." She withdrew a paper and unfolded it. "It's my father's handwriting.

"'Dearest Wren. If you are reading this, it means that a great misfortune has befallen our family and I am no longer around to care for you and your mother. A while ago, Lord Floris, a great lover of clocks and a good friend, gave me something precious to look after for him. I do not understand its nature but I know that it is of great value and power. He told me that if ever something bad were to happen to him, or if I found myself in danger of arrest, then I was to pass it to Ambrosius Blenk. He can be trusted to use it for the good of everyone in Nem. I now know that that time is near. A close friend of Lord Floris's in the House of Mysteries has warned me that I am about to be taken. I do not know why and I do not have much time. I have tried and failed to pass this thing to Ambrosius and now I fear I will be caught with it still in my possession. Under no circumstances must it be allowed to fall into the hands of the Fifth Mystery. I have hidden it here in the certain knowledge that you will be looking after this great timepiece that you love so much and will eventually find it. It is too late for me but I beg you to pass it to the great master. Know that wherever I am, my thoughts are with you. Kiss your mother for me. Your loving father, Thomas Delf.'" Wren stared at the letter in silence.

"I'm sorry, Wren." Mel placed his hand on hers and gave it a squeeze. He looked in the body of the figure. "There's a bag in here." He pulled the small sack out and loosened the drawstring that fastened it, tipping a little of its contents into his open hand.

"Mel! It's *iconium*!"

"Yeah, it is." Mel carefully poured it back into the bag, refastened it, and handed it to her. "Here, you take it. We should go."

When they arrived at the master's studio, the door was ajar and sitting in the ornate chair was Green. His head was bandaged and he looked haggard. In his lap rested the bloody and lifeless figure of his tiny, piebald creature. Mel pushed the door open a fraction more. Standing next to Green were Ludo and the angels. Ludo looked up at him in alarm.

"Run, Mel! They're going to kill you!"

32. out of the frying pan ...

MEL GRABBED WREN'S wrist and pulled her back down the corridor but blocking their way was Blue, with two other rebels. They had their crossbows leveled at the youngsters' heads.

"That's far enough. Back inside, *traitor*," said Blue. "Keep your hands where I can see them."

Green shifted painfully in his chair. "You've got a nerve to turn up here. But it saves us having to hunt you down like the two-faced cur you are."

"I don't understand." Mel looked around, suddenly very afraid. There were four more wounded rebels leaning in the corner, so bloodied that he hardly recognized them. They stared at him with an unblinking gaze, charged with malice. On the floor between them, bound and gagged and struggling, was Jurgis in his red robes. His face still bore sucker marks like oversized measles.

"Don't play the innocent with me," said Green. "We know what you've been up to. I should have let Blue slit your gizzard the first time we met."

"I think there's been some mistake. I haven't been—"

"Oh, there's no mistake. I have a confession signed by your own hand." Green pulled a crumpled sheet of paper from inside his bloodstained jerkin and held it up for all to see. It was Mel's sketch of the mirrormark.

Ludo said, "*No!*" He was deathly white.

"Your friend's guilty, all right." Green pointed to the signature in the lower right-hand corner. "Your name's Melkin Womper, isn't it? Or are you going to deny that, too?"

"No, the drawing's mine." Mel fought to control his breathing.

"So you admit it?" said Green. "You *are* a traitor."

"No. Someone stole it from my locker in the dormitory." Mel heard himself. He sounded very lame.

"He's lying," said Blue. "How else would the Fifth Mystery have known where to find us? He's the only one to have been to our hideout."

"The Fifth Mystery found you?"

"Don't pretend you don't know," said Green. "They were waiting in ambush for us beneath the House of Thrones. They killed most of my men. We're all that's left. Eight of us. The entire Rainbow Rebellion is here in this room. Now you're going to pay for it. You'll pay for it in blood." He lay the still body of his creature on the floor beside him.

"This can't be true," said Wren.

Ludo's eyes darted around the room. He was sweating.

"But I didn't tell anyone!" Mel was seized from behind and forced to his knees. His hair was grabbed and his head yanked backwards. A hand—Blue's hand—held a knife to his bared throat. Mel whimpered as he felt its cold, sharp edge, and a trickle of warm blood run down his neck as the blade was pressed against his flesh. "We're on the same side. Why won't you believe me?"

The angels tried to push forward.

"You two. Stay where you are," ordered Blue. He twitched the knife. Mel's eyes grew wide with terror and an involuntary moan escaped his lips.

Wren cried out. "*Don't!*"

"Shut up! Or are you in this, too?" asked Green.

"No one's in this. Not me and especially not Mel. He's been with us all the time. He couldn't have betrayed you."

"She's covering up for him." Blue pressed his blade harder against Mel's throat, making him cry out.

"No, I'm not. If you only knew what Mel's been through, trying to rescue the master. If we don't get back to him soon he'll be killed."

Green looked hard at Wren. His expression was stony. "I don't believe you." Then to Blue, "We're wasting time. Kill him."

"*No!*" screamed Ludo. "Mel didn't betray you. *I* did!"

"*What?*" said Wren.

"Ludo?" Mel's jaw dropped and he tried to turn his head towards his friend before it was yanked back by Blue.

"It won't work, son. Your friend's going to die." Green nodded at Blue. "Do it!"

"No, it *was* me!" insisted Ludo. "Groot made me do it. He's been blackmailing me. His uncle was going to arrest my family if I didn't help him. I'm sorry, Mel. I told him everything you told me—about the rebels' camp and everything. I took the drawing from your hiding place. That's how Groot got into the Mirrorscape."

"I thought you were our friend," said Wren.

"I'm *sorry*, Wren. I had no choice. Groot followed us all the way. He must have shown Mel's sketch to his uncle. Ask *him* if you don't believe me." He pointed at Jurgis.

Green nodded at the men guarding the renegade apprentice and one of them bent and loosened his gag. "Well?"

"He's lying. Smell's one of us, has been all along. He gave

Groot the sketch with his own hands." Jurgis's eyes darted shiftily from side to side.

Jurgis's guard drew his dagger and held it at the boy's throat.

"Let's hear it again. The truth, this time," said Green.

The dagger bit deeper. "All right, all right. Don't hurt me. It's true. Smell's got nothing to do with it. Ludo's been helping Groot all along. Just don't hurt me." He started crying.

Green looked at Jurgis long and hard. "That's better." Then to Blue, "Release Mel. There's our traitor." He pointed at Ludo.

Blue let Mel go and grabbed Ludo savagely by the throat. "Why you little . . . Don't think I have any qualms about killing youngsters."

"*Stop!* Don't do it." Mel tried to force himself between Blue and Ludo. Another rebel dragged him away.

"Give me one good reason why not," spat Blue. He gripped Ludo harder still until his eyes bulged.

"*Please* wait," pleaded Mel. "We all know how the Fifth Mystery works. This is just what they want; to see us destroying ourselves. Put yourself in Ludo's place. What if they threatened *your* family? And there's a battle going on in there." He pointed emphatically to the canvas of *The Empire of Sleep* leaning against the wall. "The master is fighting for his life while we're here fighting among ourselves. We have to get back to him at once."

"We need brushes and oils and easels," said Wren. "And we need every artist we have to fight what's in there. Including Ludo. The Fifth Mystery's got a terrible weapon."

"That's right," said Bathor, "terrible."

Farris nodded.

"You'd better believe it," said Mel. "They can create as many monsters as they want. If we just stay here they'll have won. With the master out of the way, the Mysteries will never be stopped."

"So, they got hold of the iconium after all," said Green.

"You know about that?" said Mel.

"We knew they were trying to get some," he said. "The most recent escapees from Kig told us about Brool's special mining team. There's only one thing they could have been looking for. So, Ambrosius Blenk's in danger, is he?"

Mel looked anxiously at the canvas and then back at Green. "He's as good as dead if we don't act quickly. The master and Lucas Flink and Swivel. If we go now, we'll be behind the Mystery men. You can take them by surprise—ambush them like they ambushed you. They'll be so busy attacking the master they won't be expecting you. But we must go now. *Please*."

Green shifted uncomfortably in his chair, his forehead creased with pain and indecision.

Blue looked at his leader, uncertain what to do. "Boss?"

Green looked at Mel. "Ordinary colors are no match for iconium—but you're right. We've got to try." He nodded at Blue. "All right, let him go."

Blue relaxed his grip and Ludo gulped in air.

Green said, "We can deal with this one later." He looked at Ludo. "But someone better stick by him, just in case."

"Let me," said Blue. "If he so much as looks the wrong way, I'll put his eyes out." He released Ludo, who slumped to the floor, clutching his throat and gasping for air.

"No. I'm more badly hurt than you. I'll stay with him." Green got painfully to his feet. "All right, Mel. Let's go. You, come here." He grabbed Ludo roughly by his collar.

"Is this why you've been acting so strange ever since we

entered the Mirrorscape?" said Wren. "You should have told us earlier. We could've helped."

"I couldn't," croaked Ludo. "I just couldn't. I'm so sorry."

Mel looked at his friend. "I know how you feel. The Fifth Mystery's got my parents."

"*What?*" gasped Ludo. "How do you know?"

Mel told him what he had told Wren earlier. "The only way we're going to get them back is to see this thing through to the end."

"I had no idea, Mel," said Ludo. "I've been selfish. Tell me what I can do to put things right. I'll do anything. *Anything.*"

"It's all right, Ludo. Let's just finish this thing together."

"Mel's right," said Wren. "Let's stick together from now on."

"Right," said Green. "Blue, you take the men and attack the Mystery. I'll go with this lot and get the materials to Ambrosius. Good luck."

As soon as they stepped back through the canvas, they could see that the enemy was winning. Dozens of flying, wraithlike creatures were surrounding Billet, attacking and retreating only to attack again. Their forms were vaguely human and looked to be made from red-hot coals bound together with dirty cobwebs. Wherever they touched was seared black. The giant baby gurgled with pleasure as it stared at the beleaguered house from across the expanse of red sand.

Billet looked to be in an advanced state of demolition. One of the great studio windows that served as his eyes, and most of the wall surrounding it, was missing, the interior open to the desert air. Flames and black smoke billowed from the other. He was stamping his giant feet in the hope of crushing his attackers but it was haphazard, and obvious he could no longer see. "Is that the best yer can do, pip-squeak?" croaked Billet, his voice nearly unrecognizable.

Blue led his men silently through the dunes behind the baby to await their moment to enter the camp from the rear.

Groot had made no effort to disguise the back of his hide, nearest the wall of mist. Mel could clearly see him and his companion in the strange studio inside the hollow baby.

"Here, do this creature next," said the tall man as he turned the pages of the bestiary.

"How dare you tell me what to do, you emaciated streak of snot! I'll decide what to paint next, not some jumped-up flunky." Groot threw down his paintbrush and folded his arms, stubbornly refusing to continue.

"Have some more wine. It might improve your temper," said the skinny man, proffering the bottle. "No? If you don't want any more then I might as well pour it away."

"Wait!" Groot held out his goblet and drained it greedily once it had been filled. "More." He held out the empty vessel again.

"Can we continue now? Or have you run out of inspiration?"

"What would the likes of you know about art?"

"Not much—but I know what I like. And what I like is more monsters. Now, if you want some more wine let's see another one."

Mel could see from the way Groot now tipped the chest to recharge his palette with the iconium that he had used up most of it. "Come on," he said, "we've seen enough here." He led the others towards Billet, making use of the giant heads that rose out of the sand as cover. Carrying their bundles of materials, they got as close as they could without being observed.

"We're not going to make it across the last patch of sand without being seen," said Green.

"We will if we're quick," said Wren. "Look at the wraiths." As she spoke, the highly fugitive pigment that had created them started to fade and, one by one, they blinked out of existence. "Come on."

Mel, Ludo, and Wren bolted for the postern door. Much to Farris' annoyance, Bathor left his fellow angel to help Green while he spiraled up into the air and wreaked some serious devilry on the last of the fading wraiths.

There was so much smoke drifting over the desert battlefield that the Mystery men could not have seen them from their camp. When they entered Billet, they found his interior also filled with smoke, but they made it up the stairs to the library where Swivel had constructed a barricade in one corner from a mountain of books.

"Hello! Master?" At Mel's shout, three smoke-blackened faces appeared over it.

"Womper! We thought you'd never get back. Did you bring all we need? Who's that with you?"

"It's me, Ambrosius."

"Green? Is that you? Damn this smoke. Did you bring your men?"

"They're out there now—what's left of them—preparing a nasty surprise for Brool and his men. Things don't look good, Ambrosius."

"It's just as well you came. We could use another artist."

"You're an *artist?*" said Mel.

"Green used to be my apprentice," said the master, "just like you. Billet's in a bad way. I see you've brought the materials. They'll be a poor match against the iconium, but now at least we can try to fight back. Even if we fail, we'll have given a good account of ourselves. Swivel, set up the easels here. Brushes and oils next to them. Where're the colors? Womper, you didn't bring any colors."

"No, Master, we brought this instead." Wren produced the small sack. "Lord Floris gave it to my father to give to you."

The master took the proffered sack and eased the drawstring to look inside. "Oh, my word! Lucas, look! More iconium!"

"No one has seen it for hundreds of years and suddenly we seem to be awash with the stuff," said Lucas Flink.

"Now we're in with a real chance," said the master. "To work! All of you."

Swivel set up the five light easels with blank canvases, while Ambrosius Blenk divided up the iconium into equal portions.

"I'm not about to let you have all the fun this time around, Lucas."

"Please don't rub it in, Ambrosius," said Lucas Flink.

"How about you, Green?" asked the master. "Are you up for this?"

"Iconium? Just try and stop me."

"I'm sorry, young lady," said the master. "There are not enough easels or brushes for you."

Wren smiled bravely to conceal her disappointment. "I think this work calls for real masters and apprentices."

Once it was shared out, there was much less of the pigment than Mel had supposed. "There seems barely enough for one good monster each."

"As long as they *are* good monsters, it's all we'll need," said Ludo.

"Right. Lucas, Green, Womper, Cleef. An easel apiece, I think." The master handed them a brush each.

Mel looked at his canvas, the brush in his hand and the iconium. He was about to paint the most important picture of his life with the rarest of pigments, alongside two of the greatest artists who had ever lived. *Mum and Dad, this is for you. And Fa Theum.* He had his picture already worked out in his head. He held his brush poised over the iconium.

Then he lowered it. "Here, Wren, you take my place. Groot's got lots more iconium than we have. We're never going to match him monster for monster. If I can't steal his supply, then I can at least destroy it."

"You can't go back out there."

"I have to. It's the only way to even things up."

"Then let me go. The best artists are needed here."

"You're one of the best artists. Besides, I have unfinished business with Groot."

He dashed from the library.

"Be careful, Mel," said Wren to the empty doorway. "Be careful."

Mel had just made it to the cover of the nearest giant head when it began. From the mouth of the massive baby flew a host of monsters. They were horrifying, but Mel could see they were sloppily imagined and imperfect. Groot was obviously drunk. Mel retraced his steps until he was abreast the baby again. The giant illusion of the baby was vanishing before his eyes. Its creator could no longer be bothered to renew the small image on canvas that maintained the phantasm.

Then there came cries of alarm from Lord Brool's pavilion

as smoke billowed and flames blossomed. Blue and his men were beginning their attack. Mel watched as the tall man said something to Groot and ran through the fading image of the baby, back towards the camp.

"It's just you and me now, Groot. And pretty soon there'll just be me." Mel felt in his doublet and withdrew his bodkin. He stood up straight and walked towards the head apprentice.

"Groot. *Enough!*"

Billet was beyond fighting back. He was visibly crumbling away, and it was all he could do to remain upright. His cries of defiance now sounded like creaking timbers and falling rubble, the words lost in a chaos of decrepitude.

A ghoulish croak split the air as a new creature approached. A great toadlike apparition with evil, hooded eyes swooped towards them on green, webbed wings, its back poxed with poisonous warts. Immediately, Lucas Flink counterattacked with a writhing mega-serpent that encircled the attacker. The toad creature burst apart like an overripe melon and the air was filled with flying gobbets of flesh and milky strands of toad spawn, the black embryos within stirring menacingly. They landed on Billet and burst forth. Thousands of newborn tadpole monsters with fat, rasping tongues tore chunks from the house as Billet began to dissolve like a sugar cube in hot tea.

Ludo's and Wren's inventive creations—a heron-headed crab and a voracious parrot-fish—attacked the tiny tadpoles, destroying them by the dozen. Hundreds of the squirming creatures were wiped out, but even more remained and continued the relentless assault as they visibly grew into toadlets. They swarmed over the crocodilian creature Green had created, smothering it by sheer numbers.

Ambrosius Blenk's riposte was in the form of a giant, rainbow-hued hummingbird. It hovered in the air next to Billet, its wings noisy blurs, picking off the attackers with its long bill and sticky tongue. The desert below was fanned into towering dust-devils by the downdraft. But even this inspired conception was inadequate to tackle the sheer number of Groot's creatures. A great many invaded the wreck of the library, where the fierce turbulence of the hummingbird's wings whipped them into their own darkly swirling vortex amid a storm of paper from ruined books. Within this miniature tornado, the toadlets fused and combined with one another until a new and powerful monster dominated the remains of the room, with an ovoid toad head attached to massive shoulders covered in toxic carbuncles. Powerful arms ended in webbed claws. Its potbellied torso was supported on two legs with fat, amphibian thighs and splayed feet. Its black tongue darted in and out.

"The iconium's spent," shouted the master. "Everyone back to the barricade. Where have those angels got to now?"

"If you'll permit me?" Swivel, cutting torch redeployed, shielded the master and his companions but was effortlessly brushed aside by one swipe of the monster's powerful arm. He lay in the corner twitching, his many faces swiveling out of control.

The creature's predatory instinct was to go for the weakest and it seized the injured rebel leader. Green swung his sword but this was snapped like matchwood by the monster, which shook him as if he were a child's plaything.

"*No!*" cried Ludo as he climbed on to the barricade. "Let him go!"

"Ludo, don't!" screamed Wren.

"I must. Everyone has suffered enough because of me." He leaped and encircled the creature's neck and they whirled around in a macabre dance. Some of the carbuncles burst under him and the acidic poison they released burned through his doublet. Crying with pain, he hung on and his fingers scrabbled over the toad's face, clawing deeply at its eyes. The toad-monster howled with pain and dropped Green. It spun around, smashing Ludo against the library wall.

Still the apprentice clung on, tormenting the apparition with his probing fingers. As the beast attempted to rid itself of Ludo, the wall cracked and rubble cascaded from the ceiling. Then the monster lurched backwards. The wall gave way and the creature, Ludo still clinging to it like a limpet, fell through the gap and plummeted to the desert floor.

"Ludo!" Wren ran to the gaping hole and stared down. There, far below, lay the lifeless, spread-eagled body of the toad creature. Of Ludo there was no sign. The master and Lucas Flink joined her.

"Where's Cleef?" said the master as the monster began to fade.

"There he is," said Lucas Flink. As the dead creature grew more transparent they saw a terrible sight. Lying beneath it, mauled by the monster and shattered by the wall, lay the unmoving form of Ludo.

"Ludo," said Wren. "Oh, Ludo."

33. . . . and into the fire

"**GROOT.** *ENOUGH!*"

Inside the rapidly fading image of the baby, the head apprentice turned at the sound of Mel's shout. At first, his drunken eyes refused to focus. He blinked rapidly several times and looked harder. Wide-eyed, he dropped his palette and backed clumsily into the easel. The canvas toppled to the ground. So did the small chest. What little iconium was left disappeared into the desert sand, to be trampled underfoot as he fought for balance.

"*Smell!* It can't be. You're . . . you're dead." Groot put out a hand to steady himself. The easel fell and so did he.

Mel said not a word.

Groot scrambled to his feet. "Stay away from me." He turned and fled.

Mel followed Groot across the burning camp and into Lord Brool's pavilion, where he was met by a solid wall of heat, as if he had walked into an oven. Anything that was not already burning freely was smoking. Overhead, the ceiling appeared to be made of a rippling mass of smoke.

Groot rushed, coughing, to one of the large paintings, its surface cracking and blistering in the heat. He made the mirrormark and pushed at the canvas, thinking that he could pass through it as easily as a door. He screamed with pain as the molten paint on the unyielding canvas stuck to his hand. He had chosen the wrong picture. He crossed to the other. Its surface was also beginning to bubble. He turned for one last look at Mel and, as he did so, the hem of his scarlet robe brushed the side of the tent and caught light. Groot tore it off and threw the blazing missile at Mel. Then he turned, made the mirrormark, and vanished.

Disentangling himself from the burning robe, Mel made for the painting that had swallowed Groot. Its surface was now so badly blistered that it was impossible to discern what it depicted. No matter: Mel made the mirrormark.

He fell facedown into soft snow. Blessed, cooling snow. Coughing uncontrollably, he rolled over, extinguishing his smoldering clothes and soothing his burned head. He grabbed a fistful of snow and brought it to his mouth, chasing away the acrid taste of smoke and soothing his scorched throat. For a moment more he lay there, enjoying the blissful, cleansing iciness. Then he heard a fluttering sound and felt a chill breeze on the back of his head, and he lifted it and looked around to get his bearings. Behind him, he could feel the heat coming off the wall of mist and through it the faint sounds of battle. As he rolled over, the wall of mist bubbled and disappeared. In its place was a seamless continuation of the silent, snowy scene all around. He knew then that the painting had at last been consumed in the flames on the far side. There was now no way back. If he was ever to get home, he would need to find another exit.

He moistened a corner of Groot's charred robe in the snow and used it to wipe his face. The icy shock temporarily banished his fatigue. He got unsteadily to his feet in the lightly falling snow. He did not need to guess which way Groot had gone. His footprints led off into the distance as clearly as marks drawn on paper. Mel followed them with his eyes and saw a stumbling figure, black against the pristine whiteness, running as fast as the deep snow would allow. But there was more than one set of footprints. Several people had also escaped this way. Mel wrapped the remains of Groot's red robe around his neck as a scarf and set off to follow them across the too-perfect terrain of the Mirrorscape.

He soon lost sight of Groot, but continued to follow the trail. After a while, the tracks veered off to one side. Mel followed them until he found himself in front of a thick, impenetrable wall of thorns. The high hedge seemed impassable. Groot and whoever else he was tracking had evidently felt the same way, and the footprints set off in a new direction.

Presently, he arrived at a flat area that was obviously a frozen body of water. The footprints led out on to this but after a short distance stopped in a confusion of imprints next to a hole in the ice. Someone seemed to have fallen through. It could not have been too long ago as the surface had yet to refreeze completely. There was a flattened area nearby where someone had been hauled out, evidently with some difficulty. Then the trail led off again back towards the shore and in yet another direction. After several of these random changes of course, Mel came to the conclusion that whoever he was tracking was hopelessly lost.

He began to feel hungry. The last thing he could remember eating was dinner with the phantasms of his parents.

Mel wished his friends were there with him now. Ludo would have something funny to say and Wren would have practical advice. With them by his side, his trek would be that much easier. But he was alone. He shivered.

Mel trudged on, following the footprints as they led into a wood. His breath formed pale clouds in the air in front of him as he labored through the deep snow. A little way into the wood, Mel's attention was caught by a large, solitary icicle sparkling where it hung from a branch. He went closer. As he gazed at it, the colors refracted through it changed. The pure white of the snow and the blue of the shadows vanished as if a curtain had been drawn over them. A curtain the color of blood.

"Lost are we, Smell?"

Mel's reaction was instantaneous. At the sound of the High-Bailiff's voice, he turned to flee but tumbled headlong over the body of the dwarf crouching directly behind him.

"The oldest trick in the book and he fell for it, Mumchance. That's a joke, you may laugh."

The tiny man blew an ululating trill on his whistle as he sat on his captive's back. He ripped off Mel's tabby sash, bound his hands tightly behind his back, and dragged him to his feet. He patted him down and found the bodkin.

"We've so looked forward to renewing Smell's acquaintance, haven't we, Mumchance? There's so much to catch up on. So much unfinished business. There's even a debt to be repaid. Repaid with interest. Of course we don't have our Instruments of Interpellation, but we can always improvise. Why even a delicate thing like this icicle here"—the High-Bailiff snapped it off—"can work wonders in the right hands." Adolfus Spute held the glistening point at Mel's eye. The cold air between them was filled with clouds of condensation, Mel's coming rather more rapidly than his captor's. "What do you think, Mumchance? Up for a spot of improvisation, are we?"

The dwarf blew a questioning note on his whistle.

"Do you really think so?" asked the High-Bailiff with surprise.

Another blast.

"You know, that's not a bad idea. Not bad at all." He looked Mel up and down with an appraising stare. "Come along, Smell. Things to do, people to see. No dillydallying." He strode off through the snow, hitching up the hem of his long robe with one hand as he steadied himself with his multicolored staff of office. Mumchance followed behind, urging Mel forward with the bodkin.

A chill colder than the icy Mirrorscape ran through Mel's body. The first time he had encountered the High-Bailiff, Dirk Tot had saved him, and the second, Green. Now he was on his own. All he could do was hope that an opportunity to escape presented itself. This thought sharpened his senses. He felt his mind ease into the same state as when he drew, and he began to study his surroundings with his artist's eye.

He noticed at once that something had changed in the texture of the scenery around them. It was not very evident in the thick snow, but there was less detail to be seen in the Mirrorscape. It was the kind of simplification seen in the background of a painting. Even the light was different: it had stopped snowing and had grown darker. He was sure they had crossed into another painting. At one point there was a muffled thud behind them as snow fell from a high bough. A flapping of wings told Mel it had been dislodged by birds. Eventually, the wood thinned out and they looked down on to a natural hollow surrounded on all sides by jagged mountains. The sun was setting and the evening star was visible. Nestling in the lee of a rocky outcrop was a group of strange-looking buildings. Their exact shape was difficult to see, as they were draped in thick snow. As they approached, Mel could see yellow lamplight on the ground outside a door.

Adolfus Spute entered and Mumchance forced their prisoner inside with the point of the dagger. As soon as his eyes had adjusted to the dim light, Mel could see that they were inside the frozen carcass of some huge animal, its ribs and backbone like the vaulting of a great building. At one end of the long space a fire had been built. Smoke snaked upwards and escaped through a hole in the ceiling. Incongruously, there was a table and two long benches. They seemed to be made from frozen entrails and discarded bones. Seated around it, close to the fire, was an obscenely fat man draped in the outer garments of the other two people who sat shivering in their shirtsleeves nearby. One was hiccuping repeatedly. A huge set of scarlet robes were propped in front of the fire, steaming as they dried.

The fat man sniffed loudly. "Ah, Spute, about time. And who's this?"

"Introductions. Of course, how remiss of mè." Adolfus Spute bowed. "This is Lord Brool, the Lord-High-Master of the Fifth Mystery and his private secretary, Skim. I believe you are already acquainted with my nephew, Groot."

Groot sneered as he cradled his burned hand.

"And, of course, my assistant and I need no introduction."

"Yes, Spute, very nicely done. But who's this?" asked the fat man impatiently.

"This," said the High-Bailiff with a theatrical flourish of his hand, "is *dinner*."

"*What?*" choked Mel.

"There's not much of him." Lord Brool eyed Mel up and down. "When I sent you out to trap something I was thinking more along the lines of a nice, juicy deer. That unintended dip in the lake has left me famished. Oh, well; if that's all there is on the menu. A leg for me, I think—and maybe the kidneys for garnish."

Mel was dragged outside and Mumchance tied him to a tree. He drew Mel's bodkin from his belt and felt its edge. He seemed dissatisfied and held up one gloved finger as if to say *don't go away* and went towards a nearby rock. As he crouched down with his back to his prisoner, Mel could hear the ominous *shick-shick-shick* sound of the blade being sharpened.

Mel felt his last reserves of courage ebbing away. He could see the glow from inside the building growing brighter and thick smoke issuing from the chimney as the fire was stoked. The sound of the sharpening knife grew more insistent. Mel struggled frantically against his bonds.

"Stop fidgeting or I'll never get these knots undone."

"Farris?"

"No, I'm Bathor. Farris is waiting up by the trees."

"Where did you two come from?"

"We've been following you since we left Billet. Our master distinctly told us to stay close and to look after you. We thought you would have noticed. We made enough noise. Besides, we thought you might be up to some—"

"Devilry?"

"Exactly. There, that's it. This way. We've found one of those walls of mist. It's up here." Bathor led Mel up to some trees where Farris was waiting.

"So you found him," said Farris. "What kept you?"

A shrill whistle blast sounded behind them, followed by shouts from Groot and the others. The snow had drifted deeper there and Mel struggled to lift his feet higher and higher as they made their way uphill. He was puffing loudly and great clouds of steam came from his mouth. He looked back. Mumchance and Lord Brool were having as much trouble with the deep drift as he was, but Adolfus Spute and the partially clothed figures of Groot and Skim had overtaken them and were gaining on him rapidly. Mel stumbled.

"Oh, humans. *Really*," said Farris and Bathor in unison. They each grabbed one of Mel's arms and rose into the air. Their wings caused a mighty wind that fanned the snow into a blizzard in front of their pursuers, who cowered in the downdraft.

Mel felt exhilarated, but his flight was short and they soon landed in front of the wall of mist. With the angels still holding his arms, he formed the reverse mirrormark in the air. There came the familiar sensation of tingling as the snowy world around them whirled and they were through.

They emerged into a strange space. A long gallery stretched away to the right and left, its wall hung with many paintings.

"The pictures . . . ," said Farris.

"They're leaking light," said Bathor.

Light flooded the floor in front of the canvases and strange vegetation grew out of them. Water splashed from the pictures on to the floor and flowed away down the gallery. Suddenly, Mel recalled Green's warning about the Mirrorscape: *The seal's not permanent. After a few hundred years it breaks down.*

Mel said, "We must be in the oldest part of one of the Great Houses."

"What's that mean?" asked Farris.

"The portal between the worlds is open—"

A distant roar echoed from the darkness at the end of the gallery.

"—and things can come and go."

"*Look!*" Bathor was staring back at the painting of the snowscape. It was the only picture in the gallery with its seal still intact. Bathed in the light shed by the angels, they could clearly see the painted images of the High-Bailiff, Groot, and Skim near the foreground as they ran towards them. Farther behind them, in the middle ground, was Mumchance, and behind him waddled the gross figure of Lord Brool, now back in his red robes. "Why don't we wait for them here? Then, when they come through, we can get up to some . . . you know."

"There's no time for that now," said Mel. "Come on." No sooner had the words left his lips when the animal roar came again, closer this time. The trio ran, splashing, following the direction of the water as it flowed down the gallery.

By the time they had reached the darkness at the end, they heard Mumchance's whistle behind them and then Adolfus Spute's enraged voice. "After them! Don't let Smell get away. After all he's done to me, I've plans for *him*." Their pursuers were through.

As they ran on, the stream became stronger as tributaries joined it from other dark corridors that they passed. Ahead, they could hear a continuous thundering sound growing louder with every step. The passage they sped along ended abruptly and they skidded to a halt.

They had arrived at a cavernous stairwell, the top and bottom of which were lost in darkness. By the angel light, they could see many staircases, some clinging to the side of the space and others vaulting the void to landings on the far side. The steps were carpeted in running water that cascaded in foaming cataracts, each adding to the others until they met in a deafening cacophony of roaring, white water far below.

Farris and Bathor flew up into the great void, the spray forming luminous rainbows around their glowing forms. But rather than define the space, the light of the angels only emphasized its vastness. By their glow, Mel could dimly make out the intricate carving of the crumbling masonry. Stone faces and mythical beasts looked down on them disapprovingly. A great many old paintings lined the stairs. The angels glided back down to rejoin Mel.

"Which way?" Mel looked back along the corridor and saw bobbing lights. His pursuers had made flaming torches. "*Up!*" he shouted. The angels smiled, grabbed his arms, and took off. They had not risen far before a great black shape swooped down at them from the darkness. Its horrific roar could be heard even over the thundering water. Mel was able to make out huge wings, a gaping maw, and massive eyes with a glowing blue light at their nexus. The angels flew to a landing on the far side of the stairwell and set Mel down. He had to grab a carved banister to help stay upright in the swift-flowing current.

Just then, the High-Bailiff and the others emerged from the corridor into the far side of the stairwell and their torches fizzled out in the spray. The shining angels marked Mel out for them clearly, and they began battling up the stairway that connected them to the landing where Mel stood. They linked arms and formed a chain as they hauled themselves against the rushing water. The dark shape of the winged creature circled menacingly overhead.

Mel looked around for an escape route. There was no corridor leading off the landing and only one exit suggested itself. The large painting hanging behind him was cracked and its surface was beaded with spray. Mel made the mirrormark but nothing happened. He tried again but without result. All the while, his pursuers were drawing nearer. Why was the mirrormark not working? Again, Green's words came back to him: *Not every artist can make the mirrormark. Lesser artists can mark the canvas but it won't open a door into the Mirrorscape, and not every painting even bears it.*

Mel heard Mumchance's whistle over the crashing water. Then, from the depths of despair, rose the shining bubble of an idea. Mel unwound the remains of Groot's robe from his neck and frantically searched the pockets. His hand closed on something powdery. The last iconium in the world. He dipped his finger in, and with it drew the Mirrormark on to the surface of the inert canvas. *The Mirrorscape recognizes its own.*

There was a great whoosh and a loud roar as the black creature swooped.

"Farris! Bathor!" But the angels had gone, plucked from the landing by the beast. Mel watched, horror-struck, as all three spiraled into the air, the angels struggling against the black beast. For a fleeting moment, he caught a glimpse of the angels' faces. They were laughing and had a devilish glint in their eyes. Then down, down, down in a mortal spiral until they disappeared into the thundering foam below. Mel stood for a moment in the sudden darkness feeling more alone than he had ever felt in his life.

A piercing blast on the whistle told him how close his pursuers were and jerked him back to the moment.

Mel turned and traced the mirrormark in front of the canvas. As he completed the gesture, he felt a tug on the robe he still held.

"Smell!"

Then he was through. But his enemies were also drawn through by the power of the mirrormark.

Mel was the first to recover. They were in a dismal landscape shrouded in mist, a gray world with indistinct shapes. It reminded him too much of his own ill-conceived world. The shapes of his enemies stirred nearby as they scrambled to their feet on loose shale. Wrapping his scarf back around his neck, Mel began running up a steep hill. A shape at the summit, dark gray against a paler background, resolved into a ruined semaphore tower. Its skeletal arms hung uselessly, creaking in the breeze, and a rusty weathervane on top made a lonely squeal as it turned slowly. A large bird perched on the tower cawed a melancholy cry. Behind him, he could hear tumbling rocks as the clumsy posse climbed after him.

Mel reached the tower. As he ran his hands over the rough, clammy stones, two thoughts occurred to him simultaneously. One, that sooner or later his enemies would gather there at the only landmark in the desolate wasteland. Two, how was he to find the wall of mist again in a land of mists? He had to find it soon before the iconium faded. He heard sounds; a muffled shout, an answering whistle, and a foul curse as the High-Bailiff stumbled. Then there was the sound of a hiccup off to his right. *Time to move.* He descended the hill on the far side and lay flat on the ground. As he looked back up the hillside, dark shapes assembled at the ruined tower.

"Smell, I know you're out there. I know you can hear me. Show yourself," called the High-Bailiff. "There're five of us and we've got all the time in the world."

Oh no, we haven't, thought Mel.

Adolfus Spute seemed to be looking in his direction and Mel carefully edged to one side. But not carefully enough. Loose stones beneath him rattled away down the hillside. Adolfus Spute gestured with his arms and three other shapes, two tall and one short, spread out and slipped away to each side.

Mel scuttled, crablike, to the side, always keeping the outline of the tower as a fixed point. At the sound of falling stones, he froze. A tall figure was coming towards him. He grabbed a stone and threw it over the shape's head. It landed with a clatter behind the shape.

"Smell? I can hear you. I know where you are." Groot's shadow stalked off in the direction of Mel's missile. A little later there came the sound of a scuffle. "Got you, you little scrot!" There was a whistle blast. "Sorry, Mumchance. He must have gone the other way."

The same ruse worked a second time as another tall, hiccuping figure was sent chasing shadows. Mel continued to circle the indistinct form of the tower, hoping that he would find something—anything—that would indicate where the wall of mist was. Then he heard it; the faint roaring sound of cascading water. As he edged in its direction, it became louder. When it was at its loudest, he began to back down the hillside. Soon he felt resistance behind him. He turned. "The wall of mist!"

"We thought we'd find you here, Smell." Adolfus Spute and his nephew emerged from the grayness to Mel's left.

Groot shouted, "Over here. We've got him!"

Mel turned, the wall at his back. He could feel the resistance of the mirrormark that sealed them in press against him like invisible hands. He could hear Mumchance's triumphant whistle blasts and the wheezing complaints of Lord Brool as Skim helped him over the rocky ground towards where Mel stood cornered. He stooped and picked up a stone. The High-Bailiff shook his head as if disappointed with this last, pathetic show of resistance. Mel threw the stone high over the heads of the High-Bailiff and Groot.

"Missed, Smell."

"I don't think so." There was a clang as the stone hit the weathervane, followed by an angry cawing and flapping of wings from the direction of the tower. In the dank air it sounded like the beat of angels' wings. As the two men turned, so did Mel—but in the other direction. He made the reverse mirrormark in the air.

But nothing happened. He had left it too late. The iconium had faded. He pushed against the force field and it gave slightly. He pushed harder, almost willing himself through. It was like walking into a wall of treacle.

"Oh no, you don't," cried Adolfus Spute. "*Got you!*"

Mel felt his scarf seized and strong arms hauling him back. He strained against it with all his might. Then it suddenly slipped from his neck and the additional momentum propelled him through the wall.

He fell to his knees in swiftly flowing water. It was dark. As dark as night.

Almost.

He held his hand in front of his face and could see its outline. Lying on the crumbling balustrade before him, he found the source of the soft light. A single glowing feather: an angel's feather beaded with spray. He picked it up, turned it, and held it to the canvas, wiping away the moisture with his other hand. By its light he could see several murky figures in front of the ruined semaphore tower. They were looking back out of the painting, their hands gesturing wildly in the air as they struggled to trace the mirrormark. The mirrormark that was no longer there.

Mel watched the frozen image for a while. Then he turned from the canvas and, by the light of the glowing feather, began the long climb up the staircase towards the world above.

epilogue

FAR AWAY IN Borealis, the northernmost of the Seven Kingdoms, the first snows dusted the flanks of the mountains like sprinkled icing sugar, while farther south in Nem the faint whisperings of autumn could already be heard by those that cared to listen. But for the time being, the days remained warm and bright, the blue canvas of the sky only lightly scumbled with small white clouds.

A large crowd had gathered in the square outside Ambrosius Blenk's mansion. They were dressed in their Sunday best and a carnival atmosphere prevailed. They jostled in a good-humored way for a position that gave them the best view, and some of the more adventurous youngsters had even clambered on to the fountain, not caring that they got wet in the process. Word had been circulating all week that the famous clock adorning the facade had been refurbished. It had been stopped for two days as craftsmen had toiled inside to replace key elements in time for its inauguration at noon that Sunday. The crowd had begun gathering shortly after dawn to ensure a good place from which to witness the event. Throughout the morning this had grown until, with the hands of the great clock at five minutes to midday, the square positively thronged with citizens.

There was a loud buzz of conversation among the assembly. They had much to talk about.

"I can't believe you haven't heard. It's been the talk of Vlam for the last few weeks. Where've you been—Pyrexia?"

"Not nearly so far. I've just this hour returned from Issle."

"So you won't have heard. There's been a secret election in the House of Mysteries. Everything's changed. The High-Council of the Fifth Mystery's fallen and the other Mysteries have tumbled along with them."

The traveler looked skeptical. "If the election's so secret, how come you know?"

"I just do. Lord Brool, the High-Bailiff, and other influential members of the High-Council have been voted out of office and have gone into exile. Every last one of them."

"You're pulling my leg. If that's the case, who's running the Mysteries?" asked the traveler.

"Lord Floris is back and—"

"And what? What's put such a smile on your face?"

"—all of the most outrageous Pleasures have been abolished!"

"*What?*"

The hands of the clock moved one minute nearer the hour.

"Hello, neighbor," called a pasty-faced woman. "I didn't expect to see you and your family here, what with travel being so difficult of late."

"It would take more than a lack of trams to keep us away."

"I heard they'll be back to normal soon enough. My cousin's friend's brother's been employed dismantling the treadmills in the winding sheds, and he has it on good authority that they are to be replaced with a new kind of engine that runs on boiling water."

"Boiling water. Whatever next?"

A wheelwright and his family passed close by.

"Mummy, why have those men got red hands and faces?" asked their smallest child.

"Hush, poppet. Don't point," said her mother.

"They're released prisoners, sweetie," said her father. "They used to work in the mines on Kig but they're all free men now."

"My friend says there'll be no more color from now on?" persisted the child. "Is it true?"

"Bless you, no," said her father. "Quite the opposite. The Fifth Mystery's warehouses have been thrown open. They've been stockpiling pigment for years. There's color enough for everyone now. Pigment that we can all afford."

Every strata of Vlamian society seemed to be represented in the throng.

"There are Lord and Lady Cleef and their youngest son, Ludolf, the one in the wheelchair," whispered a baker to his companion. "I heard that he was injured in a fall. But he's mending fast."

"So who's the green man pushing him?"

"Search me."

"You mean you don't know?" said a stranger interrupting. "He was once one of Ambrosius Blenk's apprentices. He had a run-in with the Fifth Mystery and ended up on Kig. Don't tell a soul, but I heard," the stranger leant closer and lowered his voice, "that he was the leader of the Rainbow Rebels."

"I don't believe you. How could he have escaped from Kig?"

"Apparently there was an original Blenk hanging in the Governor's quarters and there was some kind of hidden doorway behind it."

"You mean, like a secret passage."

"Of course. What else? Anyway, several more prisoners used it to escape before Lord Floris was removed as Governor."

"And then what?"

"I heard that some important man was helping them. Supplying them with money and documents. Someone big—*very* big."

"I think you're having us on. I don't believe a word of it."

Nearby, a prosperous burger leaned close to his plump wife and said, "I know for a fact—for a *fact*, my dear—that Lord Smert's son, Groot, has finally graduated from Ambrosius Blenk's studio and had gone to seek his fortune elsewhere in the Seven Kingdoms as a journeyman artist."

"About time, too."

Vlam had become a city of rumors.

Alongside the well-to-do there were also people from other strata of Nemish society and from much farther afield than Vlam. Marked out by their clothes were a provincial weaver and his wife.

"I hear their son's one of Ambrosius Blenk's apprentices," commented a fashionably dressed woman. "And quite talented for a Fegie, by all accounts. But look at them, my dear. You never see tabby in Vlam. It's so dowdy."

"Do you really think so, darling?" said her companion. "You know, I'm getting fed up with all this color. Now that the Pleasure's been abolished, even hoi polloi will be able to afford it. Can you imagine? I rather like what they're wearing. It's so restrained, so natural, so *unaffected*. I think I'll ask my dressmaker to see if she can source any tabby—especially if it's as well made as theirs. Mark my words, it'll be all the rage by next season."

Overhearing this, an astute merchant introduced himself to the Fegish couple and inquired about the availability of tabby of such quality as theirs. The merchant was also introduced to the couple's companion, an elderly priest in a wheelchair.

"So you're to work in the Maven's library? You'll certainly have your work cut out. I've heard that his collection of books is the biggest in the entire Seven Kingdoms," said the merchant.

The clock now stood at three minutes to the hour and a murmur spread through the crowd as Thomas Delf, the clockmaker, entered the square. He and his workshop were responsible for the revamped timepiece they had all come to see. People stood aside and greeted him warmly.

"Is that his daughter, do you suppose? The one in the Blenk livery?"

"Surely you've heard. She's been admitted to the Blenk studio—as an apprentice."

"A girl apprentice? Whatever's the world coming to?"

"Don't be so fuddy-duddy. Personally, I think it's a splendid idea. I'm sure we'll be seeing more female artists in the future."

Times certainly were changing in Nem.

The windows of the houses on the three sides of the square that faced the mansion were crowded with people, the owners in the upper floors and their servants below. The younger and more energetic of both classes had climbed to the rooftop turrets and even crowded into the semaphore machines that crowned several of the grand edifices. They watched sweetmeat sellers with handcarts as they worked the square below, selling foods concocted from delicacies that only a short time ago would have been prohibitively expensive due to the Pleasures levied on them. Now they were selling like the hotcakes they were. Hurdy-gurdy men strolled about playing newly Pleasure-freed tunes to the delight of the crowd.

"Look! There's Ambrosius Blenk. Up there at the window."

"Who's that with him?"

"That's his wife and Lord Floris."

The master waved an acknowledgment to the throng.

"And look. There's whatshisname."

"Dirk Tot. Come closer. Swear you won't tell, but he's the man who's invented all the new and cheap pigments that you can now buy."

"Really? Such beautiful colors from such an ugly man. Who'd have thought it?"

"I hear he lost half his face and his hand while he was experimenting with those new pigments."

As the hands on the clock reached one minute to the hour, an expectant hush fell throughout the gathering. The street musicians fell silent and all that could be heard was the musical gurgling of the fountain. Everyone turned expectantly to face the mansion.

Then the moment arrived. The minute hand eclipsed the hour hand and the familiar carillon began echoing across the square. The many doors around the clock face swung open and from them appeared what everybody had come to see. The first figure to appear was a minstrel. It was as if he was singing a ballad of the figures that were to parade beneath his window. Then a giant emerged, pursued by a scarlet carriage. Halfway across the clock face, the rear wheels of the carriage fell off, causing a wave of laughter to ripple through the crowd. Then three small blue-clad figures led a strange creature on a leash across the face. Suddenly, in a coup de théâtre, the mechanical beast sprung apart and transformed itself into a larger and more frightening creature. There was applause as the three figures succeeded in dragging it to the far side and disappearing back into the clock.

Then there came an interlude in the automated tableau as dozens of tiny scarlet automata chased a band of multicolored figures across the clock face, only for the tables to turn and for them to be chased back again. It ended with the humorous spectacle of a green figure repeatedly kicking a skinny red figure in the behind.

Then came the finale. It was a grand battle involving a veritable bestiary of monsters. The first out was a skeletal creature with a dinosaur's head and many feet, its huge jaws opening and closing rapidly as it chomped a bevy of hybrid monsters that seemed to be as much machine as beast. A window on either side of the clock opened to reveal a bearded artist in each, working at their easels. Below them processed a strange, human-looking house assailed by monsters. First the monsters would gain the upper hand, only to be thwarted by the house before everything was reversed. Repeatedly, a figure with many rotating faces lent a hand. As the mechanical battle continued, more and more of the house dropped away until finally it was gone. Then, in a final flourish, a masterpiece of the clockmaker's art, the pieces of the house suddenly flew back together until it was whole, and it triumphed over the monsters.

All the while, two illuminated angels flew around and around overhead, harrying the attackers and generally behaving in a very un-angelic manner. As the house, the swivel man, and the angels bowed to the onlookers, they were carried back inside the clock and the chiming ended. Only those with the sharpest of eyes for detail noted that during the whole of the mechanical performance three small, blue-clad figures, two male and one female, remained on stage playing their own part in the conflict. Throughout the entire spectacle, the stars and planets whirled overhead as they always had done and always would. When everything finally disappeared back into the clock face, the crowd broke into spontaneous cheering and applause.

Hardly anyone noticed a blond-haired, blue-eyed apprentice dressed in the Blenk household livery in the corner of the square. While everyone was lost in baffled admiration of the clock and its enigmatic procession of figures, he was busy sketching the scene. He held open a new sketchbook of expensive paper and cradled a pot of the very best ink in one hand. With the other he held his drawing instrument. The finest he would ever own. It was a quill made from a brilliant white feather that appeared to glow with its own inner light. It seemed to dance in the air as it moved across the page.

Only once did he pause and look up from his work. That was to exchange a wave and a knowing wink with a couple of friends in the crowd.

~

Mel, Ludo, and Wren's adventures will continue in
mirrorstorm.

Turn to the back of this book for a sneak preview.

~

Glossary of Artistic Terms

ACHROMATIC COLORS—Black, white, and gray

APPRENTICE PIECE—A picture made by an apprentice to graduate as a journeyman

AZURITE—A blue mineral pigment

BACKGROUND—Distant elements in a picture

BODY COLOR—Opaque color

CANVAS—Linen or cotton fabric used to paint on. Also a finished painting on canvas.

CARICATURE—Exaggerated depiction of a person

CARTOON—A preparatory drawing

CARTRIDGE PAPER—Inexpensive white drawing paper

CHARCOAL—Drawing material made from burnt wood

CHIAROSCURO—Bold depiction of light and shade

CINNABAR—A red mineral pigment

COLLAGE—Picture made by sticking various elements onto it

COMPOSITION—The visual organization of a picture

CRAQUELURE—Cracking, or a network of fine cracks, on old paint or varnish

EASEL—Stand or support for a painting

FOREGROUND—Pictorial space close to the viewer

FORESHORTENING—The compressing distortion caused by perspective

FORMAT—The shape and size of an art piece

FUGITIVE (COLOR)—A color that fades in daylight

GALLERY—A room or building used to display pictures

GESSO—White ground used to paint on

GILDING—Application of gold leaf

GLAZE—Transparent color

GOLDEN MEAN or GOLDEN SECTION—Harmonious ratio for dividing a picture

GRADATION—Smooth and gradual change of tone or color

GRATICULATION—Grid used to enlarge, reduce, or otherwise distort a drawing

HATCHING—Tones formed by closely spaced parallel lines

IMPASTO—Thick, layered use of paint

INDIAN INK—Dense black ink

JOURNEYMAN—Stage between being an apprentice and a master

LANDSCAPE—Picture of an outdoor scene

LANDSCAPE FORMAT—Wider than it is tall

LAPIS LAZULI—Blue semiprecious stone. Basis of ultramarine pigment.

LINSEED OIL—Oil commonly used as a medium with oil paint

LOCAL COLOR—The inherent color of an object

MALACHITE—A green mineral pigment

MASTERPIECE—A picture made by a journeyman to graduate as a master. A picture worthy of a master.

MEDIUM—Liquid mixed with pigment to make paint. Also, materials used to create a work of art.

MIDDLE GROUND—Pictorial space between the foreground and background

NOCTURNE—Depiction of a nighttime scene

OCHRE—A rich brown or yellow natural earth pigment

OIL PAINT—Paint made from pigment mixed with oil

OPAQUE—Impervious to light

ORPIMENT—A yellow mineral pigment

OUTLINE—The drawn boundary of an object or color

PAINTING KNIFE—Small-bladed knife used to apply paint

PALETTE—Surface on which paint is mixed. Also, a range of colors.

PALETTE KNIFE—Flexible knife used to mix paint

PERSPECTIVE—Artistic technique for depicting depth

PICTURE PLANE—The surface of a picture

PIGMENT—Natural or synthetic coloring matter

PORTFOLIO—Folder for transporting drawings

PORTRAIT—Picture of an individual

PORTRAIT FORMAT—Taller than it is wide

PRIMARY COLORS—Red, yellow, and blue

PROFILE—Something rendered from a side view

QUILL—A sharpened feather used as a pen

REALGAR—An orange mineral pigment

SCUMBLE—Pale, broken color over a darker one

SECONDARY COLORS—Green, orange, and purple, made by mixing two primary colors

SEPIA—Brown color derived from cuttlefish ink

SFUMATO—Technique of softly blending tones or colors

SGRAFFITO—Scratching through a layer to reveal another beneath

SIZE—Liquid glue used to prime a surface

SKETCH—A rapid drawing

SPECTRUM—Red, orange, yellow, green, blue, indigo, and violet. Also, a range of colors.

STRETCHER—Wooden frame on which canvas is stretched for painting

STUDIO—Workplace of an artist

SWATCH—A small sample of color

TERTIARY COLORS—Colors other than primary and secondary colors

TONE—The lightness or darkness of a color

TRANSLUCENT—Allowing light through

TURPENTINE—Common solvent for oil paint

ULTRAMARINE—Deep blue color made from lapis lazuli pigment

VANISHING POINT—Imaginary point in a drawing where parallel lines converge

VARNISH—Transparent protective layer on top of a painting

WASH—Diluted paint or ink

WATERCOLOR—Water-soluble paint

Turn the page for
a sneak preview of

Mirrorstorm

Coming from Egmont USA
in Fall 2010

1. The Hall of Awakenings

IT WAS THE creaking that was so unnerving. When Mel had first climbed into the large wicker basket, the noise had not bothered him. In fact, he had not noticed it, such was his excitement. But that was at ground level. As he was hauled higher and higher up the towering facade of the House of Spirits, the sound of the creaking became ever more insistent. Now, at several hundred feet above the dwindling rooftops, the noise became impossible to ignore. Suddenly Mel realized it was not just the basket; it was the rope itself that was creaking. Creaking with the strain as if it was about to break! He reached up and grasped it firmly in his small hands. It felt fat and substantial, as taut as a bowstring, as thick as his wrist. *It couldn't possibly break. Could it? I don't weigh much, and the basket even less.* Then he realized something else. The hempen rope was not only bearing the weight of him and the basket but also its own weight. He tried to calculate how long the rope might be. *Hundreds and hundreds of feet. A fat rope that long must weigh—ever such a lot!*

Halfway up he passed a stone counterweight attached to the other end of the rope as it descended. More weight! *Calm down, Mel,* he heard the voice of his mentor, Fa Theum, say inside his head. *Get a grip on yourself. You're thirteen years old—too old for this nonsense.* He took a deep breath and ran a hand through his blond hair as his own inner voice joined in reassuring him. *The basket's been used to lift blocks of masonry up to the works, hasn't it? I weigh nothing compared to them.* It worked for a moment. But his relief was short-lived as he realized yet another thing. *The rope must be worn out and knackered by now. It's not going to last forever. It's going to break.*

Then a pigeon soared by, close to the basket. Silent. Graceful. Effortless. Mel followed it with his eager blue eyes and his fear receded as he took in the stunning view over the city of Vlam. As the basket spun on its rope, Mel was treated to a slowly revolving panorama. In a magical moment he saw everything afresh.

Seeing the city for the first time, a stranger might have supposed that it was built upon three steep hills, each surmounted by an immense palace that reached skywards like a monumental stalagmite. In fact, Mel knew what few others did—that the hills on which these ancient structures stood were composed of the very buildings themselves. For, as generation had succeeded countless generation, each had added to the original structures as their wealth and self-importance grew. First, they spread outwards and then, when they could spread no more, upwards. As each addition was completed, the older apartments and their contents were abandoned and the most recent inhabited and furnished anew. The core of each of the Great Houses consisted of nothing but vacant galleries and chambers, as hollow as an abandoned termitarium, empty and forgotten.

After a great many years, the original structures had become impossible to discern due to the countless arcades, domes, turrets, spires, towers, and minarets that encrusted the outer parts. These were laced together with such a collection of passerelles, bridges, and flying buttresses and sprinkled with such a profusion of tracery, gargoyles, and folderols that they seemed like insanely tall wedding cakes that had been iced by a demented confectioner. The towering and precarious structures loomed over the rest of the bustling city. By night, with their windows lit, they appeared as columns of stars; by day, as great, dark gnomons that slowly cast their shadows, hour by hour, over the surrounding districts.

At Mel's back, in the eastern precincts, stood the Maven's palace, the House of Spirits, the golden diaglyph crowning its topmost pinnacle. In the west of the city, beneath the purple royal banner, was King Spen's House of Thrones, while to the north, the colored banners of the five Mysteries—secretive guilds representing crafts governing each of the five senses—fluttered from the lofty towers of the House of Mysteries. The rest of Vlam occupied what space it could as it tumbled down the hills beneath the three Great Houses only to be checked by the high city walls.

Mel took in the River Farn dividing Vlam into unequal halves. Its course looked like a steep-sided canyon as it carved its way through the city, exposing ever older strata of buildings as it cut deeper. From his vantage point he could clearly see the city's seven bridges in the early-autumn sunshine. Swirling patterns of people and carriages could be seen crossing them like ants scurrying to and from their nests, while underneath the dark shapes of wherries and lighters were busy plying their trade on the silver water. Jittering highlights flecked the river, the brightest notes in the composition. The masts and rigging of many craft and riverside cranes were silhouetted starkly against it.

Mel was startled as the basket slowly revolved and he briefly came face-to-face with a hideous gargoyle, its stony expression pockmarked with pale lichen. The revolution completed itself and he was staring into the sky once more. *That strange-looking cloud's still there. It reminds me of something, I'm sure it does. It almost looks like . . .* Mel stared harder. *A great city. I can see towers and battlements and . . .* He stared harder still. *What are those swirling lines underneath it? I've seen castles in the air before but never one as clear as that. And those lines could almost be . . .*

Suddenly, the basket reached the end of its upwards journey with a sudden jolt, cutting his thought off before he could complete it.

"Here you go, lad. Mind your footing as you step out."

A powerfully built mason took hold of Mel's arm and guided him onto the covered wooden platform that jutted out from the side of the building like a temporary balcony. On the platform was a treadmill that worked the hoist that had raised Mel from the city below. Inside the wheel were two more masons, stripped to the waist and glistening with sweat from the long pull. The fact that all three men had brightly colored skin—one red, one blue, the other green—did not surprise Mel at all. He recognized them as recently freed prisoners of the Fifth Mystery who had earned their vivid hues from a cruel spell in the mines on the island of Kig where they, like thousands of others, had hewn pigment from the chromatic rocks.

"You'll be for the new hall, I guess. Your friends are back there," said the red mason, jerking his thumb over his shoulder.

"Is it still there, mate?" called one of the men in the treadmill.

"Aye, that it is," answered the red man, glancing skywards. "Skegging odd, if you ask me. I've never seen a cloud that stayed put before. It's been there for days. Hasn't budged an inch in spite of the breeze. Just keeps getting bigger. It ain't right." Then, looking down at Mel, "Come on, lad. Jump to it. We've got work to do, even if you haven't."

With a last glance up at the cloud, Mel smiled his thanks to the masons and threaded his way through the piles of building materials to the rear of the platform and through the open window that served as a temporary doorway into the House of Spirits. Standing waiting for him were Ludo and Wren, his best friends and fellow apprentices. All three wore the deep blue velvet doublets, white silk shirts and tight-fitting hose that made up the livery of their master, Ambrosius Blenk, the greatest artist in the Seven Kingdoms.

"Come on, slowcoach, there's still a way to go yet," said Wren as she led the trio down a corridor.

"You haven't crushed the drawing, have you, Mel?" said Ludo. "We've sweated blood over that."

"It's fine. *See.*" Mel waved the large rolled drawing, squeezing it slightly to pop out the kink caused by his too-firm grip during the ascent. "Anyway, I was the one who was up half the night finishing it."

"You lost the cut," said Ludo.

"I still think those cards of yours are marked. Whenever we cut for anything, you never lose. It's always Wren or me."

"Stop bickering, you two. Save your breath—you're going to need it," said Wren. "Look."

They stood in the entrance to the incomplete Hall of Awakenings, craning their necks to take in the ordered forest of scaffolding that filled the space right up to the lofty ceiling. A small army of masons in their leather aprons were scampering over it and up and down the scores of ladders that threaded their way through the poles and planking that formed the many platforms. Several more treadmill hoists were also in evidence, lifting bundles of timber and blocks of dressed stone. The hall was filled with the echoing sounds of wood being sawed, nails being hammered and stone being chipped.

"Shall we ask if we can go up in one of the hoists?" said Wren.

"No, let's use the ladders," said Mel. "One trip in a hoist's enough for today."

"What's the matter? Scared?" said Ludo.

"Who, me?"

"Stop it, you two."

By the time they had climbed to the top, Mel wished they had taken a hoist. "Nobody told me that ladders wobble so much."

"It's not the wobbling so much as all that climbing." Wren rubbed her aching thighs. "And it's so dusty in here." She shook her long, auburn locks, making a tiny snowstorm of fine stone dust. "Where's Ludo?"

"I'm here." Ludo's dark-haired head emerged through the scaffolding and his hazel eyes widened. "*Scrot!* I didn't realize it would be so big." He reached the top of the ladder and stepped onto the planking that formed the temporary floor of what seemed an enormous low-ceilinged space. The vaulting arched overhead, giving the impression they had entered a vast cavern—an effect reinforced by the dozens of candles and oil lamps that lit the scene with puddles of yellow light. The three friends stood there, suddenly realizing the scale of their master's latest commission to decorate the ceiling of the Hall of Awakenings. "It's going to take us *ages*," said Ludo.

"Not really," said Wren. "This high up there won't need to be as much detail as there would if it was a painting on canvas."

Mel looked down through the ladder hole at the receding

platforms and increasingly smaller workmen. "Wren's right. Any fine detail will be lost when seen from down there."

Ludo looked down and abruptly took a step backwards. "*Whoah!* We are high up, aren't we?"

"What's the matter, Ludo? Scared?"

"Don't start that again." Wren walked towards the far corner of the platform. "Unroll the cartoon, Mel."

Mel held his end of the working drawing as Wren unrolled it against the arched niche they had been allotted in one corner of the master's grand, overall design, most of which was already marked out in bold, simple lines. Huge sleeping figures—human, monster, and everything in between—populated a mythical landscape over which the sun was rising. The far side of the composition was to be in darkness and, as the dawn stole across the scene, the shadows receded, the daylight increased and the figures awoke. The friends' small contribution depicted a three-headed monster. Each of them had designed one of the heads: one sleeping, one stirring, and the other fully awake. After much argument they had decided on a common body.

"You've made it too small, Ludo. It doesn't fit." Wren shook her head.

"It's not my fault. The architects must have made a mistake with the scale."

"It couldn't have been you that made the mistake, by any chance?" said Mel.

"Let's not start blaming each other," said Wren. "The point is the drawing's too small. Bex won't be too pleased." Mel and Ludo knew she was right. The new head apprentice was better than Groot, the cruel and bullying former incumbent, but was a stickler for accuracy.

"We can't mess this up," said Mel. "The master only gave this niche to us because we rescued him from the Mirrorscape."

"The question is, what're we going to do about it?" asked Wren.

"If we just put a bit more space between the monster's heads and stretch out the body, it won't show," said Mel.

"But that's even more work for us," complained Ludo. "Today's supposed to be our day off."

"We wouldn't have to work today if we'd agreed about the creature sooner," said Mel.

"It's got to be done before the real work starts tomorrow," said Wren.

"Nag, nag, nag," said Ludo.

"She's right, Ludo. But we can't all work on it at once," said Mel. "We'll only get in each other's way."

"Why don't we cut for it? Loser stays behind and reworks the drawing." Ludo pulled a pack of cards from inside his doublet.

"Not with your dodgy cards," said Mel. "We all know who'll win. Look, I don't mind resizing it. I'll meet you back at the mansion later."

"Are you sure?" said Wren.

"He said so, didn't he?" said Ludo. "Let's go. It'll be suppertime soon."

Before Mel had time to change his mind, his friends had disappeared down the ladder.

After he had painstakingly altered the drawing and transferred it to the fresh plaster of the niche, Mel tidied away his materials. As he gathered his courage and prepared to make the long descent to the floor of the now deserted hall, his unfinished thought about the mysterious cloud completed itself and elbowed its way into the front of his mind. *It's a mirrormark! The swirling lines underneath the cloud city look just like the first few strokes of a mirrormark! There's no way a mirrormark could have got there by chance.*

About halfway down the scaffolding, he heard a peal of bells calling the Fas to their evening prayers, followed closely and nearer by another and then another. *Squit, vespers. I didn't realize it was that late. That's why there're no masons about.* He hurried on down. As he reached the last platform, no higher than the upstairs story of a house, he heard approaching footsteps. They halted beneath his platform and two female voices began talking quietly. He looked down. Just visible between the gaps in the planking stood two figures, one very large and the other small. They wore long gray robes with deep cowls pulled forward, hiding their faces.

"It's quiet—we can talk here, Tunk."

"How goes our Great Project, Mudge?"

"Now that the first obstacle is locked away in the House's dungeon, it goes well, sister."

"And work in the Paper Belfry?"

"That also proceeds well. Since our allies in the world beyond joined us with their skills and cunning, the sisterhood's great plan has at last become reality. We have been ignored for too long. Soon the people will realize our true worth. Work proceeds apace. The alignment of the crystals will be perfected within the next few days. I'm sure you've seen the first results."

"So has everyone else in Vlam."

"So what? They're blind fools, every last one of them. They wouldn't know what they were looking at. Soon the sign will be complete and the wound into the world beyond can open. The first storm will begin."

"And then?"

"We will create a storm over each of the Great Houses. Three storms to engender the final storm and then the great wound between the worlds will fester and ooze demons. Our mistress can have all the demons she desires. The city will be overrun with them. There will be more demons in the streets of Vlam than fleas on a dog's back. Our allies can join us and together we'll vanquish the demon invaders and save the city. The people will be so grateful. They'll give us all we desire."

"Soon the realm will topple. All of Nem will be ours!"